I0823827

# THE WOODEN HORSESHOE

# THE WOODEN HORSESHOE

*A Novel by Leonard Sanders*

*with an Afterword by Charlie McMurtry*

---

TEXAS CHRISTIAN UNIVERSITY PRESS
*Fort Worth*

*The Wooden Horseshoe* is Number 24
in the Texas Tradition Series.
James Ward Lee, series editor.


First Published by Doubleday & Company, Inc. 1964

*Library of Congress Cataloging-in-Publication Data*

Sanders, Leonard.
The wooden horseshoe : a novel / by Leonard Sanders : with an afterword by Charles McMurtry.
p. cm.—(Texas Tradition series : no. 24)
ISBN 0-87565-178-X (pbk.)
I. Title. II. Series.
PS3569.A512W66 1997
813'.54—dc21

97-14794
CIP

*All of the characters in this book are fictitious, and any resemblance to actual persons, living or dead, is purely coincidental.*

Cover design by Barbara Whitehead

For Flo
. . . and Flo knows why.

Whosoever will be great among you,
shall be your minister.
And whosoever of you will be the chiefest,
shall be servant of all.

*Mark 10:43-44*

## FOREWORD

When James Ward Lee, director of the Center for Texas Studies at the University of North Texas, in 1987 named this 1964 novel a classic of Texas fiction, I felt moderately safe. The first printing of the original edition sold out within weeks of publication. Doubleday, for internal reasons, declined to go back to press for a second printing. The title was changed on the mass market paperback and it also disappeared quickly. The book thus entered the rare book category soon after publication. I was confident that few people had read the book, and that far fewer remembered it.

So I view this new edition with some trepidation. Virtually every writer cringes at the mere thought of his or her earliest works, certain they are filled with awkwardness the writer has long labored to lose. But a request from Judy Alter, director of TCU Press, for material surrounding the original publication sent me into a dig that could be termed archeological. Long-forgotten letters saw the light of day for the first time in three decades. With mounting surprise, I relived the stir the book caused on publication, and rediscovered incidents that had passed from memory. The letters made plain that the setting of the book in city government had struck a common chord.

Among the unsolicited letters:

> A district judge in Texas, who was former county and district attorney, called the novel's characters "close to home" and the political issues "realistic and characteristic."
>
> A councilman in Ridgecrest, California, wrote that he

found "immediate association of the characters to our own city councilmen." He said he was passing the book along to the other members of the council "to see if their comments are similar to mine."

A friend reported from Wichita Falls that the novel had been mentioned in a meeting of the Executive Committee of the Wichita Falls Chamber of Commerce and "became the subject of general discussion." He said all of the participants apparently had read it. He reported that opinions were favorable and that most termed the novel "a fine piece of work."

The mayor and city manager of Oklahoma City both wrote that they were having fun joshing each other as to which most resembled characters in the book. The city manager added: "You are certainly to be commended for your most apt description of the City Manager's environment, and I must admit it was like being on 'a busman's holiday' while reading your novel."

A professor in the Department of Political Science at the University of Kansas at Lawrence wrote a letter that was passed on to me. His opinion: "*The Wooden Horseshoe* is wonderful. It has all the elements of a good story well written." He said he could not understand why a mutual friend in city government should be worried about it.

A former department head in a Texas city wrote that she was "delighted and amazed" by the book, and that "its likeness to grim reality is almost as stunning as that reality itself." She revealed that a year in city politics sent her into a six-month stay in a psychiatric hospital "trying to forget." She said she was unable to do so and added that the book "should be required reading for my innocent fellow citizens."

All of this long-buried praise once again fell like Biblical manna among the Israelites.

At the time of publication, the North Texas City Managers Association was meeting in Fort Worth. I was presented as a curiosity—the author of the only known novel with a city manager as a protagonist.

Towns as diverse as Johnson City, Tennessee, and Panama City, Florida, identified with the novel. Since I had served on newspapers in Enid, Norman, and Oklahoma City in Oklahoma, and in Fort Worth and Wichita Falls in Texas, some residents in each of those cities believed I had borrowed elements of that Town's government for the plot and characters. But on the *Enid News-Eagle* I was a photographer-feature writer and seldom entered City Hall. On the *Norman Transcript* I was news editor. On *The Daily Oklahoman* I was chained to the rewrite desk, freed occasionally to cover the police beat. On the *Fort Worth Star-Telegram* I was a copy editor, writing nothing but headlines (and novels). Only while on the staff of the *Wichita Falls Record-News* had I covered City Hall. So Wichita Falls became the prime suspect for the setting.

Texas was never an unknown quality to me. One of my great-grandfathers brought his family to Texas after the Civil War. His experiences at Murfreesboro (Stones River), Chickamauga, and on Johnson's Island—a horrendous Yankee prison for Confederate officers—left him soul-seared. He came home a fiery Campbellite preacher. He turned his seven sons into ministers. He is buried in a rural cemetery west of Graham in Young County. His descendants are now scattered in a diaspora across West Texas, western Oklahoma, the Panhandle and eastern New Mexico.

My boyhood was spent on a ranch twelve miles from the Texas Panhandle and twenty-five miles from the Red River. The region was first settled by Texans, organized as Greer County, Texas, and considered to be a part of Texas for thirty-six years —a fact now lost in a peculiar historical amnesia. The nearest legal liquor store was in Electra and—irony of ironies—residents of the bone-dry Texas counties to the south streamed across Red River on Friday and Saturday nights to partake of Oklahoma's legal 3.2 beer. In those days the air was saturated with Texas radio fare, such as W. Lee O'Daniel and the Light Crust Doughboys from Fort Worth, the Stamps-Baxter Quartet, and the Man on the Street from the Kemp Hotel corner in Wichita Falls. My grandfather subscribed to the livestock editions of *The Fort Worth Star-Telegram*, *The Daily Oklahoman*, and *Kansas City Star*. We knew as much about the political issues in Texas as those in Oklahoma. This early sense of dual citizenship has enabled me to regard the often-fierce chauvinism of both states with a degree of detachment.

At the city managers' convention in Fort Worth, H.A. Thomason, longtime city manager at Wichita Falls, seized my neck in a firm hammerlock, pulled my head down to chest level, and whispered directly into my ear, stressing each word: "*I-know-where-you-got-every-idea-in-that-book*." He probably did. Friends on the staff of the *Wichita Falls Record-News* wrote gleefully that a memo had come down banning mention of the book in the newspaper. They were chortling because the memo mirrored incidents in the novel. Channel 5's Bobbie Wygant surprised me on-camera live by asking if it was true that the book had been banned in Wichita Falls. I said that was my understanding.

But in the writing, I prudently had changed the plot away from all the skulduggery I knew about. or suspected, or had heard about. Not until later did I learn that the skulduggery cooked up in my imagination was close to real-life skulduggery elsewhere.

The idea for the novel came in the wake of James Drury's runaway best-seller, *Advise and Consent*. Drury's ponderous novel dramatized conflicts in the U.S. Senate and other high levels of government. Experience had taught me that while often passionate, U.S. senators, congressmen, and principals on that level tend to treat issues with professional objectivity. Experience also had taught me that in smaller, local governmental bodies, conflicts often are played out amidst vicious, gut-wrenching, face-to-face drama. Perhaps newspaper and television news reports today of city councils, school boards, and commissions demonstrate that this concept remains valid. And it could be that this aspect of the novel is what Jim Lee and my long-ago correspondents found true to Life.

Leonard Sanders
Fort Worth, 1997

# *Part One*

## CHAPTER ONE

The city rose out of the morning mist, sprawling and unreal. The sun, low on the horizon behind them, sent the plane's shadow racing far ahead, its warmth chasing the lingering mists of dawn from the ranchlands below.

To the southeast, David could see the smoke of the oil refinery, drifting northeast before a gentle spring breeze. Far to the south, almost hidden in the morning haze, lay the Air Force base, its nuclear-loaded bombers lined up near the ready shacks.

Below, the highway was heavy with inbound traffic, workers headed for the distant downtown section where the naked steel of four new buildings knifed the sky.

David checked his altitude, then went into a glide. The lowering of the plane's nose put the whole panorama of the city before them. His city.

He never tired of seeing it from the air. Only at this altitude could one see the full extent of what man had dared to build on the face of God's creation.

The view seemed to have his three passengers spellbound, so David left the nose down while he hunted for the intersection of the highway and the blacktop ranch road. When he found it, he went into a wide, lazy turn, the right wing low, using the intersection as a pylon.

"There's where the northeast cloverleaf will be," he said, pointing.

Beside him, the mayor turned to look. Behind them, the two councilmen leaned toward the window, studying the intersection as if the cloverleaf were already there.

David held the plane steady in the turn, looking past them, yet seeing them, anticipating their reactions. Their support on this thing had been important. He had gotten it. Now he had to convince them he was right. For soon he would need their support on other things. The new lake, for instance.

He understood their misgivings. This proposed interstate highway bypass had never been popular. And the hard core of merchants still wanted all the traffic they could get downtown. But he had convinced the council that the expressways, originally designed for interstate use, too, were already clogged in intracity traffic, with the city still growing. So they had gone ahead and voted the state engineers' bypass plan on David's recommendation as city manager. Balloting on the bond issue had been close, debate bitter.

Now, doubt persisted in the minds of the councilmen that this had been the answer. The strong opposition was asking a delay for further study. The councilmen were hesitating on the final, irrevocable action they would take tomorrow night—approval of the final agreement and authorization of right-of-way purchase. But he knew it wouldn't do to oversell. For he knew these three men well.

The mayor, Hiram Milner, lean and gaunt and troubled, his long spidery legs doubled up, big bony hands covering his knees and massaging them nervously. The Gray Ghost, they called him, sometimes in jest, sometimes in tones akin to awe. Thick silvery long hair and a law office pallor to match. A lifetime of hunting misplaced commas, the vague word or the missing clause. The mayor couldn't be rushed into anything.

In the rear seat, by the right window, Walt Weatherbee, realtor and developer. There was little left of the itinerant carpenter of the Depression now. The last twenty years had been easy. They showed in the ample waist, heavy face, and soft hands that hadn't touched a hammer since World War II and Walt's first Air Corps contract for six houses. Now Walt Weatherbee thought in terms of blocks of houses and moved carpenters in platoons. And traffic to and from those houses was of vital concern to Walt. He studied all the angles.

In the seat behind David, leaning toward the opposite window, Cal Masters, the old rancher. Skin the color of new saddle leather from the winds of eighty-odd winters and the heat of the summers. Huge, ancient Cal Masters, who as a boy had helped drive cattle up the trail through the Indian Nations when the city had been a hamlet. A whole history telescoped into one gentle old man. Wide Western hat hiding his snowy mane, the sky-blue eyes beneath heavy white brows seeing the present, living in the past. Cal, the councilman he knew and loved best. But the most ornery, suspicious of progress, the last to accept change.

"You still think we did the right thing, David?" the mayor asked.

"No doubt in my mind," David answered quickly. One of the first things he had learned as city manager was that once a decision is made, it must be presented to the council with confidence. Day after day the council members faced a doubting public. They needed reassurance.

"Shouldn't we have brought the separation point in a little closer?" the mayor asked. "I'd like for people passing through to see more of the city."

"They'll have a good view of the skyline," David told him, completing the full turn. He leveled off and pointed. "If they want to stop, they'll be less than seven minutes from downtown on the freeway."

"But it's so desolate-looking out here," the mayor protested, looking down again at the mesquite-covered ranchland.

"It is now," David admitted. "But that's an advantage. All that undeveloped right-of-way will be ripe for motels, service stations, restaurants, everything needed to service interstate traffic. The site availability will attract them here, rather than somewhere on down the road."

The mayor grunted, and David knew he had made a point. Any mention of new industry was strong argument with the mayor. But not with Cal Masters.

"I see no reason to bring them close to town at all," Cal said.

"Tourism is getting to be big business," David said, gently chiding the old rancher.

There was a rustling of paper in the back seat, and David knew without looking that Weatherbee had the proposed highway map spread out on his knee.

"I'm still afraid that big a highway will shut off development to the north and east," Weatherbee said.

David was ready for that one. He had been gathering statistics for the last two weeks and had them bundled on his desk, waiting.

"Traffic arteries like this have little influence, I understand," David said, trying to sound casual. "What effect they have as a natural barrier is offset by the accessibility the new routes give the area. I have some material on that somewhere. I'll hunt it up and send it over to you."

Flying to the left of the blacktop road, giving his passengers a good view of where the bypass would be located, David checked the altitude, airspeed, and searched the sky around them for other air traffic. They had the sky alone. An airliner he had seen earlier had disappeared in the direction of El Paso.

When they came to the second separation point, where east-west traffic again would pass a cloverleaf and the option of a city freeway, David didn't have to mention it. Weatherbee had located the site on his overlay map and explained the landmarks to Cal and the mayor. David again made a sweeping turn, letting them examine the huge cloverleaf that wasn't there. Then he turned down the north-south segment of the future bypass.

He opened the throttle, feeling the engine take hold. He eased the wheel back, rising steeply to get enough altitude for the more-populated section, making the engine work.

Weatherbee leaned over the mayor's shoulder, and the two began studying the map and the tie-in points below, the access roads and the area each would serve. David let them discuss the pros and cons of the program without taking part. If they would convince themselves, so much the better. Cal was silent. Whether he was monitoring the discussion or lost in the past, David had no way of knowing.

He concentrated on flying, feeling the luxury of his own plane. And it was a luxury. Aside from an out-of-town meeting now and then he had no practical use for one. But he liked to keep it, for being up here occasionally, seeing the entire city, gave him a perspective of his job he could get no other way.

As they approached, the downtown section gradually changed from a silhouette on the skyline to individual buildings of brick and stone with graveled and tarred roofs. Below, the green and brown geometric pattern of blocks began to take form with houses and streets, broken by schools, playgrounds, and parks.

Down there, he knew, a hundred and ten policemen were on duty, supervising traffic, getting ready to check into the minor and major crimes of the night before. Two other shifts were off, more than fifty percent of them working at another job. Eighty-seven firemen in six station houses were on the last leg of a twenty-four hour stint; another shift was on call. Ninety-six city employees would be getting ready for their day at City Hall, and another two hundred would be preparing for a day of repairing streets, signal lights, painting curbs, fixing sewers and water mains, picking up garbage, planting trees, mowing weeds. . . .

The city was its own biggest industry. And he was its manager. He had been selected unanimously by the city council from a field of twenty-two applicants eight years ago. Since then, no succeeding council had voiced dissatisfaction with his work. Any other executive in town could tour his operation in a brief walk; David had to get up here to see the extent of his.

As he looked down upon it, the city actually seemed to be growing minute by minute. And maybe it wasn't all just illusion from the plane's movement. Since 1950 the city had doubled in size. A gain of 4.3 water meters per day, average; 12.8 new residents daily, 4672 persons a year. This gain was in addition to the new residents who checked in through the hospital maternity wards, unconcerned with new water meters. Somewhere, he had statistics on them, too.

Across his desk came reports of every happening in the whole metropolitan area worth his notice. Out of his office went the information from which the city council made its decisions. His desk was the hub upon which the whole city turned. No one, he was sure, knew the city as he did.

They reached the Southwest Industrial Park, where the future highway was destined to fade into the distance. David waited until Weatherbee and the mayor had talked themselves out.

"Had enough?" he asked. He wanted to get them back to the airport before pressing for a commitment; standing on solid ground would add confidence.

"No, I'd never tire of this," Weatherbee said. "But I have a confession. I slept so late I skipped breakfast. Now my big guts are eatin' up my little guts."

"I only had some coffee," the mayor said. "What about going in to the Petroleum Club for breakfast?"

"I have a better idea," David said, swinging toward Municipal Airport. "How about my house? I can phone from the terminal, and it'll be on the table by the time we get there."

Weatherbee's answer came a little too fast, too loud, and too forceful. "Oh, no, Dave. Hell, we don't want to put you to any trouble. Let's just grab a bite at the terminal."

David wished he could see Weatherbee's face. Had he imagined it? He didn't think so.

"No trouble," he said. "I've got to change clothes before going in to the office anyway."

"Some other time, Dave," the mayor said, too easily. "Come to think of it, I do have a nine o'clock appointment this morning. The airport restaurant sounds fine with me. Cal?"

"Early risin's one of the bad habits of old age," Cal said. "I had breakfast two hours ago. But I'll have a cup of coffee with you."

Since he couldn't see their faces to judge their reactions, David decided to leave it at that for the moment.

He crossed the edge of town to the airport, got clearance from the tower, made the pattern, then brought the plane in, setting it down a few feet from the end of the runway and letting it roll. He taxied up to the ramp at the edge of the terminal building, lined up with the tie-downs, and cut the switch.

The airport attendants hurried up to chock the wheels and fix the tie ropes. Cal was the last one out of the plane, swinging down backward as if from the saddle, using the step as a stirrup. Weatherbee stood by the wing, refolding his map.

"Well, how does the over-all picture look to you gentlemen?" David asked. "I hate to push you for an opinion, but the state engineers have heard some opposition has developed. I'd like to be able to reassure them the council still intends to approve the final agreement tomorrow night, so they can go ahead with their work."

For a moment, as they hesitated, David was afraid he had asked for a commitment too soon. But Weatherbee came through.

"Looks all right to me, David. Of course, there are a few things I want to check into, probably a few questions I'll have to have answered, but right now the program, taken as a whole, looks good."

The mayor was more cautious. "I think we ought to go slow until we hear all sides. If we do something wrong, it's going to be wrong for a long time."

This seemed to strike a responsive chord in Weatherbee, and he suddenly switched sides.

"That's right, like the way the lots were laid out in the old Bonham Addition. There wasn't any way I could line up the streets and sewer lines when I built Miramar. Cost me a goddamn fortune. The council that approved those Bonham plats ought to be dug up and shot."

"Cal, what do you think?" David asked. Cal had to be asked directly. He never volunteered his thoughts.

Cal swept off his Stetson with his left hand, ran his right through his white mane, then examined the hat's sweatband critically. "Way I see it, we've given them our word in the preliminary agreement. It's been approved at the polls, and there's no way we can back out now unless we scrap the whole idea. That bunch should have spoke up earlier."

David had counted on the old rancher's strong sense of honor. Cal had opposed the program, originally, but once committed in principle, he would see it through.

"Yes, I would question the legality of any change at this late date," David said for effect.

Weatherbee and the mayor exchanged glances.

"Well, as I said, the over-all picture looks good," Weatherbee said.

"As Cal mentioned, it has been approved at the polls," the mayor added. "I suppose our problem really is a public relations problem from here on in."

"That's the way I see it," David said. "I thought maybe the council could set the public hearing date on the right-of-way purchase, and take care of any ill-feeling then. I think that when the chips are down, there are few that'll actively protest."

The mayor nodded. "I've learned a long time ago you can't please everybody. I think you can go ahead and reassure the state engineers that our opposition doesn't amount to much. After all, the chamber is behind it."

"Good," David said. "I'll phone them, soon as I get to the office." He turned then to face Weatherbee so he could see the big realtor's expression. "Sure you three won't come out to the house for breakfast? Be glad to have you."

Weatherbee's reply was smooth this time. "No, thanks, Dave. Some other time. Why don't you join us here? Nothing at the office you can't do later."

David looked at his watch. "In forty-five minutes," he told them in mock seriousness, "a little ol' lady on the North Side is going to call and say her garbage wasn't picked up yesterday. I don't want her to think the city manager isn't on the job either."

They laughed, and started on up the ramp toward the terminal building. At David's side, the mayor slowed, letting Cal and Weatherbee move on ahead. The Gray Ghost was frowning, and at first David thought the bright sun on the concrete was making him squint. Then he realized it was the expression he'd seen often when the mayor was worried about something and was trying to think out how to put it into words.

At the corner of the building the mayor took his arm and stopped. "I understood you to say on the phone the other day the consulting engineers are ready with the lake site recommendation. I just assumed at the time you'd have the report on the agenda for tomorrow night. Any reason why you left it off?"

"I didn't know there was any rush," David said, a little surprised at the mayor's firm tone. Cal and Weatherbee, out of earshot now, glanced back, hesitated, then went on into the terminal.

"Well, as you know, the chamber, the newspaper, a number of people are very impatient to get going on this lake program. Would you have any objection to taking it up tomorrow night?"

"No, of course not," David said, searching for a way to make the mayor understand. "I just figured it'd be better to give the ill-feeling raised by this highway dispute time to cool."

The mayor's frown deepened.

"Yes, I was hoping all this would blow over sooner. But as you said, the highway opposition probably won't amount to much. Sour grapes, because they lost at the polls. And I had hoped the lake program would be finalized during my administration. I was thinking that if we could just set the date tomorrow night to hear the report . . . that'd let them know we're still working on it."

"If you want," David said. He would have preferred a breathing spell between the two projects, but again he was in that twilight area of his responsibility. "I'll contact the consulting engineers this morning, find out what arrangements would be best for them, and call you back."

"Fine," the mayor said. "And maybe you better make the announcement of an addition to the agenda, too, so we won't be accused of anything secretive."

"All right, and I'll contact you this afternoon, then," David promised.

He left the mayor and started for the parking lot, feeling the sudden weight of a new battle shaping over the ashes of the old. But he wasn't thinking of this looming battle for a new city water supply. He was thinking of the uncharacteristic reactions he'd gotten in reply to his breakfast invitation. Weatherbee and the mayor had heard something. There was no doubt in his mind about it now.

That his home life was being talked about didn't surprise David Hartwell. What did surprise him was that the knowledge failed to stir any emotion within him. No regret, anger, indignation—nothing. Was he so devoid of personal life he no longer was capable of feeling?

That question answered itself in the remembrance of a cool, crisp night last October, long black hair in the moonlight and a blackjack grove down by the river—a night of wild, abandoned youth he should forget but he knew he never would. And there had been other nights, too.

Yes, he had feelings. But not for this talk about his wife. Why, he didn't know. David Hartwell, who prided himself on knowing what made men tick, was ignorant on the most important man of all—himself.

Pondering this, he walked across the blacktop parking lot to his car, peeled off his flying jacket and tossed it into the back seat. As he wheeled out onto the highway he turned on a radio in time to catch the 8 A.M. news break.

There was another satellite up, another threat from Russia, the

Texas Legislature was set for another day of bickering over the budget, the mayor had told a chamber committee that plans for a new city reservoir and water supply were being given top priority, two persons had been shot in a difference of opinion at a South Side bar shortly before midnight, four persons had been killed in area car wrecks, a suicide had been found in his car near the old city reservoir, and there was the possibility of severe thunderstorms and damaging winds in the late afternoon and early evening. Spring was bursting out all over.

He flipped off the radio and the air-conditioner, then put the windows down, preferring the mildly warm air to the artificiality that would be all too necessary before long. Traffic wasn't as bad as he feared it would be . . . most of the early-morning shifts already were on the job, and it was too early yet for the executives and white-collar workers. He cut off the highway onto the back streets, avoiding the freeway, and jogged around on them until he was in the broad, tree-lined avenues of the Old Town.

As he turned onto the home boulevard, he was impressed with how much greener the section was than others he'd seen this morning. It seemed as if nature favored the area where roots were deeper, the district of first families, the doctors, lawyers, respectable merchants, people with names prominent on downtown buildings.

He turned into the driveway and sat there in the car for a moment, reassuring himself with the sight of the huge old two-story colonial frame, built by the city's most successful hardware merchant in the days when wagons, barbed wire, and saddles were a sizable part of the economy. Maybe the house lacked some modern comforts. The plumbing rattled and there was no way to air-condition it properly. But to David it had a touch of the old Southwestern aristocracy no amount of built-ins could match.

Admittedly, it had been a bit pretentious for a $14,000-a-year man when he bought it eight years ago. But it had paid off, as he'd known it would.

First, he'd realized the new job's possibilities, and the city hadn't let him down. The salary was $20,000 now, and if he could get the city water supply problem solved this year, there was the promise of $22,500 or maybe even $25,000. Secondly, the house had given him the right image, the air of one who belonged. He'd made good contacts, on and off the job, and his returns from oil and electronic investments had been spectacular. The house, he was sure, had much to do with that success. And no one could blame a house for the things that had gone wrong.

As he walked in the place seemed deserted. He stood for a moment, uncertain. Then he heard noises from the kitchen and knew that at least Calla Lilly was on the job. The big Negro woman was stacking breakfast dishes in the dishwasher. "Mornin'," she said, looking up without interrupting the clatter. No protocol was more important than Calla Lilly's work.

"Morning," he said, accenting the "g." "Where is everybody?"

"You just missed the younguns," she said. "Miss Chris left about a half-hour ago. That boy friend came by for her. Ronnie left on his bicycle just 'fore you came." She suddenly stopped stacking dishes to fix him with an accusing stare. "You goin' to want breakfast?"

"No, just coffee, Calla. And maybe a couple of doughnuts or a roll." He crossed to the refrigerator and poured a glass of orange juice. "Mrs. Hartwell up yet?"

Instantly he knew he'd goofed by the way Calla cut her eyes at him.

"Mrs. Hartwell went to Dallas," Calla said, and before he'd had time to absorb that, she threw the punch line. "Yesterday. She took a plane yesterday afternoon."

Her car must have been in the parking lot at the airport. He thought back . . . there'd been that damned chamber meeting last night, and it'd been after midnight when he got home. Then he was up and out of the house before six-thirty this morning. A sudden wave of anger swept through him; damn it, she could have phoned to let him know. He fought for control of his temper.

"What did she go for?"

"Shoppin', I guess."

He sipped the orange juice and tried to sound casual. "She say when she'd be back?"

"Tonight, she said."

He tried to think how to phrase the next question.

"Was she . . . all right when she left?"

It wasn't Calla Lilly's philosophy to mince words. "She wasn't drunk, but she wasn't sober."

He put the empty glass on the drainboard. "Please have her call me when she comes in," he said.

Calla nodded without comment. She was busy measuring coffee into the small coffeepot.

"I'll be back down for that," he said.

Still fighting his anger, he went upstairs to his room. He shaved and showered. Remembering he was to meet with the parks board during the afternoon, he laid out a fresh suit. Then he picked up the bedside phone and dialed the office.

Stella's efficient voice answered.

"Morning, Stella," he said. "Have I had any calls?"

"The city attorney has called twice. He said to tell you he wants to see you as soon as possible, that it's very urgent."

"Bud?" he asked in surprise. "Well, if he calls back, tell him I'll be in within thirty minutes."

He cradled the phone, wondering. Never in the five years they'd worked together had he seen Bud Tatum consider anything urgent.

Bud Tatum came into the office breathing deeply, his normally jovial fat face intent and serious. He sank into the big leather chair by David's desk and inhaled deeply to catch his breath.

David laughed. "You look like the personification of a harbinger of trouble."

Tatum wasn't in the mood for levity. "Dave, somebody got ahold of that highway map months ago. They bought up all along the right-of-way."

Almost without being aware of it, David got up from his desk and closed the door to the outer office, the high humor of a moment ago gone. A wave of premonition swept over him; Tatum wasn't the type to go off the deep end.

"Go on," David said as he went back to his desk.

"I went down to the county clerk's office yesterday to check on the northeast cloverleaf. There was a question in my mind exactly how many parcels of land we are going to have to acquire. Maybe I was jumping the gun a little, but when people ask me for information about these things, I like to have it right at hand."

David nodded impatiently.

"Twenty-six lots along the right-of-way changed hands in three days last December."

Suddenly, David understood Tatum's concern. The proposed route wasn't made public until the middle of January. Tatum unlocked his briefcase, took out a highway map, and spread it on the polished mahogany desktop. He put a forefinger on the cloverleaf, then hunted back down the highway until he found the place.

"Right there," Tatum said.

David remembered the area from the air, choice land for motel or service station sites, the first metropolitan area incoming traffic from the west would encounter. Still. . . .

"Couldn't it be coincidence?" he asked. "Or pure speculation?"

"I don't think so. Seven separate transactions, all to the same man. A Donald Ratliff. He seemed to know what he was doing."

The name didn't mean anything. "Who is he?"

Tatum spread his hands. "I haven't found out yet. He isn't listed in the phone book or city directory. The address he gave was 204 South Main, a fleabag hotel."

"You check to see if he lives there?"

"No. I thought I'd better talk with you before going any further. I didn't run onto this until late yesterday afternoon, and I didn't want to arouse suspicion by asking questions. I tried to call you at home last night."

"Chamber dinner," David explained.

He examined his desk calendar, trying to remember the sequence of events and dates. Then a slow comprehension came to him. He didn't want to believe the working of his own mind, but logic told him this was the answer. To make sure, he called Stella in and had her look up the files on his communications with the council. He had been right.

The highway program was sent out to the council on the first Saturday in December. According to Tatum's notes, six lots were purchased the following Monday, eight Tuesday, and twelve Wednesday.

"You think anybody'd put down money just on the proposed program?" Tatum asked.

"They'd be gambling," David admitted. "But not much. I'd say there was about a ninety-to-one shot that the program would go through. The only real risk they ran was at the polls. They almost got fooled, there."

He got up restlessly and crossed to the window, looking down on the boulevard below, thinking. Maybe he was wrong. A number of people had access to that information. But the calendar sure pointed toward the council.

In the eight years he'd been city manager, there never had been any question of council integrity. Sometimes, at meetings with other city managers, he'd heard others complain of the problem, and he'd always dreaded the day when it might happen to him. For it was a weakness that undermined his whole job philosophy.

He had been making decisions for others as long as he could remember, and he had evolved his own long-thought-out theories. Even as a boy he had been the leader. He had decided what games they played, assigned roles and set the rules. It was then, as a child, that he'd learned fairness had a large part in leadership. Partiality or favoritism caused the loss of confidence of all concerned. Later, in sports, he'd developed these discoveries further. He hadn't been an exceptional athlete, but in football his quarterbacking had won him all-state honors his senior year and the knowledge that under pressure a team functions best with one brain.

The war, though, was what taught him the peculiar aspects of command.

He learned that in every emergency, every situation calling for decision, there is a distinct interval when most men hesitate, hoping the decision will be made for them. He'd learned to use that moment. A word, a gesture often was enough. Then he'd learned something else. Although his superiors in rank often accepted his decisions as their own, their subconscious seemed to know. They came to depend on him.

That had been his one secret, his one true talent. And no job was better suited to that talent than city managership. Little power was given a manager in the city charter. The council could hire and fire him; the council held all legal power. But the council was made up of nonprofessionals. When the need for decision arose, they hesitated, usually to the extent of appointing a committee, either of themselves or other nonprofessionals, to report back with a recommendation. His influence had to be subtle, for as elected officials they were his employers and often self-consciously protective of their status. Yet they knew his voice was that of a professional. The council never had voted against his wishes on any major issue.

But to function well, he had to have the council's complete confidence. More important, he had to know the council members, the way each one thought. Maybe he had grown careless.

He turned back to Tatum. "We're going to have to move carefully on this," David said. "I guess the first thing we'd better do is check out this Ratliff. Why don't you go down to the police department and talk to Chief McDowell? Tell him what we know, what we want, and get him to put a couple of detectives on it. All off the record, of course. We just want to know who this guy is, how long he's been in town, who his friends are, everything we can find out without tipping our hand."

"Then you don't want anybody to talk to him?"

"No, I don't think so. Way I figure it, he's a front, or else that address is a front. McDowell's boys probably can learn more by tapping their lower Main grapevine than they'd get from him, anyway. When McDowell gets his report, then the three of us can get together on it. In the meantime, why don't you go back down and check the records to see if there's been any other transactions. And I'll be making a list of everyone who had access to the information before that date. Maybe we can come up with something."

After Tatum left, David thought about the mystery the rest of the morning. As usual when such problems arose, there was a flurry of work to be done, so he wasn't able to concentrate fully. But while he dictated and signed letters, conferred with department heads on lesser problems and took calls from complaining residents, the puzzle never was far from his mind.

So when the noon hour came, he was impatient to get back to the mystery. Instead of going downtown for lunch, or to the City Hall cafeteria, as he usually did, he sent out for a sandwich and locked the door. Then, scratchpad before him, he began the list. Out of a sense of innate fairness, he started with employees.

Engineers?

He counted eight—the city engineer, the planning engineer, two with the consulting firm retained by the city, and four state engineers. When he began the analysis, he found they fell into the same category: dedicated career men who had handled many such projects before with no question of personal conduct. He then listed himself, his secretary Stella, and the city attorney, Bud Tatum. Beside each name he carefully put a check mark, signifying his complete trust. This brought him down to the council.

Or did it? He couldn't overlook anything. There was the actual delivery of the agendas. He had to consider each step.

A few days before council meetings, which were held every first and third Tuesday, David sent an agenda to each council member and the mayor. He had devised his own system, and it had worked well. Each councilman, upon election, was presented with a handsome hand-tooled leather briefcase embossed with his name. As David made up the agenda, he dictated all information available on each item, usually giving his views and recommendations, as well as those of the city department heads involved. The briefcases were locked and delivered by an off-duty policeman. After the council meeting, the councilmen took what they wanted for their own files and turned in the briefcases to the city secretary, who returned them to Stella. The plan had worked well, up to now.

He put down the policeman's name, considered it, then put a check mark beside it, too. The same man had been delivering the briefcases six years. Besides, any tampering with the locks would be apparent.

There was the possibility the information was returned with the briefcases and left in the custody of the city secretary overnight. That was not likely, but he had to consider the possibility. He added the city secretary to the list. And beside the name he put another check mark. This was the little man's twenty-seventh year as a city employee. That brought him to the council, and the last seven names.

The mayor?

David forced himself to consider the question objectively. No,

Hiram Milner had spent a lifetime building a good name. Now he was wearing the laurels of that lifetime in the title of mayor.

The realtor?

Walt Weatherbee was selfish in some ways. But it was a way of thinking, not dishonesty. Weatherbee protected his competitors' interests as closely as his own. He just happened to know real estate and residential construction. Every action he took as a councilman was considered from that limited viewpoint. There had been examples of Walt's honesty. David knew of one case where a young couple bought a house from Walt. A year later, after a heavy rain, the walls began cracking and the doors sticking as the foundation settled. Walt discovered that part of the house had been built over an old abandoned storm cellar or dugout dating back to the early days. Walt had moved the couple into a house with a $1000 higher price tag, absorbing the loss. David put down another check mark.

The rancher?

David had hunted with Cal Masters, drunk with him, fished with him. In Cal's eighty years of independent thinking, he had made many enemies. But no one had ever called him dishonest.

The doctor?

Dr. Travis McNiel was the council's hardest-working member. He never cast a vote on any issue until he had made his own personal, exhaustive study. His whole life seemed to be dedicated to public service, either at the hospital or on the council. He was a general practitioner in the days of specialists. If he were after money, he had the training and professional reputation to earn it easily. He could just move off the hospital staff and open a swanky suite in a clinic with a couple of colleagues. Another check mark.

The merchant?

Bill Wentworth had a personality about as complex as a newborn puppy. The council's youngest member, thirty-three, he also was the best-liked, not only by other council members, but by the voters, too. In six years, Wentworth had parlayed a backyard repair shop into the biggest electrical appliance store in town, mostly on the strength of becoming a friend of every customer. He'd been president of the Jaycees, the Lions Club, and the Miramar Parent-Teachers Association, vice-chairman in charge of the industrial division of the United Fund, and was a past grand master of a Masonic lodge. He had been elected to council last November on the most overwhelming vote in years. No, there wasn't a devious thought in Bill Wentworth's head, and he didn't need one. He had it made without subterfuge.

The undertaker?

John Byron was the council's conservative, a descendant of the town's first undertaker. Now John, third in line of Byron Funeral Home owners, called it "funeral director." His father apparently had been more than a passing student of subsurface geology, for his oil ventures during the pre-Depression boom had paid off. More of the family income now came from the ground than from what went into it. On any question, John Byron was for the status quo, and had opposed the highway program because a rejection of the plan would help curb federal spending. He had almost succeeded. On urban renewal, he had been successful, heading a movement that brought a two-to-one opposition to the polls. A Republican, Byron had run a close race for Congress a few years back. From what David had heard, Byron still had ambitions in that direction. No, John Byron had no use for motel sites.

That left David with one name—the one he'd known all along he would end up with: Max Berger, man of mystery.

David tried to be reasonable. Actually, he knew little about Max Berger. A beer distributor, Berger also was a church lay leader. He seemed to spend all his time in the shoddy, run-down section along lower Main. Yet, the very fact that he had been elected to council showed he had wide support.

Some inner instinct had told David from the first that Max Berger was going to be trouble. His dislike had been nothing he could define. He thought now of the prematurely bald, shiny skull, the restless eyes, and tiny, soft feminine hands that were never still. There was just something about Berger that David didn't trust.

Out of the twenty names on the list, there was only one he could not honor with a check mark: Max Berger.

## CHAPTER TWO

Springtime on the north central plains of Texas is a subtle thing. It consists of a few rare, uncertain days in—probably—April, between swift cold fronts sweeping more winter down from the high plains. These rare, uncertain days occur only infrequently until—again probably—May, and the first hot breath of summer. Then, suddenly, spring is gone before one is aware of its arrival.

Thomas Kencaide was reflecting on this as he pushed Old Smokey through the freeway traffic. This truly was one of those precious days, the sky clear, the sun warm, and the air vibrant.

Kencaide felt good. He had slept late, one of the few compensations of night work. And now he was on his way to a leisurely breakfast alone in accord with his mood.

The question was where. No place he knew rose to the heights of his mood. If West Texas is libeled in the existing belief it is the gourmet's wasteland, there is a truth that the finicky diner often has his sensitivities trod upon. The same restaurant that attracts the gourmet may repel the epicure. Even with the casual diner—and Kencaide definitely put himself in this class—most restaurants do not wear well. Familiarity brings discoveries. A restaurant with excellent food suddenly diminishes in stature some morning in the discovery that the waitresses have the habit of wiping each table with the still-moist napkin of the departing customer. The discovery lingers in the mind, and on the next morning is recalled abruptly when the silverware is placed on the bare table, perhaps on some suspicious moisture. At another, a piece of debris is found on a fork, and forever after their dishwashing ability is suspect. A restaurant with superb omelets inevitably lets in a trace of eggshell some morning, and thereafter each bite holds potential hazard.

No West Texas waitress considers herself a servant in any sense of the word. She is a participant in one of nature's pleasures, and she wants to share this experience. Many consider ten days' acquaintance sufficient to make the customer a confidante, and at fifteen days' acquaintance reveal what terrible things the customer's favorite dish does to her own digestive system.

These are the tribulations of the daily public diner. In five years, Kencaide had patronized and abandoned more than two dozen eateries. Now, he was almost to the end of the list.

He took the exit off the freeway and turned onto the old highway, passing four former favorites, remembering and rejecting each. Then he recalled a new place he had seen at the edge of town and had intended to investigate.

The new café passed exterior inspection, so he entered. Inside, it was clean and quiet. He picked up an afternoon paper—an early street edition—and took it back to a table.

The waitress was young, but efficient, and she treated him with the polite deference reserved for strangers. He ordered the mushroom omelet, then turned through the paper as he sampled the coffee.

There was another satellite up, another threat from Russia, the Texas Legislature was set for another day of bickering over the budget, there was a rewrite of Kencaide's coverage of the mayor's speech last night pledging top priority on a new water supply. The weather was given a two-column headline on the possibility of severe thunderstorms and damaging winds. Looked like a fair news day shaping up.

The omelet was good, the coffee excellent. He ate leisurely, savoring the new atmosphere. He knew from experience the next visit would not be as favorable, and with each time after that familiarity would grow, dangerous discoveries become imminent.

He left reluctantly, driving downtown toward the office—not because it was time, but because he felt good and there was nothing else he felt like doing.

Further indication that this was one of Kencaide's better days came when he found a parking place for Old Smokey less than a block from the office. He put two nickels in the meter and walked the block. Then, as the traffic light held him across the street, he stood studying the building, trying to see it objectively, as an outsider might see it, a mental exercise he practiced frequently.

The three-story aluminum, glass, and brick building at the corner of Main and Eighth which housed the *News-Gazette* offices was less than three years old. Already, even from the outside, it was taking on that battered, trampy look newspaper buildings usually acquire. As the light changed and he crossed the street, he noticed that the glass front was a little dingier than the other windows along the street—the result of ink dust. As he swung through the glass doors into the lobby, he could see that despite twice-weekly moppings the floors bore the indelible mark of pressroom feet. Past classified and circulation, he stepped onto the self-operated elevator at the rear. Already it moved slowly, jerkily, as if overworked and indulged in self-pity.

He punched the second-floor button gratefully. No one appreciated the elevator more. He still remembered the stairs of the old building with loathing. In normal walking Kencaide could move as well as anyone. But stairs were a problem for prosthetic feet.

As the automatic doors opened on the newsroom Kencaide continued his objective study. Here, where one would expect it least, there was a stubborn resistance to trampiness. Perhaps it was because reporters and deskmen who had worked with cast-off desks and equipment for years considered the new office furniture an elevation of status and fought to retain it.

Kencaide picked up a fresh newspaper from the rubber-tired cart by the watercooler and strolled to his desk in the far corner of the right-hand—or night—side. No one paid any attention to him. The day side was too busy, and the night side was deserted. He spread the paper on his desk and analyzed the changes since the first edition.

A verbal clash in the Legislature had moved that story into the No. 1 spot, replacing the Russian threat. The weather bureau had added the phrase "possibility of a few isolated tornadoes" to the forecast and placed a wide area—including the city—under alert.

Kencaide was still digesting the details of the new stories when a passing copy boy put a note on his spike: "*Kencaide see me first,*" in Houston Collier's terse scrawl. He folded the paper and walked over to where Collier sat at the city desk less than twenty feet away.

Houston Collier, city editor of the morning *News,* was the best newspaperman Kencaide knew. There was a story he was trained in law, a graduate of the University of Texas Law School. Upon graduation, he had taken a newspaper job covering courts until the date of the state bar examination. When time came for the exam, Collier didn't bother. He had found his life's work.

He was a small man, with a Cagneyish, wide-eyed quizzical expression of surprise, which was misleading. For nothing ever surprised Houston Collier. He sat now looking up at Kencaide's shirtfront, and it occurred to Kencaide that Collier must know every reporter's ensemble of sport shirts, belt buckles, and ties, for he rarely bothered to look up at their faces.

"What'll you have coming?" Collier asked.

"Council agenda for tomorrow night's meeting is the only thing I know of. Only item of importance will be the final contract on the highway bypass, I think. The mayor might jump the gun on the lake."

"What about the lake?"

"Consulting engineers' report is ready, I hear. They might set the date tomorrow night to hear it. I believe Hartwell wants to hold off on it awhile, but the mayor seems to be getting impatient."

Collier sighed. "Well, keep after them. Let's don't goof on this precious lake if we have to let everything else go to hell. Let's have every word you can think of to write on it."

Tom Kencaide nodded. The lake was the pet promotion project of the publisher, BeeBee Milam. For years the paper had been running "the need for" editorials signed by BeeBee. With the lake nearing actuality, BeeBee's interest had developed into a monomania.

Collier laid down his copy pencil, leaned back in his chair, and gave Kencaide a rare examination with his slate-gray eyes. "Tell me, how well do you know this new councilman, Max Berger?"

Tom hesitated only a moment. He couldn't fool Collier. "I don't know him at all," he admitted. "He's a weird fish. I've never been able to get him to talk, and as far as I can tell he doesn't talk to any of the other councilmen, Hartwell, or the mayor. He never comes to those precouncil discussions or even gives his opinion in regular sessions. He just votes."

Collier seemed to consider the answer. Abruptly, he changed the subject, a Collier habit. "There was a little tavern owner in here earlier today," Collier said slowly. "He told a strange tale about the police department harassing his place of business. May not be anything in it, but I told him you'd drop by and see him this afternoon."

Collier handed Tom a piece of copy paper with a name and address. Joe Garzek, Longhorn Lounge, 3313 Broadway—right outside the Air Force base. Tom had noticed the place, but he'd never been inside.

"Wouldn't this be police beat?" Tom asked. J. Marvin Olds didn't like other reporters trespassing in his domain.

"I think it goes beyond that, if it's anything at all," Collier said. "Sounds like your department. Besides, the little guy asked for you. But you might clue Olds in on it and work with him, if you want."

Collier leaned forward abruptly, picked up the copy pencil, and went back to work where he'd left off so quickly Tom would have been startled if he hadn't grown accustomed to the curt way of ending a conversation.

Slightly nettled by Collier's technique in handing out assignments, Tom returned to his desk. He knew from experience Collier had left many details unmentioned, for it was Collier's theory that a reporter should go after his own story, and the less secondhand information the better.

Yet, something in Collier's manner made Tom think this was more than an ordinary story.

He looked at his watch. Two-fifteen. Allowing thirty or forty minutes for the interview, he still could drive out there and be back at City Hall in plenty of time to make his news beat.

Retracing his steps to Old Smokey, Tom drove out to the air base, turned onto Broadway opposite the base entrance, and found the tavern a half block up the street. The parking lot was gravel, but the long, low building was modern brick around three sides with glass brick across the front. Tom remembered that the glass bricks were lighted with checkerboard red and green lights at night.

When he first stepped inside the tavern the semidarkness was blinding. He stood for a moment until his vision cleared. The place was almost deserted, just the bartender and two customers. Tom walked across the bare floor to the bar.

"Mr. Garzek?"

"I Joe Garzek," the bartender said.

"I'm Tom Kencaide." Garzek's handshake was surprisingly strong for such a small man. His complexion was dark, and he wore a close, pencil-line mustache above a wide, uneasy smile.

"I see many of your stories in the paper," Garzek said. "That why I ask for you."

"I'm flattered," Tom said as Garzek came around the end of the bar and pulled a chair out from a table for him. "Few people bother to notice or remember by-lines."

"You like some beer? Or coffee maybe?"

"Coffee would be fine."

As Garzek went behind the bar again for the coffee Tom took the opportunity to study the place better, now that his eyes had adjusted. The place was clean, more than anyone could say for most of the beer taverns in town. A jukebox on the far wall provided most of the interior lighting, aided only by a few luminated beer signs and a clock, set several minutes ahead of true time in keeping with the widespread practice to keep drinking well within legal curfew. An empty bandstand filled one corner, and the dance floor looked as if it might hold ten or twelve couples comfortably. Garzek brought the coffee, then took two beers over to the customers in the corner, two oil workers engrossed in their own conversation.

"Nice place you have here, Mr Garzek," Tom said as Garzek returned.

"I thank you. I try to run clean place, Mr Kencaide. No drunks, no rough talk tolerated. For two years I run the place without arrest or policeman inside until three months ago. Mr Collier tell you what they do to me?"

"No." There was no way to explain Collier's theory of news gathering. "He was pretty busy," Tom added lamely. "He just left your name."

"First, I tell you this," Garzek said. "Six months ago, a man come in here. He say, 'You not sell enough Alamo Beer.' I think he joking, so I joke back. I say 'What you mean, I sell lotsa Alamo Beer.' He say, 'You not sell enough, Mr. Garzek. When people ask for something else, you tell them Alamo Beer better. That way you sell a hundred cases every week,

Mr. Garzek. Remember, Mr. Garzek, hundred cases a week.' Then he turn and walk out."

Garzek looked at the door, like he was remembering it happening. Suddenly Tom understood why Collier put him on the story instead of Olds, the police reporter. Councilman Max Berger was area distributor for Alamo Beer.

"He ever come back?"

Garzek nodded vigorously. "I still think maybe it a joke. But two week later he come in, he look at me and say, 'Mr. Garzek, week before last you only sell seventy cases Alamo Beer. Last week you only sell sixty-five. You going to have to do better, Mr. Garzek.' I say, 'Who are you. What you want?' He say, 'I only interested in your welfare, Mr. Garzek. You sell too much other kinds of beer. If you don't sell hundred cases Alamo Beer a week, you have trouble.' I tell him, 'It's free country. I don't have to sell any Alamo Beer.' He just look at me and he say, 'Remember, Mr. Garzek. Hundred cases a week your quota.'"

"What about the regular salesman? The one you'd been buying Alamo Beer from. Did he know who the man was?"

"I ask him. He say it must be a promotion man. He not know what his name is."

"Have you talked with any officials of the distributing company?"

"I call Mr. Berger," Garzek said. "He say he sorry if there some misunderstanding, but he know nothing about it, that each salesman responsible for his district, to talk to him."

"What did the district man say?"

"He not come back. When Alamo truck come next time the driver unload forty cases. I tell him that too much, I only order thirty cases. He look at his order and say, 'You ordered forty cases, Mr. Garzek.' I say, 'Take it all back. I not take one case.' Next night, when lounge full, policemen come in, start asking all my customers for ID card."

"Did you ask why?"

"Lieutenant say someone report I selling beer to minors. I never sell beer to minors, Mr. Kencaide."

Tom nodded. "Do you know the police lieutenant's name?"

"Robinson. You know him?"

"I know him. But not well. Did anyone hear this first man threaten you with 'trouble'?"

Garzek thought for a moment. "No, we there at bar. Maybe some customers hear when I get mad and shout at him, tell him I not going to buy any more Alamo Beer."

"When the police came, that first night, did they arrest anyone?"

"Not here, first night. But they arrest two boys who leave, say they drunk driving. Two boys from the base, no father here to look after them. I go down to the jail next morning and put up the money so they won't get in trouble with the Air Force."

"How long was it until the police came back, then?"

"Next night, and every night since. Sometimes one, sometimes two, sometimes four or five policemen a night. My customers not like that. Sometimes the boys with girls, get embarrass with police pushing them around. Sometimes I have to say, 'No more beer, boys. Police waiting outside to get anyone who have more'n two, three beer.' Now all customers go somewhere else."

Garzek tried to maintain his smile, failed, lowered his head. "I sorry, Mr. Kencaide. I get so angry. I have wife, children to think of. It not fair."

"No, it isn't, Mr. Garzek," Tom agreed. "Surely there's some recourse for you. Have you talked to the Liquor Control Board?"

"I make complaint, but when I go back next time they say they talk to police about me, and that this place a 'trouble spot,' that if I don't clean it up, they going to take my license."

Tom nodded. With nightly police visits, Garzek would have a record at the police station a foot long.

"These complaints, have the police ever told you who is making them?"

"I try to find out. They just tell me 'responsible citizens, Mr. Garzek.' "

Tom glanced at his watch, suddenly realizing he was running late.

"I've got to get on up to City Hall," he explained. "I'll try to do all I can for you, Mr. Garzek, but it's not going to be easy."

"You going to write a story?"

"Not right now," Tom said, trying to find a way to bridge the gap between the newspaper profession and the public's impression of it. "You see, we can only print something we could prove in court, if we should have to do so. If we printed what you have just told me, Berger could sue you, me and the newspaper for libel. It would be up to us to prove these things happened. We have to have evidence, and that may take time."

Big tears came to Garzek's eyes. "I lose money every day, Mr. Kencaide," he said. "I not know how long I can keep lounge open."

"I'll do the best I can," Tom promised. "I'll be back out late tonight. Maybe I'll know some of the policemen well enough to talk to them. We have another reporter who covers the police station, and maybe he can help us. In the meantime, if the man who threatened you should come back, it might help if you could get his license number, or make sure someone overhears your conversation with him."

Only after he left the tavern and was on his way to City Hall did Tom begin to realize the potentialities of Garzek's story.

Garzek was telling the truth, he believed. Every instinct told him so. The more he thought about the interview, the more certain he became. And if they were doing this to Garzek, what about every other tavern in town? Surely there were others.

If there were several policemen involved, the organization must be wide, well-established. Big names must be involved, maybe even Police Chief McDowell. He would have to be very careful whom he questioned.

Getting this story wasn't going to be easy. But he had a feeling this was one of those stories a newspaper thrives on, wins respect for and gains admiration with—one most newspapermen never find in a lifetime of work.

Once, when he was a boy in the dirty Depression Thirties, Tom Kencaide's greatest ambition had been to put as many miles as possible between himself and his home town.

Two wars and the GI Bill had helped him do that. For a long time he'd had no desire to return. He newspapered other places —New York, San Francisco, New Orleans.

It was during the year he'd spent in Barcelona trying to write a novel that he first began thinking seriously of returning home.

He found he wasn't ready to write a novel. A writer has to believe he has uncorked some of life's fundamental truths, and Tom knew he hadn't. He had the questions, but questions are no good without answers.

He remembered Antonio Lopez, his Army drinking buddy, who used to say, "*La vida es como la espuma en la cerveza*" ("Life is like the foam on the beer"), and then he'd grin and blow the foam off the beer.

Life had been like that for Tony. Tom had walked away and left Tony's body lying in the snow above the Changjin Reservoir on the long retreat to the sea after the Chinese swarmed across the Yalu. In Spain, Tom had tried to write Tony's story—that life is nothing—but he found he didn't believe it himself. Maybe Tony hadn't believed it either, really. He'd never been too hung over to miss Mass, and his last living act had been to peel off his heavy gloves and take the crucifix and St. Christopher's medal in his bare hands.

The more Tom searched for these fundamental truths, the more he remembered his home town and the people in it. So he'd returned, hunting the answers.

Some he'd found . . . a few that are of this world. . . .

As a working reporter he'd had license to prowl the city in darkness and in light and discover its nature. . . .

The place to search for truth, he had found, is in the workings of the human mind and in the hopes of the human heart. That was his one secret. That was why he won prizes as a reporter and acquired a reputation far beyond his years. He never wrote of events. He wrote of people. There were many he would never forget:

The twenty-three-year-old mother who took her baby by one foot and bashed its brains into the kitchen sink one hot August night . . . the father who shot his seventeen-year-old son to death in a drunken rage in an argument over the keys to an old Ford . . . the mother who grabbed a rattlesnake with her bare hands when she saw it crawling toward her child . . . the bank vice-president who went to Saturday afternoon kiddie movies and sat next to little boys . . . the blind youth working on his master's degree in psychology . . . the wreck victims at the hospital, the relatives standing in the corridors . . . the old man who lived in the city dump and scavenged for thirty-four dogs that shared his one-room shack and low opinion of the rest of the world. . . .

There were more, hundreds more. Tom had seen them, talked with them . . . He had asked *why* and seen incomprehension on their faces. They didn't know. But sometimes Tom thought he came close to understanding.

He knew the city and its people, he believed, better than anyone else. He knew the city's past, its present, and maybe a little of its future.

And now he had to find the answer to Max Berger.

When the Kiowa-Comanche came on moonlit nights, the first families had known what to do. They put the women and children inside the walls and fought. But how do you fight the white-shirted savage? How do you fight the raid from within?

Already late in getting to City Hall, Tom tried to hurry through his run. But as he'd anticipated, it was a heavy news day.

In the city engineer's office a building permit had been issued for a new downtown motel estimated to cost a half million dollars. Tom took what facts were available so he could contact the building contractor and the owners.

In the water department, the superintendent had new figures on the failure of fall and winter rains to replenish last summer's strain on the city's water reserve. This, to Publisher BeeBee Milam, would be shocking news, proving the logic of his campaign for a new lake. So Tom gathered all the statistics.

The parks board had met and discussed routine business. No, the board chairman told Tom, they had not decided what to do if faced with a federal court order to integrate swimming pools. They would cross that bridge when they came to it.

The personnel office had a release on an examination for fire and police department applicants. The city tax assessor-collector had some new figures to release showing the efficiency of his office. The traffic engineer had a new traffic pattern going into effect at a major, troublesome intersection.

Bud Tatum, the city attorney, was the only official who failed to have some news item. For the first time since Tom had known him, the city attorney was curt, almost rude.

So as Tom went on up to the office of David Hartwell, the last on his run, he made a mental note to keep his guard up. Something was wrong. Curtness was out of character for Tatum.

Through the years, Tom and Hartwell had developed a sparring half-banter, half-serious tone in a contest of wits they both enjoyed. Even if Hartwell had a news release he wanted printed, he would be reluctant, making Tom work for the story. Sometimes Tom would pay him back by bluffing a story out of him.

Today, with the vague premonition that something was wrong, Tom went into Hartwell's office doubly alert. But he saw nothing amiss in the expression or manner of Stella, Hartwell's secretary. And Hartwell was his usual calm, collected self.

"Anything going on today?" Tom asked from the doorway, observing Hartwell's face closely.

"No, not a thing," Hartwell said easily. "But you're welcome to come in and sit a while."

Hartwell's office was more like a den, with hunting trophies and gun cabinet along the wall behind his desk, and pictures of past mayors arranged on the inside wall, facing the windows. The deep chairs and heavy carpet gave the office a sense of informality sometimes proven by the lowboy under the pictures that concealed a complete bar.

Today Tom was late, so he wasted no time in flinging the gauntlet to Hartwell. "What do you mean, nothing going on? What about the lake report?" he asked as he sank into the chair by Hartwell's desk.

Hartwell's face betrayed no surprise. "I don't know what you're getting at, Tom. What about the lake report?"

"I hear the consulting engineers have the report ready on their site recommendation."

There was only the slightest flicker of irritation on Hartwell's face, but the abruptness of his question indicated how hard the leak in his security system hit home.

"Who told you that?"

Tom grinned at the unexpected reaction. If he hadn't surprised Hartwell, caught him off base, he never would have cracked that iron reserve.

"I just heard it some place, I don't remember where," Tom

said casually. Actually, he had been tipped by one of the girls in the water department who overheard the water superintendent telling the city engineer. Tom decided to try a poker-faced bluff. "I also heard that the mayor was quite upset about the lake report not being on the agenda for tomorrow night, and asked that it be included."

But he had overplayed his hand. Hartwell hesitated only an instant, then grinned back at him. "I think I'm being put on," he said. "Boy, are you sharp today. All right, you win. A quote: The council will be asked to set a date tomorrow night on which to hear the report of the consulting engineers as to the most suitable site for the proposed new city reservoir."

Tom put the statement on his notepad, more from habit than from necessity. "Congratulations," he said. "You have just made one hell of a splash on the front page of tomorrow morning's *News*."

"Come off it, Tom," Hartwell said. "All we're going to do tomorrow night is set a date to hear the report. There's nothing new, yet."

"Anything with the word lake in it is big news where I work," Tom told him.

"I wish you would play this thing down for a while."

"I just write the stories," Tom explained once again. "I don't have any say about how they're played."

"I'm afraid publicity at this point is doing more harm than good," Hartwell said seriously. "I'd sure like to let tempers cool a little from that bypass rhubarb before we tackle this."

Tom knew Hartwell was confiding now in a friend, not speaking for publication. There is a journalistic school of thought that anything said in the presence of a reporter is privileged, but Tom never had subscribed to it. Others could use their methods, he would use his. He believed he could do a better, more intelligent job of reporting in the long run if he had the reputation of never betraying a confidence.

"You might call BeeBee Milam and tell him how you feel about it," Tom suggested. "If he could be convinced he actually is hurting his pet project by these stories, he might slack off."

Hartwell considered the suggestion briefly. "No, I don't think he would listen to me. He's never liked me, and I think he has a slight suspicion—well-founded—that I don't like him."

"Maybe someone else could convince him."

"I don't know of anyone he would listen to who is on the right side of the fence. The mayor isn't. And the chamber has a full head of steam up, so I guess it's going to be full speed ahead and damn the torpedoes."

There suddenly was a growing tide of noise outside in the halls, and in the outer office they could hear Stella closing her typewriter well and locking the file cabinets. Hartwell made no move indicating he knew it was five o'clock, quitting time. Sometimes Tom wondered if Hartwell lived in his office.

Tom remembered the stories of Hartwell's wife. Did her drinking make him reluctant to go home, or was it the other way around? Again, he glanced at the long gun cabinet. Hartwell once had explained he kept the guns in his office because he wanted to keep them away from the children. But Hartwell's boy and girl were in high school now. Was Hartwell afraid to keep the guns around his wife?

Hartwell caught him studying the gun case. "You keep denying it, but you're a gun-nut, Tom. I can tell by the way you keep looking at that cabinet. Put it down in your date book now, we're going to go hunting next fall."

Tom decided to end this continual invitation with the real reason he always declined. "I'd like to, but with these feet I can't do very well on rough ground."

"Hell, that's no problem," Hartwell said. "We could drive right out into the field."

"I don't think I'd feel right, shooting deer in somebody's pasture."

Hartwell laughed. "I'll make a confession. I never have."

They talked then, for a while, of hunting, cartridge performance, and lesser things.

Not until Tom was on the way back to the newspaper office did he remember how Bud Tatum had acted and the premonition that something unusual had happened at City Hall today. He thought back over Hartwell's relaxed manner. Maybe he had been wrong.

Later, the lake story written, he hurried to finish up the other stories. He had trouble contacting the owners of the new motel, and when he did, they were reluctant to reveal the rest of the information he needed. They would have an "announcement" ready in a few days, they explained. Finally he worked out a compromise to make the "announcement" now, with the promise of a feature story later when they had the "artist's conception" ready. He turned the story in to an impatient Collier.

"That wraps it up," Tom said. "I'll be at Harry's if you need me."

"Alone?" Collier asked.

Tom grinned, knowing he was being teased. "No, I'm going to fill Olds in on this Joe Garzek thing, and see what he thinks."

"Olds is going to steal that girl from you," Collier said. "I know that old bastard."

"Not a chance," Tom told him.

He started to move away, then saw the piece of copy Collier was working on—the lake story, guided for an eight-column wrap on page one. A line of heavy black pencil showed that Collier had made a change in the first paragraph. More in curiosity than concern, Tom leaned over and read it.

As Tom had written it, the paragraph said: "The report of the city's consulting engineers on choice of a site for the proposed new water reservoir is ready for presentation, City Manager David Hartwell said Monday. The City Council will be asked at its regular session Tuesday night to set a date to hear the report."

Collier had scratched out the "will be asked" and altered the sentence to read "is expected to set a date at its regular session Tuesday night to hear the report."

"Don't you think that 'is expected' is editorializing?" Tom asked.

Collier sighed, put his pencil down, and leaned back in his chair. "Tom, are we going to go through that again?"

It was old, familiar ground, wearing thin now.

"I think our readers know propaganda when they see it," Tom said.

"We just have one reader that matters," Collier said. "If

BeeBee Milam wants to editorialize, we editorialize. It's his newspaper."

Tom saw that his by-line had been penciled in over the story. "You can just take my name off of it, then," he said.

"Kencaide, don't turn prima donna on me," Collier warned, his voice rising.

The other desk workers had looked up, listening. There was a stack of copy in front of Collier, waiting. This was no time to make an issue of it. Tom turned and walked away.

On the way to pick up Arlene, Tom tried to recover his earlier mood, but failed. Why did he have to be such a nitpicker? Why couldn't he just ignore those things. Others did. But being on the way to see his girl made him feel a little better.

Arlene White lived alone in a small efficiency apartment in a modern two-story unit. She was the assistant advertising manager of the most exclusive department store in town, making a salary, he would guess, about half again his own. The delicate matter never had been discussed.

They had been engaged one year, eleven months, and three days. Why she had taken an interest in him in the first place, he never knew, but she had. Theirs had been a stormy engagement, explanation enough for her refusal to set a definite date. But never in the heat of disagreement had either ever considered calling the engagement off—reason enough, he thought, to make their differences domestic.

And tonight he was late as usual, which didn't help, for his continual tardiness was one of the sore points between them. When he heard movement on his first ring, he knew she was ready, waiting, and his lateness was thereby compounded.

"I'm sorry," he said as she opened the door. "I had more work than I figured, and I had another row with Collier."

"A final one, I hope," she said as she closed the door behind her. She was smiling, but there was a serious tone beneath the humor.

"No, I'm still a newspaperman," he said as they walked toward Old Smokey.

"You sound as though you think it's something to brag about."

"I don't want to fly false colors. If you'd rather not go out with a plain, honest, hard-working newspaper reporter. . . ."

"Too late now to make other plans for the evening," she teased back. "I guess one more time won't matter."

As they approached Old Smokey he watched her, feeling the almost uncontrollable pride he often experienced.

She was a well-built girl, tall and lithe, moving with the poise and sureness of a model. Modeling, she once confided, had been an early ambition. Modeling had led to a growing interest in fashions, and that eventually to fashion copywriting. Despite her contact with fashion she was individualistic in her dress, personally adopting only the trends she considered to her advantage. Now, with the bouffant hairstyle all the rage, she stubbornly let her blond hair grow long and wore it alternately loose and in a halo of braids.

Tonight it was loose.

"Do you mind having J. Marvin Olds with us at dinner tonight?" he asked in the car.

"Not if you'll keep him off murder stories," she said. "I had the heebie-jeebies for a week after that last session."

"No murders," he promised.

When they turned into Harry's Steak House driveway the radio-equipped staff car used on the police beat already was parked near the entrance, and as they entered he saw J. Marvin seated at a table, waiting for them.

No one knew J. Marvin's age. He could be anywhere from fifty-five to seventy-five, and Kencaide suspected his age on company books might be falsified. For often J. Marvin talked of ancient crimes in St. Louis, Joplin, Little Rock, Oklahoma City, and more recently, San Antonio, Dallas, Fort Worth, and Houston. He was one of the last of the old tramp newspapermen, no family, no ties. In his lifetime he'd covered scores of executions, discussed their crimes with hundreds of murderers, rapists, bank robbers, and other lesser criminals. It was his life; he had no other. He was a good reporter. There were better writers, but few better at getting the facts. Age undoubtedly had caught up with him on the bigger dailies, and he had come here, where the criminal pace was slower.

J. Marvin rose to his feet as they approached, trim and athletic in an open-collar sport shirt, his deeply tanned, wrinkled face spread in a broad grin. "I must be livin' right," his deep bass voice boomed at Arlene. "I hadn't dared hope Tom would risk his future by bringing us together again."

"Go on," Arlene said. "I know the two of you had rather be alone and talk about that damned newspaper."

"There may have been such a time for me," J. Marvin admitted. "But that was back in the days when I was young and incredibly foolish. I'm old enough now to see the error of my ways." He waited until they were seated, then laughed. "However, Tom did mention a yarn he has workin'."

Arlene groaned. "I knew it."

So after the steaks were ordered, Tom told them Joe Garzek's story, as briefly and as well as he could.

"Oh, great," Arlene said when he had finished. "Another crusade. Tom has found another idealistic, fight-to-the-bitter-end soulmate."

J. Marvin was frowning. "I always knew some of the beat cops were marginal, but I didn't dream of anything like this."

"I think the police angle is only a small part of the story," Tom insisted. "This setup must be widespread, with several higher-ups involved—Berger for sure."

"Seems likely," Olds agreed. "What I'm wonderin', if we got the story, would the paper print it?"

"It's their job to print it," Tom said heatedly.

Arlene was puzzled. "Why wouldn't they?"

Olds explained. "BeeBee doesn't believe in washing dirty linen in public."

He was right. BeeBee listened to the Chamber of Commerce leaders, and seldom made a move without consulting them. Since there was no other newspaper in town, and the newspaper also owned the television and major radio station, BeeBee had all local news bottled up. There was only one other radio station, which specialized in rock 'n' roll.

"Maybe the chamber wouldn't take kindly to publicizing that our police force has a crooked element," Tom agreed. "But it seems to me BeeBee could stand up to them every once in a while."

"BeeBee is a great admirer of civic leadership," Olds said.

"And advertisers," Tom added.

"I think you're being unkind," Olds disagreed. "BeeBee is as civic minded as you are. It's all a matter of viewpoint. He thinks he's doing the right thing. And as far as partiality to advertisers goes, remember that BeeBee is not a newspaperman in the old sense of the word. He's a businessman."

"If you two are so bitter, why don't you quit?" Arlene asked.

"I'm too old," J. Marvin said quietly. "But if I were Tom, I would consider it seriously."

"An ally," Arlene said happily. "This is music to my ears."

J. Marvin's statement worried Tom all through dinner. Later, over coffee, he brought the topic up again. "Were you serious a while ago?" he asked J. Marvin. "Do you wish you'd gotten out of newspapering at my age?"

"No, I didn't say that. We were talking about you. Now, in my day, newspapering offered the satisfaction of a job well done. For me, it doesn't offer that any more. And I don't think it's going to get any better."

"I think you're wrong," Tom argued. "I think people are losing faith in newspapers, and that soon advertisers will demand better quality from the media. They'll learn that syndicated columns and such short-cuts reduce readership."

"I hope you're right," J. Marvin said. "But I think you're being overoptimistic."

"Quixotic," Arlene said.

"When people lose respect for the newspaper, they'll lose respect for the advertiser," Tom went on. "Newspapers have a role of public service, and if they don't get back into that role, they're going to lose that respect entirely, forever."

"Tom, you're a hopeless square," Arlene said. She turned to J. Marvin. "Did you know that he actually volunteered for duty in the Korean War? He wasn't satisfied with getting all shot up in Europe. He had to go over and get his feet frozen off, too."

"It's been my experience," J. Marvin said, "that the profession of journalism is full of windmill tilters."

"I'm sure journalism isn't a profession," Arlene said. "It must be a disease."

"About this Longhorn Lounge case of Garzek's," J. Marvin said, maneuvering the conversation back on safer ground. "What were you figurin' on?"

"I thought we might go out there tonight and see what cops are in on it."

J. Marvin studied for a moment. "I guess it wouldn't make anybody suspicious, if we just went out there for a beer or two. We'd just be two young bucks, entertainin' a girl."

"Oh, no," Arlene said. "I'm a working girl, and I have a rough day ahead of me tomorrow. You boys just go on and have your fun."

J. Marvin apparently saw that she meant it. He had a knack for not making a nuisance of himself. He turned to Tom. "Well, I'll get back to the police station and see if anything's goin' on. Then, if it's all right with Collier, I'll meet you out there in a couple of hours." He grinned, and winked. "That ought to give you time to do some heavy courtin'."

But it didn't work out that way. The dinner conversation had taken an unfortunate turn. Arlene pursued the topic on the way home. "I hear there's a job opening coming up soon at Chilson Petroleum," she said.

The argument at Harry's had made him overly defensive. "I've told you before. I'm perfectly happy with the job I've got. And if I want to change jobs, I'll find one myself."

He hadn't intended to be so blunt, but through contacts at the ad club and elsewhere, she always was finding him a job. Before he could apologize Arlene's temper flared. "I've never deceived you. I told you from the first what I want out of life," she said.

"Maybe you should have married that oil man."

"If I'd wanted money, I would have. Quit twisting my meaning. I don't want luxuries. I don't think I'm asking too much."

"I don't think I am either," he shot back. "Just a home, children."

Arlene's voice suddenly took on a quality of desperation that drained him of all anger. "I've worked too hard to get the cow manure off my shoes. Maybe if you'd chopped as much cotton as I have you'd have more . . . well, ambition. There's no other word for it. Granted, perhaps you wouldn't make much more money somewhere else. I'm not objecting to your salary. If you'd watch your spending you'd be better off. We don't have to dine at a steakhouse every night, be seen at the Key Club, that sort of thing. I don't care about that. If you want to squander your money, that's your business. I'm thinking of the future. You could be somebody. You could have a job where you'd know there might be more to it than just a two-fifty-a-week raise every year or two. And I'd know when to expect you home . . . Oh, hell, I don't know why I'm talking. If we marry, with you in that job, I'm going to keep on working."

"No wife of mine is going to work," he said for the hundredth time. "I want a home and all it means. Maybe if you'd never had one, you'd want one, too."

"I'm not getting any younger," she said, her voice low, close to breaking. She would be thirty-two in June.

"Nor I," he reminded her. He had just turned thirty-seven.

Arlene turned her head away from him. "We're still where we were two years ago," she said. "I don't know what we can do about it, but I can't go on this way much longer."

But again they left it that way—the way it had been for two years.

As he left her apartment he noticed lightning to the northwest, and before he got back to the newspaper office it began to rain.

## CHAPTER THREE

The phone rang again, insistent.

Travis McNiel lay quiet, hoping it would be a wrong number. But calls never were, this time of night.

He heard Marilyn's voice answer, a pause, then "just a moment." She put a hand on his shoulder. "It's the hospital," she said. "A seventy-six."

"Tell them I'll be there in a few minutes," he said.

He swung his feet over the edge of the bed, flipped on the bedside lamp, and fished for his slippers on the carpet. Then he started dressing automatically.

"Coffee?" Marilyn asked behind him.

He was still numb from sleep.

"Please."

He moved into the bathroom and splashed his face with cold water. As he toweled off the water he felt the grate of the cloth against an eighteen-hour growth of beard. Putting his glasses back on, he examined his face in the mirror, reassuring himself he didn't look too much like a bum, for there was no time to shave.

It was an unfortunate face. Too sharp, too little flesh to soften the angular features. His eyes, a deep brown that otherwise might have saved things, were hidden behind the thick lenses that added to his owlishness. His lips were thin and tight, and when he smiled it seemed to strike others as a smile of superiority. For the same reason, his dry laugh seemed to have an infuriating effect on some people.

A cold fish, they called him. This he had heard. But they called him a good doctor, too. Nothing else mattered as long as they said that.

The beard, he decided, would have to stay. With the collar of his white shirt open, no tie, house slippers and a dark blue suit, he would appear to all just what he was . . . a doctor called out of bed in the middle of the night.

He left the bedroom and went down the darkened hall toward the distant light of the kitchen, walking softly past the children's door.

Marilyn had the coffee ready, a big mug steaming on the bar beside a glass of cracked ice, a trick dating back to the days when she was a working nurse and he was in medical school. The coffee was extra strong; the ice was to bring it to drinking temperature fast.

He was aware of her watching him as he spooned in the ice. Even after fifteen years of married life these quiet, intimate moments were nice. She was the only person in the world who knew his secret personality. Even the children—he had difficulty getting rapport with them, too. But never with Marilyn.

Drinking deeply, he forced himself to think of the job ahead. "They say how many?"

"No, it was an aide. I don't think she knew."

"Or wouldn't say," he said. Rather than risk conveying misinformation, nurses often tended to be too close-mouthed, he believed.

Marilyn smiled. This was an old, much-discussed issue. She always defended the nurses.

He finished the coffee and she followed him to the back door.

"I'll call you if it's an all-night stand," he said.

As he went out into the darkness he heard the click of the night latch behind him. She never felt safe alone at night, especially since there'd been some reports of prowlers in the neighborhood.

Travis drove fast on the nearly deserted streets, still wet from the rain earlier in the night. At the hospital, he pulled into the emergency drive, the right-hand wheels up over the curb to give the ambulances room.

When he turned off the ignition and stepped out into the calm night air he could hear the sirens in the distance, the sound reflected strongly by the two new wings of the hospital angling out on each side of him.

New wings—a misnomer. The newest was now twelve years old. The hospital was like the rings of a tree, the old parts inside, the new to the outside. The farther in you went, the farther back in time until somewhere, at the center, was the original 1933 WPA hospital. As the town grew, the hospital had tried vainly to keep up. Now it was far behind.

Travis strode rapidly to where the two wings met and walked down the half-flight into what used to be a storage room appendage to the hospital. Now, it was the emergency room. Concrete floors, low ceiling, and plaster walls. Sanitary, functional, and small.

Three patients had been brought in and now filled the examining tables. Two boys and a girl, all seventeen or eighteen years old. Dr. Wayne Callihan, the duty intern, and the duty nurse were working on the boy in the far corner. One bloody leg was exposed and they were intent on stopping the bleeding.

Travis hung up his coat, rolled up his shirt sleeves, and washed his hands. Callihan looked up, saw him, and hurried over.

"How does it look?" Travis asked, pulling on a fresh white jacket.

"I think everything's under control, for the moment. But the ambulances went back after two more trapped in a car. They called for a wrecker to help get them out, so I'm expecting the worst."

"I heard them coming back in. Any chance of making room for the next load?"

Callihan gave him a rundown. The boy in the far corner was in critical condition with a fractured skull, compound fracture of the left leg resulting in heavy loss of blood, and possible internal injuries. The lab was rushing the blood typing. Callihan hadn't had time to examine the other two fully, but the boy appeared to have just a fractured arm and two teeth broken off. The girl was in shock with a broken nose and severe facial lacerations.

An aide came in with the blood. Callihan hurried back to start the transfusion. Travis heard the ambulances again, briefly, before they cut the sirens two blocks from the hospital. He walked over to the other boy. He was a big, sideburned youth in Levis and cowboy boots, his head pillowed on his good arm. The broken one, splinted, lay parallel to his body.

"You hurt anywhere else besides your arm, son?" Travis asked.

"Mah teeth. Mah teeth hurt like hell, Doc."

Travis raised the puffed upper lip and looked. The upper front incisors were sheered off at the gumline.

"Mah arm don't hurt atall," the boy said. "It's jest kinda numb."

Travis nodded and examined a bruise across the forehead. It didn't seem to be serious. He gave the boy a shot of morphine.

"Put him in the hall, "he told an aide. The examining table would be needed, and there'd be time to set the arm later.

When he first looked at the girl's face he winced inwardly. Her nose was shattered and glass was imbedded in the deep jagged cuts across he face. That would take time to fix. The immediate concern was shock.

"Stay with her," he told an aide. "Keep her quiet, and watch her pulse and respiration. If there's any marked change, call me."

He turned then to the two new patients, a couple about fifty-five still on ambulance cots. The faces, unnatural in pain and shock, yet seemed familiar.

Travis knelt by the woman and examined her first, a medium-sized matronly woman fighting for breath. He cut away her bloody blouse and slip, and it was as he had feared . . . she had been driving. A large segment of the chest wall was floating free, broken loose by the steering wheel. The segment moved inward on inspiration and outward on expiration—paradoxical respiration. The pain, he knew, must be unbelievable, but she was conscious, fighting for breath.

While they moved her onto a table Travis examined the man. He had been luckier. His jaw was broken and he had numerous cuts and bruises, but Travis could find nothing else serious in a quick check. So he turned back to the woman to give her what relief he could.

He injected local anesthetic to block the involved intercostal nerves. There was a dullness to percussion, and the breath sounds seemed to be diminishing, so he suspected bleeding into the pleural space. With an aspirating needle, he found blood posteriorly in the seventh interspace.

But he soon saw it was a losing battle. Carbon dioxide retention and oxygen deficit were bound to be developing rapidly. She needed an automatic respirator and there wasn't one immediately available.

"Doctor!" an aide said behind him, a note of panic in her voice. He turned, knelt by the ambulance stretcher. The man suddenly was having trouble breathing.

It took Travis a moment to understand what was happening. There had been direct injury to the larynx. He had overlooked it in his first hurried examination, thinking the irregular breathing was from the pain of the broken jaw. Now the swelling and secretions were shutting off the trachea—the windpipe. It had to be opened, and quickly, or the man would die.

"Get him up here," he ordered. He turned to the duty nurse. "Fix her a place in the hall. Set up that oxygen unit there."

Callihan came to help and they performed an emergency tracheotomy on the man. They went in low, made an oval opening, and affixed a tracheal tube.

As he worked, Travis was aware of relatives gathering outside in the hall. A highway patrolman and two deputy sheriffs came in, followed by two radio station newsmen and J. Marvin Olds, the newspaper reporter. From billfolds, purses, they made tentative indentifications. Then they checked with relatives in the hall, the voices low, funereal.

Three times Travis went out to the screened enclosure where the woman fought for life. Each time she was weaker, the battle stronger. Each time he considered some dramatic effort, and another look at the crushed chest told him anything would be futile. He could only prolong her suffering. The outcome was inevitable. Yet, who was he to say what was inevitable?

Three times he went through the old debate within himself. Was it his duty to help the woman cling to life as long as possible, or to let her die easily with a minimum of suffering? The debate was academic, for he had done all he could. Still, he couldn't keep from standing beside the cot, listening to the shallow, labored breathing, waiting. . . .

The fourth time he went out, she was dead.

"Any relatives out there?" he asked the duty nurse.

"A son," she said, and gave him a name. Then he knew why their faces had been familiar. They owned a small furniture store downtown. Once they had applied for a loading zone beside the store and the traffic commission had denied the request. They had appealed to the City Council and Travis had gone downtown and visited the store to study the merits of the plea. On the basis of his report, the council had asked the traffic commission to reconsider the application. The last time he'd been by the store, the loading zone was still there.

He had heard of the son, too. Active in the Jaycees, civic clubs, YMCA. . . .

Travis braced himself for what he had to do. This was something one never got used to doing.

He walked out into the hall and called the son by name.

"Yes, Doctor?"

A crewcut young executive, probably in his early thirties, his face almost pleading. Behind him, anxious, stood a young woman, the daughter-in-law, no doubt.

"I'm sorry," Travis said firmly. "Your mother has just passed away."

The young woman gasped and said something unintelligible.

The son put his arm around her and stood for a moment, looking at Travis. "And Dad?"

"His condition is serious, but not critical, unless unforeseen complications develop." He went on, explaining briefly the nature of the injuries. But the son wasn't listening. He was staring past Travis to where a space in the screen gave them a partial view of the body.

"That her there?" he asked incredulously, just becoming aware his mother had been the one behind the screens in the hall all the time he'd waited just a few feet away.

"Yes," Travis said.

The son's face flushed with anger. His voice rose, taking on a quality near hysteria. "What in hell is she doing there? Don't you know who she is?"

"There was very little we could do for her," Travis said as gently as he could. "She got immediate attention the minute she was brought in. But as you see, our emergency facilities are limited. . . ."

"At least you could have given her a room."

"The hospital is full," Travis explained. "We could have put her down the hall, in a ward, but this was much nearer to our facilities." He checked himself, knowing this wasn't the time nor place to discuss it. He could see that the son was struggling for self-control.

"What about Dad?" he asked. "We can get him a room, can't we?"

"He will be moved down the hall to a small room just outside the ward. There's a good chance we can get him into a private room sometime later today."

"Sometime," the son exploded. "Look, if it's money you want . . ."

Travis cut him off. "It isn't a question of money. It's simply a matter of facilities. I'm sorry. Please excuse me. I must get back. . . ."

Inside the emergency room again, he found his hands trembling. He knew better than to get involved in explanations. Yet he always managed it some way.

Dr. Callihan came over, jubilant. "Well, I think I won one. I think that boy's going to make it, unless that cracked skull is worse than it looks." Callihan seemed to regard patients as baseball games: win one, lose one, the average was what mattered.

"I just lost one," Travis said.

"Oh, the woman? Too bad." The way he said it let Travis know Callihan had heard how it was: Travis is a good doctor, but he takes his patients too seriously. A little bit of Travis dies with each one.

"Yes, too bad," Travis said. He motioned toward the girl with the battered face. "I believe we still have some work to do, Doctor."

It was almost two hours later before Travis felt everything was under control enough to leave. As he walked out into the cool morning air, he realized he had forgotten to call home. Overhead, the sky had cleared after the rain, and stars still were shining. But in the east day was breaking. Travis circled the car through the ambulance driveway and started home.

Always, after witnessing death, life in its many varied forms became more noticeable to him. The buds of early spring were out, cats were ending their nocturnal forays, and dogs, traveling in twos and threes, were setting out on dawn jaunts. He passed a bakery with its deep, rich smells, waved to a paperboy returning from his morning route, and felt a trace of envy at the sight of two fishermen in an old battered car.

Time was growing short, he reflected. Two years had passed since a group from the medical association had approached him and urged him to run for council. He had protested vigorously. Politics and professional ethics don't mix, he had told them.

"This is a new era," they'd argued. "We need representation on the council. That's the only way we'll be able to make them see our problems at the hospital."

He'd agreed, reluctantly. The medical association was urging doctors, as professional men, to be more active in community life. A new hospital wing, with new emergency facilities, seemed worth the effort. And there were other problems. The city and county were supposed to split the cost of charity patients. Each griped constantly, thinking the other should bear more of the cost. Some permanent plan should be worked out.

The medical association and hospital board had given him full support in the election, and they'd seen to it he got the support of those who mattered. Sam McIntosh, the financial patriarch of the city, oil man, rancher, owner of the town's most exclusive department store and a dozen downtown buildings, had invited Travis into his home. After discussing political views, Sam McIntosh too had supported him, and when the votes were counted, Travis' total tripled that of his nearest opponent.

Now, it was spring again. His two-year term would end in the fall. And the hospital expansion was no nearer than it was when he started.

First it had been the school bond issue. "Wait until the school board gets this through at the polls; we don't want to put too much on the voter at once," they'd said. He couldn't argue. He had a boy in the second grade and a girl nearing school age. He had visited the schools and seen conditions. He knew they needed more buildings. But the medical groups weren't happy with the delay.

Then came an urban renewal plan that was defeated at the polls, and the interstate bypass plan. "If you'll just go along on this, Travis, we'll give the hospital plan top priority." "If we don't get in on this urban renewal thing now, Travis, we'll lose our chance for federal funds."

He didn't even try to explain to the medical association or the hospital board any more. His name was a dirty word with most of the medical men in town, he knew. But that didn't matter so much.

What did matter was that he'd been used shamelessly, lied to and taken for a complete fool. And all that time, patients died in a concrete hallway outside an old abandoned storeroom.

Turning into his driveway, he left the car out, knowing he'd be leaving for the office in less than three hours. As he walked up the steps to the front door, he stooped and picked up the morning newspaper. He carried it in with him, tossed it onto the sofa, and started toward the bedroom. Then the bold face type caught his attention.

COUNCIL EXPECTED TO SET DATE TO HEAR LAKE SITE REPORT said an eight-column headline across the top of the paper. Travis sank onto the sofa and read the story. When he sifted the facts from promotion and propaganda, the meaning was clear: the lake program was going to be next, not the hospital program.

He first felt the helplessness of defeat, then anger. He tossed the newspaper aside with the first foul word he had used in years.

They had better not be expecting him to help set a date tonight to hear anything. As of today, Dr. Travis McNiel was through co-operating.

"Yes, I heard about the wreck on the radio this morning," Mayor Hiram Milner said. "Terrible thing. But I'm glad it didn't happen in the city, if it had to happen at all. That boy should be charged with manslaughter, driving that way."

"I don't know about that," Travis said. "The crime I'm concerned with is the one after they were brought into the hospital last night."

The mayor looked at him warily. "What do you mean?"

They sat alone in the mayor's downtown office, a throwback to the law offices of yesteryear—a walnut rolltop desk, stark wooden chairs, bare unpolished floors, brass cuspidors and walls lined with legal volumes.

"Mayor, I had to push that woman out into the hall last night to die. Our facilities for treating her were inadequate. I'm not saying that if we'd had proper equipment she would have lived, but she would have had a better chance."

"Why did she have to be pushed out into the hall?" the mayor asked, frowning.

"Every room in the hospital was full, and we had four other patients in the emergency room."

The mayor picked up a pencil, fingered it nervously. "Any of her relatives know about this?"

"Her son was there. He saw her body out in the hall, and got pretty hot under the collar."

The mayor winced as if he had a sudden stomach cramp. When the expression went away the frown remained, and suddenly Travis knew why the mayor's pictures in the newspapers never looked natural. In the pictures, the mayor always smiled. They didn't have that expression of continual worry.

"Think he may make trouble?"

Travis was tempted to let the mayor stew over it for a while, but his better nature prevailed. "No, I think his reaction was mostly emotional release. But if you want to know what I think, I believe he has grounds to sue." He held up a hand to stop the mayor's protest. "Now I know I'm not a lawyer, but I've noticed most lawyers come into my office with their own diagnosis, so I guess I can have a legal opinion."

The mayor's smile was fleeting. "You mean sue over her death? That would be difficult to prove, wouldn't it?"

"No, not the death. For not being provided a place, a little privacy, to die. Have you seen what we have to work with?"

"I've seen it."

"We examine women patients in front of other patients, ambulance drivers, radio and newspaper reporters, policemen, whoever happens to be standing in the hall. Of course we have screens, but what good are they with nurses and aides running in and out? It's a disgrace."

"I agree," the mayor said. "Something's going to have to be done about it."

"Everybody agrees, but nothing is done."

They sat for a moment in silence. From an outer office there came the low murmur of voices and the mayor cocked his head to one side to listen. Apparently satisfied the conversation didn't concern him, he turned back to Travis. Sometimes the mayor had the exasperating habit of lecturing his listeners. Before Travis could stop him, the Gray Ghost of office law had wrapped his imaginary judicial robes about him and launched into a full-fledged oration.

"Travis, I want you to know that, personally, I agree with you. I think the hospital program should have high priority. But what you don't understand is that what I think has little to do with it. As I see it, I'm in this job to carry out the programs the majority of the people want. And you definitely seem to be in the minority on this one. I've kept asking you to put it off because I think that at the right time, when the public's attention is not diverted by something else, we can convince the public of the need."

"I gather you think it should wait again."

"I'm afraid so, Travis. If you'll get out and talk to people—as I have—the people down at the chamber, civic clubs, I think you'll find there's strong support building up for fast action on the new lake, lots of enthusiasm. It just happens to be what the public wants, right now."

"I guess that's the difference between us, Mayor. You think we should give the public what they want. I think we should give them what they need."

The mayor held up a forefinger as if the observation were his. "That's it. That's where you keep butting your head into a stone wall. Who are we to say what the public needs? Only the public knows."

"I'm not so sure," Travis said. "I think we have people in this town who would think the hospital far more important. They can spend thousands of dollars on their daughters' debuts into society, fly in name bands, take over country clubs for parties. Now you can't tell me these people wouldn't do something about it if they knew their lives and the lives of their children might be in jeopardy."

"They will," the mayor assured him. "When the time comes, they will."

"The time has come and gone, and they haven't done anything. That's why I think we've got to make the decision of what's best for them."

"No, believe me, Travis, that isn't the way. I've been in politics in one way or another most all my life, and I know. You'll get no thanks for telling people what's best for them, and no co-operation, either. There are certain ways these projects are handled. You've got to create a want."

"How would *you* go about it, Mayor?" Travis asked quietly. "I know I'm a greenhorn in politics. I'm asking for advice."

The mayor studied a small wart on the back of his left hand for a moment before he answered. "I'd start off slow. Instead of asking for the whole thing at once, as you've been doing, I'd ask first for just a survey of the hospital."

"There's no need for a survey," Travis protested. "Any doctor can tell you. . . ."

The mayor stopped him with a raised forefinger. "It's just a gimmick, Travis. I'm sure the rest of the council would support you on a survey costing a couple thousand or so, by some outside agency, with the county paying something like an equal share, of course."

"That's a lot of money to spend for nothing."

"Not for nothing. Don't you see? You've got the other councilmen, the county commissioners participating. When the outside, impartial agency makes its report on the horrible conditions at the hospital, maybe there'll be stories in the newspaper, on television, radio—you can talk to BeeBee Milam and get that done. The public will feel embarrassment that a bunch of strangers has come in and found dirty laundry—some Yankee firm would be best. With the public reaction, things will begin to move."

"In other words, the survey would be merely for publicity, a psychological maneuver."

"Call it that, if you want. But it would serve its purpose. The needs would be known, pressure put on the council. Then the council would be in a mood to set up a committee to consider what steps should be taken, maybe the whole council acting as a committee. As mayor, it would be natural that I should name you, our only medical member, as chairman."

"All right, now I'm chairman, and I still don't know what to do."

"You know what you need, the council doesn't. You could write your own ticket into the committee report, with the weight of the full council behind you, and probably the county commissioners, too. Hire an architect to do a big drawing of the new wing."

"I already have one."

"Put it away. Don't show it to anybody until it's just a step away from reality, when you have everyone involved, awaiting a result."

Travis thought the mayor's plan over. It sounded feasible. If he'd only had sense enough to seek this advice eighteen months ago. . . .

"How long would all this take?"

"Well, let's see. Say six months for the agency report, three months for your committee work—you wouldn't want to appear to be rushing it—and another three months to get county co-operation and approval at the polls. That'd make it a year, minimum."

"Too long. I go off the council in the fall."

"Surely you're going to stand for re-election. You've done such fine work."

"No. I've been too big a disappointment to too many people."

"If you got the survey started, maybe they would support you again."

"No, they expected action from the start. A survey would seem like so much wasted effort. I've got to find a short cut."

"There are no short cuts," the mayor said solemnly. "Anything to do with democratic process takes time."

On council meeting days, Travis always tried to take the afternoon off to make preparation. No appointments were made. But inevitably, something came up. This Tuesday was no exception.

After his talk with the mayor, Travis dropped by his office to pick up his council portfolio and was trapped by an overanxious mother and an otherwise healthy six-year-old boy with early symptoms of German measles. Before he had allayed her fears, his first snakebite case of the season arrived—an elderly rancher who had been clearing mesquite. Although there appeared to be no complications, there was a history of heart disturbance, so Travis made arrangements for his admission to the hospital and followed up with a visit to the bedside to make sure the old gentleman was going to be all right. Then, since he was at the hospital anyway, he checked on two O.B. patients and a gall-bladder case.

So he didn't get home until past three in the afternoon. Marilyn sent Cindy out into the back yard to play, turned off television, and Travis settled down on the couch in his study. But for once his long training in the art of cat-napping failed him. This mess he had gotten himself into kept nagging him. There just had to be a way out. . . .

Trouble was, the hospital got treated like an unwanted step-child by all concerned. It wasn't the city's, and it wasn't the county's. It was somewhere in between. Each contributed, but believed the other wasn't doing enough. The county medical association advised, but took no responsibility. The hospital board just floundered along, trying to keep both the City Council and County Commission happy, without success. Each time the bill for charity cases came up, open warfare threatened. The bill was supposed to be divided equally between city and county. But the county argued that most of the population was inside the city limits, therefore the city should pay most of the cost. The city argued that a big percentage of charity patients were victims of auto wrecks out in the county, transients from other counties, other states. Therefore, they argued, the county should pay more. When the annual, inevitable deficit had to be met, the arguments became even more heated, more complex.

And into all this Travis had been chosen to bring peace.

He couldn't make them understand—neither the members of the City Council nor the county commissioners. They listened, but they didn't understand. They talked of the doctors' "free use" of the hospital, as if the doctors should contribute more than being on call up to ninety hours a week. If he only could make them see the part the hospital had in the city's life. . . . Or, if he could make the other side—the medical association and the hospital board—understand what he had gotten into in accepting the responsibility of a council seat. . . .

When he was first elected, a year and a half ago, he had been amazed at the complexity and volume of problems that came before the council. Now, eighteen months of experience hadn't helped. Even the most trivial items, considered routine, were loaded with possibilities. The purchase of a few thousand dollars' worth of sewer pipe, he realized, could result in charges and accusations of partiality months later. And with twenty to forty routine purchases each council night, it was impossible to check each. There was nothing the councilmen could do but blindly follow Hartwell's suggestions, and these were based usually on the recommendations of department heads. Even Hartwell, Travis was sure, couldn't check on all purchases.

At first, Travis had thought competitive bidding took care of the need for decisions. But he'd found it wasn't that easy. Most calls for bids carried a complex statement of specifications, and he'd soon learned most department heads geared their specifications to the brand or make of merchandise they wanted.

In a way, this made sense. Hartwell often quoted department heads candidly as recommending a certain brand as a "superior product" or because "we've had much better service from this product in the past." There was no doubt that often the city could spend a few dollars above the low bid and save money by obtaining better quality merchandise. But who was to determine?

In his early council meetings, Travis had tried to question the department heads. Hartwell hadn't seemed to mind, but he could tell it irritated the other council members, who wanted to get on with the meeting and get it over with. Also, the department heads seemed ill at ease, and he realized they couldn't be as candid in open council, especially in front of the bid representatives. So Travis switched his questions to the bid representatives. But then the issue became bogged down again, usually, in statistics.

So now he did what the rest of the council did: rubber-stamp Hartwell's and the department heads' recommendations. But he'd never felt comfortable doing it, and he still studied as many items as he could. There just wasn't time enough to do justice to the job. This was why it galled him so when his medical colleagues came around periodically and prodded him about his progress on their project. They had put him on the council to look after one issue, and they couldn't understand that he had been saddled with a hundred issues a month.

Unable to sleep, he went to his desk and turned through his council material until he came to the interstate bypass plan. He had been a reluctant participant in the plan's narrow victory at the polls, and he still wasn't sure it was the best of all possibilities.

With a pencil, he made imaginary journeys, trying to find a flaw in the access and feeder routes. Each time, the pencil would emerge from the maze of mingled ribbons on the right course.

Who was he to question the best engineering brains in the state? He had no alternative but to accept their experience-born product. But on the one thing that he could tell the council all they needed to know, speak from his own experience, he was frustrated. They wouldn't listen.

He refolded the map, closed the briefcase, turned out the desk light, and went into the kitchen. Marilyn was tossing the salad, keeping an anxious eye on the ham in the oven. Out the back door, Travis could see Billy and Cindy playing. Marilyn heard his footsteps and turned in surprise.

"What are you doing up? It isn't five yet."

"I know. I couldn't sleep."

She studied him with practiced concern. "You're taking that council work too seriously again."

"Someone has to take it seriously."

She sighed, then turned back to the salad. "I'll be glad when it's all over."

Even his wife didn't think he would be returned for a second term.

"I may run again," he said experimentally.

She stopped work and looked up at him. "You wouldn't!"

"I may," he said again. "The mayor spelled it out for me today. He told me what a babe in the woods I've been, what I should do, how long it will take . . . another year, at least. If I do it by the book, I'll have to run again."

"You could let someone else do it."

"And admit failure? I'm not used to failure. I've never failed in anything I really wanted before. I wanted to be a doctor; I'm a doctor. I wanted a wonderful wife; I've got one. I wanted children; I couldn't have asked for better. Why should I start giving up now?"

She tonged the salad onto plates and started placing them on the table. "Think you'll be re-elected?"

"No."

"Be kind of silly, then, don't you think?"

"I guess so. I don't know what I'm going to do," he admitted. "I'm just talking."

"I still think you should try to make the hospital independent. It'll always be in a mess as long as the city and county fight over it."

This was being done in some places by setting up a hospital district with power to levy taxes and float bond issues. But the plan required a special act of the Texas Legislature and approval at the polls.

"That'd take even longer," he told her. "And both the city and county say they have too much invested. They'd fight it all the way."

"Do you know a better hospital program?"

"No. But I'm hunting a short cut to do what has to be done. The mayor says there is no short cut. I'm not so sure."

He told her, then, how the mayor said the project could be accomplished.

"That seems pretty devious," she said when he had finished.

"He's right, though. Since he told me that, I've thought back to other projects. They're all done that way. Take the lake program. They've got the demand built. Now, they're about to unveil the glorious artist's conception."

"Maybe if you talked to the association, the board, told them what you've learned, maybe they'd give you another chance."

"No, that would sound like a feeble excuse. I don't want to be put in that position. Besides, I don't want to do it that way. Like you said, it's too devious. Maybe I can think up a better way."

She slid the ham from the oven, then tested it with a long-tined fork. "Dinner's about ready," she said. "Call the kids."

He went out from the warm kitchen into the cool afternoon air. The sun was low, sending its rays up over the back hedge so he had to put an arm up to block it. Billy and Cindy were at the jungle gym in deep discussion about something. "Dinner's about ready," he told them. "Go scrub."

He once had taught them how a surgeon scrubs. Sometimes they still made a game of it. But now the mood of whatever he had interrupted hung with them.

Cindy pushed a picture card out at him. "Isn't this God?" she asked.

Travis looked at the picture, one of Cindy's Sunday school cards from her collection. The picture was of Joseph, Mary, and the Infant Child at the manger. She was pointing at the Infant Child.

"That's Jesus," Billy said from his superior eight years. "Anybody knows that."

"My teacher said it was God," Cindy insisted.

Travis looked at her earnest, angry face, trying to think of some way to tell her she was wrong without hurting her feelings. She had enough troubles with a brother three years older who knew everything. Travis sat on the jungle gym rung beside her and studied the card.

"Maybe she said it was our Lord," he suggested.

"What's the difference?"

Billy snickered and Travis gave him a stern look.

"Lord isn't a name," he told her. "It's a title of great respect, like we say our Lord God or our Lord Jesus. But there's only one God, just as there's only one Jesus."

She pointed to Joseph. "Who's that?"

He told her, and explained the Nativity scene. The explanation touched a chord in her memory, for she quickly nodded.

"And there's the star," Cindy said.

Constantly, he was amazed at the feminine workings of her mind, so like Marilyn's. There had been no women in his life before Marilyn, for his mother had died early. So the marvels of femininity, especially fledgling femininity, were a never-ceasing wonder. He looked at Cindy's angelic face, the honey-blond hair, and wished again there were some way she would never grow up, so he could keep her, protect her. . . .

"Where *was* God born?" Billy asked suddenly.

Travis turned, prepared to lecture Billy's irreverence when, just at the last instant, he saw the serious, intent expression. One of the greatest trials of parenthood, Travis had learned, was to know when to answer questions and when to ignore them. Here, plainly, was one to answer. He fished in his mind and came up with the theme of one of his father's sermons.

"The Bible tells us God is eternal," he explained. "God always was, and always will be, with eternal life."

He saw the boy's mind take the thought and struggle with it. "How could that be?" Billy asked.

"Remember the night when we were fishing down on the river, when we tried to think big, and count all the stars in the universe?"

Billy nodded that he remembered.

"There were so many stars that our minds were too small to hold the number. A hundred hundred, a thousand thousand, a million million. Remember? It's kind of like that. Our minds are too small to understand eternity, something without beginning, without end, because there's nothing we know, nothing in our lives like that. Does that make sense?"

Billy nodded again, still wrestling with the thought. Travis turned to Cindy. She was shuffling through her collection of Sunday school cards. The discussion had been over her head.

"Go scrub," Travis ordered.

They ran ahead of him to the house. Travis trailed along behind them, reflecting on his lecture—a religious lecture by a heretic. He had done well for a man who'd lost his religious credentials, he decided. He hadn't dug into his past so deeply since the last time the minister, Dr. Anderson, visited to invite him to church.

When he entered the kitchen Billy and Cindy were already in the bath, fussing over the bar of soap.

"What kept you three?" Marilyn asked.

"I think our son and heir is going to be a learned theologian," he said. "He just asked me where God was born."

"I hope you had an answer."

"For once, I think I did as well as my father would have. But of course they were his words."

"I'm glad Billy asked you instead of me," Marilyn said.

After dinner, Marilyn got Billy onto his homework and Cindy quiet over a coloring book. Travis went into his study and read through the big stack of council material carefully.

He kept thinking about his talk with the mayor. He counted up on the calendar; he had only thirteen more council meetings to serve. He thought back over the way he had been treated by the mayor, the councilmen, and other civic leaders. There was no other way to describe it: he had been lied to, used, and taken for a fool. The knowledge didn't set well at all.

Finally, he put the material back into the briefcase. He found Marilyn helping Billy with his schoolwork.

"Well, I've made up my mind on what I'm going to do," Travis said. They walked on into the living room, leaving Billy to his labors. "I'm going to serve notice on them tonight. I'm going to be the most unco-operative, cantankerous son-of-a-bitch for the next six months this town has ever known. And if they don't play ball with me, I'm going to fight their lake project tooth and nail. Maybe I won't accomplish anything, but at least people will know I've been trying like hell to do something."

A troubled frown crossed Marilyn's face. "I hate to see you do that," she said.

"You mean you're afraid I'll get the reputation of being some kind of a nut?"

"That kind of a reputation might be all right if you were a

used-car salesman. You could have a sign, something like 'come out and trade with Nutty McNiel.' I don't believe it would help a doctor much, though."

He tried to rise to her humor and failed.

"Maybe I am a nut," he said lamely. "But I have to live with myself."

# *Part Two*

## CHAPTER FOUR

City Hall had closed. The sounds of footsteps and closing doors along the hollow corridors had faded into silence. Now there came only the occasional clatter of a janitor's pushbroom from some far-off corner of the building.

David Hartwell sat alone in his office, studying the report, waiting for Police Chief Dan McDowell and City Attorney Bud Tatum to arrive and explain it to him. It didn't make sense.

The report told him that an ex-convict, living in a firetrap lower Main Street hotel, had bought suddenly and unerringly choice sites along the proposed right-of-way of a new highway at a time when its future location was secret. A one-time burglar with no known criminal associates, the report said, and no visible means of support.

David tried to form a mental concept of this man, the way he thought and acted, his way of life. But he couldn't. For he was unequipped, by nature and background, to deal with dishonesty. He realized this was a serious weakness, but it was one he seemed unable to do anything about. His mind just worked that way, trained and conditioned in childhood.

Yet, he couldn't blame his parents. Those early years in southwest Oklahoma might as well have been in a different world. Then, a man's reputation had been a prized possession if he cared about it at all. He remembered one Saturday when they arrived back home after a fifteen-mile trip to town and his mother found the grocer had given her four dollars too much change. There was no discussion. David and his father made the thirty-mile round trip in the old Model T truck over rutted roads to return the money. In those days, you just didn't keep a man's money without his permission. He might think hard of you.

This and other incidents left David ill-prepared for facing a world where honesty was a fault as well as a virtue—a fault to be exploited. In the Air Corps, at flight school, the word had gone around fast: Hartwell's a soft touch. Gradually, over the years, David had built a defense mechanism to protect his weakness, but the weakness was still there.

He heard footsteps coming down the concrete corridor. David got up from his desk to meet Tatum and McDowell in the doorway.

"Sorry we're late," McDowell said. "I was late gettin' in from the pistol range, and kept Bud here waitin' for me."

"That's all right, Dan," David said, going back to his desk. "I'm just sorry I had to call you in after hours. But I figured we better get our heads together on this thing and decide what to do."

They sat facing him, waiting for him to take the initiative. David turned to McDowell. "Your report said this Ratliff was sent up from here for burglary five years ago. Do you remember him?"

McDowell shifted his two-hundred-twenty pound frame in the chair, a frame as lean and hard as it had been on Southwest Conference football fields more than twenty years ago. "Sure, I remember him. Couple of the boys caught him inside a liquor store on a routine door-check one night."

"What kind of a guy is he?"

"He's pretty cagey. No ordinary punk. Quiet-actin', but you get a feelin' his mind's workin' all the time. I found out this afternoon he finished his parole workin' in a bowlin' alley in Dallas." He grinned sheepishly. "I'll have to admit I didn't know he was back in town."

"And no known associates or source of income," David said. "What about putting a couple of detectives on his tail?"

"No," McDowell said firmly. "He's too sharp for that. I think we'd find out more by listenin' to lower Main gossip than we would by watchin' him."

David nodded. McDowell knew his job. If McDowell said surveillance wasn't a good idea, it wasn't. Yet he knew they couldn't afford to sit back and wait for the breaks. The wait might be too long. Whatever arrangement had been made between the ex-convict and his sponsor, there was a good chance no further contact would be made for weeks, maybe months.

"Any chance of him talking if we picked him up on a vagrancy charge?" David asked.

"No," McDowell said emphatically. "That might spook the whole setup."

"I guess we can't risk it," David agreed. He decided to try a new tack. Maybe the secret partnership could be traced from the other end. "What do you know about Councilman Berger?" he asked McDowell suddenly, watching his face for reaction.

Only a slight widening of McDowell's slate-gray eyes betrayed his surprise. "I don't *know* anything about him," he said. "But what I suspect would take an hour to tell."

It was David's turn to be surprised. This was the first indication anyone other than himself distrusted Berger. "I've got an hour," he said.

McDowell hesitated, as if trying to decide how far he should go. "Mind you, I can't prove anything," he said. "But one of the first things I learned about police work is that you can pretty well judge a man by the company he keeps. Now, from little bits of stuff I've picked up over a period of time, I think Berger travels in pretty fast company."

"Let's hear it."

McDowell hesitated again. "Well, remember that night-club owner we picked up about six months ago with a carload of stag movies?"

David had to think a moment. "Yes."

"He's a bosom buddy of Berger, not that I have anything against stag movies. Point is, I think that was a financial venture, with Berger's money behind it. Remember that farm house about three miles the other side of the Northside Shopping Center the Rangers raided?"

"Yes."

"Place was owned by Berger about two months before the raid, then deeded over to the gambler. Again, no proof, just name association. Remember that phony uranium company the state attorney general broke up a few years ago?"

David nodded.

"Berger was in partnership with the president of the company in a loan shark operation on the South Side. Again, just a coincidence. But there have been too many coincidences."

David thought all this over. If there was just something to nail down, something concrete he could use. . . .

McDowell went on. "There was only one time I thought we had somethin' on him. A South Side tavern owner called in and talked to me. He said Berger's beer firm was demandin' that he sell a certain amount of Alamo Beer, for him to tell customers he was out of the kind they ordered. I asked him to come down to the station and make a statement, but he never showed up. I went out there and talked to him, but I couldn't get anything out of him. But you know, I got the feelin' he was scared off."

"What did he say about the telephone call to you?"

"He said it was all a misunderstandin'. He claimed he misunderstood the company salesman, that it was a promotion campaign."

David thought over the possibilities of that one. "Good Lord, do you suppose he would try anything as brazen as that?"

"I don't know what he could do if they didn't play ball," McDowell admitted. "Beat up his customers, maybe, or cause fights in the place and get it shut down as a public nuisance. Even an after-hours fire or bombin', maybe. We're gettin' to be a big town, now. I guess we can start expectin' that sort of thing."

David shook his head in bewilderment. "Why didn't you tell me all this before?"

McDowell spread his hands. "Now how would it have looked for me to come up here with a bunch of flimsy ideas about a city councilman? Hell, I got files on several people that would surprise you, but I can't go around broadcastin' it unless I got a court case. I think, though, that if there's any organized crime in this town, Berger's behind it. But you can see how much proof I got."

David turned to Tatum. "You find out anything?"

Tatum had been tilted back in his chair, listening. At David's question he leaned forward and opened a small black notebook. "Not much," Tatum admitted. "I contacted three of the previous owners of the property out there. None of them knew this Ratliff. He approached them with an offer, seemed eager, and paid one in cash and the other two by check. Through a friend down at the First National, I learned he'd opened an account the date of the first transaction, then closed it a few days later. I couldn't find any other purchases. It seemed to me he just wanted that one block of choice sites."

They sat for a moment in silence. Of all the problems David had handled in the last eight years, this was undoubtedly the most difficult. Also, it was the one he was least equipped to deal with. "What would you do about Berger, if you were me?" he asked McDowell.

McDowell grinned. "Way I see it, there's nothin' you can do except give him plenty of rope and try not to spook him."

For David, the answer went against the grain. Inaction was always more difficult. The hardest part would be to continue treating Berger as any other councilman. But it was important that Berger have no inkling of suspicion, for the best chance of nailing him would be to let him get overconfident, overplay his hand.

David felt his helplessness boil over into a brief flare of anger. Almost without realizing it, he brought his fist down hard on the desk top. "I want that bastard, McDowell," he said. "I don't care if we have to let everything else go to pot for a while. Just so we get Berger."

Afterward, he hurried home to shower and change clothes. He always felt more like facing the council and audience wearing a fresh shirt and suit. Tonight there was little time left, for he had promised to meet Cal Masters at the Branding Iron before council.

But as he drove home his mind began playing a trick that had become almost a habit lately. There had been a long period—the busy years of the war, college, his early jobs—when he'd seldom thought of his childhood. But lately he had begun to think of those days more and more.

Now, somehow, that life on a windswept southwest Oklahoma farm seemed to hold a key to whatever was wrong with the present. Somewhere in trying to deal with today's complexities he had lost contact with his wife, his children, and now—apparently—the council. Somewhere, something had gone wrong. He kept thinking that if he went back, maybe he could find out where. . . .

There were many things in his childhood that were pleasant to remember. . . .

The roar of a wood fire on cold winter nights with the wind baritone in the chimney. The sound of milking in the red blaze of dawn, the streams of milk singing against the bottom of the empty pail, then growing softer as the bucket filled. Hunting rabbits in the snow with a dog and the old single-shot .22. Riding in the riverbed, the horse's hoofs sharp on the gravel, looking for a stray cow. Climbing the forbidden windmill tower and lying high on the monkeyboard, hidden from the world below, the huge fan barreling in the wind, blue sky and white clouds to contemplate and the whole future to daydream about—all the places he was going to go and all the things he was going to do when he became a man.

Now, he was a man, living beyond any of his wildest daydreams on that windmill tower. But he wasn't happy, and his family wasn't happy.

Was his outlook on life all wrong? Had his father's been right?

His father had harbored no yearnings for luxuries. An old Model T truck, two well-worn pairs of overalls for work, a newer pair for town, and a single, well-preserved suit for church, weddings, and funerals were enough material blessings for his life.

Louis Hartwell had homesteaded in Old Greer County while in his early twenties, and his life had been spent in a search for security. He sought it in a well-tended garden and a cellar of fruit and vegetables laid by for a hard winter. He pursued it in backbreaking work in his cotton fields.

David once heard someone say that you've got to know cotton to hate it. He learned early. His later memories were less pleasant—long, hot days with a hoe or cotton sack, the sting of sweat in his eyes, and the pain of straightening up after pulling ninety pounds of cotton down a row.

Reward came in his father's rare words of praise. "You did real good today, David. I'm right proud of you, pacin' the hands."

That had been his father's philosophy of life: a man's worth can be judged by his work. That had been David's moral legacy from his father. Maybe it wasn't much, but it seemed to be more than David was leaving his children.

He showered, dressed, and was using the whisk broom on his suit coat when he heard Helen's footsteps. She went down the hall to her room without even a pause at his door. He heard the rustle of packages as she walked, indicating she'd just returned from Dallas. She hadn't called him at the office, and when he'd checked at midafternoon Calla Lilly had said she wasn't home yet. He waited a moment, then went down to her room and knocked.

She sat at the vanity, still in street clothes, looking up at him with that emotionless stare he'd almost grown accustomed to now. The bed was littered with packages.

"How was Dallas?" he asked, pushing some boxes to one side so he could sit on the edge of the bed.

"I didn't have any fun, if that's what you mean. It was a very dull trip."

She worked at the right earring. He knew she hadn't started drinking yet because her co-ordination was good. When she drank, co-ordination was first to go, even before her diction.

Watching her as she studiously removed the other earring, he was struck by how rapidly her looks were beginning to go. Her figure seemed fuller, less defined. There were traces of crow's-feet around her eyes. Her once unique russet hair was less well-kept, and had lost its luster. She never worked at personal appearance any more as she had in the first few years.

He tried to put what he came to say in a tactful tone. "I wish you'd tell me when you're going off on these trips."

She threw the earrings on the vanity top. "I didn't know I had to get permission," she said without looking at him.

"No one said you did. It's just embarrassing to get all my information about what you're doing from the hired help."

"She's your hired help, not mine."

He brought his fist down on the bed in frustration. "Do you always have to pick a fight? I don't think it's too much to ask. Suppose something had happened? Calla Lilly thought you were coming back last night. I've been worrying about it all day."

"Not at the expense of your job, I'm sure. I didn't get everything done yesterday, so I stayed over. And don't tell me there are so many hotels in Dallas you couldn't find me if you'd wanted."

"I suppose I could have. But I don't see why a man should have to hunt around for his wife. *If* there were something important enough to stay over for, you could have called."

She turned and looked at him. "The 'something important enough' was the fact that I hadn't found the birthday present I was hunting for Christine. Or had you forgotten her birthday?"

He hadn't been aware it was so near. Today was the fifth. That would put the eighth on Friday. Christine would turn sixteen Friday.

"I thought you would be making big plans," Helen said. "If I had known you weren't going to take care of it in your usual high-handed fashion, I might have had the temerity to do it myself."

He spoke quickly to keep her from suspecting how close he had let the date slip upon him unaware. "No, I hadn't planned anything. But I suppose we should have a party or something. I remember that turning sixteen seems very important at the time."

"I'm surprised you would remember anything as tender as that," she said acidly. "And it's a little late to be planning anything now. Three days isn't enough time."

"We'll hire a caterer," he said, thinking rapidly. "It's warm. We can use the back yard." He grew more enthused as he thought about it. "I'll see about getting a combo of some sort, something the kids would like."

"What about invitations? Even if they were mailed in the morning they wouldn't be delivered until Thursday, probably."

"We'll use the telephone. Nothing wrong with that. And remember how Christine talked about that little foreign convertible when she was queen candidate at the Auto Show last fall? I'll go down and see about getting her one of those little cars."

"Don't you think that's going overboard for a birthday gift?"

He wanted to make her see how he felt about it. "You said a minute ago you were surprised I remembered how it was to be a child. Well, I remember. I have some good memories of my childhood, despite what you thought of my father. And when I get to thinking about them I have the feeling we're cheating Christine and Ronnie out of something. Maybe a car is a poor substitute, but at least I've made an effort."

"You can't buy what they're missing." She slipped out of her suit jacket, went to the closet, and found a hanger. "But do you know of anything we can do about it?"

"For one thing, you might stop acting so distant toward me in front of them. You could act . . . well . . . more normal."

She sighed. "We can't act normal in front of the children because we don't have a normal relationship. This isn't a normal house, it is not run in the normal manner, we are not normal people, and this is not a normal marriage."

"And where did we begin to leave the norm?"

He meant her drinking. She turned the question back on him.

"I know of one place, and I'll give you an example. Will you be home for dinner tonight?"

"No. I have to get together with Cal Masters before council," he admitted. He glanced at his watch. "And I'm late now."

"There, you see? The normal thing is for a husband and father to be home evenings."

"That's just part of my job," he said. "Plenty of men put in as long hours as I do and their wives understand, make allowances. I don't see why you can't."

"Why don't you take my failings up with the council tonight? Maybe they'll appoint a committee to study them."

Anger drove him to his feet. At the door he turned, glaring back at her. She had returned to the vanity bench and was removing her stockings. "If you can't talk sensibly, there's no use trying to discuss it," he said.

He turned and walked out, closing the door hard behind him. As he neared his room he heard the drawer of her vanity slide open. He stopped, listening, and heard the unmistakable tinkle of glass on glass. She was starting. By the time he came home tonight she would be past conversation or anything else. If he came home.

He smiled grimly to himself. The knowledge that just one phone call, just one word, would bring him more of a woman than most men dreamed existed was a soothing comfort, and at the same time an almost irresistible temptation.

But he knew he couldn't, mustn't. For if he let himself go one more time, there might be no turning back.

If Cal Masters was annoyed at David for being late in getting to the Branding Iron, he gave no sign. His smile was as broad, his grip as warm as ever. He waved aside David's apologies.

"I knew you'd be along in a minute. But since we don't have much time, I did go ahead and turn in the order. I hope a club will be all right."

David assured him a club steak would be fine. Feeling the need of a pickup, David asked for coffee while they waited.

When Cal had called earlier in the day, saying he had something he wanted to discuss before the council meeting, David had realized from his tone that Cal was concerned or worried about something. But he'd never seen the old rancher so preoccupied. Cal, one of the most conversant of men, was unusually quiet.

He had selected a booth at the rear, where the dim lights made the brands burned into the knotty pine walls darker. As the waitress came with the coffee, David studied Cal's face. By the faint, shielded bulbs in the wagon wheel chandeliers overhead, David marveled once again how well Cal had retained his age. His white mane was as thick as ever, his posture still ramrod straight.

But when Cal spoke it was not right to the point. David had noticed that was the way with old men. "I rode down into the bottomland this mornin'," Cal said. "It's just workin' alive with baby quail."

"That's good news," David said. "I'll be looking forward to fall."

He remembered how it had been last fall, he and Cal striding across the rugged bottomland, the cold wind of a norther in their faces, and suddenly three quail flushed from a clump of sage, Cal's shotgun coming up, following them, then three quick shots and three birds dropping. A triple, with eighty-year-old eyes and eighty-year-old reflexes. And later, Cal like a boy in trying to mask his pride.

"I'll bet you rode that dark Quarter Horse, didn't you?" David asked.

Cal grinned slightly. "Wanted to work the fat off him."

"You ought to stay off those half-broke horses."

Cal finished his salad, moved the dish to one side and picked up his coffee, spurning the handle and holding it mug-style in deference to two missing fingers, casualties of two long-ago roping accidents.

"When you get older, David, you'll welcome every chance to indulge in the few pleasures you have left. Horses are one of mine. When are you goin' to bring those two youngsters of yours back out to see me?"

David had taken Christine and Ronnie out to the Masters Ranch one Sunday afternoon two years ago, and they'd all had a memorable day trying out Cal's horses, looking over the ranch. Cal had seemed to enjoy the visit immensely, and still talked about it. David had kept intending to take the children back out, since they'd had so much fun, but it seemed there never was another opportunity.

"We'd like to some time, Cal. But you know how it is . . . the kids have their own activities, and I keep busy."

"Yes, I know how it is," Cal said slowly. "More than you know, maybe. You stay busy, and suddenly life's about over and you've missed out on the really important things."

David looked sharply at Cal, wondering at the similarity between Cal's remark and his own thoughts along the same line the last few hours. Apparently Cal, as a friend, was trying to warn him.

"I wouldn't have thought you'd have any regrets," David said.

"I suppose any man my age has, if he's got any sense a'tall."

As the waitress brought the steaks, David debated what to do. He hated to prod Cal, but only forty minutes were left before they were due at City Hall for the pre-council meeting, and he knew Cal's way of taking his time. He waited until the waitress had left the table.

"Is there something coming up tonight I should know about?"

Cal seemed nettled at being pushed. He sliced his steak with a knife and studied the meat critically before answering. "It's about this lake, David. Couldn't we put off action on it for a while?"

David tried to keep his concern from showing. "I thought

everyone was ready to go ahead with it, Cal. I'll admit I would have held off a few weeks, if the mayor hadn't insisted. But I thought I knew your views on it. Something change your mind?"

"Well, I was just surprised to see it on the agenda this time. Or at least I read in the papers it's goin' to be on the agenda. I hadn't expected it to come up this soon, or I'd have talked it over with you. I've come to the conclusion there may be other things we need a hell of a lot more'n water."

"You sound like the doctor," David said.

"I could be in worse company. And in this instance I think perhaps Travis is right."

David decided to take the initiative. "Granted, there are things we need badly, Cal. But without water, there's nothing. The town's just got to have it. You've seen the reports."

Cal nodded. "They all say we need water if the town is to grow. Point is, I'm not sure I want the town to grow any more."

They ate for a while in silence, the argument hanging heavy between them. David tried to think of a way to avert discussion for the present. "All we're going to do tonight is set a date to hear the consulting engineers' report," he reminded Cal. "There'll be no commitment in that."

"Don't try to softsoap me, David. I know the pattern. I know how the chamber puts the spurs to the council. But the chamber doesn't want water for homes. They want it for more industry. I was mayor back when we built the present reservoir. We thought it'd do for a long time. But do you know there's less water for the homeowner now than when we built that lake?"

Cal did have a point. The chamber's industrial committee already was beating the drum for new industry with pamphlets and statistics on the city's upstream watershed rights and the news that "a new reservoir is under study which, when completed, will give the city one of the biggest per capita water supplies in the Southwest." The chamber also was planning a new campaign of sending "civic salesmen" back East to contact potential industry and to spread the good word.

David could see Cal wasn't in the mood to be put off easily. "All right. How about getting it in writing that a certain reserve per capita be allocated. Industry would be secondary. Right now, with the project in the planning stage, I think the chamber people would compromise on that. Is that what you want?"

Cal thought it over for a moment. "I'll tell you what I want. I want to leave my grandchildren a town with a good police force, clean, paved, well-lighted streets, schools, parks, fire protection. We can't seem to take care of the people we got. Why do we want more? David, one of my daughters bought a house from Weatherbee. The contract said there'd be streetlights within six months. That's been three years ago. The city hasn't lived up to its bargain."

"You know our budget problems, Cal. There's no reason to go into that. But the beauty of this water program is that it won't even touch the city budget. All we'll do is enter into a contract with the water district to purchase so much water at a certain rate. They'll float the bond issue."

Cal snorted disgustedly. "It's still the same taxpayer. Whatever you label it, the same man gets the bill. Governments are limited on their bonded indebtedness. But who's looking out for the taxpayer? He's got his city, county, state, federal taxes to pay, the school levy, and now a water district. And most of them going up. What's the limit on that man's bonded indebtedness? We're ridin' a good horse to death."

"I don't think anyone will object to paying a few more cents for water," David insisted. "All we have to do is remind them of the drought of the Fifties. Remember? Odd-numbered houses water lawns on odd days, even on even days? No car washing? No street cleaning? Is that what you want for your grandchildren? Not enough water to have green lawns?"

"I think it's quite apparent the good Lord didn't intend for this part of Texas to be very green," Cal said wryly. "I keep thinkin' about my grandson bein' sent home from school some days at noon because there's not enough classrooms. I keep thinkin' about how there's no sidewalks in any of these new additions. No, David. People are wrong in thinking bigness is greatness. Hell, if it's population they want, let them move to China. I'd rather have a good little town like we had twenty years or so ago than have Dallas, Fort Worth, San Antonio, and Houston for suburbs."

"Cal, all we are going to do tonight is set a date to hear the engineers' report," David said as firmly as he could. "That's all. I don't think anyone intends to discuss it."

"I'd rather put it off a while," Cal said stubbornly.

David lowered his voice to a confidential tone.

"I agree that you have some good points. Those things certainly should be taken into consideration. But Cal, I think you would be defeating your purpose if you start arguing against it tonight, before you've even been told what the plan is."

Cal's eyes widened slightly, and David knew he'd struck home. He had talked Cal out of immediate action.

"It's seven now," David said. "I guess we better be getting on up there."

But as they left the restaurant for City Hall, David realized that he'd only won a skirmish, with the major battle still looming. He felt a growing sense of apprehension.

Cal apparently was going to be an opponent. Right-winger Byron, slow to decide on any issue, was still on the fence. If Dr. Travis McNiel couldn't be mollified again, the water project was in serious trouble.

## CHAPTER FIVE

Darkness spread over the city. To the north, almost unseen, a thunderstorm formed, moved slowly southeastward, and disappeared, leaving the supper hour quietness undisturbed.

Tom Kencaide sat at his desk in the *News-Gazette* city room penciling in the finishing touches on a long description of the lake program. He read the story through again carefully, watching for typographical errors, making sure the phraseology was right, the continuity smooth. This description would be the main body of his City Council story tonight. After the meeting, he would write a beginning, using whatever action the council took on the lake, and an end, using other, minor decisions of the council. But this, the backbone of his story, would be in type, waiting.

For there was never enough time between council meetings and the final edition deadline. Often, with a long session, there would be no more than twenty or thirty minutes for the whole process, from typewriter to the press. When this happened, Tom only had time to phone in a few paragraphs.

And tonight's meeting had a long agenda.

Satisfied with his work, finally, he wrote "*lead to kum*" across the top and at the bottom penciled in "*add to kum*," then took the story across the room to Collier at the city desk. Without looking up, Collier picked up the copy and gave it a quick, preliminary inspection, reading only the first few words of each paragraph. Then he slipped the story under a stack near his left elbow.

"Good enough," he said. "Tight paper tonight, so keep the rest as short as you can. And Tom, if there's any controversy on the lake, for God's sake play it down. The setting of the date will be the important thing, not that they haggled over it."

Tom should have kept quiet for once. The clash he'd had with Collier the day before over the change in his copy still smoldered. And Collier could have a nasty temper sometimes. But Tom spoke before he thought. "I don't see how we can completely ignore a big hassle if one should develop."

Irritated, Collier swiveled around and glared at Tom's belt buckle. "I didn't say you had to ignore it. I just said play it down so I won't have to rewrite your lead at the last minute."

The deskmen beyond Collier were listening again. The sting of Collier's words on the still-smarting memory of yesterday's rebuke brought Tom's reply out before he could stop it. "Maybe you'd rather send someone else."

Collier slammed his pencil down on the desk and whipped the cigar out of his mouth. "That might be a good idea," he said, raising his gaze to meet Tom's.

They glared at each other for a long, uncomfortable moment. Then Tom turned and started toward the elevator.

The numbness in his mind suddenly changed to hope as he heard Collier's voice behind him, calling his name. He stopped and waited for Collier to catch up.

Collier's face was still set with anger, but his voice was lower, softer. "Come on, let's go get a cup of coffee."

They rode the elevator down, the silence heavy between them, and walked to the Silver Dollar Café next door. No one Tom knew ever ate at the Silver Dollar, but the coffee was tolerated because it was nearest and quickest. They went to a booth in the corner away from the jukebox, and Collier waited until the waitress had brought the coffee and left before he spoke.

"Don't ever pull that walkout bit on me again, Tom. I might not trot along after you next time."

"I'm sorry. But you've been very unhappy with my writing lately. Maybe we ought to come to some sort of an understanding."

"Not unhappy about your writing, Tom. It's your thinking that's all wrong. I don't like some of the things we have to do any more than you do. But damn it, when you work for a man, you have to do the work the way he wants it done."

"Even if it goes against every canon of professional ethics you've ever known?"

Collier sighed. "The ethics of journalism is a good phrase. It has a good solid ring to it. But when you work for a paper that doesn't believe in it, you just have to work out your own code, one that fits."

"Have you worked one out?"

"I'll admit it gets strained to the limit sometimes. I imagine even the lowest factory worker has his personal standards offended at times when he's ordered to do substandard work. But he does it because he's working for the factory, not for himself."

"But we're not making bedsprings or something like that," Tom protested. "We're dealing with informing the public, a part of the democratic process. I don't see how . . ."

Collier cut him off with an exasperated grunt. "I don't know why I thought I'd be able to talk some sense into you. What in hell am I going to do with you, Tom? You give me more trouble than all the rest of the staff put together."

"I know. It's just that I don't feel like a reporter any more. I feel like BeeBee's hired spy and propaganda writer."

"Well, I'm serving notice on you right now to quit taking your frustrations out on me. If you want to go over my head and take your gripes to the managing editor or to BeeBee, feel free. But remember that I've got frustrations enough of my own."

"I've been childish," Tom admitted. "I realize it, and I promise that I'll try to do better."

"Good enough," Collier said. He glanced at his watch. "I've got to get back. You have anything else coming?"

"No. I thought I'd run out to the Longhorn Lounge and see Joe Garzek for a few minutes before council."

Collier had started to slide out of the booth. He stopped on the edge of the seat. "I meant to ask. What did you and J. Marvin find out last night?"

"Nothing. We stayed about two hours. Two cops came in, and J. Marvin followed them out and talked to them. They said the Longhorn Lounge is a trouble spot and they have standing orders to keep a close watch on it."

"That may be all there is to find out, you know."

"No, Garzek's telling the truth. I'm sure of it."

"I had that feeling. But I have been wrong once or twice in my life."

"Isn't there any chance of working up a story now? We could tell Garzek's side of it, the police side, and maybe I could get a statement out of Berger."

Collier scowled. "No, it's going to have to be nailed down much better than that. Fifteen years ago we'd have done that and the devil take the hindmost. But now . . ." His voice trailed off and his fingers drummed the table. "Maybe we better just forget about it," he said finally.

"If you don't mind, I'd like to keep after it," Tom said. "I've been thinking that if they've pulled this on Garzek, there must be others who are afraid to talk. I might be able to find them."

"Suit yourself," Collier said. "But remember, I'm promising nothing. Before we run anything it'll have to be cleared by BeeBee's lawyer, and you know how much of a chance we have in getting a story like that past him."

"Well, I'd never feel right about it if we didn't try," Tom said.

Afterward, as he walked the two blocks to where he'd left Old Smokey, one phrase of Collier's kept resounding in Tom's mind: "Fifteen years ago . . ."

Fifteen years ago Thirty-Thirty Milam, BeeBee's father, had been alive, running the paper the way a newspaper should be run. Tom had known him, and Tom's youthful admiration of

Thirty-Thirty's newspaper had influenced him in his choice of a career.

Since the death of Thirty-Thirty changes at the *News-Gazette* had been swift—typical of the whole newspaper industry, but faster. Tom had been there to see some of them.

Maybe he worried about the changes because he understood them better, saw them in their long-range perspective. Tom had spent hours in the old yellowed files in the basement, going clear back to the newspaper's beginning. . . .

James "Shotgun" Milam founded the *News-Gazette* in 1887. He got his nickname from the double-barreled editorials he wrote and the real article he kept by his desk to back them up. Shotgun and his son, John "Thirty-Thirty" Milam, were strong-willed men in a strong-willed era. They ran their publication from the newsroom with the idea a newspaper earned its keep. They did not solicit advertising. As late as 1930 advertisers shoved their ads through a slot in a side door, where they were picked up daily and set in type only if the Milams felt the words and spirit therein were worthy of the newspaper.

Shotgun's views on any subject were no secret. They appeared regularly in ten-point editorial type, often on page one. The opposition was given its say in regular type on the news pages. Tom often thought he would have loved to work for Shotgun Milam.

Thirty-Thirty carried the tradition into the mid-Forties. His editorials showed more education and were more conservative in tone. But his news pages bore the same standards of fair play.

Ironically, Tom reflected, it was in the story of Thirty-Thirty's death that things began to change.

Thirty-Thirty died of a heart attack in the midst of copulation with a mistress of several years' standing. The first edition carrying his obituary stated he "died in the home of an old friend." The second edition said he "was stricken while conversing with old friends." The presses were stopped, however, and the last of the press run said he "died on a public street."

Although he had known Thirty-Thirty but slightly, Tom believed the man would have sacrificed his privacy—and that of his mistress, wife, and ex-wife—for accuracy in his newspaper.

With his death, titular control of the newspaper went to Thirty-Thirty's son, Arthur Milam, nicknamed "BeeBee." Tom sometimes felt a twinge of guilt in taking pleasure that whoever nicknamed BeeBee skipped over several calibers.

BeeBee was past forty when he got the newspaper after, as one staffer put it, "sitting down there twenty years, looking out the window, waiting for his daddy to die."

The changes came with BeeBee.

In all fairness, Tom reflected, maybe BeeBee wasn't entirely at fault. He faced problems Shotgun or Thirty-Thirty never would have believed could exist.

In the late Forties, production costs began to climb. Newsprint, labor, circulation, prices on all phases of operation rose, and continued soaring, faster with each passing year, through the Fifties.

And unlike Shotgun and Thirty-Thirty, BeeBee no longer was in full control. His mother—Thirty-Thirty's first wife—had willed some stock to a brother, and Thirty-Thirty's widow still retained a seat on the board. BeeBee's much younger half-sister, Sharon, also got a portion. A few shares had been awarded to faithful long-time employees by both Shotgun and Thirty-Thirty, and this stock had passed to heirs. BeeBee had to answer to stockholders who demanded a reasonable profit on investments even in the face of rising expenses. The newspaper had to support more people in a time of higher costs of living.

Inevitably, control of the newspaper passed from the editorial department to the business office. Shotgun and Thirty-Thirty had their private offices adjoining the newsroom and left the doors open. BeeBee's private office was now next to the business office, and it had been years since Tom had seen him in the newsroom.

The editorial department now struggled along on a tight budget dictated by the business office, and without any significant increase from year to year. Since this was an industrywide problem, solutions and economy discoveries made by any newspaper were adopted by others.

Newspapers had found it cheaper to fill news columns with syndicated features: comics, advice to the lovelorn, puzzles and word games, bridge and chess columns, cartoons, religious exhortations of all faiths, Hollywood and Broadway trivia, columns on care of the garden, house, hair, children, pets, beauty—any copy that could be written at one source and sent out to hundreds of newspapers. It seemed to Tom the newspaper was trying to be all things to all people, and succeeding with none.

Now, they used wire-service news instead of sending someone from the staff to outlying areas. The staff was reduced, but not enough to suit the business office, for salaries also had increased. There was only one solution: a less-experienced staff, sprinkling the older employees in key positions, hoping they would catch errors before they got into the paper.

In the mechanical department, changes were slower, for there the business office had to buck the unions. But in time, they managed. Now all news copy was punched onto tape and fed through automatic typesetters. It wasn't as accurate, but it was cheaper and faster. With so much syndicated material, more and more pages could run through all editions, cutting stereotyping costs. In the mailing room, where men used to insert sections by hand and wrap and tie by hand, machinery now did most of the work. Income tax depreciation could be declared on the machines, not on the men.

All this resulted in a shoddy product, and even if Tom had been blind to it he only had to talk to a few readers to know how much prestige the newspaper had lost.

Yet, he still had hopes it would change. Surely, sometime, the public was going to get tired of this shabbiness, realize the repetitious garden-beauty-child-pet-household-lovelorn columns were a penalty, not a prize, and start demanding news again.

Joe Garzek was alone behind the bar, watching two young airmen playing the shuffleboard machine. When he saw Tom, he broke into a broad smile. "I knew you coming," he said exuberantly. "I got fresh coffee made. Or do you want beer?"

"No, coffee's fine," Tom told him. "I just dropped by to see if you've had any more unwelcome visitors."

Garzek shook his head, his smile fading. "Nobody at all here today, hardly, customers or anybody." He turned to get the coffee.

Tom leaned against the bar, one foot on the brass rail, and studied the airmen. They played without spirit, without interest, switching the beer bottles to their left hands to shoot, the lead pucks making a soft swishing sound with an occasional solid thunk as one dropped into the gutter. But they were far enough away they couldn't eavesdrop without being obvious about it.

Garzek set the coffee on the bar. "You ready to write the story now?"

"I'm afraid not, Mr. Garzek. In fact, the paper is giving me even less support than I'd hoped for." He paused, trying to think of a way to explain. "We can't blame the paper too much, though, because it'd really be going out on a limb to print a story now, no more facts than we have."

"You mean we got no proof," Garzek said sadly.

Tom nodded. "I've got several ideas on how we might get some proof, maybe. For one thing, I'm going to rent a tape recorder in the morning, and maybe we can put it behind the bar, there. If this man comes back, or anyone from the Alamo distributors, you can make sure you're standing where you can flip it on."

"I don't know," Garzek said dubiously. "How much this cost?"

"Don't worry about that. I can put it on the newspaper expense account," Tom lied. "Is there a good place back there to put it?"

They examined the shelves and found a place at the end of the bar, away from the sink, to serve the purpose. The location also had the advantage that it would seem natural for Garzek to walk to the end of the bar, away from customers, if any happened to be in the lounge.

"Good," Tom said. "Now, do you know any other tavern owners . . . anyone else who might be having the same trouble?"

"No, nobody. I think about going to talk with somebody else, long time ago, but I afraid I talk to wrong one, somebody that tell on me."

"Is there an association of tavern owners? Any kind of a trade group?"

"I don't know of one."

Tom hadn't been able to find a trace of one, either.

"Well, there are probably others in your fix," Tom told him. "It's just a matter of finding them. If you can think of any tavern that's gone downhill, or gone out of business in the last few months, jot the name down and I'll look into it tomorrow. I know of a few prospects. If we could just get two or three to side with us, I don't think we'd be the underdogs very long."

"You think the paper would print it then?"

"Maybe. But there's a good chance they still wouldn't. I think our best bet would be to turn what we get, if anything, over to the district attorney. If we could get a grand jury indictment, then the paper would have a legal leg to stand on in printing it."

"How long you think all this take?" Garzek asked.

"Depends on how long it takes us to turn up some support."

Garzek shook his head sadly, lowered his gaze, and his mouth began to quiver. "I don't know what I going to do, Mr. Kencaide. Used to, this time of day, I have fifteen, twenty boys here drinking beer, having good time. Later, more come, maybe with girl friends. Used to, I have a band play on Friday, Saturday nights, whole place full."

The financial problem apparently was even worse than Tom had guessed. "I'm sorry," he said gently. "If you can just hold out awhile . . ."

Garzek's eyes suddenly filled with tears. "Today my little girl go to dentist. The doctor say her teeth growing all wrong, have to be fixed. I tell him to go ahead, do what he have to do. I pay some way." He started sobbing openly, his head cradled in his arms on the bar.

Embarrassed, Tom glanced at the two airmen, but they were intent on the shuffleboard game. He tried to think of something to say to make Garzek feel better. It'd been a long time since Tom had seen a grown man cry.

"If you should have to sell, it seems to me you will do all right," Tom said hopefully. "It's a good location, good building."

"Mortgage," Garzek said between sobs. "I got big mortgage." He raised his head and blinked at the colored glass front, long bar and empty booths. "When I come to this country, I think it going to be different."

"It is," Tom said. He started to say more, but there was no way to express what he felt. If he talked all night there wouldn't be enough time to explain all he'd seen in the world, the way this had affected him. He would have to use such jaded terms as democracy, free enterprise, national heritage.

Slowly, Garzek got control of himself, pulled a white handkerchief from a hip pocket, and wiped his eyes. "I got no right to ask you to do this," he said. "You start asking questions, maybe you get into trouble."

Tom grinned. "I guess that's a risk we'll just have to take," he said.

On his way to City Hall, Tom passed an outdoor theater with a thirty-foot Bardot pouting in the evening sky, acres of suburban shopping centers, the beer and hamburger drive-ins with their malmufflered cars, loud horns, jukeboxes, and nerve-jarring sounds of tires digging out on gravel.

A restless people. That was their heritage.

They told the story of a Tennessee mountaineer who heard of the Texas struggle for independence, grabbed his rifle, and said: "I'm goin' to Texas and fight for my rights."

These were his children. Theirs was a turbulent history of continual conflict: the War for Independence from Mexico; the Civil War, the border disputes, the Indian wars, the county seat wars, the range wars, the oil booms, the battle of the Depression, the world wars. . . .

The Super-Americans, *New Yorker* writer John Bainbridge had called them.

They didn't like all he said, but they liked that title.

Now, there was no outlet for their restlessness but to work, build, make changes, acquire. . . .

For a time Tom had thought his fellow Texans were not aware of their heritage, of the world conflict going on around them. He thought they were too busy building, making changes, acquiring.

Then in an October crisis, when the threat of nuclear holocaust hung in the air like a fog, he had learned different.

They were aware. That was a part of their restlessness.

Tom parked Old Smokey in the municipal parking lot behind City Hall. He was walking across the blacktop toward the walk when he heard someone call to him from the shadows of the building. As he stepped into the semidarkness he recognized Dr. McNiel's car.

"Could I see you a minute?" the doctor asked through an open window.

Tom went around to the other side, and the doctor reached across the front seat to push the door open for him.

"I'll just keep you a minute," the doctor said, his face serious under the domelight. He waited until Tom was in the car, the door closed, and they were in darkness again. "I'm going to make a little speech tonight," he said. "I just want to make sure it won't be misunderstood as far as the newspaper is concerned."

"I'll do my best," Tom promised.

"I want it understood that I'm not against the water program, *per se*. It's just that I believe hospital improvements should come before we do anything else. I'm going to propose tonight that we either take up the hospital program first, or at the same time as the lake program. My stand is that if we can't afford to safeguard the health of our citizens, we can't afford the lake. That will be the basis of my voting against the lake program."

Here it was, opposition. Tom's first thoughts were of the extent, the organization. But he caught himself. The doctor wasn't that much of a politician.

"Think you might have a chance for a majority?" Tom asked.

"No. I haven't talked to any of the other council members, so I doubt if it will even come to a vote, for lack of a second. But I'm going to do it because I want to go on record."

Tom had long realized some of the pressures Dr. McNiel must be under for his failure to accomplish any of the objectives he was put on the council to achieve.

"I'll put it in the story," Tom promised. "But I can't guarantee it will be left in." A couple of paragraphs, deep down in the story, probably wouldn't be considered dangerous to BeeBee's project.

"That's all I can ask," the doctor said. "I guess we better be getting on up there."

They walked up to Hartwell's office together, the doctor matching Tom's slow pace on the steps without comment. All the other councilmen were there except Berger, who never attended the pre-council meetings. The councilmen, Hartwell, the city secretary, and four department heads were standing around waiting, talking in groups of twos and threes. As Tom and the doctor walked in, the mayor broke off his conversation with Weatherbee and announced in a raised voice:

"Well, we're all here. Let's get started." As usual, he ignored Berger's boycott of the pre-council discussion.

Bordering on illegality, these pre-council sessions dated back beyond the memory of any council member. They were defended as being private, rather than secret, giving the councilmen "a chance to iron out differences in opinion" and to "get the benefit of each other's thinking" before facing the public upstairs in the council auditorium. Thus the council could "present a united front on important issues."

True, no voting or formal action was ever taken at these meetings in the city manager's office. But since individual opinions were voiced freely, the real tests on issues often came here, making the official, public session upstairs an exercise in play-acting. Only recently, with Berger's refusal to participate, had there been any element of uncertainty on the outcome of the official votes upstairs.

Tom was allowed to monitor these sessions, probably to guard against any future cry of secret sessions. However, the rules were clearly defined: he was not allowed to take notes, nor quote anything said. What he heard, it was explained, was for "background" information.

Now, they took chairs in an odd protocol Tom never quite understood. Hartwell sat behind his huge desk, the mayor on his right, with Cal Masters on the other end. On the north side, next to Cal, Travis McNiel and Walt Weatherbee. On the south end, next to the mayor, Bill Wentworth and the undertaker, John Byron. Tom, the city secretary, and four department heads sat in straight chairs in front of Hartwell's desk, completing the circle.

There was a rustle as all the councilmen dug into their briefcases for the agendas and manager communications.

"If the city manager will start down the agenda," said the mayor, "we can take an item at a time." He leafed through his papers nervously. "It's a rather long agenda tonight, so we'll have to hurry."

Hartwell picked up a copy from his desk. "I think we can lump the first eight items," he said. "They're all bids received at the last session, and you all have the recommendations of the department heads. Are there any questions concerning these?"

The doctor shifted in his chair. "This Item Three. I notice the recommendation is not the low bid. Is there any reason why we shouldn't accept the low bid?"

Tom looked at Item No. 3—water meters.

"John, you could probably answer that better than I," Hartwell said to the water director, sitting on Tom's right.

"Well, Doctor, we're just geared for that brand, with our testing equipment and all," the water director said. "If we switched back and forth, we'd have to keep changin' connections, equipment, and that'd run into considerable money."

"Has this brand always been higher?" the doctor asked. "Or did they jack up their price after we geared for their equipment?"

"Sometimes they're low bid, sometimes not," the water director said. "Over the years, I think it about averages out."

"I'd like to see the bids on this equipment tabulated over the last two or three years before the next purchase," the doctor said. "I think we should find out if that company is taking advantage of us." He turned to the mayor. "Should I put that in the form of a motion upstairs?"

Hartwell broke in before the mayor could answer. "I hardly think that would be necessary," he said. "It's an administrative matter, and as you say, Travis, should be done. John, will you see to it that the purchases and bidding on this are tabulated for the last three years?"

The water director nodded. Taking a small notepad and ballpoint pen from his shirt pocket, he ceremoniously made a notation. Tom couldn't resist peeping. He wrote one word, *"bids,"* and put the paper and pen back into his pocket with a flourish.

"Are there any other questions on these items?" Hartwell asked.

There were none.

Hartwell went rapidly on down the list, getting little discussion. The manager-communication portfolio must have been complete, Tom realized. Even the much-debated highway plan brought only a single question from Weatherbee about an access road's intrusion on facing lots.

It was eight-fifteen, a quarter of an hour before council time, when Hartwell finished the agenda.

"I talked to the consulting engineers in Fort Worth again today," Hartwell went on without pausing. "I tentatively set next Tuesday, a week from tonight, as a date to hear the water report. Of course, that's only a suggestion. I thought the council might prefer to set an off night so other business wouldn't interfere, and the mayor had requested an early date. Does this conflict with anyone's plans?"

McNiel leaned forward. "Before we go any further, I want to make my views known on this," he said with a deep, forceful tone that brought the full attention of all in the room on him. "The speed with which this water program is being pushed is quite a surprise to me. I've yielded before on other programs against my better judgment, but I've gone as far as I'm going. If we can't afford a few thousand dollars to improve our hospital, I don't see how we can afford a multimillion-dollar lake. I will oppose it."

The mayor glanced hesitantly at Hartwell, then back at McNiel. "Now, Travis, the hospital program will be taken care of in time. We can't do everything at once."

"I believe the hospital program should come first, or at least simultaneously. I plan to make that into a formal motion upstairs tonight," the doctor said firmly.

There was a moment of silence, with everyone still looking at the doctor, who glared back at them unflinchingly from his owlish hornrims.

The mayor broke the silence with a cough. "Travis, of course you would be fully within your rights to make that motion upstairs. But don't you realize that division within the council jeopardizes all our programs—the hospital improvement too? I hope you will reconsider."

"You have no hope for a vote," Weatherbee said bluntly.

Cal Masters' bass voice was so loud in the closed room that the mayor actually jumped at the sound. "I agree with the doctor," Cal said. "I must say that I deeply resent the high-handed manner in which this program has been forced upon us."

The mayor turned to Hartwell again for help, but got no response. Tom had noticed before how Hartwell had an effective way of treating council division as a family spat, with himself as an outsider. He put the technique to good use now.

"Gentlemen," the mayor said. "If I've offended anyone in planning the lake report for early consideration, I apologize. I thought we were of like mind on this."

"That isn't the point, Hiram," Byron, the undertaker, said. "We all know we need water. But I, too, am concerned at the pressure being placed upon us by the newspaper and the chamber and civic groups. This lake involves federal funds. If we're not careful, we'll have federal control, too. I think we should proceed slowly and cautiously."

"We have to work with others on this," the mayor said quickly. "The water board here, the State Water Commission, and we must depend upon the chamber and civic groups for support. We can't set our own pace."

"The pace was set, agreed upon," Byron argued. "When I voted for this survey, I was told it was necessary to retain our water rights on the river. I understood it was a long-range study, and probably wouldn't be ready until next fall, or maybe even next year. Then after we contracted for the survey, the date began to get earlier every time it was mentioned. Now it's ready, at least six months ahead of schedule, and we suddenly get it shoved in our face for action. I guess we're supposed to be happy at having our own timetable altered."

The mayor frowned. "Well, I wasn't to say anything about this, but I'm sure that under the circumstances it will be permissible. Yes, there has been some pressure placed on the engineers to speed up the report, and I did ask the city manager to arrange an early date, and with good reason." He lowered his voice to a confidential tone. "The chamber has some representatives of a New Jersey industrial firm coming in next week to inspect a site in Industrial Park. They're definitely going to move a major portion of their operations to the Southwest, and we are among the top three of the cities being considered."

"I figured it was something like that," Cal said.

"This plant would involve four or five hundred workers—a thousand or more new residents," the mayor went on, ignoring Cal. "We would be the top choice, the chamber believes, if the company wasn't worried about the future water supply. If they could be given concrete evidence we are hard at work on the problem, it probably would remove their one remaining doubt."

"What kind of a company?" Byron asked suspiciously.

"I'm not at liberty to say." The mayor raised a bony finger. "You all please understand this has been a well-kept secret. They don't want any publicity." He shook the finger in Tom's direction. "Is that understood?"

Tom nodded affirmatively, knowing that BeeBee would have been informed of the news blackout and would enforce it.

"I imagine it would impress those visitors more to show concern over the medical care of the community," the doctor said.

"Ten hospitals wouldn't help them if we have another drought and have to cut their water off," Weatherbee said curtly.

"Gentlemen, this bickering will get us nowhere," the mayor pleaded. He glanced at the clock on the north wall. "We're five minutes late upstairs now. But I suppose it would be wise to determine the majority opinion before acting on the matter tonight. Walt, are you for going ahead and taking up the lake project now?"

Weatherbee spoke firmly. "I see no reason for delay."

"Bill?"

His ears turning red from the sudden attention, Bill Wentworth, the council's youngest member, spread his hands and shrugged. "I'm one hundred percent for the new lake," he said. "The sooner we get started on it, the better."

"Cal?"

"I side with the doctor."

All attention shifted to Byron even before the mayor asked the question.

"John?"

Byron studied a moment before answering, and Tom could see his Adam's apple working on a dry swallow. When he spoke his voice conveyed his uncertainty. "Well, I made my views known. I think we've got to do something about outside meddling in council work. Lord knows, I would have preferred to wait. But if the report is ready now, I guess there's nothing left to do but decide whether we want to commit ourselves, or give up the water rights on the river."

Tom knew from the mayor's frown that the loaded answer displeased him even more than the earlier flat refusals.

The mayor looked again at the clock. "We better be getting on upstairs," he said.

Tom stood to one side to let the councilmen file out. As he waited for them to gather their material for the trip upstairs, Tom realized that, for the first time in his memory, the pre-council session had failed to resolve an important issue before the council faced the public. And the mayor hadn't even taken a poll on the doctor's proposal for a double ballot.

Cal Masters came by, his leathery old face wrinkled in a peculiar meditative frown, his cowboy boots making a solid sound on the floor. Sam Weatherbee followed, serious as always. Dr. McNiel had a stubborn set to his jaw. Wentworth was wearing his Jaycee president's smile. Byron's face was even more somber than his dark suit. The mayor looked as if he wished he could call the whole thing off. Only Hartwell appeared unperturbed.

"Could I use your phone?" Tom asked Hartwell.

"Be my guest," Hartwell said, gesturing toward his desk. "Just latch the door when you leave."

As they filed on out Tom picked up the receiver and dialed the office. He had a brief wait before he got through the PBX and heard Collier's gruff "City desk, Collier speaking."

"I thought you might like to tell BeeBee he can hit the panic button," Tom said. "Looks like his lake project is in hot water, if you'll pardon the pun."

"You don't have to sound so damned happy about it. What happened?"

Tom told him briefly. Collier listened in silence.

"How does that stack up?" he asked when Tom had finished.

"Two siding with the mayor, and two against, with Byron undecided, I think." He remembered the other reason he'd phoned. "You know anything about some New Jersey industrialists coming to town next week?"

Tom was honor-bound not to write a story on it, but he had no compunction about tipping off the reporter on the Chamber of Commerce run and letting him dig into the story, using another source. But Collier's impatience confirmed his suspicions that BeeBee already had the blackout in effect.

"Yes, but just forget it. We're supposed to hold off on it awhile.

What I want to know now is, what's going to happen up there tonight?"

"I haven't the slightest idea," Tom admitted. "It'll be up to Byron . . . and Berger."

## CHAPTER SIX

Before Travis McNiel was asked to run for council, he never had attended a council meeting. He had read the newspaper accounts and was aware of most civic issues. But he never had occasion to take a protest or plea into the council chamber.

While he was considering the idea of becoming a candidate, he attended two sessions out of curiosity. At the time, he considered those the dullest evenings of his entire life, and the boredom almost prompted him to give up the idea. But then, as he thought over what had occurred at those meetings, he began to get an insight into the strange mechanism of this form of government.

The City Council almost could be called rule by default. The laboriously long meetings continually played to a near-empty house. Of the platoons of titled Chamber of Commerce members who met with their varied committees and subcommittees over luncheon and dinner and dreamed great dreams for the city, none braved the tedium of a council session.

None left home and hearth on cold winter nights or air-conditioned comfort in the depths of summer to listen to the drone of the city secretary's B-flat monotone voice reading long pages of bid specifications. For to do so would violate every concept of the Big Operator, Civic Leader, and Power Behind Progress. Council pay of $10 a month wasn't much of a lure.

Only those who wanted something or believed their rights were being violated came. An assessment for street paving might bring ten or fifteen to protest. The mention of a tax increase might yield a crowd of thirty for a night.

The council agenda was arranged to make their suffering minimal. Matters involving members of the audience were scheduled early so they could tiptoe out after a decision. Only two or three eccentrics who made a hobby of council and letters-to-the-editor ever sat through an entire session.

Yet, such were the peculiarities of public concern that on four nights Travis actually had seen the auditorium packed, with many standing along the side aisles for lack of seats. Out of this came what was still known as the Comic Book Ordinance.

It had happened almost a year ago. A sudden, widespread movement among the women's clubs had spawned an organization called the Committee to Wipe Out Newsstand Trash. This group brought representatives down on the council en masse demanding an ordinance. To back up their case, they loaded the council table with nudist magazines, bedroom novels, and sadistic comic books they claimed were available to children on most every newsstand.

Travis checked. What they said was true. But he also learned, through the city attorney, that there were state laws against pornography. Informed of this at the next council session, the Committee to Wipe Out Newsstand Trash retreated, conferred, and returned the next week, saying the state laws were ambiguous and apparently incapable of being enforced. They demanded a City Board of Censorship. The city attorney advised against it. Every action of such a board, he said, might have to be tested in court with considerable expense to the city. "And personally," he added, "I believe any such board would be a violation of Freedom of the Press. If you find truly pornographic material, it can be prosecuted under existing state laws."

The council voted not to act on the petition.

Every councilman had sheer hell for the next two weeks. Travis had to put an extra receptionist in his office to screen calls. At home, he installed a separate, unlisted phone to guarantee an open line when the hospital needed him. The persistence of the campaign kept Marilyn busy night and day, and he could only hope that when a patient tried to reach him at home the call would come during an infrequent lull. Letters, many containing the accused pornography despite postal regulations, piled up unread on his desk at home, at the office.

After two weeks, the councilmen knew they were defeated. They passed the ordinance creating a City Board of Censorship to cheers from a full council chamber. Then the women went away, apparently satisfied.

In the year since, the mayor had not appointed members to the City Board of Censorship, nor had there been a single demand that he do so. Members of the Committee to Wipe Out Newsstand Trash presumably had gone back to whatever they were doing before the crusade. And the council went back to routine, with a nightly average of ten in the council audience.

So Travis was not surprised when he entered the council chamber and saw only a dozen bid representatives and two loafers for an audience. He had known his speech would be delivered in a public vacuum. It would be intended for only two people: the city secretary putting the meeting into shorthand, and Tom Kencaide, the *News* reporter. Kencaide was the only newsman covering council sessions, usually. Most council decisions were too late for television's ten o'clock news, and both TV and radio seemed to lift their early-morning newscasts from the newspaper.

Travis took his seat at the end of the long, horseshoe-shaped council table. His was the best seat available, he believed, with the possible exception of Berger's on the far end. It gave Travis a view of every face, both at the council horseshoe and in the audience, for the ends of the horseshoe projected almost into the first row of auditorium seats. On his left sat Weatherbee, then Wentworth, then Hartwell next to the mayor, who occupied the center of the horseshoe rim. On the mayor's left sat the city secretary, then the city attorney whose presence was required in case a legal question should arise. Then Byron and Cal Masters, with Berger on the far end. To aid in this far-flung arrangement, each had a microphone.

In the curve of the elevated horseshoe, below the mayor, Tom Kencaide sat alone at the press table. Angled into it, forming a T, was a longer table with a podium and microphone for the use of anyone coming forward from the audience to address the council.

Travis' view of the whole chamber was complete. But the greatest advantage of his position was that it gave him a full-faced view of Berger. From the first, Travis had experienced a vague uneasiness about Berger. There was something about the man that held a unique fascination. Tonight, as he had many times in the past, Travis covertly watched him while waiting for council to begin, studying him, trying to determine what there was so disturbing about the man. Berger sat now watching the mayor and Hartwell, who were conferring in low tones in the rear doorway behind the council table. He had a right to be curious about tonight's delay, Travis supposed, but the close-set eyes seemed overly bright, and his small, white feminine hands rolled the cigar around in his babyish mouth even more nervously than usual. His mouth seemed no bigger than a nickel, and he always had a cigar in it, even while talking. Berger's gaze kept flicking about the room, his face expressionless, his bald head shining in the overhead lights, but his attention kept returning to Hartwell and the mayor.

There definitely was something in Berger similar to the psychopaths Travis had seen in the state mental hospitals while in training. He tried not to let his personal dislike of the man stand in the way of his evaluation. But every action of Berger bore this out . . . the antisocial behavior, the paranoiac suspicion Travis had occasionally glimpsed in him.

However, there was a difference. The mental patients were possessed by delusions, compulsions, obsessions, diseases of the mind. The more Travis watched Berger, the more convinced he became that this illness was not of the mind. It seemed more a deformity of the soul, outside the realm of medicine. . . .

Mayor Hiram Milner tapped the table three times with the gavel.

"Meeting will come to order," he said, leaning forward, close to the microphone. "Our guest minister this week is the Reverend Robert Wolff of Crockett Avenue Baptist Church, who will lead us in prayer. Reverend Wolff."

Reverend Wolff came forward from his front-row seat, Bible in hand, and paused a moment before the microphone, then raised his face to the ceiling and closed his eyes.

He asked the Lord's blessing on the council and heavenly guidance in its decisions. The theme of council prayers never varied, just the denomination and choice of words. Travis raised his eyes to check on Berger. As usual, Berger had not lowered his head, but sat boldly studying others in the room. This, Travis supposed, put himself and Berger in the same class—a couple of heretics. At least Travis hoped he wasn't hypocritical about his religion. He had heard Berger was a church lay leader, but somehow this seemed incongruous with the man's actions.

"Thank you, Reverend Wolff," the mayor said. He fumbled through the papers before him to allow a decent interval between the prayer and earthly routine. "Will the city secretary read the minutes of the last meeting?" he asked finally.

The city secretary, a dried-up little man in his mid-fifties, arranged his notes, leaned forward into the microphone, and started reading in his monotone.

Reverend Wolff arose, smiled, exchanged an understanding nod with the mayor, then tiptoed to a side aisle and out the back of the auditorium.

The city secretary's voice droned on to the end.

"Are there any corrections to be made in the minutes of the last meeting?" the mayor asked.

There was no response.

"I move the minutes of the last meeting be accepted," Weatherbee said.

"Second the motion," Byron said.

"Motion has been made and seconded that minutes of the last meeting be accepted," the mayor said. "All in favor say aye."

"Aye," the council said.

"All opposed nay."

No response.

"First item on the agenda," the mayor said slowly, "is purchase of tires for city vehicles. The list of sizes and specifications is quite lengthy, and since it has been read before, I don't believe there is necessity to repeat it. Low bid is from Davis Tire Company in the amount of three thousand, seven hundred and fifty-six dollars. Do I hear a motion?"

Travis leaned forward to the microphone. "I move that the bid of Davis Tire Company in the amount of three thousand, seven hundred and fifty-six dollars be accepted," he said.

"I second the motion," Cal Masters said from the other side of the council table.

"The motion has been made and seconded that the bid of

Davis Tire Company in the amount of three thousand, seven hundred and fifty-six dollars be accepted," the mayor said. "All those in favor say aye."

"Aye," the council said.

"All opposed nay."

No response.

"The bid of Davis Tire Company, in the amount of three thousand, seven hundred and fifty-six dollars is accepted," the mayor said. "The next item on the agenda . . ."

Travis' mind wandered from the myriad of pipe fittings and conduit lengths which followed. He had made a minor contribution to the session. Now he could relax a while, just voting on cue. Looking out across the wide expanse of empty seats, he thought of how it had been on those four nights the comic-book crowd came before the council. He could sure use that audience and enthusiasm tonight.

If there were only some way to make them as concerned over medical care for their children as they had been over what their offspring read. If an auditorium full of women could get an impractical ordinance through the council, surely the same burr under the saddle would get a rational one through. Medical care wouldn't have the attraction of nudist magazines, but it should arouse an even stronger protective maternal instinct. If he only knew how to reach them, how to get the same simultaneous groundswell movement among the women's clubs throughout the city. . . .

Travis was thinking about this, oblivious to the routine of the council session, when he became aware of someone entering the chamber. He could hardly believe his senses as he saw his wife walk down the near aisle and take a seat in the third row. Marilyn had given no indication she planned to be here.

On the far side of the council table, Cal nodded a greeting to her, then turned to Travis and winked. There wouldn't be much of an audience for his speech, but it would be a friendly one.

The session ground on. Approval of the bids took more than an hour, so it was after nine-thirty when the bid representatives tiptoed out. The rest of the routine items, zoning board action approval, plat approval, a report from the planning board, an administrative change in the parks department and a proposed traffic change, took more than an hour. At a quarter to eleven they finally took up the highway program. After all the bitter words and long months of debate, the approval of the final agreement with the state on the loop bypass was anticlimactic.

Walt Weatherbee asked a few last-minute questions, and—surprisingly—there were a couple from Berger concerning the flow of traffic in the vicinity of the northeast cloverleaf. Then they voted, unanimously, to enter into the final contract, and the highway battle was over.

"I believe this brings us to the final item on our agenda," the mayor said. "This is to set a date to hear the report of our consulting engineers on the municipal water program. The city manager has informed me that he has been in contact with the engineers, and that next Tuesday, a week from tonight, would be satisfactory with them. Does that conflict with any plans of the council?"

It now was a few minutes past eleven. Travis knew everyone was tired and bored. This was a poor time to make his stand, but he had no choice.

"Mayor, before we go into this, there is something I would like to say."

Travis felt all eyes upon him.

"Very well, Doctor."

"I want to say that I am surprised and concerned over the speed with which this reservoir project has been pushed. I voted, a few months ago, with the rest of the council, for a continuing study because it was my understanding we must keep our program in motion in accordance with our contract with the State Water Commission. If we don't, we put our water rights to the river in jeopardy."

"I believe that is correct," the mayor said.

"With this in mind," Travis explained, "I voted for a continuing study, seeking a program to be put into effect at some future date. Therefore, I was most surprised to learn this week an election is planned soon on the water program. My point is, I believe the expansion and improvement of our hospital should either come before, or possibly at the same time as the water program."

Beside him Walt Weatherbee came to life. "Apparently the

doctor doesn't remember the drought of the Fifties. The town has grown twenty percent since then. We've got to have water, and we've got to have it before another drought cycle. We can't act fast enough, in my opinion . . ."

"Gentlemen," the mayor cut in. "I see no use of wrangling over the matter. The important point Dr. McNiel has overlooked is that the water program has been researched and prepared. As far as I know, there has been no impartial study of hospital needs."

"I can give you any facts or statistics you want," Travis said.

"He said impartial study," Weatherbee put in.

Suddenly, Cal Masters' voice boomed out over the council chamber. "I believe Dr. McNiel still has the floor."

The mayor was the first to break the surprised silence. "The doctor has the floor," he said.

"I admit I can't be impartial," Travis said. "I have to work in that hospital, and if you want to know the truth, I'm ashamed of it. Any statistics you want will show you why. A city should have between five and six hospital beds, minimum, per thousand population. Taking in the area we serve, we have slightly less than three, counting the Catholic hospital and the various doctors' clinics. You mentioned growth, Walt. Our hospital facilities are the same now as they were in 1950, and they were considered inadequate then. Our budget is virtually the same. The recommended average is two point six staff members per patient. We have one point seven, which means that our nurses and ward attendants are overworked, and I'll leave it to your imagination to think what that means in lessened medical service, and how dangerous it is to have an overworked person dealing with human lives. . . ."

He went on, knowing he was talking too loud and too long, but they were listening.

"If we were going to be practical, it would be a good idea to pass an ordinance that only two persons be allowed to ride in each car within the city limits, because if two cars collide and all four persons are injured, that would fill our emergency room. Just a simple automobile collision. I'm not talking of a tornado like the one that brushed town three years ago, with dozens of injured. You saw what happened then. We have no hope of meeting any minor calamity without outside help."

He told them of the need for static-free flooring in the operating rooms, about the spinal blocks and Pentothal Sodium used as anesthetic often because the surgeon disliked using ether with the danger of an explosion always present. He told them how it was necessary to pass through the surgical section and operating rooms to get to the recovery and intensive care unit, and how a relapse in recovery could affect an operation in progress. He went into other, minor things: the need for more isolation space, for a small security section to confine mental and criminal patients.

"I'm not asking anything for the medical association," he concluded. "I'm asking for facilities for proper care of the people of this city. As it is now, we are underequipped to offer your families the best possible care in the event of accident or illness. And I think you, or any citizen, would want this."

Travis could tell that he had gotten through to them, probably for the first time. The mayor stared at the table in silence for a moment before he answered.

"Doctor, I agree with you that something must be done. But as I said before, we are not prepared to go forward with it. Now, suppose we appoint a committee to go ahead and obtain estimates of needs, to work out a plan of co-operation with the county commissioners. . . ."

The mayor was going back to the schedule he'd proposed earlier in the day.

"No," Travis said. "If we can rush the water program, we can rush the hospital program. It isn't as if we were starting from scratch. Plans for expansion were drawn at the last addition twelve years ago. All that needs to be done is to update the costs, and already a preliminary estimate has been made out of the hospital board's budget. The national average cost of hospitals is figured at twenty-one thousand dollars per bed. Our estimates show we can provide fifty-two more beds, plus all the other improvements I mentioned, for slightly more than seventeen thousand dollars per bed, utilizing existing construction."

He paused, giving them time to absorb this.

"I therefore make the motion that we retain an architect immediately to draw up specifications and estimates based upon existing plans, and that this be submitted to the commissioners court and a vote of the people on the same ballot as the water program, whenever it be set."

"I second the motion," Cal Masters said.

"You're crazy, both of you," Weatherbee exploded. "We can't put a tax rate item on the same ballot with the water program."

"Yes," the mayor said. "Surely we would have to raise the tax rate, which certainly would have some effect at the polls. The water vote is merely an agreement with the water district, financed out of revenue. Also, the hospital item would have to be a countywide vote."

"Mister Mayor," Cal said forcibly, ignoring the microphone, "the only way I could conscientiously vote for the water program would be to start providing, at the same time, some facilities for the people of this city, and the people this new lake would bring here. I will not vote for the lake program unless it is understood we will make a start in that direction."

"We can't put them on the same ballot," Weatherbee argued. "Look what happened to Fort Worth. Remember the Gruen Plan? They were going to turn the downtown section into shopping malls, the city of the future, an idea that made headlines all over the country. But they loaded up the ballot with some other projects and lost the whole damned thing at the polls."

"Yes," the mayor agreed. "And this being a tax-increase item, I certainly don't feel we should risk them both on the same ballot. . . ."

Cal's voice boomed again. "I believe you have a motion before you, Mister Mayor, duly seconded."

Confused momentarily, the mayor glanced at Hartwell, who sat impassive, aloof to the squabble. Then, taking a deep breath, the mayor repeated Travis' motion.

"It has been moved and seconded that the city secure the services of an architect immediately to draw up specifications and estimates for expansion of the city-county hospital, and that said expansion proposal be placed before the voters of the city on the same ballot as the water program, whenever that shall be set." He turned to Travis. "Am I quoting you correctly, Doctor?"

"Close enough," Travis said.

"All those in favor say aye."

"Aye," Travis and Cal said together. And, almost like an echo, Travis thought he heard another.

The city secretary thought he heard it, too.

"I didn't get the vote," he said. "Dr. McNiel and Councilman Masters, and . . ."

Byron raised his hand solemnly. "Teaming these two programs would give us adequate time to study both," he said. "I am convinced of the need of Dr. McNiel's program. I am not convinced on the other. To my mind, more study is yet to be done on the lake project than on the hospital program."

Everyone's attention turned to the mayor in the sudden realization that this was going to be a tie vote, the first since the mayor was elected. From the frown on the mayor's face, it was apparent he already knew he was going to have to break a deadlock. But he went ahead with his duties as if he hadn't noticed.

"Opposed nay."

"Nay," said Weatherbee, Berger, and Wentworth, almost in unison.

The mayor's frown deepened. He gazed studiously at the table for a moment in silence. Travis knew the mayor was not thinking of how he was going to vote, but how he would go about it. Cal Masters was grinning broadly at the mayor's discomfort.

"Before I cast my vote to break the council's tie," the mayor said finally, "I would like to say that I'm in sympathy with Dr. McNiel's motives and his objectives. I, too, believe that the hospital expansion program should have high priority. However, I do not believe we should endanger both programs by combining them on a single ballot. Therefore, I say nay."

He sighed deeply, as if completing a distasteful task. "If there are no further objections, then," he added, looking at Travis, "I hereby call a special session of the City Council for eight o'clock next Tuesday night for the purpose of hearing a report from our consulting engineers on our proposed water program."

There were no further objections.

Afterward, Travis was pleasantly surprised by the reaction to his speech. Even before he left his council seat Weatherbee turned and offered his hand.

"No hard feelings, Doctor," Weatherbee said. "If this lake didn't mean so much to the city's growth, I might be willing to risk it for your project. When it comes up later, I'll give you full support."

The mayor came around the council table and gave Travis one of his rare smiles. "Maybe I was wrong today, Doctor, when I told you how to go about winning council support. If you had given that speech eighteen months ago, maybe things would be different now."

Byron had no reservations. "You've won me over. Anything I can do to help, let me know."

Cal Masters walked down to the parking lot with Travis and Marilyn. "Maybe you think you lost the battle tonight," he said. "But you didn't. As I see it, that was a victory. You got them to considerin' the hospital project seriously. That's a start."

Travis knew this was true. And he knew he should feel some sort of elation, but he didn't. He only felt a sharp disappointment in coming so close, yet failing. "How about coming by the house for a nightcap?" he asked Cal.

They were by Cal's old white pickup truck in the parking lot. Cal stopped and faced them. "No thanks. It's late, and for some reason I've got quite a pain right here in my breadbasket again tonight."

Travis looked at him closely. Even in the dim light there was an appearance of fatigue not in Cal's nature. And Cal's ramrod posture seemed to have yielded slightly; nothing takes the starch out of a man like a severe stomach pain.

"Again?" Travis asked, concerned.

"Been botherin' me right smart lately," Cal said. "Been intendin' to come in and see you about it."

"Any time," Travis said. "But if you're uncomfortable, I can take Marilyn home, meet you down at the office tonight."

"Oh, no, tomorrow will be soon enough," Cal said, opening the door of his pickup.

So they said good night to Cal and walked on to the car. All the way home, Travis worried about him, the persistent stomach pain, other outward symptoms.

Beside him, Marilyn felt the elation he should have felt over the council meeting. She, too, had seen the look of new respect in the faces of the other councilmen. She, too, had heard him change opinions with his own.

But for him, the effect was unsettling. Never before in his life had he talked so much, so violently.

Marilyn was full of praise for his accomplishment. "I didn't know you could lecture people like that," she said. "You really stirred them up."

He tried to pass it off lightly. "Advantage of being reared in a revival tent," he told her.

Later, after he had taken the baby-sitter home and while Marilyn was getting ready for bed, he tried to regain his composure with Scotch and water.

There was one way, he knew, to organize the comic-book crowd. But it would take far more effort than that speech tonight. He'd have to make thirty, forty, maybe even a hundred speeches. Could he do it?

His deep introversion had ceased to worry him long ago. From the works of Freud, Jung, Adler, and Menninger he had arrived at a simple explanation: he had been overexposed to crowds before his personality was able to cope with the situation. He had retreated into his self-made shell.

In the quiet of the house, thinking back, he could remember those crowds, the women especially—big hats and print dresses, large bosoms and stern faces. It wasn't a memory, exactly. It was more a moving kaleidoscope of impressions, always of strangers, smiling down. . . .

The son of a traveling evangelistic preacher continually faced strangers. There were many invitations into the homes of each congregation, and his father felt duty-bound to visit as many families as possible. In those formative years Travis seldom ate two meals at the same table or slept two nights in the same bed. The children in these communities regarded such an alien way of life freakish. In time, Travis began to accept himself as a freak.

This barrier kept him from meeting other children on their terms. The worst words Travis knew were "you kids go out and play," for he never knew exactly what to expect from his hosts' offspring, especially from the males. The challenges ranged all the way from seeing who could urinate the farthest to actual combat.

And when it came to fighting, Travis always lost, for he was no match for the husky rural opponents. Also, he was hampered by the knowledge that his father was going to give him another whipping for fighting.

So Travis soon learned to use silence, the only real weapon he had. If he let his tormentors get the best of talk, things seldom moved to the combative stage before some adult intervened.

Meals, too, were a trial. With most families, dinner for the revival preacher meant digging deep into the larder, and Travis faced formidable tables constantly—fried chicken, heavy gravies, mashed potatoes, corn bread, turnips and greens, pies—food for ranch, farm work. Gauged by his hosts' children, Travis' intake was meager.

"Why I declare, Brother McNiel, that boy don't eat enough to keep a bird alive," he'd heard more than a thousand times.

"It was the Lord's will to take his mother in childbirth," his father would reply solemnly. "I suppose he needs a home, a woman's care."

This remark usually was taken as an open invitation by some overly maternal church worker who then saw to it his tie was right, shoes shined, hair combed and that proper foods were forced upon him. Travis came to dread these attentions, but he found they protected him from combat.

Later, when he went to live with Aunt Ida, he used his teachers as guardians. For him, becoming the teachers' pet was easy. He could recite much of the King James version of the Bible from memory, and once he connected the letters of the alphabet with the words in his mind, there was no holding him back. Teachers recognized him as a natural scholar.

His many hours with books didn't disturb Aunt Ida, nor did she worry about his lack of normal activities. Reading books kept him quiet, which was in accord with her way of life.

When war came, his eyesight kept him from that great social integrator, military service. Now, he felt keenly the denial of even that camaraderie. He had spent the war a myopic 4-F, studying, aloof from the war as he had been from other problems.

Looking back, now, he could see the vast adjustments he had made in the last few years.

He eventually had learned to accept the public life of a doctor, and to face the demands of his patients. In some ways, his deep reserve had been to his advantage. For there were many patients who preferred an objective, clinical relationship with their doctor. Especially women. Despite his shingle of general practice, much of his work was in obstetrics and gynecology.

Service on the hospital board had pushed him further into public life. A few years ago, he would have considered City Council work impossible for himself. But tonight, he had made a speech. His adjustments were testimony to the flexibility of human character. He had come to understand his deficiencies and had surmounted them. He knew his reluctance to appear before gatherings was more than simple stage fright. It was a deep aversion nurtured in early childhood.

Maybe voicing his convictions to strangers was another adjustment he should make. His talk tonight in familiar surroundings, before a dozen people he knew, would be nothing compared to getting up and speaking in a roomful of women. But if that was what needed to be done, maybe he could do it. . . .

Finishing the Scotch, he rinsed out the glass in the sink and left it on the drainboard. He switched out the lights in the front part of the house and went through to the master bedroom. Marilyn already was in bed, but he could tell from the way she lay that she was still awake.

"What women do you know who are active in clubs?" he asked.

Her eyes opened slightly, and she raised her head to see the expression on his face. "Mae Coates, up on the corner, is something or other in the Federation of Women's Clubs," she said after thinking it over. "And there's Alice Post, she's president of the Junior League. Almost everybody's in PTA or something. Why?"

"I want you to do me a favor," he said. "Tomorrow, I want you to make a list of every woman you know even slightly who's even remotely connected with a woman's organization. Then I want you to call them and tell them I want to make a speech to their group, soon."

She sat up in bed, fully awake now. "Don't people usually get invited to make speeches?"

"Well, ask them to invite me, then."

"What about the men's clubs? Mr. Arnold across the street is tail-puller in the Downtown Lions."

"Tail-twister," he corrected her. "No, men would just agree with me, just as the council has done, and do nothing, thinking about higher tax rates. Men are gamblers. They're sure that no accident or illness is going to happen to them. I want the mothers, the comic-book crowd. I want to put that mother instinct to work."

"Dr. McNiel, that sounds like dirty politics to me."

"I suppose it is. But if I could just get them half as interested in the hospital, they'd probably build that new wing with their bare hands."

"If you could keep them interested long enough."

"That's true," he admitted. They had been like quicksilver, there one minute, gone the next. Directing that power, keeping it in check, would be difficult.

He stepped into the bathroom and brushed his teeth. Through the door he could see her still sitting up in bed, thinking.

"Do you think it's worth it?" she asked when he came out. "I hate to see you do anything like this. So many people seem to misunderstand."

He knew what she meant. There were always those who said a doctor made speeches, got his name in the paper to drum up business because his profession wouldn't allow him to advertise any other way. Unfortunately, sometimes the worst critics were fellow physicians. Already he might have gone too far. When word of his council speech got around, he wouldn't be surprised if a delegation came around with the theme: "Travis, we know you mean well, but we believe it will do more harm than good to undermine public confidence. . . ."

"I think my reputation will survive," he told her. "And this isn't what I want to do. It's what I feel I have to do."

He turned off the light and lay for a long time in the darkness, striving to adjust to his new circumstance.

# *Part Three*

## CHAPTER SEVEN

The telephone assault on City Hall began Thursday afternoon. David was confused by the first three calls, but on the fourth one he learned of Travis McNiel's speeches and was prepared for the onslaught during the rest of the afternoon.

The number of calls was disturbing enough. The identity of the callers was even more alarming. Almost without exception they were leaders of the well-to-do women's clubs, the study groups, the torchbearers of enlightenment. He knew from experience there wasn't a more uncompromising element in the world to deal with.

He did his best to mollify them . . . yes, conditions were inadequate at the hospital . . . that was just one of the many problems the city had to solve . . . no, he couldn't promise anything, for this was a council policy matter, not an administrative one. . . .

Either David's refusal to accept responsibility rerouted a few calls, or else the attack was on a wide front, for before nightfall the mayor phoned.

"David, I'm afraid we've got trouble."

"Yes, I know. I've been getting calls, too."

"We've got to put a stop to this," the mayor said, his voice rising to a falsetto on some syllables. "He's going to wreck everything."

David didn't like the "we." He shouldn't get involved in intracouncil differences. But the mayor was right. If the lake program was to be saved, Travis had to be stopped.

He tried to put his suggestion subtly.

"I wonder if the medical association knows of these talks Travis is making."

He could almost hear the mayor's mind working over the phone. "Say, that's right. I bet they wouldn't like this any more than we do. I'll contact them and see if they can stop him."

Late in the afternoon Chief McDowell dropped by to report that his investigation on the highway plots had gleaned no new information. There was nothing to do now except await developments, he believed. Reluctantly, David agreed.

That night, David went over the notes Stella had taken on the day's telephone calls. Travis was setting a fast pace. He had talked to the Thursday Study Club at noon, and was scheduled to speak to the Junior League during the evening. He was booked at the Woman's Club for a talk Friday noon, with the Trowel and Error Garden Club due to hear him in the afternoon and the Fine Arts Club Friday night.

Also, David learned, Travis was having a commercial photographer make color slides of the hospital facilities. So there was no doubt he was planning a long campaign.

The division of the council on the water program Tuesday night had surprised David, but he had felt no immediate concern. The sudden revolt was just an unfortunate series of mistakes, he believed. The mayor had ignored his warning and brought the matter up too soon. They had underestimated the doctor, and they had failed to see a sudden aging, senile trend to Cal Masters' philosophy. This, combined with the doctor's evangelical swaying of Byron's support, had almost brought disaster. But he had been confident these mistakes could be remedied until Travis' latest move. Now, he didn't know.

The next morning, he saw the mayor at a traffic signal light dedication. He knew from frequent glances that the mayor was eager to talk to him, but there was no opportunity during the strange ceremony.

A young matron returning home after taking her two children to school one foggy, misty morning had pulled in front of a loaded gravel truck at the intersection and was killed. It was the first serious accident in the intersection's twelve-year history, and traffic counts showed the flow far below the minimum meriting signals. The city would have dropped the fatality as an unfortunate incident, but the dead woman happened to have been the wife of the popular vice-president of a suburban Lions Club. The club had waged a six-month battle for the signals over objections of the traffic engineer and the Traffic Commission. Finally, after petitions signed by 1269 registered voters, the council yielded. Now, the signals had been installed, and the dedication ceremony was a weird combination of a victory celebration and memorial service.

David hadn't known quite what to expect. As a precaution, he had asked for a police detail to block off the neighboring corners and route traffic around. Now he was glad he had, for the attendance filled the intersection.

A TV service shop had donated the use of a loud-speaker, a lumber yard a flat-bed truck, and a funeral home some folding chairs to seat club officials and visiting dignitaries. The truck was angle-parked in the intersection with a long red ribbon running from one traffic light pole diagonally across to the other, passing over the truck bed.

When David climbed upon the truck to take his seat, he estimated that two hundred people were jammed around the truck—about four times what he had expected.

The Lions Club president, a beefy-faced supermarket manager, spoke first. He praised the new signals as evidence of the section's growth, thanked the city for its co-operation in alleviating a hazard, and reminded the audience in sad tones of the tragedy which had taken place there less than a year ago. The mayor responded. He, too, lamented the death of the fine young mother. He praised the section's growth and civic spirit and finished—rather lamely, David thought—with an apology that the controller for the signals hadn't arrived, but should be installed within the next few days. He was followed by a Methodist minister, who offered a brief prayer.

Then the Lions Club sweetheart, a red-haired high school senior, stood, shed a long cashmere coat, and stepped forward in a cherry-red bathing suit. She handed the mayor a pair of long-bladed scissors. The ribbon had sagged almost to the bed of the truck. When she stooped to pick up the ribbon, David saw an appreciative reaction sweep through the males in the audience. She blushed slightly. The mayor, uncertain as to the source of the sudden levity, frowned. Flashbulbs overrode the bright sun as the mayor and the Lions Club sweetheart posed for a moment, both pairs of hands at the task. Then the ribbon was snipped, parted, and the audience around them burst into applause.

Afterward, the mayor was delayed by handshaking and small talk. David walked to his car and waited. In a few minutes the mayor broke free and hurried after him, walking so fast that he came up to David out of breath.

"I was afraid you'd gone," he said. He looked around to make sure no one else was within earshot. "I've contacted the medical group," he said in a low voice. "I have a dinner meeting set with them tonight to explain our problems. Will you be free?"

David almost said yes before he remembered. He hesitated. "Do you really need me there? I did have something planned."

The mayor's surprise showed. "Well, I don't know, David. I *had* counted on you. . . ."

"This is my daughter's birthday," David explained. "I've planned a party at the house, with some of her high school friends."

"Maybe you could drop by the meeting for a few minutes, then leave early," the mayor suggested.

Again, David almost gave in. He had promised to let Helen supervise the refreshments, the decorator seemed competent, and the combo had been hired. Yet, he couldn't keep from remembering what Helen had said: any other father would be home nights. For Christine, this would be something special. And he had been trapped in "leave-early" meetings before.

"I'm sorry, I just can't make it," he said. "Surely you understand. Of course, if there are any questions, anything I can do later. . . ."

"Sure, I understand," the mayor said. But from his expression, David knew he didn't. The mayor walked on toward his own car slowly, as if puzzled.

Afterward, David had a few bouts of uneasiness over turning him down, for never before had he failed to do anything the mayor expected of him.

Then, to top that off, he spent most of the afternoon outside the office.

The little convertible for Christine cost more than he'd expected, but he bought it anyway. He wanted to give her something to make her sixteenth birthday an event she would remember all her life.

Financially, there was no problem. They lived within his salary. At the moment, he happened to have more than enough money free from oil investments.

When his father had died, after the war, he'd gotten a little more than thirty thousand from the sale of the Oklahoma farm. Through the years he had invested the money, dividing it between oil long-shots and electronic firm stocks. There were those who called him lucky. But his coups in speculation couldn't all be attributed to luck. Surely, an investment in his daughter's happiness would be as good as any he could make.

He hunted through three dealers, walking over the lots in the hot afternoon sun, before he found the exact model. The salesman let him test-drive a sedan, and he was amazed at the simplicity of the small machine. The tiny engine had a nostalgic sound, and it took him awhile to realize why: it was four-cylinder, like the old Ford cars and Farmall tractors he'd worked on as a boy. He found himself thinking ahead to when he could tinker with it, keeping it tuned for Christine. He hadn't had a set of tools in his hands in a long time.

He wrote a check for the car and drove it home himself. A Negro garage flunky followed him in the Olds, towing a three-wheeled motorcycle. David guided the whole caravan into the driveway, knowing it was too early for Christine to be home from school. As the Negro unhitched the motorcycle, David put the small car in the seldom-used garage, confident it would remain hidden until the proper time.

The decorator was still at work in the garden. He was arranging creped hoops over a small platform constructed for the three-piece combo, giving it a miniature-bandshell effect. His assistant was wrapping the refreshment table legs in red and white crepe —school colors.

"Looks very nice," David said to the decorator.

He stepped down to survey his work. He was tall and thin, and had a slightly effeminate manner. "If there'd been more time, we could have done much better," he said with an offended air.

"It looks nice anyway," David insisted. "And I'm sorry I didn't call you sooner. The date just slipped up on me."

The decorator picked up another curved stave and began shaping it hurriedly, as if too much time had been wasted already.

David walked backward a few steps, shading his eyes against the sun, to get an over-all impression of the garden. Not bad at all, he decided.

A shame, really, that they hadn't used the garden for so long. The back lawn was one of the best features of the house, an entertainment area designed in the days before air-conditioning when garden parties were not only more popular but more practical. Flagstone walks led from the quarried limestone patio to stone loveseats in the far corners. Long ago, evidently, these walks had been lined with rose bushes. Now, most were gone. The Mexican gardener who worked Thursday afternoons in season had spaded the earth of the gaps and planted flowers. The grass was well-watered and green, a thick carpet between the flowerbeds.

He tried to imagine how the yard would look now by floodlight. Shouldn't be bad at all, he thought.

He went through the French doors and on into the coolness of the kitchen. Calla Lilly and Helen were working over trays of hors d'oeuvres. He had wanted to hire a professional caterer, but Helen had insisted this would be simpler. The hum of the air-conditioner in the back window had masked his footsteps so that the sudden sound of his voice startled them.

"How are things going?" he asked.

"We're about ready," Helen said, smiling. "We want to have plenty, though. With teen-agers, you never know what their capacity will be." She looked at David with an expression akin to warmth.

"That's the truth," Calla Lilly said. Then, as Helen picked up a tray of sandwiches and carried it across the room to the refrigerator, Calla Lilly grinned at David and nodded. Everything's fine, she was signaling.

"Can I be of any help?" David asked.

"No," Helen said, closing the refrigerator door. "Honestly, we're about through."

"Well, if everything's under control here, I'll go on up and check back with the office."

He went to his bedroom and phoned Stella. Aside from a near-constant barrage of calls from women's club members, everything was quiet, Stella said. He knew he should be there to receive them, but right now he didn't feel inclined. He would return the calls tomorrow, he told Stella. He cradled the phone, stripped to his shorts, and lay across the bed, relaxed, thinking.

Helen's footsteps came up the stairs, slowed almost imperceptibly at the door of his room, then went quickly on down the hall to her room. He lay for a long time, trying to nap, but he found himself listening for a sound that never came: the tinkle of glass on glass.

Finally, he got up, pulled on a robe, and went down the hall in his slippers. He knocked twice softly, then went in at the sound of her voice.

She was on the bed, partially resting on one elbow. The room, with its western exposure, caught the late afternoon sun. Needles of light and pure heat filtered through a tiny opening of the drawn drapes.

"Damn but it's hot in here," he said. "I didn't know there was this much difference." He crossed to the windows and felt the heat on the blinds. "I'll get some metal awnings put up. That'd help some."

"I don't care any more," she said. "I used to, but I don't any more." There was an alert, guarded manner about her that made him believe he had interrupted something. Maybe she had been about to take a drink.

He sat on the vanity bench and examined the bare calf of his left leg. He had picked up a couple of chiggers somewhere. He rubbed the red welts viciously, knowing this would only make them worse. "I didn't think about it being so hot this time of the year," he said. "Maybe I should have planned the party inside."

"No, it's cool out there at night," she said. "No matter how hot it is during the day, the garden's cool. Except in the late summer, of course. I used to go out there a lot, spring evenings."

The realization there was another little facet of her life unknown to him left him strangely unsettled. He changed the subject. "I wanted to tell you before the party. I got Christine that little foreign convertible. It's out in the garage now, if you want to sneak out and look at it."

She laughed without humor. "I should have known you'd do it, even when common sense told me you wouldn't. Well, that'll certainly make my gift look like two cents."

"It'll be from both of us," he said quickly.

"Sure," she said, her voice heavy with sarcasm. He ignored it.

"What did you get her?"

"A simple little party dress."

"All right, you put the dress down as from the both of us, and the car will be from the both of us, too."

"If you want. But Chris will know. She's not that dumb."

Helen shifted her position on the bed, changing the weight from one arm to the other. As she moved, he saw something on the bed behind her, partially hidden by her body. He had to search his memory for a moment before he realized what it was—the big leather photograph album. He had bought it for her the Christmas after Ronnie was born. They had talked, then, of how they must take and keep pictures of the children as they grew up. He hadn't seen the album now in years and had forgotten it existed.

"What are you doing with that?" he asked.

She followed his gaze and slowly brought the album from behind her. "Just looking at it."

"Let's see."

She handed the album to him reluctantly. The first few pages were filled with half-forgotten, half-remembered baby pictures of Christine and Ronnie. He turned through them as she watched. There was a page, then, of pictures taken on a weekend jaunt, his senior year at the university. Christine was a toddler, Ronnie still a baby. He had just finished his finals, he remembered, and they had driven down to Turner Falls and camped out the whole weekend, the sound of the water soothing in the distance, everything green with spring.

"We were happy then," Helen said.

"Why aren't we happy now?" he asked, slightly nettled. "We're at the place now we were working toward back then. A good job, two fine children, a good house. There's no reason not to be happy now."

"Happiness isn't a place you arrive at," she said. "It's how you travel along the way."

"You read that somewhere."

"Yes, but that doesn't keep it from being true."

He leafed on through the album. There were pictures of their tiny prefab house in Sooner City at the university, the children on a pallet, the stands at a football game, the campus, their first house after he got a job, the children on other outings. . . .

There were more. But he didn't want to see them. He felt a strong sense of regret, a sadness. Those *had* been good days. He closed the book.

"What are you doing with this out, anyway?"

"I told you. Just looking, remembering how things were when I was young."

He studied Helen closely, thinking maybe Calla Lilly was wrong about her being on the wagon today. But her eyes lacked the telltale signs, and there seemed to be no impairment in her speech and no unco-ordinated gestures, always an early indication.

"I didn't know you were becoming decrepit."

"Christine is sixteen. That makes me thirty-eight, almost thirty-nine. But I look past forty-five, and I know it."

"No, you don't," he said.

But she did. He knew she took his protest for what it was, a feeble courtesy.

"Yes, I do," she said. She opened the album and looked at the pictures of their weekend at Turner Falls. "I wish we could go back there again and camp out some weekend, like we did before."

"Maybe we can, sometime."

"I didn't mean sometime. I meant next weekend. Couldn't we?"

He thought of the lake program, Travis' speeches, Berger. Something might break at any time. He had almost let things get out of control. Being out of touch for two or three days right now might be disastrous.

"I really can't get away, now," he said. "But maybe we can, before long."

She sighed. "I guess it wouldn't be the same, anyway."

"For one thing, it'd probably be more crowded," he said. "But we'll try it, sometime."

He left her and went downstairs for a dinner of cold cuts, ordered earlier so Calla Lilly could devote more time to the party. He was standing in the hallway, monitoring Calla's movements through the door to the dining room where she was setting up the buffet, when Christine came down. For a moment, he felt some of the sudden aging that had hit Helen.

His daughter had managed to achieve the ultimate in teenaged sophistication without striving for too much maturity. She wore a dark short formal cut lower than he would have chosen for her, but he had to admit that with her russet hair in a long, modified bouffant, and the necklace he had given her for Christmas, the effect was disturbing. This was, he realized, a turning point in his life, too, like the day he himself was sixteen, or twenty-one, or forty. His daughter definitely was coming of age. She stood for a moment, awaiting his comment.

"Ravishing," he told her.

"Thank you," she said, and curtsied. He kissed her forehead. With her high heels, he no longer had to stoop.

"Who's the lucky man tonight?"

"Don't be silly. You know."

He knew. But he had hoped otherwise. Although David had tried, he couldn't find it in himself to like this boy, Buddy Nowell. He thought he could detect in him a certain disrespect for elders, a hint of meanness, something subtle that escaped definition.

He realized, though, that the dislike might spring from jealousy, for he recognized this in himself. He probably would feel the same way about any boy who happened to be his daughter's first "real love."

Remembering that he hadn't thought to compliment Helen on her appearance, he made it a point to do so when she came down. "You look very nice," he said, trying to make it sound sincere.

"Well-preserved is the term, I think," she said. She took a step backward. "Seriously, how do I look?"

"I told you, fine," he said. Although she had become careless about her appearance in the last few years, it was evident she had made a real effort tonight.

The band arrived before David was through eating. He went out and showed them where to set up, three tired-looking men in their forties, all wearing identical sport coats and string ties. The sax player, who seemed to be the leader and business manager, asked him what kind of music he had in mind.

"You probably know more what these kids want than I do," David said hopefully.

"Yeah," he agreed.

The drummer began tightening and trying out his drumheads and David winced inwardly, wondering how far the sounds would carry in the still night air. There was no help for it now, though; he could only hope that the neighbors would enter into the spirit of things.

Ronnie came out, then, and stood watching the combo set up. He looked even taller and more ungainly in his dark trousers, and the white sport coat accentuated the length of his arms.

There was a problem about Ronnie. Slightly more than a year younger than Christine, he was two years behind her in school because of an unlucky birthdate. Almost as old as Christine's high school crowd, he was still in junior high, a world apart. He hadn't wanted to go to the party, but David had insisted, offering to let him have the car to pick up his date. The use of the car had been too strong an incentive for Ronnie to resist.

David went over and handed him the keys to the Olds. "Stay off the main streets," he warned. "We'll both be in trouble if you get picked up for driving without a license."

Ronnie nodded. David had noticed he never seemed to talk any more unless pushed into it.

As Ronnie hurried off toward the car, David went back inside to get a sandwich, trying to put the worry out of his mind. For the last six months, Ronnie had been begging for a motor scooter. David considered scooters too dangerous for city streets, but he couldn't make Ronnie understand. Somehow, tonight, he'd had the feeling that if he showed the boy he had confidence in him, gave him some responsibility, he would get his point across.

David answered the door when the Bannings arrived. In planning the party he had asked them—parents of one of Christine's girl friends—to help chaperone.

Banning was an affable, rotund, easygoing guy, the vice-president in charge of the installment loan department at First National. David had talked with him several times at chamber committee meetings. His wife was a rather stern, businesslike woman.

"Isn't there something we can do to help?" she asked abruptly before David had a chance to make small talk.

"I think everything's about ready, but we'll go through the kitchen and see," he said.

He led them through the house, and from Helen's hesitant greeting to them, David knew something was wrong. Calla Lilly was ladling punch from the brimming bowl into a silver pitcher.

"What's wrong?" David asked.

"I don't know what I was thinking of," Helen said helplessly, more to the Bannings than to him. "I mixed the punch in here, and now the bowl is too full to carry out to the back yard without spilling."

Calla Lilly had the pitcher full now.

"That doan take it down much," she said dubiously.

David tried to keep his anger from showing, remembering again that he had wanted to hire a professional caterer, but Helen had insisted.

The guests would begin arriving any minute.

"Calla Lilly, what's the biggest container you have in the kitchen?" he asked.

She blinked at him. "That ice cream freezah, I reckon."

"Get it out," he told her.

He went to the cabinet and found a paring knife. He cut about two feet of hose from the sink spray and rinsed it under the faucet. He then plunged one end down into the punch, waited for the liquid to flow into it, then milked the other end sharply with thumb and forefinger, starting the siphon into the freezer can Calla Lilly had ready.

"You can order a new hose tomorrow," he told Calla Lilly. "That one was about worn out anyway."

"Nice to have a genius around the house," Helen said to the Bannings, making a joke out of it.

"Elementary. Any first-class professional engineer could have done it," he told her.

When the hose took the punchbowl level down past the halfway mark, he stopped the siphon and carried the bowl out to the garden. Calla Lilly followed with the ice cream can, and Helen and the Bannings brought up the rear with the trays. Calla Lilly covered everything with cloths for protection from insects. The garden had been well-sprayed recently, the Japanese lanterns strung around the garden were armed with anti-bug bulbs, and there was a fair breeze, so David had hopes bugs wouldn't be a problem.

The children began arriving, then.

There was the inevitable ten or fifteen minutes of inertia, but when it finally got started, the party warmed up quickly.

The music wasn't quite what David had in mind. Aside from a few irritating moments in drive-ins and cheaper restaurants, he'd never heard anything like it. But Christine assured him this was what the high school crowd wanted to hear.

There were no wallflowers. All the teen-agers were good dancers—even Ronnie, which surprised David, for Ronnie hadn't shown much interest in girls. Soon couples filled the patio, and some were dancing out on the lawn.

Up to a certain point, the party was a big success. Then, suddenly, it began to disintegrate right when it should have been reaching a climax.

He didn't know when Helen started drinking. He first realized she was slightly drunk when he saw her standing by the punchbowl talking to the Bannings. There was something in her manner, that extra bit of animation, that gave him warning.

Afterward, he danced with her and smelled vodka—she seemed to believe vodka couldn't be detected, for she used it in sneaky drinking. Knowing that arguing about it would only make her worse, he said nothing, deciding the best thing to do would be to slow the process enough to get the party over before she reached the final stages. He went to hunt the bottle.

Calla Lilly was alone in the kitchen, stacking dishes in the washer.

"Where's Mrs. Hartwell getting her liquor?" he asked.

Calla Lilly's eyes widened. "I doan know. She went upstairs

awhile ago, but I doan think she had anything when she came back down."

He went up, searched her room, and found nothing. He'd long since stopped keeping liquor of his own around the house. She must have a flask or pint bottle in her purse, he reasoned, or else one hidden away about the driveway or garden. He went out and searched her car. He found two empties, both bourbon, but no vodka.

There was nothing else to do but bring the party to an end as soon as possible, he decided.

Turning out the driveway lights, he eased the garage door open and pushed the little convertible out. Then he went to get Calla Lilly to help with the unveiling.

"I'm going to get everyone out to the driveway. When I give the signal with my flashlight, turn the lights on."

But as he moved through the dancers toward the bandstand he saw Helen. She'd progressed fast in the short time he'd been gone. She was ladling punch, and he could tell now she was at the losing-control stage. The combo was playing a number with a wild, heavy beat, and she was keeping time with the drums as she ladled, missing the cups with about half the punch. He saw that the youngsters around her were laughing. He felt a tug at his sleeve.

"Mother's drunk," Christine said.

He tried to shush her.

"It's no secret. Everybody's laughing. She was doing the twist a minute ago." He saw that she was crying. She ran across the patio to her boy friend and put her head on his shoulder. He put an arm around her and looked at David defiantly.

David's frustration left him weak and sick inside, but as his anger mounted it gave him new strength. He went over and took Helen's arm, jerking the ladle from her hand.

"Come into the kitchen. I want to talk to you."

She went with him as far as the kitchen before she realized what he was going to do. Then it was too late. He tightened his grip on her arm and got her into the dining room before she started protesting. From then on, it was a battle. He heard Calla Lilly close the kitchen door behind them, and he took Helen on up the steps, half-carrying her. She fought him every step of the way. Once, near the landing, she got one arm free and raked his face, her nails biting deep. Between her incoherent outbursts he could hear the band out back, and he hoped the noise would be enough to cover the sounds of battle.

By the time he got her into her bedroom he was exhausted, and he felt blood running down his cheek, collecting on his chin. But she, too, was exhausted, and the exertion had made her sick. She messed the bed and the wall beyond. He knew then that it was over. This was the final phase.

In his room he assessed the damage to his face at the bathroom mirror. With cold water and styptic pencil he got the bleeding stopped, then he covered the scratches with narrow strips of flesh-colored adhesive.

There was blood on his white shirt, so he changed. Then he went back downstairs.

"Mrs. Hartwell is sick," he told Calla Lilly. "I'd appreciate it if you'd help her."

He got Ronnie to do the business with the lights, and the car-surprise came off fairly well. Christine's pleasure over the car seemed to ease her embarrassment about what had happened. But Helen's abrupt exit had cast a pall over the party, and it never recovered.

When the guests were saying good night he felt their discomfort. They were too young to keep their poise. Most ignored Helen as if she never existed. Only three said to "please tell Mrs. Hartwell I had a wonderful time," and one, a tall basketball player, said he was "sorry Mrs. Hartwell became ill." If they had been older, he would have attempted apologies for Helen. But under the circumstances, he thought silence was best.

As the Bannings left, he thanked them for their help. They must have been rehearsing their lines. Smoothly, she said she knew what a strain teen-aged parties could be, and Banning said he hoped Helen felt better soon.

David gave Christine permission to stay out with her date until one, but Ronnie disappeared with the car before David could put a curfew on him.

Afterward, he helped Calla Lilly carry the dishes in. They piled them on the big table in the center of the kitchen and left them.

He felt he shouldn't leave Helen, so he called a Negro cab for Calla Lilly and gave her the fare.

He checked on Helen, then, and found her still in a deep sleep, the smell of vomit heavy in the room despite Calla Lilly's efforts to clean it up. On the vanity bench lay Helen's gift—the party dress—still wrapped. He had forgotten it in the confusion.

Feeling suddenly very tired, he went to his room and lay down, knowing he wouldn't sleep soundly until both Ronnie and Christine were in. He regretted now that he'd let Ronnie have the car, that he'd granted Christine the extra hour.

The phone call came a few minutes after midnight. He had been dozing, and hearing Police Chief Dan McDowell's voice on the phone was a jolt. David's first thought was of some important break in the highway plot investigation.

"Could you come down to headquarters a few minutes, David? I just got a call that they've got Ronnie down there, and I'm on my way now."

As David's sleep-numbed mind began to clear he remembered Ronnie and the car. His next thoughts were of a car wreck and what Travis had said about emergency facilities at the hospital.

"Ronnie is where?" he asked.

"Down at headquarters," McDowell said patiently.

David couldn't get the idea of a car wreck out of his mind.

"Is he all right?"

"He's O.K. Probably scared, but that may do him good."

"What's it all about?" David demanded, growing more awake. "Look, if it's driving without a license, there's no need . . ."

Dan interrupted him. "David, it's not that. As I understand it, he wasn't in the car. Now, I don't know the details, but it's something about window-peeping. That's all I know. Why don't you meet me down at the station. Then we'll both find out what it's all about and get it cleared up tonight."

The force of Dan's voice made it an order, more than a suggestion.

A barrage of protests that it couldn't have been Ronnie welled up in David's mind, but in him was the deeper realization that Dan McDowell was in an unusual position. Under the city charter, the police chief was appointed by the city manager.

Technically, David was his boss. But as police chief, Dan had an undeniable responsibility.

"I'll be down in fifteen minutes," David said.

He started down the stairs before he realized he didn't have a car. Ronnie had taken the Olds. Christine's date had left his old jalopy in front of the house and they were out in the new convertible. David went to Helen's room and hunted through three purses before he found the keys to her Buick.

On the drive down, there was a numbness of disbelief in his mind that drove out all rational thoughts. Ronnie must have taken the girl home, then picked up some young hoodlums that got him into this, he decided. He began to see what he was in for when he walked into the police station.

"Chief's waiting for you in Juvenile Division," the desk sergeant said, and almost grinned openly. The story would be all over the police force and City Hall by Monday noon. And Juvenile Division involved. Surely Dan could have taken care of this in his office.

Ronnie was sitting on a metal folding chair in the far corner of the bare room, looking pale and scared. Dan and a detective were standing over him. David felt his anger returning—they didn't have to make a federal case out of it.

"David, I believe you know Rogers, Juvenile Division," Dan said, nodding toward the detective.

"We've met," David said curtly, shaking hands with him. Rogers looked more like a college professor than a policeman—a lean, studious face and hornrim glasses. But he wore the customary snub-nosed .38 of a detective on his belt, left side for a cross-body draw.

Dan walked over and closed the door. He came back, picked up another metal chair and spun it around. He eased his weight into it backward, his arms resting on the chair's back.

"It's your department, Rogers," Dan said. "I'll let you acquaint Mr. Hartwell with the facts."

David interrupted. "Where are the other boys? Shouldn't we have them in here, too?"

"There were no others," the detective said softly, but with force. "Isn't that what you told us, Ronnie?"

Ronnie's voice was barely audible. "Yes, sir," he said.

David sank into a chair the detective had pushed out for him. The detective leaned back against a desktop. Ronnie sat staring at the cement floor.

"As I understand it, Mr. Hartwell, Ronnie took his girl straight home from the party, because she had to be in at eleven. He drove around for a while, on back streets, then parked the car. He walked up the alley between Calhoon and Parker, went through a gate, and was hiding in some bushes behind the residence at 3808 Calhoon, watching the back of the house."

"Good Lord," David heard himself say.

"We got a call from a resident across the alley. He'd gone out to turn off his lawn sprinkler and saw a prowler. Patrol cars blocked both ends of the alley, and when one pair of officers flushed him, Ronnie ran right into the arms of the other pair at the other end. Isn't that about the way it happened, Ronnie?"

Ronnie didn't look up. He nodded, his lower lip trembling.

"Good Lord," David said again, still trying to accept it all. He got up and went over to Ronnie, looking down at him. "Why, Ronnie? That's all I want to know. Why?"

Ronnie still wouldn't lift his head. "I don't know," he mumbled.

David took him by the shoulders and shook him. "Goddamn it, boy, don't you know someone might have blown your head off? Anybody snooping around a house at night is just asking for a load of buckshot. Don't you know that?"

Ronnie began to cry silently. The detective laid a hand on David's arm. "I've been talking to him. I think he realizes now the seriousness of what he did."

"Are you going to file charges?" David asked.

Ronnie looked up then for the first time. The detective turned to meet Ronnie's gaze as he answered. "No, I don't see any purpose in it. Ronnie's not a bad boy. He's done something wrong, but one mistake doesn't make a delinquent. If he understands this . . . and I think he does . . . I believe we can let him go this time with the understanding he's got to get himself straightened out."

"I can't have any favors," David said. "I can't afford to have it dropped because of my position. You know that, Dan."

"Well, hell fire, you wouldn't want us to prosecute your boy just because of who you are, would you? That wouldn't be fair to him. I think this is standard for a first offense. Isn't it, Rogers?"

"We usually can tell from talking to them," the detective said. "If we think there's a good chance we won't have a boy back in here again, we don't file on him. I don't think we will have Ronnie back again."

"You sure as hell won't. I'll see to that," David promised. "Come on, Ronnie, let's go."

They rode most of the way home in silence. David was too bushed emotionally and physically to puzzle it out. But the question kept hounding him. "Why, Ronnie?" he asked again. "I still want to know why."

"I don't know," Ronnie mumbled.

"Damn it, if you're that curious about women, we'll fly down to the border. Any whore'd be better than that."

He heard Ronnie's intake of breath. "Oh, no," he said quickly. "I wasn't doing anything like that. I mean, I wasn't watching anyone . . . undress."

"What in hell *were* you doing, then?"

Ronnie stammered for a moment.

"Just listening," he said finally.

David dropped the subject, then, unable to grasp any reasoning behind the answer. Clearly, this was a job for a psychiatrist.

He remembered, then, that the Olds was still down where Ronnie was arrested. But he couldn't bring himself to drive down there tonight. Tomorrow morning, early, he would take a cab down there and get it.

## CHAPTER EIGHT

Tom had often observed that Texas was born with enough street names to last most of its towns a hundred years. Among the estimated one hundred and eighty-seven fighting men who died in the Alamo, such names as Travis, Bowie, Crockett, and Bonham still live as geographical facts. Other battles and the struggle of the new republic added more: Houston, Rusk, Burnet, Fannin, Milam, Lamar. . . .

Ironically, he had noticed, many of these streets bearing the names of Texas heroes are now among the shabbiest. For they were the first-named, the old town. As the cities thrived, new buildings sprang up, the center of business edged away, and the old sections became the home of those acquainted with life's economic miseries.

Tom Kencaide reflected again upon this as he walked the streets of the old neighborhood, his memories bitter. The old scenes hadn't changed much. Lower Main Street still cut a red neon gash from the railroad tracks to the river. Cheap bars, dusty pawnshops, dirty hotels, drunks and prostitutes, sudden death and precarious living.

Two years ago, a Chicago industrialist, visiting to inspect a potential site for a new plant, was quartered in an uptown hotel as a guest of the Chamber of Commerce. Arising early Sunday morning, as was his habit, he had taken a long walk. With no chamber official present at that hour to guide his steps, he had strolled down Main Street, all the way to its gaudy end. Fascinated, he reported to the chamber that the city must have twice as many derelicts per capita as his home town of Chicago.

The horrified chamber had taken two immediate steps: Orders were given that never again would important visitors be left without escort, and top priority was voted to instigate an urban renewal program.

Under the proposal, the old town and its worn-out buildings were to be razed. But Councilman Byron and a hard core of conservatives had waged an active campaign against accepting federal funds. The proposal had been defeated at the polls.

The *News-Gazette* had supported urban renewal. Secretly, Tom had sided with Byron, certain most people in the old neighborhood would succeed in making a slum out of new low-rent homes within five years, federal help or no federal help. Some people just belonged in slums. He knew. His father had been one of these people, here in the old town.

Tom hadn't wanted to come here. All weekend he had been visiting taverns and bars, systematically. Saturday night, with Arlene, he had roamed the night spots around the air base, ordering Eastern beer. Usually he got Eastern beer. But twice he had been told the refrigerating unit was broken, that only Alamo Beer was cold. Both times a followup interview with the tavern manager had been a total loss. But he had seen fear. He was sure of that.

All the time, in the back of his mind, there was the knowledge that if corruption existed it would be found in the old neighborhood. Down here, corruption was old, familiar, and well-entrenched. Here he knew the language. He also had known, though, that his return would reopen old wounds, revive painful memories.

Lower Main was quiet, now. He had almost forgotten how quiet the Sunday nights were. The new week always started off slow. Saturday nights were the climax. He crossed Lamar, Burnet, Crockett. He was almost there.

In the doorway of a walk-up hotel a panhandler stepped in front of him. "Frien', could you lemme have a quarter for a hamburger? I ain't had nothin' to eat for two days."

Tom stopped and studied him. A dirty white shirt and a two-day beard, ragged, baggy pants. About forty, maybe younger. Back in the shadows of the stairway Tom could see another one waiting. Tom gave him a quarter. "Don't forget to take the cork out of that hamburger."

The wino laughed, a short, explosive sound. "You're a wise one, ain't you."

"Not totally dumb, anyway."

The wino seemed to accept this. The other one, a smaller, baldheaded gnome, came out of the shadows. "I'd like one of them hamburgers too," he said.

Tom gave him a quarter. He saw their restlessness, then, and knew the reason. They had fifty cents now, enough for a bottle of cheap wine. The liquor stores were closed, but they would know a bootleg place. Tom spoke quickly before they could turn away. "Who's running things down here now?"

The tall wino looked at him suspiciously. "What you mean?"

"Just that. The stud that keeps the best girls, the best crap games, who looks after everybody—the guy to get word to if you're in trouble."

The wino considered this and apparently didn't like the sound of it. "I don't know nothin' about anything like that," he said, and they shuffled on off up the street.

Tom stood watching them go. He remembered the contempt they felt for a soft touch.

A police car cruised slowly down the street and the driver turned to examine Tom curiously. In the old days, there'd been a beat cop who knew everyone up and down the street, and who put an arbitrary limit on what he considered normal sin. Now, two young cops in a squad car, superior, apart.

He walked on up to the next corner and looked down into the darkness of Deaf Smith Street. Deaf Smith had been one of Houston's scouts. Now there was a county named for him, this street, and maybe some other streets elsewhere. Tom stood under the streetlight, hearing the sounds of the night, seeing the street the way it was and trying to remember how it had been. Deaf Smith Street was blacktopped now. Back then, it had been gravel. The house was gone. They had torn it down during the war. When he'd returned a printing shop was in its place. Most of the old rooming houses were gone, too. That had been where the old ones lived.

Across the street now there was a bakery. There used to be a big rooming house there, he remembered. He couldn't recall much about the other people in it, but there had been an old man, a tall, gnarled cottonwood of an old man with snowy white hair and a hypnotic eye. . . .

"I soljered, boy," he'd say. "Ever hear of Fort Phantom Hill? Ever hear of Adobe Walls? The Buffalo Wallows Fight?"

If you said you had, he'd assume you heard it all wrong and tell you anyway. If you said you hadn't, he'd correct your abysmal ignorance.

Later, when Tom began to learn about such things, he realized the old man had been a historic find. The Adobe Walls he'd talked about was the Second Battle of Adobe Walls on June 27, 1874. He had faced seven hundred Comanche, Kiowa, and Cheyennes. He'd seen Quanah Parker and Lone Wolf on the warpath, and surely he'd known Billy Dixon, the scout. But by the time Tom learned of the importance of the old man's memories he was dead. And now his ghost was out there with the rest of them. The old man believed in ghosts. For a time, he'd made a believer out of Tom.

"They're out there, boy. You'd better believe it. Ever' creek bottom, ever' blackjack grove. Other things there, too, if you could just find 'em. Injun bones, spurs cowboys lost, old guns the Spanyards lost, all sorts of things if a body knowed where to look. Dobie kin tell you. Read J. Frank Dobie. His the only books worth readin', 'cept the Bible, of course."

And now the old man was gone, and even the house where he lived was gone. But the old man had been right. There were ghosts. There were ghosts all over the place.

From down the street he heard the thump of a jukebox, reminding him of what he was after. He walked on down the half block and studied the tavern across the street. The exterior was new, but the location and the name were the same: Fowler's Bar. There had been a Fowler's Bar here twenty-five years ago. Inside, there were changes, too. The booths were newer, the chairs and tables were more modern, more functional. But the railed bar was the same, and the collection of horns behind it. A young red-haired woman was polishing glasses. Tom asked for an Eastern beer.

"Only bottle beer we got cold is Alamo," she said. She would have been pretty if she hadn't had a certain harsh quality to her features.

"Well, Alamo then." He waited until she brought the bottle and glass and made change. "Is the owner in?" he asked.

She gave him a quick, hard look, then turned her head. "Al," she called over her shoulder. There was a shuffle of feet, and a heavy-set man about his own age swung out of a conversation at a booth and circled behind the bar. This wasn't the Fowler Tom knew. Al came up and leaned his forearms on the opposite side of the bar.

"I was looking for the Fowler that owns this place," Tom explained.

"That's me," Al said.

Tom hesitated a moment, confused. "The Fowler I remember here was older."

"That would be my dad. He died in 'fifty. I been runnin' the place since then."

Then Tom remembered. There had been a boy, a year ahead of him in school. Alvin Fowler.

"Sure, I remember you now," Tom told him. "We went to school together. Remember Tom Kencaide?"

Al frowned, rubbed a scar on his chin, then grinned. "Pepper Kencaide's boy."

Pepper, a nickname dating back to his father's Texas League baseball days. Pepper Kencaide. It had been a long time since Tom had heard that name. Somehow, it sounded good. The old antagonisms had faded.

"Right," Tom said, and they shook hands.

They talked, then, about the changes that had come in the years since the war. Al showed the pictures in his billfold of a blond wife, two boys and a girl. He asked what Tom was doing. Tom told him.

"I'll be damned," he said. "I'd noticed the name in the paper, and I wondered if it could be you. I remember, you was always readin'."

Tom decided the time was ripe. He glanced around cautiously, making sure he wouldn't be overheard. Two customers were drinking at the far end of the bar, so he lowered his voice.

"In fact, that's what I'm doing down here. I thought maybe you are having the same trouble as some of the other bars in town."

"What trouble is that?" Al asked softly.

Tom finished his beer, put the empty bottle on the bar between them, and pointed to the Alamo label. "The quota," he said.

Al studied him for a moment, then glanced at the two men at the end of the bar. He reached into the box behind the bar, pulled out two bottles of Alamo and opened them. "Let's go into the back where we can talk," he said.

Tom followed him past the rear booths, through a partition, and into a small, beaverboard storeroom in the corner of the building. The restrooms occupied the other corner, and there was the faint smell of urine and the stronger smell of urinal cakes.

Al checked the men's restroom to make sure it was unoccupied. He wasn't worried about the women's apparently, because the only woman in the place was the redhead tending bar. He leaned against an old tin-topped desk, facing the storeroom door so he could check traffic to and from the restrooms. He turned the beer up, drank, and made a wry face.

"I guess I'll have to start drinkin' the damned stuff. I can't keep up with the quota any other way. Get a few cases behind every week." He waved the bottle around the storeroom, and Tom saw that most of the stock was full cases of Alamo. Al looked at Tom seriously. "You goin' to write a story about this thing?"

"If I can get enough information, find enough people willing to fight back."

Al snorted. "You not goin' to find anybody that crazy, man."

The fact that Al would knuckle under to such high-handed tactics surprised Tom. "I remembered you as a guy who wouldn't take anything off anybody," he said.

Al shoved himself away from the desk. "What in hell can you do? This ain't kid stuff, Tom, where you can just bust somebody's nose an' he'll leave you alone."

"I know," Tom assured him. "But there are laws to protect people from this kind of highway robbery. Do you have anything in writing? Any witnesses that they've set a quota?"

Al laughed bitterly. "Hell, no. It's called a 'promotion campaign' or 'contest' but when the truck comes, that's how many cases they set off. They've got it all set up, I'll tell you."

"You talk to the police or anyone about it?"

Al snorted again. "You can't trust these local cops. I did think about goin' to the state, the Rangers, or the Liquor Control Board, but what in hell could I say? I've had a couple of shootin's in here and I damned near got my license lifted on the last one, about six months ago. I ain't in any position to ask favors. Besides, if word got back to certain people, I'd wind up in the hospital."

"You know of anyone that has happened to?"

"Sure. Sy Blackmon, used to have a place a block down, on the corner. He told 'em to go to hell, and two nights later he was beat up and robbed after he closed up. When he got out of the hospital, he didn't have any business left." Al saw the direction of Tom's thinking. "No use talkin' to him. He's learned his lesson."

"What about the district attorney? Would you make a statement to him? I've got another tavern owner who will, and with the two of you, we probably could get an investigation started."

Al scowled. "I don't know, Tom. I wouldn't be a damned bit surprised if the DA isn't in on it, too."

"You have any reason to think so?"

"Just common sense. This is a big setup. It couldn't operate like this unless they have it fixed."

"I just can't believe a brazen thing like this could be protected," Tom said.

"Then you don't believe the stories about Beaumont and Port Arthur printed in your own newspaper. They had worse setups than this fixed."

"I guess you're right. But we got to start somewhere."

Al's eyes widened. "Where do you get that 'we' stuff. Man, I don't want any part of anything like that. We're just talkin', see, just you an' me, an' I don't want it to go any farther than that. I got a wife an' three kids, man. I can't get involved."

"Somebody's got to get involved," Tom told him. "Those stories about Beaumont and Port Arthur wouldn't have come out if somebody hadn't bucked the system."

"Well, it doesn't have to be me. I lost a sister in a deal like this. I know what they can do to you."

Tom had a brief, fleeting recollection of a girl in his class in grade school, a memory of pigtails, skinny legs beneath a thin, faded dress. "Kathy?"

"Yeah. You remember what happened to her, don't you?"

Tom shook his head negatively.

Al looked like he was sorry he had brought the subject up. "Well, Kathy went kinda bad. There wasn't a damned thing we could do with her, the war and all the servicemen around. She went kinda nuts. I was in the Army, overseas, an' Ma couldn't handle her. Dad just refused to believe the stories he heard about her. But when she got drunk, she talked too much. She talked once too often, I guess. They found her in 'fifty-two, floatin' face down in the lake."

"Murdered?"

"Your paper had some stories on it. Autopsy showed she didn't drown. She was hit on the head with something, then thrown in the lake."

"I'm sorry. I didn't know. I must have been in Korea then. You think it was the same organization?"

Tom saw by Al's reaction that the thought was new to him. He rejected it. "No. That was a long time before this beer thing came up."

"Sounds to me like the same outfit," Tom told him. "They couldn't operate so efficiently if they hadn't been in the shakedown game a long time. They're probably just branching out a little all the time."

Tom watched him struggle with the idea. "Kathy never knew but one guy—the one she paid the money to," Al said thoughtfully. "An' he disappeared. Course, I knew there were others. Hell, man, I talked to half this town, tryin' to find out. It might be the same setup. I never thought about it before."

"If they're not the same people, they're the same *kind* of people," Tom told him. "The only way to get them is to fight back. I think getting the DA interested would be the first step."

Al studied his empty beer bottle silently. Then he looked at Tom, eyes narrowed. "Would it be confidential? No story in the newspaper or anything like that."

"Nobody will know but you, me, and the DA's office."

Al put the beer bottle on the desktop beside him, glared at it for a moment, then brought both fists down on his thighs. "All right," he said. "I'll do it. But I hope you know what you're doin'. I still think this is liable to get us both knocked in the head."

Shortly after nine the next morning, Tom was admitted into the inner sanctum of the district attorney in the old courthouse. With some misgivings, he explained his interview with Joe Garzek, his search through taverns and bars, and the finding of Al Fowler.

District Attorney Mark Matthews listened with only an occasional flicker of more than passing interest. Matthews was a tall, heavy-set man in his mid-forties, his thick dark hair trimmed long, with impressive touches of white at the temples. His face was set in serious contemplation. He wore expensive suits, and he spoke with a rich, well-modulated voice. Unfortunately, this distinguished appearance was a sham. Before his successful political campaign two years ago, Matthews had never been connected with a criminal case. Since then, his record had been less than marginal, punctuated with frequent clashes with the district judges. Matthews publicly blamed the judges for the growing backlog of cases. The judges blamed Matthews.

As Tom explained Garzek's troubles, his misgivings began to mount. It occurred to him that Matthews might be too wrapped up in his feud with the judges to investigate anything outside the courthouse. But Matthews nodded solemnly when Tom had finished.

"I'll be glad to take their statements," the district attorney said. "But I can't promise anything until after I hear what they have to say."

"Of course," Tom said. "I just hope it will be enough to start a good case."

"When can they come in?"

"Just about any time. What about this morning?"

"No, I'm due in court in a few minutes. But the case should go to the jury late this afternoon. Tell you what. When they start to send the jury out, I'll get word to you, and you can get Garzek and Fowler down here. I'll talk to them while we wait for the jury to come back with a verdict, and from the looks of that jury, that'll probably be plenty of time."

Later, when Tom stopped at the city desk and told Collier of his talks with Fowler and the district attorney, he didn't get quite the reaction he expected.

"Damn it, Tom, I wish you'd let that alone," Collier said irritably. "With the doctor out raising hell about this lake project, you're going to have to stick pretty close to your beat for the next few days."

That was Tom's introduction to the newspaper's prize weekend boo-boo and the resulting tirade of Publisher BeeBee Milam.

One of the society staffers had written a feature for the Sunday paper on a speech by Dr. Travis McNiel. Unfettered by the political aspects of the story, she had donated the better part of a column of type to the doctor's description of the hospital's dire needs and his hopes for getting an improvement program on the next municipal ballot.

Since reporters and deskmen in the city room seldom looked

at the society section, the story went unnoticed until a copyreader, turning through the section wistfully studying pictures of brides, happened to see the headline.

The presses were stopped, the story jerked, and the hole plugged with an Associated Press story on the migration of whooping cranes. But the makeover came late in the press run. Despite the precautions of destroying all early editions around the newsroom, BeeBee Milam happened to get one of the early papers.

Only after a two-hour session in Milam's office Monday morning did the society writer tearfully convince Milam that she wrote the story in all innocence, that no one had encouraged her. During the first hour, BeeBee fired her three times, apparently so upset he didn't notice the repetition. But during the last hour, he relented and hired her back.

BeeBee's edicts were handed down rapidly throughout the remainder of the day. The doctor's purpose, BeeBee announced, was to get his name before the public for professional reasons. Therefore, the newspaper was not to aid and abet the doctor in this pursuit by printing his name.

BeeBee decreed that in the future when the doctor spoke, the newspaper would carry a story on the meeting as usual, but without mentioning the speaker's name or topic. If possible, some other aspect of the meeting was to be featured. For his own purposes, BeeBee wanted a full report on the doctor's activities: each talk he gave, the organization, who attended, what was said, the organization's reaction. This chore was assigned to Tom.

So Tom spent most of Monday afternoon backtracking on the doctor's last few days. The assignment was easier than he first figured, because many of the women's club membership lists overlapped. By steady telephoning, he had a fairly complete dossier compiled in three hours, along with the doctor's itinerary for the next week.

That day, for the first time in years, Tom covered his beat by telephone, never leaving the office. At four-thirty, the DA's secretary called, relaying the information that the judge had started his charge to the jury, and the DA probably would be free within the next thirty or forty minutes. Tom was able to mingle his calls to Garzek and Fowler in with the others, concealing from Collier that he hadn't dropped all his plans at BeeBee's bidding.

He also called for a dinner date with Arlene, planning vaguely to meet J. Marvin Olds at the steakhouse. Her coolness over the phone didn't surprise him. She didn't like to have him call her at the department store, and she apparently still was miffed over their Saturday night date being turned into a bar-hopping, beer-drinking spree. She had asked him to take her home early. Resenting her lack of co-operation, he had accommodated her. She had gotten out of the car without speaking, and he hadn't called Sunday, partly because he was busy, partly because he figured time would help heal the discord. It always had before, so he didn't worry. They'd had spats worse than this.

Now, he realized he'd been wrong. She must have been brooding about their differences. From the tone of her voice he knew this was more than just another quarrel.

"I don't think I'd better plan on having dinner with you," she said with an unfamiliar inflection. "I'm not in the mood."

Immediately, he sensed the urgency of the situation. He felt, somehow, that if he could just talk to her, everything would be all right again.

"Couldn't I see you for a few minutes?" he pleaded.

She didn't answer for a moment.

"If you want, you can take me home," she said finally. "It might be a good idea for us to have a talk."

He finished the report for BeeBee and wrote the few stories he'd gotten from his beat, then hurried over to the courthouse.

The district attorney had finished taking the statements. Garzek and Fowler had already left.

District Attorney Matthews seemed disappointed. "Very strange, I'll admit. But I'm afraid there's not enough to prosecute or to turn over to a grand jury."

Tom thought he had made it perfectly clear he knew that from a legal standpoint the value of the information was limited.

"I didn't think there would be enough," Tom told him. "I'm sorry if I led you to believe there was. I only hoped there'd be enough to merit further investigation."

"Well, of course I'm grateful for the work you've done, and

we'll keep this information on file. If anything else comes along, it might be the beginning of something."

"But you plan no aggressive action on it?"

Matthews smiled. "Not to the extent that you can write one of those 'it has been reliably learned the district attorney's office is investigating' stories, if that's what you have in mind. Understand my position. We have fourteen murder cases alone on the dockets, not to mention lesser assorted crimes."

"And in the meantime, Garzek is run out of business."

"Let's be realistic, Kencaide. You must admit the whole thing sounds pretty preposterous. Garzek admits there've been numerous arrests in his place. He has no proof that any of these alleged conversations took place, or even who the other party was. He sounds like a paranoiac with a persecution complex. And Fowler is even worse. He readily admits there never were any direct threats. He just 'knew what would happen' if he didn't go along."

Tom understood, then.

"You mean you don't believe them."

Matthews spread his hands. "I'm not in any position to believe or disbelieve. But I'm a lawyer, and I think like a lawyer. Let's just say I haven't been convinced."

Tom knew he was getting nowhere. "I'm sorry I took so much of your time. I won't come back until I have something to convince you."

Matthews left his desk and followed Tom to the door. "If I were you, I'd just forget about it, Kencaide. I don't think there's a story in it."

"I started out after a story," Tom admitted. "But right now, all I'm after is a little justice."

Being fifteen minutes late for his date with Arlene didn't get Tom off to a good start at reconciliation. She was standing alone on the sidewalk beside the shuttered department store, waiting for him in the glare of the late afternoon sun. So he had to begin his fence-mending with an apology. "I'm sorry I'm late. I had to go by the district attorney's office."

"I should have known you'd still be more concerned about Joe Garzek than me," Arlene said. She rolled down the right window as he squeezed Old Smokey through rush-hour traffic.

"Won't you reconsider and have dinner with me?" he asked, trying to establish the old rapport. "I'll get J. Marvin to tell some murder stories you've never heard before."

"No."

She dabbed her face with a white handkerchief. He couldn't take his eyes from traffic long enough to see whether she was wiping away tears, or perspiration from the heat.

"How about a cold drink? I could stop at a drive-in."

"No," she said again, her voice curt. "Just take me straight home."

He kept his mind busy seeking some way to atone for the way he had treated her during the weekend. But as he pulled Old Smokey to a halt under the shade of the elm in front of her apartment, he had nothing to offer her except another apology. "I'm sorry about Saturday night. I hoped you'd understand. Finding someone to back up Garzek's story was very important."

"Did you find anyone?"

"Yes."

"Did it do any good?"

"Not yet," he admitted. "But it may eventually."

"You still think, though, that what you did this weekend was more important than . . . you and me."

"Nothing is more important to me than our future," he said.

She just looked at him and shook her head sadly.

"I would do anything to make you happy," he said.

"Anything?"

"Anything."

"Anything except changing jobs, you mean."

He hesitated, hunting for the right words. "I don't believe making me over into something I'm not would make you happy. And that's what you're trying to do."

"If you'd just consider the idea. . . ."

"I have considered it."

"You haven't investigated another job. You haven't talked to anyone else. I wouldn't call that considering it."

"If I did get out and scare up some job possibilities, get some offers, would that convince you that I'm sincere?"

"It would convince me you're not sacrificing our happiness to your stubbornness."

"All right. I'll do it. I'll bring you a list of jobs I've hunted up, considered, and rejected, giving you the reasons why."

"That's a fine attitude to start job-hunting with. But I believe that when you look around, you'll get an entirely new perspective."

"I doubt that."

"I know you do, now. But I'll tell you a place you can start that might change your viewpoint right quick. I was going to tell you Saturday night, and that's why I got so damned mad—you were too interested in bartenders to listen to me. I talked to the vice-president in charge of public relations at Chilson Petroleum Friday at the Ad Club. He was very interested in you."

Suddenly, the tensions of the last hour turned to anger. He drove the flat of his hand against the steering wheel. "Damn it, Arlene, I've told you not to mention me to anyone. If and when I want to change jobs, I'll go out and find one myself."

She matched his anger. "I didn't approach him," she said heatedly. "He spoke to the Ad Club, and afterward we got to talking. Your name just came up naturally."

"I don't care how it happened. I told you not to mention me to anyone."

She turned away from him. When she spoke again, there was a tremor to her voice. "Tom, I can't wait forever."

He tried to make her see how he felt.

"Arlene, doesn't it make a difference that I happen to like the work I'm doing?"

She turned back toward him. There were tears in her eyes. "You like your work. That's just great. Maybe when you're as old as J. Marvin you can sit and tell some young reporter about all the hoodlum councilmen you've known and advise him to get out of journalism. It'll be too late, then, Tom, just like it's too late for J. Marvin now."

"That can't be the real reason you want me to change jobs," he said. "And you insist it isn't the money. What is it?"

She hesitated, as if arranging her thoughts. "I somehow have the feeling that I wouldn't be marrying you, I'd be marrying that damned newspaper. Call it jealousy, if you want. I suppose it is. But I know that if you keep on working for the newspaper, you'll give it far more time and attention than you give me.

This last weekend was a good example of what I can expect. That's why I would keep working. I'd still have some life of my own."

He suddenly felt very tired. Her long argument had worn down his resistance. "What would this job be at Chilson Petroleum?"

"No, forget what I said. I wouldn't want to be a factor in your doing something you'd regret." She sighed deeply. "I can't understand it. You gripe for hours on end about how newspapers are going to hell, yet you believe it's your life work."

"That's part of the reason," he explained. "I feel I've got to do whatever I can to help. You accused me the other night of being a square. Maybe I am. I believe a free press, with public confidence behind it, is essential to democracy. I'm afraid the public is fast losing that confidence, and if that happens, it may be the collapse of everything, our whole way of government."

"What do you think you can do about it?"

"I can write as objectively and accurately as I can, try to keep my own personal standards."

"I've read your promotion pieces on the new lake. They sure are objective. They make me want to throw up."

He winced inwardly. "As Houston Collier points out to me almost every day, I do work for BeeBee Milam."

She lowered her head and wiped her cheeks. The sun had set, now, and in the twilight he couldn't see the expression on her face clearly. "I was mistaken, I guess. You're not square. I'm beginning to think you're just a little bit crazy."

"That's the way I am, whatever it is."

She moved toward the door on the far side of the car, then paused with her hand on the handle. "I think we had better not see each other for a while," she said very quietly. "I want time to think things over."

Her remark about his being a little bit crazy still stung enough to make him retain his pride.

"If you want," he said.

"Maybe you'd rather call the whole shootin' match off," she said.

"That's up to you."

They glared at each other for a long moment in the gathering darkness.

"I guess that's the only sensible thing to do," she said quietly.

She pulled the engagement ring from her left hand, put it on the seat between them, and got out of the car. He stepped out to stop her, but by the time he rounded the car she was already up the steps and running along the walk to the building. He stood and watched her hunt for the key, open the door, and go into the apartment.

Slowly, he got back into the car, picked up the ring, and sat holding it. He felt no emotion, only a sort of numbness. For a long time he sat there in Old Smokey, looking at the apartment house, unable to follow her, unable to go away. No lights came on at her windows.

Finally, he drove off.

He should have known what to expect from J. Marvin Olds. Arlene became the topic of conversation the moment Tom walked into the restaurant.

"Alone," J. Marvin said, shaking his head sadly. "If I'd known you weren't bringin' that gal, I wouldn't have come."

"Me you got," Tom said.

For a time, he managed to turn talk away from Arlene by telling J. Marvin of his failure with the DA. J. Marvin was not among the DA's admirers.

"I wouldn't be a damned bit surprised if that son of a bitch isn't in on it," J. Marvin confided. "Seems mighty odd he didn't show more interest."

"I don't know what I'm going to tell Garzek. I had him thinking this might be the end of his problem, and I don't have any further hope to offer him. What do you think about going to the sheriff's office?"

"No, he'd be reluctant to move in on the city's domain. I'd be more inclined to go to Chief McDowell. I trust him. He might not be able to indict Berger, but I bet he'd clean house."

"That'd just be a temporary solution," Tom said. "I want to get Berger. If we talked to Chief McDowell, or Hartwell, everything would be taken out of our hands, hushed up. I think I'll go talk to Berger, see what he has to say about it. I'd like to see him explain all these coincidences."

J. Marvin raised his eyebrows. "That sounds like a pretty good idea—as long as it's you doin' it, and not me."

They went on to other topics, then, the weekend booboo, the repercussions, BeeBee Milam's newest tirade. But when a lull came in the conversation, J. Marvin went back to his favorite subject.

"How come Arlene couldn't make it tonight?"

Tom tried to be evasive. "She said she wasn't in the mood."

Before Tom could take the talk into another field again, J. Marvin came out with the old, familiar question. "Tom, when you goin' to marry that girl, anyway?"

It was a question he had asked many times in a joking, teasing way, and they'd bantered good-naturedly about this so long Tom was at a loss now as to what to say. Suddenly, in a wave of resignation, Tom just told the simple truth.

"You may as well know. I guess everyone will before long. The engagement's off." He took the ring from his coat pocket and tossed it onto the white tablecloth between them.

J. Marvin looked at the ring for a moment before answering. "Me and my big mouth. I'm sorry, Tom."

"That's all right. You had no way of knowing."

They lingered over a second cup of coffee in an uncomfortable silence.

"Damn it, I believe I feel as bad as you must," J. Marvin said finally. "Is there anything I can do? I don't believe I ever would forgive myself if I didn't ask."

"No, I don't think so." Tom suddenly felt like talking about it. J. Marvin's obvious concern made it easier. "I guess we're just not suited for each other—not compatible. You've heard most of our differences discussed right here at this table. I don't see any solution. She knows what she wants in life, and I know what I want. And they're just not the same things."

"Do you? Do you really know what you want, Tom?" J. Marvin held up a hand to ward off a reply. "I'm going to give you the benefit of my experience. I've spent most of my life in newspapers trying to puzzle things out, and I believe I have some of the answers. Tell me. Did you ever see a newspaperman, especially a reporter, accurately portrayed in a movie, on television, anywhere?"

"No."

"You know why? It's because they try to put a reporter into the story, into the stream of life, try to make him a part of the scheme of things, and he just isn't."

Tom didn't understand. "What do you mean?"

"I mean we go out and talk to killers, politicians, celebrities, officials, people that make the news, and pretty soon we get to thinking we're a part of the news. But we're not. We're observers. A reporter gets to living vicariously, and if he doesn't watch himself, he'll come to have no life of his own. I know. This has happened to me. You grow to be like those guys who get their kicks by going to whorehouses and paying to peep through gimlet holes to watch the other guy."

"Oh, come on, now," Tom said. "I think newspapering deserves a better label than that."

"Maybe so," J. Marvin admitted. "But sometimes I wonder. Observing may be more fun because you don't have the resultant worries of participation, but it isn't very productive, and it sure doesn't get you anything. There's the danger, I guess. We have more fun than most people. We have the opportunity to observe life around us and enjoy it. Then too, it seems to me most of us are better equipped by nature for having fun. But we're not living our own lives. We don't affect life's stream."

"I've made things happen," Tom protested. "And what about the murders you've solved?"

"Exceptions that prove the rule. That's what I call the Great Search for Identity. The police are better at solving murders than we are, but we keep trying to prove we exist. We do all kinds of things—interpretive reporting, columns, first-person features—attempting to put ourselves in the lifestream. But when you come right down to it, we're just observers."

"I don't agree at all," Tom insisted. "By getting out and working, publicizing injustices, crimes, the human things in life, I think a reporter has more influence than most anyone."

J. Marvin sighed in apparent resignation. "I didn't think you'd see it. Maybe you will, when you're my age, no home, no wife, no children. Nothing but a stack of by-lines, all talent, energies burned and nothing to keep for yourself. I don't know if Arlene has thought all this out, but I imagine that with a woman's intuition, she knows that she'd be competing with this vicarious life."

Tom felt hemmed in, confused, helpless. He tried to come back with an argument, but he couldn't get his thoughts organized. "Then she's completely right, and I'm completely wrong?" he asked, the question sounding more sarcastic than he'd intended.

But J. Marvin took the question seriously. "At the risk of our friendship, Tom, I'm afraid I'll have to answer that I think so."

## CHAPTER NINE

Travis sat in the Almeron Dickenson Room of the Woman's Club, awaiting the introduction. Around him, forty members of the 1934 Study Group were dawdling over the remnants of their low-caloried lunch. Those at his table had given up in their polite attempts to engage him in idle chatter. Travis didn't feel like conversation. He couldn't keep his mind from the things he should be doing and the two big tasks still ahead of him today.

He sipped the lukewarm coffee and thought of the lab reports on his desk back at the office. He had known, almost from the first, that Cal Masters' trouble was serious. Still, the arrival of the results this morning had been a shock.

The possibilities had been numerous, and Cal was not an ideal patient. In the beginning, he had stubbornly refused to cooperate. His symptoms were revealed grudgingly, vaguely—his pain had been there for "some time"; no, he couldn't remember exactly when it started; sometimes the pain was sharp, sometimes general; sometimes it seemed in front, often it felt like it was toward the back, near the spine.

Only by persistent grilling had Travis worked up a fair case history. Other possibilities had been ruled out, one by one, in an intense series of tests. Now, he had the answer.

Telling Cal would be the day's first big job. The appointment was right after lunch. Breaking the news to Cal probably would be one of the most difficult things Travis ever had to do.

He put the lab report out of his mind and concentrated on preparation for the second major item on today's agenda—the initial test in council tonight of his speaking campaign. There hadn't been much time, and he wasn't ready. He had to get at least some of these women out tonight to help.

The study group's president called the meeting to order. She got right to the point.

"I'm sure you all know that we have a distinguished guest with us today. Since his time is limited, I will turn the meeting over to the program chairman without further ado."

The introduction by the entertainment chairman, a rather attractive young brunette matron, was much less than the length Travis had come to expect.

"We are honored to have with us today Dr. Travis McNiel of the City Council, who will give us a report on conditions at the city-county hospital." Referring to her notes, she read a resume of Travis' services with the hospital board and medical association committees. She folded her notes and smiled at Travis. "Ladies, Dr. McNiel."

In the midst of applause, Travis walked to the microphone. As usual, he felt the inner queasiness of stage fright, but the words of his speech had become so standardized that, after the qualms of the first few moments, he quickly regained self-confidence.

Using a trick he'd read somewhere in a book on public speaking, he selected individuals on the far side of the room and spoke to them. Some he recognized—the overdressed wife of a prominent lawyer; a school principal's wife; the widow of an oil engineer, now a grandmother; the wife of a rancher.

Again, as he talked to the serious, intent faces, he felt he was obtaining a rapport. If he could make these women realize the need for hospital improvements, perhaps he would be doing more for the medical profession than anything he'd accomplished on the council.

After his talk, the room was darkened while he showed the color film slides he'd had prepared. Then he answered a few questions from the audience.

In closing, he invited them to visit the council and show their support for these needed improvements, either at the special session tonight, or at the next regular meeting week. But he especially invited their attendance whenever the council met to set a date for the water bond election—he would notify their club officers beforehand as to the exact night. It was his hope, he explained, to have the hospital improvements voted upon simultaneously with the lake proposal. In the meantime, if they would call or write the other members of the council, the mayor, the city manager, he was sure their views would be well received.

After the closing applause, the entertainment chairman explained that the doctor had a busy schedule, that she was sure everyone appreciated his coming to give them this information, and that she knew they all would understand that the doctor preferred to leave now, rather than sit through the upcoming business session.

So, with a burst of laughter and applause as his exit cue, he left, thankful he didn't have to endure another treasurer's report. He hurried back to his office to face Cal.

He had the reports on his desk, studying them, when Cal arrived in the reception room. Travis had his receptionist keep Cal waiting a few minutes while he thought desperately of some way to put all the technical jargon into plain words, regretting his promise that there would be no secrets. He had given Cal the promise that first day in his office. And Cal had made him repeat it when he'd had to keep Cal in the hospital overnight for the biopsy of a lymph node. Now, there was no alternative.

Travis went into the reception room, met Cal, and escorted him back into the office. He made an attempt at small talk to put Cal at ease. "They treat you all right up at the hospital?"

"Fine, considering the terrible shape they're in, to hear you tell it."

"How are you feeling today?"

"I still got the pain. Otherwise, I couldn't complain."

At least Cal was admitting now that the pain was constant. Travis had suspected it from the first.

"How's your appetite?"

"I haven't been eatin' too hardy for some time," Cal said. "But from all those tests, you ought to know more about me than I do."

Suddenly, Travis realized that Cal knew he was stalling. He opened the folder on his desk. Then, with the report in front of him and Cal facing him, Travis simply lost the power of speech.

Cal seemed to sense his trouble. "Judgin' from the expression on your face, you must have some bad news."

"I do," Travis managed to say.

"It's cancer, then," Cal said simply.

Travis nodded.

Cal's right hand moved up experimentally to cover his solar plexus. "Where is it?"

Travis understood then that Cal was confused. The pain was in his middle, sometimes radiating into his back, but they'd taken the biopsy from his groin. Travis explained:

"We found cancer cells collected in the lymph node we took from your groin. We found cells which we recognize as being from the pancreas. This indicates the pancreas is the primary site of the malignancy."

Cal's hand rubbed his solar plexus again. "So it is here?"

Travis nodded again. "The pancreas lies behind the stomach."

Then Cal understood. "The sweetbreads."

"Yes." Cancer of the sweetbreads. There should be a special course in medical school on how to explain illnesses to ranchers; they have a knowledge of anatomy all their own.

"Can you cut it out?"

Travis hedged. "I want you to have the benefit of other medical opinion, but I would say that, on the basis of these preliminary tests, surgery is not indicated."

"How long have I got left?" Cal asked gently.

Travis was certain now that Cal had known. The diagnosis had been no surprise. Cal had come to hear the answer to this one question.

"Don't try to pin me down on that, Cal," Travis pleaded. "We're not that all-knowing. Too many people, including too many doctors, tend to look upon medicine as an exact science. We don't heal people, we only help heal. The more I practice, the more experience I get, the less I feel like putting anything down as certain."

Cal listened, his face expressionless, his blue eyes unwavering. "But what looks probable?" he insisted. "Weeks? Months?"

"I told you, I don't know. Nothing is for certain. Each case is different. A malignancy of this type progresses at different rates of speed in each patient. We'll do comparative studies on you, from time to time, and maybe we'll know more. Also, we have some new drugs that show a marked tendency to retard the advance of cancer in some patients, but these same drugs seem to have no effect whatever in others. So you see, Cal, I just can't say."

"A year?" Cal asked determinedly. "Do I have a year? You promised there'd be no secrets."

Travis had given the promise in order to get Cal's co-operation. Now, there was no turning back. "If the malignancy is as far advanced as our tests indicate, I would guess six months . . . at the maximum," Travis said, finally. Then, suddenly, his personal feelings burst through his professional veneer. "Damn it, Cal, why didn't you come in when you first began to notice this pain?"

Cal grinned sheepishly. "Plain cowardice. You see, Travis, I've seen so many of my friends spend their last precious days in that hospital. I just put it off, day by day, enjoying each one, because from the very first, I think, I knew."

"If you'd just come in earlier. . . ."

"Travis, I don't mind dyin'." Cal pushed a forelock of white hair back from his forehead, then spread his hands in an inarticulate gesture. "Anyone who has lived eighty years has thought a great deal about death. And believe me, if the Lord wills, I'm ready to go. It's just a simple matter of . . . certain arrangements."

"Well, don't give up. There are many things we can do."

"Yes, I know. I've seen some of them. And I'm tellin' you right now, Travis, while I'm able, that I don't want to go like some of my friends went. When my time comes, I don't want it to be with a tube down my nose, another up my rectum, a needle in my arm, a tent over me, and all the other gadgets I've seen used. I want to meet my Maker still feelin' like a human, if at all possible."

"Cal, I can't promise. . . ."

"I mean it," Cal interrupted. "And I'm not goin' to the hospital until I absolutely have to."

Travis decided to avoid the topic for the moment. "Did you get that prescription filled?"

"No. I'm not goin' to go around all doped up. My mother bore me in pain, and I guess it's only proper that, if God wills it, I can stand to suffer some to see her now."

"Cal, I'm going to warn you. Pancreatic pain can be as severe as any known to man. As a favor to me, if nothing else, will you have that prescription filled and carry the pills with you?"

Reluctantly, Cal agreed.

Travis' duties as a physician were over, for the moment. But he walked out through the reception room with Cal to the pickup truck at the curb. Somehow, he felt he should express his personal feelings. "Cal, I'm sorry," was all he could say.

"Don't be," Cal said as he climbed into the truck. He looked at Travis through the open window and grinned. "I'm not sorry. Why should you be? Use your sorrow on those who haven't had as long a life or as full a life." He started the truck. "I'll see you at council tonight."

Travis stood and watched Cal back the pickup out, shift gears, and gun the truck off down the street. Then he went back into his office to tell his next patient, a twenty-year-old housewife, that her pregnancy test was positive.

There was a quality to Cal's acceptance of the diagnosis that left Travis greatly troubled. He had seen the effect of faith in the face of death before, and he had seen the strength of religion. But Cal's faith was a calmness, unlike anything Travis had known. He wondered how he would react if their roles were reversed. The religion Travis had known was one to be worn as a personal adornment. The church permeated every thought. The church was a fraternity, the members even addressed as "Brother Jones" or "Sister Smith." The strength was in the church. But Cal's strength was within himself, a personal faith born of long communion. Faith was a word Travis associated with the sounds of a summer breeze in a brush arbor, the hiss of a lantern, a crowd worked into a high emotional pitch, men, women on their knees, faces upturned, begging the Lord's forgiveness. . . .

When millionaire Sam McIntosh, the power that got Travis elected to council, phoned during the afternoon to express his displeasure at Travis' speeches, and urged him to reconsider his lake views, Travis firmly told McIntosh he was sure he was doing the right thing. When a group of doctors dropped by at the close of office hours with a complaint he was undermining public confidence in the hospital, Travis refused to be swayed. He told them that if the medical profession lost face in the revelation of conditions at the hospital, perhaps that was just what it deserved.

Afterward, Travis was impressed by the self-confidence he had shown in dealing with his fellow men. Why couldn't he get up the courage to set himself right with God? Was it fear? Some latent, traumatic experience of childhood?

He considered that possibility. There might be some such repressed event. Certainly there was enough in his memory to make other, hidden incidents plausible. His father had been a stern disciplinarian where religion was concerned. And Travis had spent his boyhood listening to hellfire and brimstone sermons on what awaited sinners.

He remembered his first sin, and the effect it'd had upon him. . . .

They were holding a revival at a brush arbor in a small southwest Oklahoma town. Across the street there was the playground of a school. One afternoon late, while his father readied his sermon, Travis went over alone to play on the swings. When half a dozen neighborhood children came up, Travis knew from experience that the best thing to do was to remain aloof, rather than retreat. So he stayed in the swing, watching.

There was one boy who displayed an amazing athletic skill. He would shinny up a bare steel pole to the top of the swing, then walk hand over hand the full length of the swings to the other side, then slide down. He did this two or three times, showing off, as Travis watched.

Then, as the children moved on to a slide a few feet away, Travis decided he would attempt this feat. He went hand over hand up the pole to within a few inches of the top before his grip began to fail. Frantically, he sought to find purchase with his legs on the pipe. As he did, a strange thing happened.

Suddenly, his whole body was consumed by overpowering sensations from his loins. He began losing his grip on the pipe.

Again he tried to grip the pipe with his legs. This time the sensations sent him sliding slowly down the pipe to a comatose heap in the grass.

As his head began to clear, an older, wiser boy was standing over him, laughing. The other children, two boys about his own age and two skinny little girls, stood in a semicircle, staring at him, apparently as puzzled as he. But the older, wiser boy cleared up the mystery in gutter terms. Overcome by confusion and embarrassment, Travis fled across the street, their giggles and peals of laughter ringing behind him.

For the first time, Travis knew what his father meant by sins of the flesh. That night he stayed hidden in the car during the sermon. When his father came searching, Travis said he didn't feel well.

Fortunately, it was the last night of the revival. The next was more than thirty miles away. And Travis' illness wasn't all feigned. The horror within himself actually made him sick.

It was then he learned the chasm between himself and God. He tried to pray. He realized, then, that his saying of grace and bedtime prayer had been empty mouthings. He tried, but he knew it wasn't real prayer, not like his father's. For his father, prayer was as easy as picking up the telephone. He was on intimate terms with God. He had long consultations with the Deity on all important matters.

If Preacher McNiel knew hellfires were raging in his small son, he never gave indication. And Travis never found the courage to confess.

Every time his father ended his sermon with a call for all sinners to come forward and repent, Travis felt the urge to go. Twice he mustered enough backbone to go down the aisle, but when he saw the rows of adults on their knees before the altar, many weeping, all awaiting prayer and words that would make them whole, Travis backed out and turned aside, pretending to be seeking a better seat.

Then, that fall, his revival life ended.

Leaving Oklahoma alone one night after a Saturday night service, Preacher McNiel was driving to deliver a Sunday morning sermon across the Red River in Texas. As he drove his old roadster down the hill toward the river, a carload of celebrants from a roadside tavern pulled onto the highway, right into his path, with no lights. Witnesses at the scene said he prayed over a drunken corpse before he, too, died.

So his father's counsel was gone, unused. Travis stayed with Aunt Ida and kept his sin. Through the years, he'd acquired others, and he'd never been able to bridge the chasm to God.

Travis didn't leave home for the special council session until the last minute. Since this was not a regular council night, there would be no warm-up meeting, and he didn't want to get buttonholed in the hall and lectured by the mayor or Weatherbee about his speeches.

His first real hope of success in his women's club campaign came when he saw the full parking lot behind City Hall. As he entered the crowded chamber and took his seat on the far end of the council table, his hope was tempered by the realization that only about two-thirds of the audience was from the women's clubs. This unusual representation of femininity occupied the rearmost two-thirds of the chamber. Down front was an even rarer representation from the Chamber of Commerce.

The mayor called the chamber to order and opened the meeting. With such a large audience, the Gray Ghost felt called upon for more oration than at a routine council opening. He explained the purpose of the meeting, then went on into the background of the lake program: when it was first conceived, when preliminary work was started, the progress over the years. . . .

Again, as he usually did during dull openings, Travis studied faces.

At the other end of the horseshoe council table, Berger was more fidgety than ever tonight, perhaps because of the crowd. He sat hunched forward on the table, rolling a pencil over and over in his hands, darting quick, nervous glances at first one, then another of the council, the audience.

Beside Berger, Cal sat patiently, showing no effect of his death sentence. On Cal's right, Byron appeared half-asleep. This was his fourth term on the council. He must have some working philosophy on long speeches.

The city attorney and the city secretary sat quietly, earning their pay. On the mayor's right, Hartwell sat exuding confidence from his perfectly tailored suit, well-barbered face and cool, poised reserve. Only three scratches on his left cheek marred the Man of Distinction image. To Travis' experienced eye, the marks suspiciously resembled fingernail gouges. If so, they failed to shake Hartwell's smooth composure. He gave the appearance of knowing more about what was going on than could be told tonight, of being here only to make sure all went well.

Councilman Wentworth saw someone he knew in the audience, waved, and grinned boyishly. Councilman Weatherbee turned and glared at him in disapproval.

In studying the audience, Travis was amused to notice that there were several husbands in the Chamber of Commerce section who matched wives in the female delegations. The lake-hospital clash—if he could bring it to that—might split some homes right down the middle.

The mayor finished his historical lecture and introduced the first consulting engineer, who came forward to speak into the microphone. Below Travis, the news reporter, Kencaide, picked up a pencil.

The first engineer explained much that Travis already knew: Three sites had been under study for the proposed lake—the Spur Site, the Singletree Site, and the Lone Grove Site. Each, he explained, had its own advantages and disadvantages. A complete cost and yield study had been made of each and compared against another study of the city's future requirements.

The Spur Site, the engineer said, was nearest, and would be the most economical to build. But the lake would be smaller, shallower, with more per-gallon loss to evaporation. Adding to the economy, the water could be brought into the city mains by gravity flow. Unfortunately, he added, this small, ideal lake would be only a stopgap measure. From their studies, the engineers estimated the city would outgrow this lake within ten to twenty years.

The Singletree Site had the advantage of low-cost dam, deeper lake and less evaporation. But the conduit would be longer, more costly, and with the lake below a certain level, pumps would be necessary. Also, there was some oil activity on one fringe of the lake, raising a pollution problem. The cost of isolating the oil pool would be prohibitive, they believed, making the Singletree Site the least feasible of the three.

The last, the Lone Grove Site, had the advantage of the biggest lake and an ideal dam location. Farthest from the city, conduit costs would be high, and pumping would be necessary unless a certain level were maintained. Two ranch roads would have to be rerouted and a railroad line would have to be raised an average of three feet for a distance of two miles. Yet, even with this additional cost, they believed this site would be the most feasible. Federal funds would be more easily obtained for flood control, conservation, fish and wildlife and recreational facilities, they believed. Best of all, the lake would continue to fulfill the city's water needs for a long time to come, perhaps even into the twenty-first century. The cost, they estimated, would be in the neighborhood of $9,200,000, compared with $7,650,000 for the Singletree Site—which was not counting isolating the oil pool—and $5,200,000 for the Spur Site. This, of course, was in addition to a recommended outlay of $3,000,000 for repairs and increased facilities for water treatment and distribution within the city.

There was an electric stir of excitement through the audience at the engineer's description of this Herculean project. But this was quenched by the introduction of the second engineer, a small, smug young man who seemed to be the firm's statistician.

He mesmerized the audience with graphs on the per-capita rise in water use, graphs on the growth of the city, graphs on the per-thousand-gallons cost of water on delivery at the city treatment plant. He broke down the financial outlay for each proposed site, estimating costs of diverting small salt water streams, raising railroads, rerouting blacktop roads, availability and cost of earthen fills, and the size and estimated price on the required dams. He compared watershed areas, long-ranged rainfall records, stream flow studies and silt estimates, and the amount of water estimated available at each site.

Then, to complicate matters further, he presented a series of proposals on combinations of the three sites—a small lake now, a bigger one later, with the huge downstream lake as the eventual goal. This would involve greater loss from evaporation, he explained, and a much higher conduit cost. Then he produced the statistics to back up this conclusion.

Looking around him, Travis could see he wasn't the only one confused by the onslaught of figures. Alongside this, his little hospital program was nothing. He noticed the general stir of relief as the engineer wound up his presentation.

"And so, with all things taken into consideration, there is no doubt but what the Lone Grove Site is the most feasible."

"And the most expensive," Cal said.

There was a burst of laughter from the audience.

The engineer smiled indulgently. "Well, yes, speaking in terms of the initial cost. But in projecting our figures to the year two thousand, considering the average cost per thousand gallons of water delivered, the Lone Grove Site is the most economical and will provide the most water. I think that's what we're interested in, isn't it?"

Cal didn't answer. He was studying some notes he'd made. "I've been tryin' to break your rather detailed figures down into somethin' an old man like me can understand," Cal said finally. "As I understand it, the city now uses about twenty million gallons a day on peak days of summer. Our conduit from the reservoir carries only about sixteen million, the deficit bein' made up from in-city storage. Now, this big lake would supply another fifty-five million, which added to our present sixteen, would give us a potential of seventy-one million gallons a day, three and a half times our use on the hottest day of the year. Now tell me, what in the world are we goin' to do with all this water?"

The engineer turned back to his graphs.

"As I explained here, our projected curves of growth indicate the city probably will catch up with this water supply about the year two thousand. Of course if there's something we can't plan on—some per-capita boost to water use like home swimming pools and automatic washers have been—the city may run out of water before then."

"How big do you think the city will be by the year two thousand?" Cal asked.

"Our growth curve shows something like three-quarters of a

million population," he said matter-of-factly. He smiled with pleasure at the excited murmur of surprise from the audience.

"In other words, we'll be bigger than Dallas?"

"Bigger than Dallas is now," the engineer corrected him. "Of course by then, Dallas will be bigger than Chicago, probably, and Houston will be bigger than New York City, if the present trends continue."

There was another buzz of excitement through the audience.

"You'll have to pardon me," Cal said. "I find this all rather frightening. You see, I can remember the time when I knew everyone in town by their first names. I also remember when we put in the first municipal water system, a deep well out where the airport is now. Back then, we thought that would be all the water this town would ever need. But bigger than Dallas! I just can't believe that. . . ."

His voice trailed off. He sat looking out over the audience as if he couldn't think of what he started to say. The engineer waited, uncertain if Cal had finished.

"Then you have seen the changes brought by the last forty or fifty years," the engineer said finally. "I see no reason to doubt that the next forty or fifty will bring more."

Travis thought he sensed what Cal had been attempting to put into words. "How can you be sure the city will continue its growth curve?" he asked.

As the engineer turned to face Travis, there seemed to be a faint glimmer of recognition before he answered. "Well, the only way I can answer that, Doctor, is that all of our estimates are on the conservative side."

Since they'd never met, the title "doctor" caught Travis off guard. Then he realized the engineer must have been briefed—the thin, sharp-faced guy on the end of the council table's the one you got to watch, they'd probably told him. That's the doctor; he's apt to give you the most trouble.

If he had the reputation, Travis decided, he might as well use it. "You admit, then, that this rate of growth is conjecture?"

For the first time, the engineer seemed uncomfortable. "I suppose you could call it that. Conjecture based on fact. We know the city's growth rate in the past. We know the city's potential. All we have to do is project these figures into the future."

"Let's suppose, just for further conjecture, that the city's growth halts, even reverses. Would the proposed reservoir pay for itself?"

The engineer laughed. "Doctor, with this city's consistent rise in rate of growth over the last few years, and its vast potential, I just can't conceive of such a thing happening."

There was a burst of appreciative applause, concentrated mostly in the down-front Chamber of Commerce section.

Travis stuck to his point. "But if it did happen, would the lake pay for itself?"

The engineer shrugged slightly, as if trying to explain an irrefutable fact to an uncomprehending child. "Just supposing, as you say, I don't suppose it would. I don't know exactly what the critical drop would be, at what point loss would begin. But let me add my professional belief that such a thing is not going to happen."

"Could you give us the figures?" Travis asked. "The figures on what you call the critical drop?"

"If you want. It would take a few days, but we could work them up." He turned to the mayor questioningly.

The mayor took his cue. "Do you want to put that into the form of a formal motion, Doctor?"

Travis thought quickly. Cal would second it, probably, but that might be his only support. Yet, a formal motion would be a matter of record for all time that he had made an effort.

"Yes. I move that the council request the firm of Hilton and Harriman, consulting engineers, to provide the council with figures on the critical financial point for the proposed city reservoir, showing at what point in a loss of growth rate the city would experience financial loss."

Travis had underestimated Weatherbee.

"I second the motion," Weatherbee said. Then, as he saw the expressions around the council table, he apparently realized the need of clarifying his stand. "I agree with Dr. McNiel that we should examine every aspect of this program. It might be reassurance for the voter at the polls, if nothing else."

There was a moment of silence while the political aspects of the motion sank in.

Then the vote was unanimous.

From there the discussion went into the expanded distribution system, with Weatherbee doing most of the questioning. The needs for enlarging key water mains were almost as complicated as the different lake possibilities. Also, since the city's water treatment facilities were working at capacity now, another plant would be needed. It also would be financed out of the lake program, technically owned by the water district and leased to the city under a token arrangement.

With the debate drifting on into the various-sized conduits and relative costs, Travis was unable to maintain his interest. He sat plotting ways to use his newly found hospital support, waiting for the opportunity to give the council a sample tonight.

Finally, the technical discussion slowed. The mayor frowned at the clock on the opposite wall. "Well, we're running late," he said. "Are there any other questions from the council?"

"Just one, Mister Mayor," Travis said. "It has never been quite clear to me exactly where we stand in this project. The bonds will be issued by the water board, and they will call the election. It seems to be their project, their responsibility, but we seem to be taking all the initiative. Could someone straighten me out on this?"

The mayor turned to Hartwell. "Mister Manager, I believe you could answer that better than I."

Hartwell seemed to think the question was for the audience's benefit. "I have a detailed report on this, Doctor, and I'll get a copy out to the council in the next day or two. As you know, the idea is simple, basically. The water district allows the city to use its credit facilities. But when you get into the step-by-step process, it's quite complicated. However, we've researched this plan carefully, and I'm certain we are on solid legal ground."

Travis clarified his question. "I'm especially interested in the legal time lapses."

He could tell from the way Hartwell answered that the city manager knew now what was in Travis' mind.

"First, of course, we'll have to firm up this program," Hartwell began. "A public notice of hearing, legal publication, and a decision on what program we are going to pursue. I'd say a month minimum for this."

"But maybe longer?"

"A month, perhaps six weeks. The water district will have to convert itself into a water control and improvement district. This can be done without an election. The board just adopts a resolution and conducts a public hearing. Twenty days' notice is required for this."

Travis added another twenty to his scratchpad.

"Then the water district calls an election on the question of the bonds for the lake, the bonds payable solely from payments received from the city under a water supply contract. Thirty days' notice is required and a simple majority carries. Our own election would be on the same day, on the question of entering into a contract to purchase a certain amount of water at a specified rate upon completion of the lake. Only two weeks' notice is required for our election, but of course we would have to wait for the water district's time lapse."

"That would throw us into the summer before we could possibly hold an election. June, July, and August are heavy vacation months. Why not wait until September?"

The mayor intervened. "Well, I think we can put the question off until later, Doctor. Plenty of time left to decide."

Travis spoke quickly to make his point. "In any event, we cannot have an election before midsummer. I have been in contact with the architects who worked on the last hospital expansion. As I informed the council at the last meeting, the necessary plans for the proposed expansion are in existence. All we need is up-to-date cost estimates. I have been promised these figures could be available in six weeks. Even with thirty days' election notice, that would give us plenty of time to get the hospital program on the same ballot. . . ."

The mayor interrupted, his voice rising with sudden anger.

"Travis, we voted on your proposal last council night, and I can't see where anything would be gained by bringing it up again. In fact, I think there is a certain length of time before a question can be resubmitted, under the city charter. . . ."

"Unless there is new information," Travis corrected him. "I have just given you that new information. I therefore ask that the city manager place the proposal on the council agenda for the next regular meeting."

"Travis, we'll have another busy night scheduled. . . ."

"I believe I'm well within my rights as a councilman in requesting that the matter be placed on the agenda."

The mayor turned to the city attorney, who nodded affirmatively.

"Very well, Travis," the mayor said.

There was sudden applause from the rear two-thirds of the auditorium. The mayor looked up, startled, and the chamber executives down front turned in their seats in surprise. The discussion and argument had been so intent even the councilmen, facing them, had forgotten the women were there. As the mayor waited for the noise to subside, Travis could see that he was shaken. Beside Travis, Weatherbee was looking apprehensively at the audience.

The mayor tapped the council table with the gavel. "Are there any other questions from the council?" he asked as the disruption faded. "From the audience?"

There were none.

The mayor recovered his formal, official tone. "If there are no further questions, do I hear a motion from the council as to action on the engineers' recommendations?"

Weatherbee was first. "I make the motion that the engineers' report be taken under advisement for further study."

"Second the motion," said Wentworth.

The vote was unanimous. Since there were five Tuesdays in the month, the next regular council session was still two weeks away, adequate time, it was decided, for the council to study the lake recommendations. The mayor thanked the engineers, complimented them on the report and the manner in which it was presented, and invited them back for the next session, when the council would take action on the report. He thanked the chamber officials for coming to hear the report. Then he paused.

"I also would like to thank all the ladies for attending tonight." He lowered his head in a coy way Travis had never seen before. "I was going to invite you back to our next session, but I gather you've already been invited."

In the appreciative laughter that followed, the mayor looked at Travis with a self-conscious grin. It was the most droll thing Travis had ever seen the mayor do. Travis smiled back to show he could take a joke. On this note they adjourned.

As the session broke up, most of the councilmen moved down to shake hands with the two engineers and to politic with the chamber executives. Travis crossed around behind the council table to talk to Cal. Berger had left by the back door, and Byron had gone down into the audience, leaving them momentarily alone at the end of the table.

"Well, I believe we won a round tonight," Travis said.

Cal pushed his chair back from the table and stood. In the movement, slow and trembly, Travis saw how fatigued he was. "You mean *you* won a round." Cal laughed. "Two weeks ago I wouldn't have given you a Chinaman's chance, but I'll be damned if I don't believe you're goin' to do it."

"We'll give it the old college try, anyway. How are you feeling?"

"Who's askin'? The friend or the doctor?"

"Both."

"I'll answer the doctor. I feel poorly. Haven't got any strength."

Travis nodded. "Part of that could be emotional reaction, and loss of sleep the last few nights. How about dropping by the house for a nightcap?"

"Now who's askin'? The friend or the doctor?"

"The friend. The doctor would probably tell you to quit drinking."

"In that case, I accept." Cal looked past him to where a circle had formed around the two engineers. "I guess we better go shake hands with that smart-aleck little bastard."

They stepped down from the platform, mingled with what was left of the audience, shaking hands, exchanging idle comments. Finally, they got to the engineers.

"I'm sorry if I gave you a rough time," Travis said to the small, smug one. "I'm the problem child of the council."

The engineer chuckled. "I'm used to politics, Doctor, and I understand. I wish you luck with your project."

"Thank you," Travis said.

The engineers went on out ahead of them, and since Cal had

to go back to the council table for his hat, Travis and Cal were the last to leave the building.

As they walked across the parking lot, the last of the cars were pulling out. Only his car, Cal's pickup truck, and two other vehicles remained—the older cars of custodial employees. But in the far corner of the lot, almost hidden in the shadow of the building, there was a newer, bigger car he didn't recognize. Even while he was wondering about it, the dome light flashed on.

He saw Hartwell entering the car on the driver's side, and at first he thought the girl waiting was Hartwell's daughter. Then he saw that it was an older girl. Just as the dome light went out, he recognized her. BeeBee Milam's younger half-sister, Sharon.

The car started and moved on out into the street on the far side of the parking lot.

Apparently Cal hadn't seen. Maybe his eyes weren't holding out as well as he'd been pretending. No use jumping to conclusions, Travis cautioned himself. Besides, it was none of his business. But he couldn't keep from hoping it wasn't what it appeared to be on the surface.

Surely Hartwell had more sense.

# *Part Four*

## CHAPTER TEN

David drove fast through the night, the car lights making a tunnel in the darkness. Just David, the speeding Cadillac, and the girl on the white, empty highway.

He had no plan and for the moment felt no need of one. There had been tempting thoughts earlier of the border, but he hadn't taken them seriously. Mexico and a hideaway were a good dream, a temptation of the night. At dawn, on some wind-swept plateau north of the Rio Grande, reality would return.

"Where are we going?" she asked.

"Anywhere, nowhere. Where do you want to go?"

"I don't care." She snuggled down against his shoulder, her head resting against his.

An alarm sounded somewhere in the rearmost recesses of his mind: back out, Hartwell. You've goofed, you've made the phone call. But no harm done yet. Turn around. End this before it's too late.

That, too, was just a thought. He held the car on course down the lonesome road. The memory of their last time together was still strong.

Sharon rolled to where her face was against his chest, her arms around his waist, her long legs on the seat.

A Thoroughbred. A Shotgun Milam champion, sired by Thirty-Thirty Milam out of a cultured Boston filly. He had no right to be running around with such valuable property.

He asked her a question that had been troubling him. "With all the young bucks floating around, fine eligible young bachelors, why do I rate in your affections?"

She looked up at him, pondering the answer. "Because you're

a man. A real man, I mean. All the others I've known just try to act like men. Cheap imitations."

"What qualifies me as a man?"

"Now you're teasing me."

"No, I'm not. I really want to know."

She thought some more about that. He tried to study the expression on her face, but there wasn't much light from the dash, and the car demanded too much attention.

"The way other men respect you, listen to you," she said slowly, as if thinking it out as she talked. "The way you're always in control of things, running the whole city."

"At the risk of your affections, I'll let you in on a little secret. I'm sure as hell not in control of things now."

"You will be," she said firmly. "Everyone expects it, and you will be. That's what I mean. You're a leader, and they all know it."

"That's a trick," he told her. "You can learn to handle people the way you put those horses of yours over the jumps."

"No, it's different," she argued. "You couldn't make people like the mayor, those councilmen, the chamber people do what you say unless they respect you, unless they have a high regard for your abilities."

"Or a low regard for their own," he said. He wondered what they—and she—would think of his abilities if they knew the mess he'd let things drift into, and the helplessness he felt at the stalemate in the highway land investigation.

Ahead, the lights of a small town came into view and he slowed. Sharon raised her head from his shoulder and watched. They rode silently through the deserted town. At the far edge, ablaze with neon, was the motel.

He hadn't consciously driven toward it, but he would never make her believe it, now. He looked at her. She was smiling, and when he widened his eyes in question, she nodded.

They drove on beyond the town, made a U-turn, and went back. Shooting the car up the drive, he parked away from the office, yet close enough so the Cadillac could be seen in profile.

The fluorescents of the office were bright after the road, and the room clerk was different this time. A square-built, unsmiling man with a cigar and a bowtie laid down a paperback novel to give David the register. David put down a name and paid the nine dollars in advance.

Then he followed the Negro bellboy to the far end of the court and the upstairs room, luckily out of sight from the office. He gave the bellboy a half dollar.

"Don't bother with the bags. There's only a few, and I'll have to sort out what we'll need."

If the bellboy was wise to the deception, he gave no hint. He acknowledged the tip without enthusiasm and went back to the office.

David walked to the car and drove it across the court to the parking space below the room and they went up. Inside, you could almost imagine it was the same room.

But it was different: the mood was different, and they were different. Before, there had been the adventure, the suddenness, the excitement of the unknown. Now, there was none of this.

Sharon walked across the carpeted floor to the television, and from the movement he realized that she, too, knew the futility of trying to re-create things as they had been. For there had been no television before. The screen came on white. She flicked the channel selector several times, then turned the set off.

"I forgot how late it is," she said.

"Would you like a drink?" he asked. There had been no drinks, either, before.

"I think I would like that very much," she said. "But it's so late. . . ."

"There are ways. But it may take a few minutes, and I hate to leave you alone."

"I'm used to keeping myself entertained."

He walked across the asphalt court to the office and motioned the bellboy over to the door. The clerk looked up briefly, then went back to his paperback novel.

"Any way of getting a fifth of good whiskey this time of night?" David asked the bellboy.

A profitable sideline depended upon the bellboy's ability to recognize a state liquor control board agent. David could almost see his mind working, putting it all together . . . the girl, the big car, no bags.

"Maybe," the bellboy said noncommittally. "Co'se it'll be a

little high, this time of night, but I got a friend might have some. What kind you likes?"

"Any kind of good bourbon." He gave him a ten-dollar bill. "And we'll need some ice and a bottle of mix."

The Negro walked to an old car stashed behind the office, started it, and roared away toward town.

David knew from experience there would be a ten- or fifteen-minute wait. Someone would have to be roused out of bed, and there would be the problem of making change.

He leaned back against the brick wall at the side of the office and waited. He lit a cigarette and thought of the girl, his whole body warm with anticipation. It had been a long time since he'd felt so alive. Once, years ago, there'd been something like that between himself and Helen.

There should be some way, he thought, to warn young people of marriage. There ought to be a way to analyze each person with a computer and say: No, this marriage is not right. In time, love's warmth will cool. These two lives will not progress in the same direction. This marriage should not be.

A problem of engineering. Take two components, test their reactions upon each other, analyze the results. But it wasn't that simple. There were other things—outside elements—hundreds of unforeseen catalysts that would begin to work upon the two personalities involved.

All the factors were there, though, even the outside influences, if one only had the imagination to see them. These factors must have been there from the beginning in his own marriage. There'd been no danger signals on the surface. They had both thought they knew what they wanted out of life—a home, children, a comfortable living. They had much in common—a rural background turned urban by the war, a childhood of hard work, a realistic attitude toward life. They'd looked past the wartime glamour—Randolph Field, the movies with the trainers passing over the field in huge V formations, Keep 'Em Flying, Into the Wild Blue Yonder. . . .

The blame wasn't there. Nor could he find it in his actions in the years since. He'd given her everything he'd promised. But the marriage hadn't worked out. All the potentialities had come down to this: Helen home drunk and he philandering with a girl half his age while dreading tomorrow's appointment with his son's psychiatrist.

A divorce? He'd thought about it many times. Always, there had been the children to consider. Now, the children were growing up. Another three years and most of the home influence would be over—for better or worse.

David studied the window of the motel room, the only one lighted. If he did get a divorce, could he make another start? Others did. Sam McIntosh, the local oil millionaire and department store tycoon, had begun a new life in his late fifties, and a damned good one, too. When Sam's first wife, plain as a mud fence, died of a heart attack, Sam put thirty years of bickering behind him, made a foray into the East, and brought home a New York model half his age. There was no doubt the second marriage was much better than the old one. Sam looked younger every day, and was leading an even more active life. It could be done.

Alcoholism was not grounds for divorce, but there were stories that would sway the mind of any judge . . . the night of Christine's birthday party. Or the time two years ago when they'd fussed at dinner over Helen's drinking and she'd gone upstairs and returned with a loaded shotgun. Only the cross-bolt safety had kept the gun from going off while they struggled for it in front of the hysterical children. Calla Lilly had seen that incident. She could testify he couldn't even keep a gun in the house.

There'd been other incidents, many others. But that alone ought to be enough. . . .

The bellboy's old car came rattling up the motel drive and passed him to turn in behind the office building, where he heard the squeak of ancient brakes. The bellboy had an excellent "friend." Packed in a twenty-pound paper bag was a fifth of good bourbon, a small bag of ice and a bottle of mix.

The bellboy fished in his pocket for change.

"Let's see, the whiskey's six and a half, an' the mix . . ."

David cut him short. "This is fine. Just keep the change."

When he got back to the room, Sharon had the radio going, a Mexican station. She had peeled down the bedspread and blanket and was lying on the topsheet, her shoes off, listening to the radio. She had turned off the overhead light for the indirect lamps on each side of the room. Raising on one elbow as he entered, her long, sorrel hair spread across the pillow behind her, she watched him unload the whiskey and the mix.

"That was fast work," she said.

"As I said, there are ways," he reminded her. "One of the first things a man learns in this world is that when you want liquor or a whore-lady, ask a porter or a taxi driver. If they can't help you, they at least can steer you in the right direction."

"I'll remember that, if I ever need liquor or a whore-lady."

He laughed.

"That's the first time you've laughed tonight."

"First funny thing you've said tonight."

He spread a complimentary newspaper over the dresser to make a semisanitary bar. The motel glasses were sealed in waxed paper and guaranteed sterilized. He had no jigger or swizzle stick. For a man who used to take pride in his mixed drinks, this was a hell of a way to do business. But on a clandestine, midnight date, he supposed, one couldn't be choosy.

The highballs weren't bad, considering. He pulled a chair up alongside the bed, opposite her, shed his coat and tie, and sat facing her so he could see the full bronzed, tawny length of her.

BeeBee Milam must have inherited the worst qualities of Shotgun and Sharon the best. And what she'd inherited, she'd cultivated—a year at an exclusive girls' school in Switzerland, art in Paris, music in Vienna. He had read about her and admired her long before he'd ever seen her—writeups of society balls in Washington, New York, Dallas, San Antonio, of her attending bullfights in Spain, road races in Italy, a steeplechase in England.

"What have you been doing with yourself all this time?" he asked.

"I placed second in the hunter stakes at the Fort Worth Stock Show on Foxy Boy."

"I know. I saw your picture in the paper."

She grimaced. "That was a horrible picture. I'm never going to allow a photograph of me in riding clothes again. I look too masculine."

His laughter at that was so spontaneous she joined in.

"You can't spend all your time riding," he said. "What else do you do?"

She toyed with her drink, rocking the glass from one side to the other, making the ice clink. "I swim, sometimes, in the indoor pool at the club. I read quite a bit, and watch television. And believe it or not, I have a few dates."

"I believe it," he said; he had thought, often, of her out with men . . . younger men. . . .

"I went up to Colorado ten days in January," she went on. "And I've been to Dallas a couple of weekends. But mostly, I'm just bored, bored, bored." She looked up at him suddenly. "Why don't you get me a job up at City Hall? I can type. I would make a good secretary."

He didn't know whether she was joking or not.

"How would we know you weren't a spy for the *News-Gazette*?"

She winced disgustedly. "I'm sure you know more about what goes on down at that newspaper than I do. I haven't even been inside it in six years. I can't even attend board meetings. Father believed business is for men, and that women should . . . well, be women. All executive powers were left to Arthur, and when I go down there I'm treated like a guest."

It took David a moment to realize Arthur was BeeBee's real name. Although he saw the name in the paper all the time, it didn't register, because one always thought of him by his nickname.

"But you did get an equal share, didn't you?" David asked before he realized how personal the question was. "I mean, it would be terribly unfair if . . ."

"Oh, sure, I got an equal share. But you see, everything was all decided before I came along. I was kind of an afterthought. Arthur was out of college and on the board of directors when I was born. Everything was cut and dried. Arthur was to take over the paper, and Father never could readjust his mind to the fact that I'd grow up some day. I was eight when he died."

Atop his favorite paramour, so David had been told. He wondered if Sharon had heard that choice bit of gossip.

"Couldn't you get a lawyer and fight for your rights?" he

asked. "If the stock's in your name, and now that you're of age, I don't see how they could keep you out."

"I guess I could. But Father handed out shares right and left to long-time employees, and once when he got in a pinch he sold some to a banker. Mother willed some of her shares to a younger brother, and Arthur's mother got a cut. It's all sliced up into a lot of pieces. If I split up what we have, nobody would have control. And the paper isn't making much money any more, anyway. If Father hadn't had some other investments, I guess we'd be broke."

The news that the paper wasn't making big money was more surprising to David than anything it'd printed lately. "What's wrong with it? I thought circulation was higher than it's ever been, and it seems jammed with advertising."

"Costs. Newsprint is humpteen times higher, labor is something point something or other higher, and so on. All newspapers are in the same boat, I hear. But mostly, they need my father down there to tell them what to do. They were so used to his making all the decisions nobody left has any initiative. They just stand around like they keep expecting him to get a message through to them on what to do now."

"He must have been quite a guy," David said, thinking of the stories he'd heard.

"Oh, he was," she said enthusiastically. "People just don't know. When he talked everybody listened. The governor used to call him up and ask what he thought about things, what the people up here would think if he did so and so. I'm not kidding. And when he walked into a room, people turned and looked. You just got the idea he was a cut above other men."

Her enthusiasm for the subject left him slightly uncomfortable. He got up to refill the glasses. She seemed to sense his discomfort and changed the topic back to her earlier question. "Seriously, why don't you get me a job at City Hall? Any piddling job, I don't care. I just want to get out on my own and do something."

Handing her the fresh drink, he went around to the other side of the bed, untied his shoes, and sat on the bed, leaning back against the headboard. He sipped his drink while he thought over her request. The idea was probably a passing fancy, but he wasn't certain how he could fend off the request without hurting her. He decided the truth was best.

"You've put me in a position where I'll have to puncture that image of my sitting in my office running the city. I have very little say-so about the hiring of city employees, except the department heads. The personnel office takes care of all applicants."

"Couldn't you recommend me?"

"It would be highly unorthodox, and there'd no doubt be some raised eyebrows. But if you're really interested, why don't you go down to the personnel office and apply? All jobs are prorated as to experience, and they have aptitude tests you'd have to take. The results would be the same whether I said anything or not."

"They wouldn't take me seriously."

"I'm not sure I do either," he admitted.

"There! See?"

"If you need something to do, why don't you insist on your rights in handling some of your family money? Surely that would be far more responsibility and executive power than you could get anywhere else."

"They don't take me seriously either. Besides, I wouldn't be proving myself that way. I just want to be somebody's little secretary, or maybe even a receptionist—you know, to flirt with the callers and keep all the men in a good mood."

He laughed again, confident now that the idea was a toy of the moment. Placing his glass on the night stand, he rolled across the bed, took her by the shoulders, and pulled her against his chest. "Show me how you would flirt."

She finished her drink and placed the empty glass on the other night stand. "Oh, you're just like my father. He said women ought to spend all their time being women."

The remark was unfortunate, for it started a mental process in David.

Locked in each other's arms, they struggled against the limitations of anatomy, clothing, and gravity. And all the time as he approached his ultimate goal, David was thinking.

He remembered how she had compared him to her father all evening. Now that he thought about it, there had been a couple of references to his resemblance the first time they'd been together.

"What's the matter?" she asked.

Her head was nestled down in the pillows, her face in the shadows of her tousled hair. In the dim light, for a moment, she was an older, more mature Christine. All desire left in him froze. He rolled away from her, swung his feet to the floor, and began fumbling with his shoes.

She sat up in bed, alarmed. "What's wrong?"

He answered without looking at her. "It just occurred to me that we're both being very foolish."

In the mirror, then, he could see her fumbling, uncertain, with the topsheet. "What do you mean?"

"I mean get your clothes on. We're going home."

She came to her knees in the middle of the bed, her voice rising. "Look, if you can't make it, that's all right, there'll be another time. But don't take your frustration out on me."

He started to lash back in anger. But the memory of her lying there almost the living image of Christine stopped him. He was in no position to cast stones. And he didn't want to hurt her. "It's nothing like that." He turned to meet her puzzled stare. "Believe me, it takes more of a man to do what I'm doing. Get your clothes on."

Silently, she obeyed. The radio had been playing low, unnoticed. But now it began to grate on his nerves. He went over and turned it off. Sharon went into the bathroom and locked the door behind her.

He put on his suit coat, adjusted his tie, picked up the bottle of whiskey and went down to the car to wait. When she came down the steps a few minutes later he went around the car and opened the door for her. As he got behind the wheel, she was studying his face in the dome light.

"Is it something I've done?"

"No. It's just what I've done to you."

On the way back, she sat on the far side of the seat, and they didn't talk until they were entering the outskirts of town, heading for City Hall and his car.

"Then it's all over between us?" she asked.

"Yes. You have your whole life before you. I have my family.

We have no business jeopardizing our futures for a few minutes of pleasure."

Her mouth opened and closed, but she made no sound. He knew she still did not understand.

His Olds stood in front of City Hall, alone on the deserted street. He had left the lights on in his office so anyone seeing his car would assume he was toiling over the new city budget—which he should be doing. He had gone out the back door and met Sharon in the dark of the parking lot behind the building.

He angled the Cadillac in beside his Olds and left the motor running. "I know you're angry with me now," he said. "But there may be a time you will thank me for what I'm doing."

"I'm not angry. I just don't know what's wrong. First you want me, then you don't. It doesn't make sense."

"I do want you. But there is no way in the world that I could make you happy. There is nothing I could give you but grief. The best thing to do is admit we've both made a mistake."

"If I said that I love you, enjoy being with you more than anyone else I've ever been with, would that make a difference?"

"Yes, it makes a difference. But it only makes me more sure I'm doing the right thing. Can't you see that if I didn't care about you, I could just take the fun and not worry about the consequences?"

"I don't care about the consequences," she said, her voice quavering on the edge of tears.

"I do," he said. "Enough for both of us." He leaned across the seat and kissed her cheek. "Goodbye, Sharon," he said.

She didn't answer. He stepped quickly out of the car, closed the door and walked away.

He was circling behind his car when the Cadillac suddenly came to life, shot backward into the middle of the street, stopped with a squeal of rubber, then roared forward, the tires gnashing the pavement with Sharon's anger. David watched the car picking up speed until it went over the hill toward the freeway, leaving him standing alone in the night.

Almost as an act of penitence, David went up to his desk and worked more than an hour on the new city budget. By then the eastern sky outside his window was beginning to show the first graying of dawn. He was tired, but still not sleepy.

On impulse, he drove out to the airport and had his plane pushed out of the hangar. After two cups of coffee in the terminal to remove the last lingering effects of the whiskey he'd had earlier, he put the plane into the air.

Again, as he had many times, he watched the new day come upon the sleeping city. Usually he liked to see the freeways and service roads gradually fill with inbound traffic and the downtown parking lots change from blocks of asphalt and pavement to squares of shimmering chrome.

Today he had a different inclination. He turned the plane toward the open country to the west.

In that direction the ranchlands flattened out, the mesquite, prickly pear, and soapweed thinned, leaving wide pastures of lush grass and grazing Herefords. David throttled back and lost altitude so he could inspect the ground better.

When he came to the river he turned upstream, following its path, mostly, cutting across only a few of the stream's more violent meanders. Then, as he came over the Masters Ranch, he dropped even lower. He didn't take his eyes from the steep clay bluffs to check his airspeed or altimeter. He flew by the seat of his pants, watching the topography of the river, pulling up to miss the red tentacles of earth that reached up at him, then going down again over the long sandbars where the riverbanks were eroded away. He felt a strange exhilaration. He hadn't flown this recklessly in years.

At the sharp bend of the river he turned away from the stream and crossed Cal's big pasture. The Herefords had bedded down around the salt lick for the night and now were grazing out fanwise in the morning sun. As he zoomed low over the herd, the cattle raised their heads in unison, seeking the source of the strange sound, and some of the calves started running and bucking, kicking their heels out behind them. David laughed, banked, and made another run over them. But this time some of the grown Herefords went into an awkward trot, scattering to escape the sound. So David quit his game with the calves. He didn't want to run the fat off Cal's steers.

He gained more altitude for the run over the ranchhouse. The old pickup wasn't alongside the house, indicating Cal had spent the night at his place in town. As David passed over the bull trap below the corral, he saw a figure on horseback rein in and watch him fly over. Knowing it must be one of Cal's hired hands, David rocked the plane, wiggling the wings. The rider swept off his hat and waved.

Again, as he often had in the past, David considered liquidating all his assets and buying a spread something like Cal's. He had managed to run the inheritance from the Oklahoma farm into more than a hundred thousand dollars, he estimated. There was nothing he'd like better than to put the whole wad into a good ranch.

That might be enough capital, with his sound reputation, to get bank financing for the rest he'd need for what he had in mind—he didn't want any poor-boy setup. But his business sense told him there was no good justification from the financial standpoint. He would be going from a secure, money-in-the-bank existence into a precarious, mortgaged venture. Good paying ranches were rarely for sale. And taking an average ranch and turning it into an operation like Cal's took years.

Still, he liked the idea. The change from his office and its vast responsibilities to rural relaxation would be tremendous and welcome. A little hard work might give Ronnie some confidence in himself and remove that hang-dog look. Christine liked to ride, and once, long ago, when he'd confided his long-ranged dream to Helen, she'd expressed a nostalgia for the country scenes and smells of her girlhood.

There was one other big drawback: the city manager job was too time-consuming. There was no way he could continue making twenty thousand a year while he got spudded in on the ranching business.

He flew back to the airport and landed, then drove home for a shower and fresh clothes. All things considered, he still didn't feel too bad. He'd always been able to get by without much sleep. In college, he'd sometimes averaged only four or five hours a night for weeks. Before examinations he often had stayed up all night studying. But today, as the hours passed, he began to suspect age was catching up with him.

By three in the afternoon, time for his meeting with Ronnie's psychiatrist, he was so tired and sleepy he thought of making some excuse and postponing the appointment. Only his curiosity to learn what the doctor had discovered kept him on his feet.

For a man who charged in the vicinity of twenty dollars an hour, Dr. Fishbein was surprisingly relaxed and easygoing. He met David in the reception room and stood chatting pleasantly about the weather, the day's headlines, and the possibilities of war. Finally he led the way through his medical suite to his office in the far corner, still talking about the Russians.

"They're bluffing," he said. "If we'll just stand up to them again, like we did on Cuba, or in the Berlin airlift, they'll back down. Don't you think so?"

Half-listening, David said he supposed they would. He had no strong feelings on the subject. He'd never been to Cuba, but he'd seen Berlin from the air three times. All he remembered about it was that the flak wasn't nearly as bad as Hamburg or Cherbourg or Hanover, and the last time they'd gotten two ME-410s, new ones so fresh from the factory they had no paint.

He followed the doctor into the corner office. For a man who must gross close to a hundred and fifty a day, Fishbein didn't have much overhead. The suite was small—a reception room, his office, and two tiny side rooms. Only one of the side rooms had the traditional couch.

The office, too, was plainly furnished—just a desk, two chairs, diplomas, and a wartime picture of some officers standing in front of a turret on a battleship or heavy cruiser. The picture was too far away to see the faces, but David recognized the doctor's square build.

"I can't keep from believing the horrible weapons we've got now will scare nations away from war," the doctor said. "But of course that's what we thought the last time. Were you in the war?"

David nodded. "Air Corps," he said.

"Pilot?"

David nodded again. "B-17s."

"Which theater?"

"Europe. Eighth Air Force."

"I was in the Pacific myself," the doctor said. "Navy Medical Corps."

David felt a wave of irritation. At twenty dollars an hour, Fishbein already had talked about five dollars' worth.

"About Ronnie," he said insistently, knowing he was being rudely blunt. "Is it anything serious?"

Just a flicker of interest behind the doctor's steel-rimmed glasses made David suspect the rambling chatter hadn't been pointless. Suddenly he felt he had been undergoing some sort of a test of his tensions, his threshold of irritation. This suspicion was increased when the doctor's manner changed abruptly to a more businesslike tone.

"I'll put you at ease right off about Ronnie's mind. As far as I can tell, he's a normal, growing boy, with normal, healthy anxieties."

"Then what made him do what he did?"

Dr. Fishbein rubbed his stiff, iron-gray crewcut. "There's no easy answer to that. But let me explain what we've learned so far. As I told you, these first two two-hour sessions were diagnostic. I've given him a series of tests, none significant alone, but taken over-all, they give us a definite pattern. Ronnie's act was not the result of anything, but symptomatic of a deep-seated insecurity."

In his tired condition, David was growing confused. "I thought you said he was normal."

There was only the slightest hesitancy before the doctor answered.

"I did. But it's impossible to isolate each individual. Whether we like it or not, our personalities are made up largely of our environment, molded by persons around us. Now, take a normal boy, put him in an abnormal situation, and before long the situation is going to wear on the boy's normalcy. You follow me?"

"You mean Ronnie's mother should be getting the treatment, not Ronnie."

Fishbein's reaction was emphatic.

"No. I certainly did not say that at all. I'm in no way qualified at this point to comment on your family situation. All I know is that from two brief talks with Ronnie and the results of this series of tests, I see the effects of some disturbing influence in his life. Family counseling is out of my line. I deal almost solely in personality disorders. To put it briefly, Ronnie has a strong feeling of insecurity at a crucial period in his life, right when he's striving to become an adult."

"His mother is an alcoholic," David said. "I don't know if I could get her to come down for treatment or not."

"I won't accept an alcoholic as a patient," Fishbein said, his tone hardening. "Not unless one comes to me of his own free will, without any pressure from family or friends, because otherwise, it's just a waste of my time and his money. There's something in an alcoholic's life that makes him drink. Unless he wants to quit badly enough, or that cause is removed, there's little chance."

"But you do think Helen's drinking is the cause of Ronnie's trouble?"

"Please, I said I'm in no position to comment. But one thing is significant to me. That is Ronnie's motive for what he did. He didn't say so right out, understand, and he's not aware of it himself, probably. But I pieced it together from several things he said. He was curious—curious as to what goes on in other families."

"You mean sexual relations?"

"No, nothing like that. He could hear through the open windows of that house. He was curious as to the role of the father, the role of the mother, the role of the children in the family. He was eavesdropping, not peeping."

David couldn't make his mind absorb this new line of thought. "What can I do about it?" he asked.

"I'll recommend a family counselor. I see no reason why I should see Ronnie again, unless there are other serious, overt acts. I think you should tighten your discipline on him, know where he is at all times, that sort of thing, and give him mild punishment—confining him to his room or something—when he misbehaves. Believe it or not, that will help ease his feeling of insecurity."

"I can't be at home as much as I probably should be, but I will try," David said.

"I also believe you should have your family relationships thoroughly evaluated. There's nothing I can do for Ronnie now. If you should fail in correcting this situation, and a crippled personality should begin manifesting itself in some strange ways five or ten years from now, he will be the type of patient in which I specialize. But right now, there's nothing wrong with him that you can't correct through proper parental procedure."

David thanked him, took the name of the family counselor, and left, knowing the gesture was useless. A marriage counselor couldn't cure a drunk either.

## CHAPTER ELEVEN

By virtue of an eleven-hour day covering the special council session Tuesday, Tom was released from work three hours early the next day so the newspaper wouldn't have overtime pay added to its many other financial burdens.

Ordinarily, he looked forward to this time off with high anticipation, for it meant an evening with Arlene—a drive-in movie, beer, and dancing at some night spot, or best of all, drinks and records in her apartment. But now, on the second night after their breakup, just when the full impact of his loss was beginning to hit him, he had a whole evening to himself to think about what he'd be doing if it hadn't happened.

He avoided J. Marvin Olds at dinner. He didn't want to be reminded of the usual threesome. He had no inclination to hang around the newspaper and watch it being ground out without him, nor did he desire to squander a perfectly good spring evening in his apartment. So in one of the few instances in his life, he premeditatedly and with malice aforethought set out to get drunk.

For some inexplicable reason, he started his quest with six beers at Joe Garzek's Longhorn Lounge. This was a mistake. Garzek's sad face and empty establishment only compounded his misery. Here was another of Tom Kencaide's failures.

Once again he drilled Garzek in the use of the tape recorder hidden behind the bar. Garzek was practically devoid of mechanical ability, and even the push-button controls confused him. Tom wished now he had hunted around for an easy-to-operate model, even at the expense of performance. He led Garzek through the step-by-step procedure of walking down the bar and starting the tape recorder without being obvious about it.

"And try to get their names, or some admission of who they

work for," Tom told him. "I talked to the district attorney again, and he said that although the tape wouldn't be admissible in court, any information we can get will help in an investigation."

"I don't think they come back, anyway," Garzek said ruefully, looking at his deserted tavern. "They already done what they want."

"Sure they'll be back," Tom assured him, voicing an enthusiasm he didn't feel. "And when they come, we'll be ready for them. You just remember what to do."

"I remember," Garzek said. "But I don't think they come."

Tom tried to cheer him up. Tomorrow, he promised Garzek sincerely after his sixth beer, he would call up that sonabitchin' Berger and rake him over the coals. There were some mighty pertinent questions still unanswered, Tom confided to Garzek, and he was just the man to ask them.

Garzek seemed on the verge of tears again, and Tom began to fear he might join in any weeping, so he left.

Restlessly, he drove back uptown.

Beer was far too weak for his thirst tonight. He stopped at a liquor store and was searching for economy priced bourbon when he happened to notice an aisle display of flyspecked, marked-down rum. Good Puerto Rican rum, now well-aged in the bottle, unappreciated by these *Norte Americanos.* He bought a fifth. Then, while the clerk was making change, he went back and got another, shrewd in the knowledge this was a real bargain.

At the Corral Drive-in restaurant, across the train viaduct from town, he ordered a pint of fountain Coke, sipped some to make room, then added rum for a king-sized drink which proved a powerful companion for six beers.

He sat behind the wheel of Old Smokey for a while and tortured himself with speculation about what Arlene would be doing at the moment. She was probably out with some public relations man, he figured, some "information specialist" in a Brooks Brothers suit, dining at a swank restaurant or dancing at some private club.

If that's what she wants, he thought bitterly, she's welcome to it. He'd seen that type glad-handing about the office, and many times he'd dealt with them. He couldn't do that kind of work. He was no hail-fellow-well-met. Glad-handing wasn't his nature, and he was damned glad of it.

What hurt was Arlene's evaluation that he wasn't a success. Everybody else thought he was a good reporter, damn it. He had plenty of prizes and awards they didn't hand out to just anybody. He had always considered himself a top newspaperman, and even had been a little bit proud of it. Never in the depths of his most frustrated moments had he considered changing professions.

But now, as the rum began to tingle the more sensitive fibers of his brain, he began to be plagued by nagging doubts. He had a high opinion of Arlene's intelligence, and she said he was wrong. J. Marvin Olds, who'd apparently been through something like this himself, seemed to have regrets that he'd chosen to stick with his newspaper career.

Tom sat and watched the wiggly-tailed carhops and wondered if he *was* wrong. He wanted Arlene for his wife, and he guessed he should be thinking of ways to make her happy.

But public relations? Never.

He considered advertising. Again, that was something he couldn't imagine himself doing. The gap between news and advertising was too wide.

The difficulty was plain: He had grown into adulthood with the newspaper as a father-fixation, and he knew nothing else—except soldiering.

He remembered that the newspaper had been just a job, at first—work and money for a lean, hungry thirteen-year-old from lower Main who needed shoes and clothes for school. Someone had told him they needed boys in the mailing room on Saturday nights. He'd had enough sense to lie about his age and they'd hired him.

Later, when he heard of a carrier route open, he applied, this time lying not only about his age, but also about having a bicycle. After he'd badgered them for several weeks, he got a route.

The newspaper route had been his first real taste of independence. He no longer had to hunt up his father in a bar when he needed money and risk public refusal.

He was fifteen when he won the circulation contest. That was in the days of Thirty-Thirty Milam. Tom had worked hard, building his route, and was awarded top prize in the contest for the highest rate of circulation per block, the most efficiently run route, and the fewest complaints from customers.

The prize had been a trip to Washington, and he was to "send back his impressions" of the nation's capital by Western Union, press rates. This responsibility staggered him more than the news of winning the contest. Before the trip, he read all he could find on the capital and points of interest. On the tour, he was one of the few to take the dispatches seriously. His research showed through. The stories had the sincere quality of a talented, impressionable boy seeing his nation's capital for the first time.

On his return he got word that Thirty-Thirty wanted to see him. He still remembered that brief conversation with the flamboyant, leather-lunged publisher.

"You the boy that wrote those stories from Washington?" Milam demanded, his slate eyes fixed on Tom.

"Yes, sir."

Milam looked like the legend he was . . . dapper clothes, gold-headed cane, heavy watch chain, mustache.

"Good stories," Milam said. "What do you want to be when you become a man?"

"A writer," Tom said. He'd never before made this admission to an adult.

Milam had looked at him so fiercely that Tom feared for a moment he had sounded too brash. But Milam seemed to admire his conviction. "Good. How would you like to be a writer some day on my newspaper?"

"I'd like that very much, sir."

"Good, good," Milam said. "Come with me."

He took Tom out into the city room and introduced him to Houston Collier, and Tom had started his journalistic career as a copy boy. His time spent reading Kipling, London, Hemingway, Faulkner, Wolfe, and others soon paid off. They started letting him do two-and-three-paragraph stories and found he had a way with words.

It was only natural when he came back from the war with the GI Bill and college waiting that he'd majored in journalism.

Since then, there'd been other papers, other jobs, but this was home. . . .

He finished the rum and Coke and ordered another pint. Suddenly, he realized this was his first solitary drunk. The knowledge went against the grain. Even his father, Pepper Kencaide, one of the most accomplished drunkards in lower Main's past, never drank alone.

Climbing out of Old Smokey, Tom went to a phone booth at the corner of the building, dialed the police station, and asked the dispatcher to put a Code Fifty-two, Corral Drive-in, on the radio for J. Marvin Olds. There was a radio in the staff car to monitor police calls, and sometimes they sent messages to J. Marvin that way. As Tom got back into Old Smokey, he remembered that they monitored police calls in the office, too, and Houston Collier would know Code Fifty-two meant "meet a party." Well, to hell with Collier.

Two police cars passed in the next three minutes, curious as to who wanted J. Marvin at the Corral Drive-in. One of the officers waved when he recognized Tom, but they didn't stop. They must have thought J. Marvin was fooling around with some waitress. Nosy cops.

J. Marvin wasn't too far behind them. He drove unerringly alongside Old Smokey and stopped. Tom transferred his bottles to the staff car, knowing J. Marvin would be reluctant to leave the radio. J. Marvin looked at him poker-faced and shook his head.

"I had a premonition of this. I presume you're the party I'm supposed to meet."

Tom held up the rum. "Here's the party," he said. He confessed to the terrific bargain he'd found.

J. Marvin examined one of the labels and sniffed experimentally. "Not bad for mouthwash. But I gather you're actually drinking the stuff. How do you feel?"

"A shame you're still on duty and so critical," Tom said. "I was about to suggest you share this windfall with me."

"On such a dull night, there is no duty, and my taste buds were dulled on bathtub gin while you were wearing rompers." He pointed to the pint cup. "Are you cutting it, or drinking it straight?"

Tom tapped the horn and ordered two more pints of Coke. J. Marvin waited while he parked Old Smokey beside the building, out of the service area. Then they started cruising around in the staff car.

J. Marvin wasn't wrong about it being a dull night. There wasn't an armed robbery, wreck, anything all evening.

"Hell, let's go down to The Cave and see if we can't stir up some life," Tom said after the final edition went in. That, too, was a mistake.

The Cave was the last remnant of the coffeehouses that hit town during the beatnik era. It was in the basement of a downtown liquor store, and usually came to life about the time the rest of the town's nightspots closed. But tonight only a dozen regulars made the scene.

For the customers The Cave served various coffees and a more popular drink laced with rum extract. For insiders—and the newspaper staff was considered such—the bearded proprietor served from a pitcher liberally spiked with 180-grain alcohol, compliments of the house. Texas law forbid sale by the drink in public places, but there was no law to prevent giving a drink away.

Most nights a jazz combo held forth, the audience stretched out on cushions. And sometimes, when the mood was right and the crowd receptive, the doors were bolted from the inside and the beatchick waitresses took turns in a strip show.

A shooting and two knifings had given The Cave an aura of evil, but Tom had heard fine poetry read to an appreciative audience, and the music was often original and exciting.

But tonight the moon was in the wrong phase, or something. A bearded folksinger in a Mexican poncho was stuck on plaintive ballads of unrequited love. He had drifted into town from San Antonio a week ago. He had a soft, true voice and an impressive repertoire of Child. He was good, but awfully sad. His songs weren't very conducive toward Tom's forgetting his own troubles. In fact, they led him into some realistic thinking. . . .

He knew he'd never find another girl who fit into his life as well as Arlene. Not just anyone possesses a disposition harmonious with newspaper people.

It wasn't that the newspaper staff was a clique. Others had

been invited to the parties over the years, but things didn't work out. The little theater group had been too exhibitionistic, officials from the news beats too staid or currying, the TV and radio staffs too talkative. . . .

But Arlene had fit in, right from the first. That should prove something.

The singer's dismal ballads began to wear on Tom's misery. He kept remembering all the wonderful times he'd had here with Arlene.

"Let's get to hell out of here," he said to J. Marvin finally. "I can't take any more of this."

They bought a six-pack of Coke at an all-night grocery and went to Tom's place.

His landlord had built the garage apartment to live in while building a house. But for some reason or another, he never got around to the house. Now the apartment sat alone on the back of an empty corner lot. The tract next door was empty, too, and the one across the street, leaving Tom with what was probably the biggest residential parking facilities in town.

The remoteness made the apartment ideal for parties, and Tom had been host—both welcome and unwelcome—to most of the staff blowouts.

J. Marvin got out of the car and went on up the steps ahead of Tom like it was his second home. Tom followed at his slower pace, vowing once again to move some day to a ground-floor layout.

J. Marvin waited on the landing. Tom unlocked the door and pushed it open for J. Marvin to go in. It swung too far and collided with the bucket of bones behind it.

"What in hell's that?" J. Marvin asked.

Tom fumbled for the light switch. "That's the Indian," he explained. With his foot, he shoved the bucket farther into the corner. He'd gotten into a series of buried treasure stories last fall. All he'd found was this skeleton in a dry wash—a Comanche, judging from the copper ornaments.

"I forgot about your roommate, or I wouldn't have intruded," Olds said. He leaned over the bucket and peered into it. "Ever decide what in hell you're going to do with him?"

Tom put the Cokes on the drainboard of his kitchenette and

went to the refrigerator for ice. "I don't know," he said. "Bury him somewhere, I guess. I thought some museum would want him, but they don't."

J. Marvin prowled through Tom's bookshelves while Tom mixed the drinks. Then, for a while, they sat and regaled each other with tales of other places, other newspapers—the stories they'd covered, the people they'd known.

Inevitably, though, they fell to discussing BeeBee Milam and the sad state of their present newspaper. Tom confessed that he had been considering the idea of changing jobs.

Tom was drunk, but he wasn't so far gone he didn't notice the effect of liquor on Olds—a slight inclination for more talk, a little more tendency to use his years as a vantage point for profundities. J. Marvin seized on Tom's admission instantly. "Way I see it, the newspaper has deserted you. It's the one that's changed, not you," he argued. "If I were you, I'd quit tomorrow."

Tom wasn't so drunk that he could be tricked by sneaky logic. "I ought to do what I can to keep things from going to hell," he protested.

J. Marvin made a sound that could have been either a snort of disgust or a dirty word. "How many stories have you dug up on your own time in the last year and had BeeBee Milam kill them before they got in the paper?"

They got bitter for a while, then, thinking about all the unprinted stories, most of them common knowledge around town in gossipy circles: the $12,000 stolen out of the United Fund office and subsequent halt of police investigation, the YMCA director fired because his interest in boys was too physical, the First National Bank cashier charged with misapplication of funds, the city judge forced to resign when his friendship with prostitutes and lenient fines became suspect, the funeral home sued for picking up a more-profitable body at a wreck scene and leaving a badly injured man, the local legislator—well-known in Austin for his absenteeism and scrapes with women—being named corespondent in a Methodist minister's divorce suit. . . .

"There's an old sayin' that you'll never be completely happy on a newspaper until you own one," J. Marvin expounded. "And I would proudly donate my left testicle to the cause of forming an opposition publication to run BeeBee Milam out of the profession."

It was a remark that Tom had heard, in one form or another, more than a hundred times. A competitive newspaper was an old, wistful subject around town. There'd even been a move in that direction a few years ago by a group of moneyed residents. But after an investment-profit study the idea was quietly dropped.

Now, the idea suddenly ignited in Tom's fertile, alcohol-fueled mind. "Somebody could, you know," Tom said, seizing the thought excitedly. "There are plenty of people in this town with money, and there are plenty of them that hate Milam enough to go all-out."

J. Marvin didn't understand what he meant. He gave Tom a scornful glance. "It'd take a million dollars to put in a newspaper big enough to compete with Milam. Anybody that's got that kind of money is a businessman. And no businessman's goin' into the publishin' game the way it is these days."

"I'm not talking about competing," Tom hurried to explain. "I'm talking about a little weekly, covering like a blanket all the news Milam ignores. Nothing except the local scene, reported in depth."

"Still take money," J. Marvin insisted. From the way he slurred the words, Tom knew J. Marvin was getting drunk.

"Not as much as you'd think," Tom said, his mind racing ahead with startling agility as the vast potentialities of the idea unraveled. "You'd be surprised how little a good offset, tabloid-sized newspaper would cost."

"Fifty to a hundred thousand," J. Marvin guessed, still not understanding.

"No, I'm not figuring on buying a whole damn publishing plant," Tom explained. "We wouldn't want any equipment. That'd be the beauty of it. All capital would go into production. We could get a commercial shop to print it for a few hundred dollars a week. That way there'd be no overhead except a little office, a telephone, and the printing bill."

"That bill'd be more'n a few hundred dollars," J. Marvin insisted.

"Six hundred at the most," Tom said adamantly. "I know. I got stuck putting out a post newspaper for a while in the Army, and it was printed by a civilian plant. Our bill never ran more'n five, six hundred, and that was with enameled paper. Printing may have gone up since then, but for a cheaper grade paper, it shouldn't run higher than five or six hundred now."

"What about income? I trust this would be a profitable enterprise."

"Advertising. There's hardly a store in town that hasn't had trouble with Milam's horsy ad salesmen. Arlene knows every advertising director in town, and I bet she could drum up plenty of welcome for a new outlet. She'd know how to manage that end of it."

"If you just knew how to manage Arlene," J. Marvin said wryly.

Tom had temporarily forgotten about that. J. Marvin had him there. And before he could think up a suitable reply J. Marvin threw another wrench into his plans. "There's also the problem of circulation, even with a throw-away."

Tom straightened him out on terminology. "It wouldn't be a throw-away. People don't respect what they don't pay for." He thought about the problem for a moment. "We could do it by subscriptions and newsstand sales—a circulation of seven or eight thousand would be pretty good for a weekly, and there are at least that many people in this town that'd like to know what's going on."

J. Marvin thought it over. "Might be done," he said grudgingly. "But it'd take a financial angel and plenty of work."

While J. Marvin went to the bathroom, Tom got up to refill their glasses, jubilant he'd finally gotten an admission out of J. Marvin that the plan was a good one. He got the last ice tray from the refrigerator and braced a knee against the cabinet for support as he knocked the cubes out onto the sinktop. A few stuck and he banged them out with the small ball-peen hammer he kept handy for the purpose. In manhandling the tray, he knocked an empty Coke bottle off the sinktop to the floor. He didn't feel capable of bending over to pick it up. He kicked it into a corner so it wouldn't constitute a hazard.

"Why don't we try it?" he asked enthusiastically when J.

Marvin returned. "We might even get it going on the side in our spare time. Then, if BeeBee wants to fire us, well and good."

The trip to the bathroom had sobered J. Marvin somewhat. He grinned tolerantly. "All right. You want to start tonight, or wait till tomorrow?"

With indignation, Tom suddenly realized that J. Marvin thought this was liquor talk, just another bull session on the many injustices of BeeBee Milam. "I'm serious," Tom insisted. "I'm going to do it, and I can find somebody else to help me if you don't want to. It's a damned good idea."

J. Marvin seemed slightly embarrassed to be associated with a drunk who got so carried away by whims. He looked at his watch and yawned. "It's past two," he said. "I got to go home and get some sleep."

Tom protested that there was still almost half a bottle of rum left. They argued for a while, and when it became apparent J. Marvin was leaving despite the rantings of his host, Tom asked for a ride back to the Corral Drive-in to get Old Smokey.

J. Marvin refused, claiming Tom was too far gone to be out driving. So they argued a while about that. Finally, Tom let him go, not because he was convinced J. Marvin was right, but because his feelings were injured by the implication he couldn't hold his liquor.

After J. Marvin drove off, Tom had no inclination to go to bed. He was too worked up over the weekly idea. Then too, it didn't seem right to leave Old Smokey at the drive-in all night. If he slept late, it might be mistaken for an abandoned car and towed away.

He called a taxi and went back to the darkened drive-in. As he got out of the cab his feet didn't work right and he stumbled, grabbing the door for support.

"You sure you're all right, buddy?" the driver asked. Tom assured him he was. The driver shrugged and drove off.

At the moment, Tom was almost as intoxicated with the excitement of the newspaper idea as he was with rum. He began to wonder what Arlene would think about it.

The clock in the drive-in window said two thirty-five. If Arlene had been out with that public relations guy, he reasoned, she'd probably be getting home about now. Some of those country-club dances didn't break up until one-thirty or two, and then everybody went to a pancake house for breakfast. Yep, she might be just getting home. He fished in his pockets for a dime and went to the phone booth at the corner of the building and dialed.

For a girl who'd been out dancing all night, Arlene's voice sounded suspiciously sleepy.

"Oh, hell, did I wake you?" Tom asked apologetically. "I figured that guy had just about got you home."

"What guy? What are you talking about?"

She was being coy, he decided, so he ignored the question. "I got a terrific idea," he told her. "I got to see you."

The line was silent for a moment.

"Are you drunk?" Arlene demanded.

He cleverly evaded the query. But his voice betrayed his pride in the nimble brainwork. "Drunkenness is a relative term."

She sounded angry now. "I've always said there's nothing more despicable than a man who gets drunk and calls a girl up in the middle of the night."

Indignation made him turn the full force of devastating logic upon her. "I'm calling you about this good idea. It just happens that I have had a few drinks. The two facts are completely unrelated."

"Where are you?" she asked in a voice too patronizing to be sincere.

He told her.

"Go home and get some sleep," she said. "You can call me tomorrow if you still feel so inclined."

"No, I got to see you tonight," he insisted.

"What's this big idea about?"

"It's so secret I can't divulge it over the phone."

"Be a good boy, Tom. Go home."

"Please," he pleaded. "Pretty please?"

There was another moment of silence on the line, and in that interval Tom knew he'd won.

"All right, you can come over for a little while. It's obvious you're in no condition to be roaming the streets. I'll put a gallon of coffee on."

The lights were on in her apartment when he arrived, but

there was a long wait after he rang the bell. When she finally came to the door she was wearing a duster and no make-up. Her hair was loose, hanging full length down past her shoulders. She glanced at him coolly.

"If you're not a hell of a sight," were her words of greeting. She let him in and closed the door behind him. "Pour yourself onto the couch. I'll get the coffee."

The electric coffeemaker was perking intimately in the small kitchen. He watched her pad noiselessly toward it in the slippers he had given her last Christmas. Then he relaxed on the couch, listening to the clatter as she got the cups and saucers. With the lights, familiar surroundings, and a sober hostess, Tom began feeling a little foolish.

In less than a minute the perking stopped and Tom knew the red light had come on. Then Arlene came in with the coffee.

"I'm sorry about waking you," he said. "And I shouldn't have come over."

"No apologies necessary. I was wrong a while ago on the phone. There is one thing worse than a drunk who wants to see his girl in the middle of the night, and that's the girl who has so little backbone she lets him."

"I'm beginning to feel like a heel."

"You better save all your feelings for in the morning. I would imagine you're going to need all you've got. Who helped you get into this shape? Surely you didn't manage it all by yourself."

"J. Marvin stayed with me for a while. But he chickened out when the going got rough."

"I should have known. Well, what is this grand scheme you two cooked up?"

She sat on the couch beside him, near yet discreetly aloof, and listened as he explained the whole idea. As he talked, he began to get excited again. The deeper he delved into the type of coverage he planned, the better it sounded. Now, talking to Arlene, he thought of stories he and J. Marvin had missed in their discussion—stories that would have the right tone for a first issue: The way Negroes were buying into sections where elderly, retired white people lived, and the bitterness and harsh words that should not be ignored. BeeBee Milam had issued orders that nothing be written on the situation. But Tom couldn't keep from thinking that some reporting in depth, giving the views of those involved, quoting words of caution from leaders of both factions, would help each race understand the other's views better.

There was the suppressed federal housing story. One after the other, most of the big apartment house projects in town had failed. The government, backer of the mortgages, was now the biggest landlord in town. The rate of foreclosures under FHA and VA financing had also been high. Milam, at the request of the realtors, hadn't used the story because it didn't "present a true picture of the over-all economy."

He thought of other unprinted stories the public should know about . . . the new school building where the roof leaked and the walls cracked in the first year . . . the gravel that disappeared from county construction . . . the way criminal cases handled by certain law firms never seemed to come to trial. . . .

With the encouragement of his enrapt audience, Tom went on into the financial aspects of the venture. He asked Arlene what she thought of the advertising possibilities. She was hesitant.

"It might take a while. Most of the big stores are run on a close, strict budget, and the advertising managers couldn't change their media or make allowance for a new outlet overnight. But I think most of them would do all they could to help. In smaller stores, where such decisions are usually made on the spur of the moment, I think some Milam competition would be greeted with open arms."

"If I could swing the financing, would you handle the advertising?"

"Am I being propositioned to change jobs?"

"I'm proposing marriage to you for about the twenty-sixth time—and this time as a working partner. You say you want to keep on working. All right, I'm being generous. I'm compromising. I'll let you use your talents to make me rich instead of Sam McIntosh and his department store. Besides, the newspaper wouldn't be able to match your salary."

She started to say something, then hesitated.

"We're talking business," she said firmly. "Let's stay on the subject. How much capital would it take?"

"I don't know. Five to ten thousand, probably. If it can't be done on that, it can't be done at all."

"I've got about twelve hundred in a savings account. Maybe we could borrow enough from a bank."

He was encouraged by her use of the plural pronoun, but her thinking wasn't very practical.

"No, the money would all be working capital," he explained. "If we went bust, the bank wouldn't have anything to foreclose on, not even office furniture. We've got to find a financial angel, somebody that'd like the idea of going in with us as a silent partner."

"Ten thousand is petty cash to some people around here. Surely you can find someone."

The coffee was beginning to take the edge off his exhilaration. In the light of his three hundred and fifty-nine dollars in the credit union, he began to feel less temerity about dashing out and raising ten thousand.

"Who?" he asked. "I don't know anyone who might be interested, and if I did, I wouldn't know how to approach him. I don't think I'd have enough nerve."

"Don't talk that way," she said. "If you could just find the right person, getting the capital would be the easiest part of it. You would be contributing something more valuable than money—all your years of experience, your established reputation as a newspaperman."

"But I'm not a businessman. What kind of an arrangement would I ask for—fifty-fifty split on profits? Forty-sixty?"

"Don't you know anyone who could advise you?"

One person came to mind immediately.

"Hartwell. He has plenty of contacts, and he is an expert in investments, I understand."

"Could you trust him?"

"Sure."

"You would want to pick the right time to talk to him about it. Maybe you could take him out to dinner or something."

That line of thought made him remember. "We're going out to the proposed lake site this afternoon. I think we'll be alone. That might be a good time."

She agreed.

He began to get sleepy then. The coffee had taken full effect and the let-down was rapid. But he wanted to get one thing straight before he went home.

"What about my twenty-sixth proposal?"

"That wasn't exactly the most romantic one."

"I guess all my eloquence was expended on the first twenty-five."

"Maybe it's your ardor that's faded."

"You know better."

"I've led you on a long, not-so-merry chase. I haven't been fair with you at all. It would serve me right if you don't feel as deeply toward me now as you used to."

Even in his drowsiness, he could see that she was sincerely concerned. He tried to reassure her. "Arlene, ever since that first night we went out together, I've never wanted anyone else for my wife. I've been going crazy the last few days, thinking I'd lost you."

"I know," she said. "I was afraid to leave the apartment . . . afraid you might call and I wouldn't be here."

He marshaled his dwindling strength, took her by the shoulders, and pulled her toward him. Then he used his weight and the momentum to take her on down, full-length on the couch. She protested only feebly as he hovered over her.

"Arlene, I love you. If I can swing this deal, will you marry me?"

"Let's don't put it on such a commercial basis. I'll marry you, whether you swing the deal or not."

His sluggish mind couldn't adjust to the rapidly changing situation. He didn't know whether they were going back to the yes-I'll-marry-you-sometime status or to something more definite.

"When?" he asked.

"Anytime you say. I know when I'm licked. I'm through struggling."

He kissed her, but his remaining strength was fading fast. She seemed to understand, and pulled him down beside her. They lay stretched on the couch, bodies touching, her head resting on his chest.

"I don't understand it," he said. "You refuse to marry me as long as I have a good, secure job. But when I start talking about going out and starving to death, you change your mind."

"I told you, the job has nothing to do with it. I've just come to my senses or taken leave of them. I don't know which yet."

"A weekly wouldn't be much of a money-maker," he warned. "Even at best, it might be no more than a good living."

"I don't care about money. I just want to see you be somebody—something other than BeeBee Milam's errand boy."

He started to make a witty reply, but before he got the first word out he forgot what it was. While his mind fumbled for the thought, he closed his eyes to concentrate.

That was a mistake. For with Arlene cuddled in his arms, he rudely went to sleep.

The sun streaming in through the venetian blinds and onto his face woke him just before noon. He had a few orientation problems as consciousness returned—such as who he was, where he was and how he came to be there. Instead of feeling better once these hurdles were cleared, he felt worse.

It was bad enough to go to a girl's apartment in the middle of the night, but certainly no man with an ounce of sportsmanship would still be there at noon the next day.

Painfully, he attempted to get up. As he threw back the thin blanket over him, he discovered that Arlene had removed his shirt and trousers. She hadn't known what to do about the mechanical parts of his feet. She'd left them on, and now the fittings itched. He found his shirt and trousers hung neatly over the back of a chair and wrestled into them. Then, calling Arlene's name, he searched through the apartment.

He was alone. She must have left for work hours ago.

Crossing to a window, he raised a slat of the blind and peeked out. Old Smokey sat incriminatingly at the curb. Tom groaned. The resident landlady had a reputation for monitoring the lives of her renters. Arlene had always been careful—up to now.

As he started into the bathroom he found a note hanging at eye level from the doorjam, affixed to a coathanger with a clothespin. In Arlene's firm, precise penmanship:

*Dear Future Husband:*
*Now you can only do the honorable thing and marry me! There are orange juice and milk in the refrigerator, and ice water, but don't drink too much and get sick. Just plug in the coffee-maker and it will do the rest. There's some cereal in the cabinet if you feel like it.*

*I always keep a new toothbrush handy for the use of my over-night gentlemen callers. You will find it on the upper shelf in the bathroom, still sealed. I don't think any of the others have used it.*

*All My Love,*
*Arlene.*

What a wife she was going to be; the thought and its accompanying twinge of anticipation made him feel better.

He was in the kitchenette hunting a cereal bowl when the phone rang. At first he decided to let it ring. Then he realized that anyone who knew Arlene also would know she was working. So he went into her bedroom, picked up the receiver, and held it silently to his ear.

"Tom?"

When he heard her voice he sank down on her deliciously unmade bed, her subtle fragrance tantalizing his olfactories. "I'm sorry, but the lady of the house is out," he said.

Arlene laughed. "I was afraid you wouldn't wake up in time for your appointment with Hartwell, so I sneaked out of the office to call you."

He'd forgotten. He groaned again, wondering how he'd ever manage to hike miles through mesquite breaks under a hot sun with a condition so delicate. But he couldn't back out now. This was a special assignment from BeeBee.

"How do you feel?" Arlene asked.

"Terrible. But I think I can make it out of the apartment so you won't have a corpse on your hands."

"I've been thinking about your idea all morning, and the more I think, the more excited I get. I just know it will work."

He had to puzzle around some before he knew what she was talking about. Then he remembered the grand scheme of last night. Right now, he couldn't work up much enthusiasm.

"Well, we're a long way from it, yet," he cautioned.

"It's a wonderful idea," she assured him. "Someone will buy it."

"I liked the other idea better," he said. He didn't have any trouble remembering that one.

"That's a lead pipe cinch to go through now," she teased. "You have no choice but to make an honest woman of me."

Later, going back over the night before, Tom also remembered his promise to Joe Garzek. So before going to meet Hartwell, he called Councilman Max Berger to arrange an interview.

As Tom expected, Berger was reluctant, asking what Tom had in mind. Not wanting to go into it over the phone, Tom hedged.

The *News-Gazette* kept profiles on all leading citizens, Tom explained, and Berger's file was comparatively slim. That wasn't a total lie. There wasn't much in the newspaper's morgue on Berger, and it *was* Tom's duty to see that adequate files were kept on personalities on his beat.

Obviously nettled, Berger said he was preparing to leave town for a distributors' convention in San Antonio. Was it anything that wouldn't keep until next week?

It would keep, Tom told him, and they agreed on the interview the next Thursday afternoon in Berger's office.

Tom and Hartwell drove out to the lake site in Old Smokey, for as Tom pointed out, the high-framed old car was better equipped to deal with mesquite and the deep-rutted roads than Hartwell's low-slung Olds.

The proposed dam site was almost fifty miles out of town by car, for they had to make a big semicircle around the river's meandering where roads were few. They drove twenty miles on the highway to Dallas and Fort Worth, twenty miles on a blacktop ranch road, then ten miles on gravel and dirt roads into the river bottom.

In the white glare of the sun on the powdery, alkali dust in the roadbed, Tom's eyes began to feel the strain. He hunted in the camera case beside him and found his sunglasses, but they didn't help much. Hartwell had been quiet, seemingly lost in his own thoughts, all the way out from town. Now, as they neared the river, he spread the map across his knees again and studied it.

"We ought to be about there," he said. "Supposed to be a cattle guard on the left just beyond the next bridge. We can go about two miles farther on an old wagon road. Then we'll have to walk about a mile."

"I wouldn't have asked you to come, if I'd known it was so inaccessible," Tom said.

"I'm glad to have the opportunity," Hartwell said. "I'll have to bring the council out here, probably, and it'd be a hell of a note if I got them lost. We could have flown down, but it's hard to get any idea of topography from the air."

"I think I can get better pictures from the ground," Tom said.

A jackrabbit leaped from his Johnson grass cover on the left, paced them down the dirt road a few seconds, then cut abruptly across the ditch on the right and disappeared into the mesquite. That was the first sign of life they'd seen since some Herefords along a fence five miles back.

They approached the bridge and Tom slowed. After they rattled across the wooden planks, Tom eased Old Smokey across the left-hand barrow ditch, up over a metal cattle guard, and onto a narrow, heavily rutted trail leading off into a mesquite thicket. They followed it more than a quarter of an hour, winding around rocky hillsides, crossing dry washes and circling brush, cactus, and soapweed. Finally the tracks ended at a well-trampled clearing decorated by a salt and feed box and innumerable cattle droppings.

"End of the line, I guess," Tom said. He braked Old Smokey to a stop and switched off the ignition. In the sudden silence he could hear the lowing of a cow somewhere far away.

Hartwell studied his map. "Let's see. We're about ten feet under water now. The shoreline's about a quarter-mile back. We're supposed to follow this creek on down to its junction with the river. Then the dam site will be downstream a way."

Tom hadn't realized how warm the day was until he got out of the car. He peeled off his coat and left it in the front seat, and Hartwell did the same.

"The car doesn't lock," Tom said apologetically.

Hartwell laughed. "Take a very enterprising thief to steal our coats way out here."

Tom got his camera bag from the car. Hartwell went on ahead, surprisingly trim and athletic in shirt sleeves. Tom followed, feeling the full effects now of his hangover. Two aspirin tablets had faded his headache into a weak, giddy pulsation in his temples, but a resolute breakfast of two eggs and bran flakes hadn't quieted the churning in his midsection. To make matters worse, the outdoors seemed to have a rejuvenating influence on Hartwell. He started off at such a fast pace Tom was relieved when the thickening brush began to give them trouble.

They tried to walk parallel to the creek, but before they'd gone far the thorny mesquite gave way to solid, unyielding blackjack tangles, and the footwork required was too difficult, especially for Tom and his prosthetic feet. So they descended into the dry creekbed and the walking was much easier.

In about a half mile they came to a point where the river lay spread before them, with wide stretches of dry sand, a trickle of water, and thick salt cedars along the bank.

"Water'll be about thirty feet deep here," Hartwell said, studying the map again. "The dam site is about a half mile on down."

They walked along the sand of the river until they rounded a slight bend and the dam site was there, unmistakable. A long, high bluff on each side of the river made the natural start of a dam.

Tom raised his Speed Graphic and framed the bluffs in the viewfinder. The river was so wide and they were still so far upstream that the bluffs appeared deceptively low. But even from this distance Tom could barely get both ends of the future dam in the viewfinder.

"I'll have to shoot one bluff at a time, from close up," Tom explained. "Might as well take a couple here, though, for background."

He took two pictures, then they walked on down closer to the dam site. That was no good either. The bluff on the left filled the picture, but there was no perspective, nothing in the viewfinder to give the illusion of height. The hundred feet to the bluff's crest might as well be a six-foot bank by a creek, and the trees so many weeds. Tom knew how much would be lost in newspaper reproduction.

"I hate to ask you this," he told Hartwell. "But would you mind climbing up to the top of that bluff?"

"I can truthfully say that would be one of the minor tasks of a city manager. Where do you want me?"

"Right up there by that biggest white rock, I think. And you might point to where the dam's going to be."

Hartwell nodded and walked off, moving fast up the slope of the hill, circling around toward the edge of the bluff. Tom squatted in the sand, checked the camera settings, and watched Hartwell's progress. At the top Hartwell moved slowly to the very edge of the bluff. "How's this?" he yelled.

From a kneeling position, Tom checked in the viewfinder. It was just as he'd imagined it would be. Hartwell looked small up there, but when you realized it was a man, it gave you perspective of how high the bluff and how wide the river.

"Fine," he yelled back.

Hartwell pointed with his left hand, facing the camera, and Tom clicked the shutter. Then he took another.

"O.K.," he called.

Hartwell came back down the hill in long strides. He trotted up to Tom, breathing hard, and leaned over to brush dried nettles from his trouser cuffs.

"More of a climb than it looks. Get what you wanted?"

Tom nodded. "Ought to be a good one."

They stood for a while, looking over the terrain and figuring out the future shoreline. Then they started back to the car. Since they now knew the way, the return trip was easier and quicker.

Tom realized he should be thinking ahead to the story he was going to write about the visit to the lake site, absorbing description and facts while he was actually there. But the problem of broaching the weekly newspaper idea with Hartwell hung heavily on his mind. He thought about possible introductions for the topic all the way back to the car, mulling them over and rejecting them, one by one.

Then, when they got back to Old Smokey, Hartwell himself began the conversation that led to the opening. Tom had unloaded his camera gear into the back seat, wiped the sweat from his forehead with a sleeve, and eased in behind the wheel.

Hartwell stood by the car door as if reluctant to leave. "This lake is going to ruin a damned good ranch," he said.

"I didn't see many cattle," Tom said, wondering about it.

"Overgrazed," Hartwell explained. "They've run too many cattle on it in the past, ruined the grass, and the brush took over. But a good rancher could fix that. I'd put a couple of bulldozers to work and clean out all that mesquite, seed it back to good native grass, and have one of the best ranches in the state."

"I didn't know you knew ranching."

"Sure, I'm a farm boy," Hartwell said, finally getting into the car. "I may go back to one some day, too. At least that's what I have hopes of doing."

Hearing Hartwell express his personal desires was something new to Tom. He saw the opening to work the subject around to where he wanted it.

"That sounds good," Tom said as he started Old Smokey and turned around in the clearing, guiding the wheels away from the fresher cow chips. "I've got a big ambition, if I can figure some way to swing it," he confided.

"I always thought you were the one guy I knew happy at his work," Hartwell said.

"There's an old newspaper saying that you'll never be happy on a newspaper until you own one," Tom told him. "And I've been thinking in that direction—a small weekly. I've got plenty of ideas. All I need is capital."

Hartwell was studying the map and the future shoreline as they drove out of the lake bottom. "I've heard weekly newspapers are often a good investment," he said absently. "Seems to me you shouldn't have much trouble raising the money."

"That's the reason I brought it up," Tom admitted. "I want to ask your advice. Do you know anyone who would be interested?"

Hartwell looked at him sharply, then laughed. "You're a cagey bastard, Kencaide. So cagey I don't think I'd want to do business with you. But let's hear your idea."

Tom explained the whole plan as they drove toward the highway—the type of stories he had in mind, the editorial slant, the production advantages, the advertising availability.

"Sounds like a hell of a good idea to me," Hartwell said when he had finished. "How much you figure it will take?"

"I haven't gotten down to the details yet," Tom admitted. "But it shouldn't require more than five to ten thousand. If it can't be done on that, it can't be done at all."

Hartwell nodded, then rode along in silence for several miles before he spoke.

"I see one big problem. It's too small a deal for anyone who really has money. Be too much worry for the returns. If you were wanting to start a newspaper plant, several hundred thousand dollars involved, I could name a half dozen men who'd at least give you a good audience."

"I think the success of it would be in keeping it small," Tom explained. "If I started trying to compete with Milam, I'd be in trouble."

Hartwell agreed. "But the problem exists. And it isn't something a small investor would be interested in, either, because it would be one hundred percent risk."

"It would be that," Tom admitted.

"So what you need to find is someone interested in what you're trying to do. I can just think of one definite possibility, right off. Why don't you go talk to Cal Masters about it? Tell him exactly what kind of a newspaper you have in mind. I believe he might go for it."

Tom would never have considered the possibility. The old rancher seemed like a holdover from another age, inaccessible.

"He's never been very friendly with me," Tom said dubiously.

"That's just because you're working for the *News-Gazette*," Hartwell said. "He used to admire Shotgun Milam a great deal, and later even Thirty-Thirty, but he doesn't have much use for BeeBee. I'll call him for you, tell him generally what you have in mind, then you can get together and mull it over. I wouldn't be surprised if you two don't have much in common."

Afterward, at his typewriter, Tom found that the trip to the lake had given him a new perspective, a softer theme. . . .

He described the way it felt to be walking in river sand that might some day be the floor of a lake, thirty feet under water, seeing jackrabbits that would have to find a new home. He described the way it was now . . . the heat, the dust, the loneliness . . . and the way it might be . . . fish swimming along the old cowpaths, water skiers zooming over bulldozed mesquite thickets.

But the picture was the biggest lift. Out of every couple hundred photographs, if a man is good, or a couple thousand, if he's merely lucky, there will be one that defies all rules of light, shadow, and substance. Exposed as all the others, processed in the same liquids, it transcends everything the photographer saw through the viewfinder when he snapped the shutter. This was one of those rare pictures.

In it, Hartwell stood outlined sharply against the sky, a heroic figure dwarfed by the scenery around him, yet dominating it, a Washington crossing the Delaware, a Columbus sighting America, a Balboa pointing to the Pacific. Below Hartwell, the river sands had a rich, fleshy tone that would hold up in printing, and in the center the river water had caught the glint of the sun in clear detail that gave continuity to the whole picture.

Collier and the news editor decided to go a full five columns on the photograph. Collier put it into words: "That ought to make BeeBee drop his spoon in his oatmeal in the morning."

## CHAPTER TWELVE

Earlier in the week, three more envoys had come to visit Travis and express concern over his speechmaking—two members of the county medical society and one from the Chamber of Commerce hospital committee. All expressed essentially the same view: "We appreciate your tireless efforts, Travis, but really, let up a little. We shouldn't destroy the public's confidence in what medical facilities we have now, should we?"

This Travis had expected. But when the dinner invitation came from Sam McIntosh, he knew the envoys had been mere scouts. The big attack was yet to come. For Sam considered his social life an extension of his business life, and an invitation to one of his Saturday night dinners was in the category of a summons. There was nothing subtle about Sam.

Travis had learned this during the campaign for his council seat. Even with no more political acumen than he then possessed, Travis had known that he who aspires for power must have friends in high places. And when a series of social invitations came from Sam, followed by not-so-discreet discussions of civic affairs, Travis had accepted them for what they obviously were

—an opportunity to woo powerful support. Travis had not curried favor, but he had given his views frankly and earnestly, knowing his election might hinge on what he said. Later, when Sam had closed a long evening's talk with the remark, "I like your attitude, Travis; I think you will make a good councilman," Travis had taken the statement as an official endorsement. After that, the invitations stopped, proving his assumption right.

The new summons could mean only one thing. Sam wanted to talk business again. And now there was an unknown element in the relationship which bothered Travis.

How much was his indebtedness?

There was no doubt Sam had been a big factor in getting Travis elected. Sam's influence was wide—a director at First National, owner of the town's prestige department store, Chamber of Commerce director, oil man, rancher—there was hardly a sphere of business activity where Sam's opinions weren't weighed.

Travis hadn't promised Sam anything—even loyalty—in exchange for his support. But he *had* wanted that support, and he *had* solicited it. He couldn't keep from feeling a nagging sense of obligation toward Sam, and the more he thought about it, the more his doubt grew.

One night he asked Marilyn for her viewpoint on the subject. She answered without even pausing to reflect.

"You told him what you thought about things, and he gave you his support on the strength of that. I don't see that you owe him anything."

"I did seek his help," he told her. "And if he hadn't given it, I doubt if I would have been elected."

"My understanding was that you didn't ask him for anything."

"Well, I didn't come right out and ask him. But just accepting his invitations to dinner was asking, in a way."

"He was looking out for himself, not doing you a favor. Surely you don't think you were the only one he had out to his house for a miserable evening or two. He backed you in your campaign because he thought your political philosophy would do him the most good, that's all."

This, he felt, was true. Yet he couldn't bring himself to think of Sam as just another citizen. With the big department store, a half-dozen downtown buildings and his outsized new home on the tax rolls, Sam probably paid several thousand times the tax burden of the average citizen. He explained this to Marilyn.

"I thought that was one of the first tenets of democracy. All citizens are equal despite race, creed, color, or the size of their bank accounts."

"A good theory that's difficult to put into practice."

"I should think any man of conviction could do it."

"All right," he told her. "When we go down the drain, remember you were the one who insisted I hang onto my convictions."

With Marilyn's logic for support, his misgivings about the summons eased slightly. But all his doubts returned in full force that Saturday night the instant they turned into the half-mile long driveway leading to Sam's floodlighted home. Even that house tended to give Travis an inferiority complex.

It had been featured in several national magazines when completed three years ago, and was Sam's most cherished plaything —the young wife excepted, of course.

The house was nestled into what had been one side of a creek before Sam diverted the flow. That left the other bank of the stream in the way, so Sam had it removed. Long and low, the huge dun structure blended perfectly into the dismembered creek bank. "Harmonizing with the landscape" was the phrase the architect had used. Marilyn, the first time she saw it, remarked that the house resembled an old bottling plant that had sunk into the mud. The description was apt. The soft lights in the big factory-sized windows were the only hint it was other than a warehouse.

Originally, the house had looked out on a half mile of pastureland and scrub brush between the house and road. But Sam changed all that. Now the half mile was rich, rolling grass with a lake and Japanese garden placed incongruously in the center. The lake was fed through an underground conduit by gravity flow from the creek, which now flowed through Sam's living room into the dining room, where it disappeared through the mouth of a bronze dolphin.

"Now don't make fun of his house tonight," Marilyn said as they neared the parking area. Maybe the outsized domicile blended with its surroundings in the daytime, but at night, under lights, it monopolized the whole countryside.

"He likes to be teased about it," Travis told her. "It's his wife you don't joke about."

In the parking area—bigger than those at most supermarkets—the mayor's big Cadillac with the No. 1 license tag confirmed suspicions that this wasn't a social gathering. There were two other Cadillacs there beside Sam's Rolls-Royce and Jaguar, but Travis didn't recognize them.

Sam met them at the door, his young blond wife smiling like a toothpaste ad behind him. "Glad you two could come, Travis," he said, his grip firm and his left hand closing on Travis' arm. "I don't see enough of you any more. You work too hard. You ought to take it a little easier."

This was strange advice indeed from Sam McIntosh, the human dynamo. Travis had read a profile on Sam in the business section of the latest issue of *Time* magazine. In it, Sam had been credited with forming the biggest oil exploration program in recent years to open a new South American venture with himself as the kingpin. In organizing the joint effort, the article said, Sam had spent three months on the road talking to top financiers and corporate leaders in a half-dozen countries. Then, with the deal closed, he'd taken off into the Yucatán jungles hunting a lost Mayan city. Sam worked hard and he played hard. And now he stood here telling Travis he should take life easier.

"I hear you've practically retired since I last saw you," Travis said.

Sam laughed heartily and punched Travis playfully in the ribs. "Yeah, I've been out of town swingin' a deal or two. I can't follow my own advice."

"The pace must agree with you," Travis said. "You look a year younger."

Sam grinned with pleasure. The remark was no idle compliment. Travis knew Sam must be past sixty, but he appeared no more than forty-five, his small, muscular frame lean, his slate-gray eyes alert and untroubled, and his skin that peculiar golden brown some men achieve with sun, exercise, and good whiskey.

He ushered Travis and Marilyn on inside the house, complimented Marilyn on her dress, commented on the likelihood of rain before morning and told a risque joke, all so rapidly Travis had a difficult time keeping up with the changing subjects. Then, as they started into the living room, Sam suddenly stopped, listened for a moment, and turned to his wife.

"Bunny, would you take Travis and Marilyn on in and fix them up with a drink? I hear somebody else drivin' up."

"This way," Bunny said, speaking audibly for the first time since they'd arrived. She still wore the frozen smile. Travis somehow had the impression she was confused by the myriad of guests passing through her house and made no attempt to retain identities.

This second wife of Sam's was even more unique than the house, Travis reflected. The first one had died about five years ago, a coronary. After a minimal period of mourning, Sam had left on an announced hunting trip to Africa. He had returned with this blond trophy.

Apparently in her early thirties, Bunny had a figure that scandalized the matronly friends of Sam's first wife. Also, Travis heard, Sam had resorted to fisticuffs a number of times at stray eyes and remarks from his own friends, which was a useless gesture, for Bunny was the type of girl who naturally drew men's eyes and remarks.

She was overbuilt in every department, just enough so that she gave the aura of ripeness rather than plumpness. Added to this, she had a way of walking, of carriage, that attracted attention. There was one story that she had been a New York artists' model when Sam met her. There was another story that she was a ballet dancer, and another—probably spread by friends of Sam's first wife—that she'd been a high-priced call girl. No one knew. Sam talked about his other trophies, but not about this one.

As they rounded the pool into the living room Travis inadvertently began to study Bunny's walk. His side vision saw Marilyn's head turning and he lifted his gaze, but too late.

"Watch your step," Marilyn said in the overly firm voice she reserved for teasing.

Bunny glanced back at them quizzically.

"Travis was so fascinated with the pool I was afraid he was going to fall in," Marilyn said.

Their hostess stopped suddenly and looked at the pool as if she'd just discovered the creek flowing through her living room. Her voice was so soft and husky Travis had to listen intently to catch her words.

"Yes, I like the pool. Sometimes I can turn the air-conditioner on all the way and make it fog."

"That must be beautiful," Marilyn said.

"Does Sam have it stocked?" Travis asked.

Bunny looked at him blankly.

"With fish," Travis clarified.

"Oh, yes. See, there's some of the gold ones now. And somebody put an alligator in it once. Sam almost got bitten getting it out. He gave it to a zoo."

Travis had heard about the alligator episode. Two truckloads of untreated dairy loam had been mysteriously dumped and spread on the lawn of one of Sam's oil boom cronies not long afterward.

Bunny started walking again and they followed, Travis now forcing himself to concentrate on Sam's material furnishings. As Marilyn once had remarked, the interior of Sam's house would look great in the fur salon of his department store, but it was difficult to imagine anyone actually living in these surroundings.

Past the pool, they could see the other end of the L-shaped room. The mayor and Walt Weatherbee stood at the bar, and their wives were seated at a curved sectional behind them. Bunny confirmed that they'd all met before.

Cabrito, Sam's No. 1 boy and gentleman's gentleman, was bartending. A trophy of a trip to Mexico City several years back, Cabrito traveled with Sam as an interpreter-valet, and now was almost as worldly and unassuming as Sam. Marilyn asked for a martini, and Travis for a whiskey sour, remembering Cabrito's touch with mixed drinks.

Marilyn and Bunny went over to join the other wives. Lined up in a row on the sectional couch, the four made an interesting study in contrasts, Travis couldn't help but notice. Marilyn, a pretty suburban housewife; Mrs. Weatherbee, a heavy, peasant-faced woman; the mayor's wife, a haughty grande dame in pearls, and Bunny, whatever she was.

Travis turned back to the bar and tried to follow Cabrito's

motions and learn the secret of the whiskey sour, but Cabrito's hands were too adept. He mixed the drinks so fast and with such flourish that the mystery was intensified.

With a jerky head movement, the mayor signaled covertly for Travis to follow him away from the bar. They strolled over toward the pool with Weatherbee following. "You have any idea what Sam wants?" the mayor asked, his voice almost a whisper.

"No," Travis said.

Weatherbee walked up beside them. "I told the mayor I think he just wants to get caught up on all that's happened while he was out of town."

"No, he's got something on his mind," the mayor said, frowning. "Something to do with the council, it seems, with the three of us here."

"Hardly a quorum," Travis pointed out, and Weatherbee smiled. The mayor was too worried to approve of humor. His frown deepened.

Their discussion was ended suddenly as Sam rounded the pool with BeeBee Milam and the publisher's dumpy little wife.

"Hey, what's goin' on here?" Sam demanded. "Travis, you don't even have a drink."

"It's on the bar," Travis explained. "We just walked over to look at your gator trap."

Sam laughed heartily. "Think I got all the big ones cleaned out," he said. BeeBee and his wife stopped to admire the pool. Travis asked a question that had been in his mind a long time.

"What happens when the creek floods?"

"That was the big question around here about three years ago," Sam said. "Damn architects wanted to put an overflow pipe in here. Said that'd be enough to take care of it. Hell, I knew they'd never seen a good Texas rain. I made 'em put a sluice gate in about a hundred yards above the house. You know, like on an irrigation ditch. That way we can cut it off and send it runnin' down that draw between here and the road. Puts the Jap garden under water, but that's better'n havin' it in here."

"What if the creek dries up?" BeeBee's wife asked.

Sam laughed again. "Don't let this get out if we have to go back to water rationing, but I've got it piped so I can use enough city water to keep the pool from gettin' stagnant."

The mayor frowned again. Travis didn't know if his worry was renewed by the mention of the city water supply, or if he was merely expressing his disapproval of the waste.

"Lookin' at that damn pool always makes me thirsty," Sam said. "Come on, you people. Let's have a drink."

As they moved toward the bar Travis realized that Sam's undivided attention meant the guest list was complete. The party was under way.

One of Marilyn's chief objections to Sam's dinners was the segregation of sexes in conversation, and Travis also found it irritating. Tonight was no exception. The men gathered at the bar and talked, with the women seated fifteen feet away carrying on their own discussion. And Travis was left out of both groups. The talk at the bar adhered to the same topic. . . .

What'd happened to business the last couple of months, Sam demanded. Retail sales were up only four percent last month. Dallas had an eight percent gain, Fort Worth seven, and Houston and Abilene nine.

A seasonal slump, the mayor suggested.

No, there was something more serious, Sam believed. There were danger signals showing in the area's economy.

Advertising lineage was down last month, too, said Milam. He'd always found that a harbinger of a recession.

Horse manure, Sam said. Advertising didn't boost business; it was the other way around.

Housing starts were down, Weatherbee lamented. No litmus like the housing industry.

Residential sales were down, Sam said, because every damned realtor in town had overbuilt and overfinanced. Every knucklehead that could raise fifty bucks for a down payment had been saddled with a lifetime mortgage and drained of buying power. That, he believed, might be a big part of the area's trouble.

Something was going to have to be done, they all agreed. The regional economy needed a shot in the arm. Local business wasn't getting a fair share of the boom. Maybe the chamber should try for more industrial diversity. . . .

Travis stood silently and listened. He could have contributed that bronchial infections also declined last month, but that somehow didn't seem germane. And he honestly didn't know if his income was up or down, but he knew these men wouldn't believe him even if he chose to be so candid.

He tuned out of the man-talk and concentrated on what he could overhear of the feminine chatter. From the few phrases he caught, Marilyn and Bunny seemed left out, too. The mayor's wife, Mrs. Milam, and Mrs. Weatherbee were commiserating that the new look in fall fashions would do nothing for the figure, that the federation of women's clubs was not going to do well this spring in statewide competition, and that once again the symphony orchestra would fail to break even this year.

Finally, the tempo of conversation slowed. Without any signal that Travis could see, a white-jacketed Negro suddenly slid back the folding doors beyond the bar and Sam led his guests downstream into the dining room. Again Travis witnessed the subduing effect of the scene that once had been the subject of a two-page spread in a national magazine.

The vastness of the deep-carpeted room made their party of ten seem small and intimate. Silently, the guests went in single file across the narrow gangplank to the dining table on its oval platform, surrounded by water and dominated by the gurgling dolphin. The bronze had turned a deeper green since his last visit, Travis noticed. The darker color blended well with the twenty-three somber paintings lining the walls, the charcoal carpeting and the heavily stained panels on the ceiling.

As he followed his host to the table, Travis remembered the oft-quoted remark by one of Sam's roughneck friends after a first visit to the floating banquet: "I felt like a danged bullfrog settin' on a lilypad."

Travis was relieved to find that he was seated on Bunny's left and facing away from the bronze. At previous dinners, the sight of the dolphin gorging itself on water had an unfortunate psychological effect on him. But the seating arrangement didn't help much, he found. He could still hear the gurgling. . . .

Again, Sam's guests were silent, overpowered by their surroundings. The first course arrived—a soup of French origin, the unmistakable creation of Sam's Cajun chef. At the other end of the table, Weatherbee started telling Sam something about a Chamber of Commerce dinner, an incident that had happened there, but his voice was so low the dolphin noise swallowed up the words.

Travis studied the paintings on the opposite wall, and this time he noticed two new canvases, brighter than the others. One was of a golden wheatfield in harvest and the other of horses romping in a sunny field of wildflowers. The two must be Bunny's, he decided. They clashed with the others, but they eased the sensation of dining in a waterlogged art gallery.

Weatherbee's voice droned on in a monotone. Sandwiched between Bunny and Mrs. Weatherbee, facing Milam, Travis waited patiently for the end of the story. Finally, he became aware his neighbors felt awkward, too. They couldn't hear the story, but they couldn't ignore it, either. Travis turned to Bunny.

"I've been admiring the two pictures in the corner. I believe they are relatively new, aren't they?"

Bunny looked at the pictures and smiled. "Oh, thank you," she said softly. "Those are mine. Sam let me buy them."

"Very nice," Travis said.

"They're contemporary art," Bunny confided, carefully enunciating each syllable of the polysyllabic word. "Do you like contemporary art?"

"I'm not much of an art fan," Travis admitted.

"I like contemporary art," Bunny insisted. "I mean, it makes me feel bad, to look at one and know the man that did it is dead. You feel that way?"

Travis was aware of Milam and Mrs. Weatherbee monitoring the exchange. He was sorry now he'd gotten involved.

"I guess I never thought about it. Seems to me, though, that the old masters would derive some satisfaction in knowing others appreciate what they've left behind."

"But they can't see them any more," Bunny said. "That's what makes me feel bad." She looked at the contemporary paintings again longingly. "I wish I could paint."

"Maybe you could."

"No, I can't. I tried."

"Well, I suppose art appreciation is a talent in itself," Travis said.

"I think so," Bunny said. She turned to look at him. "You're a doctor, aren't you?"

"Yes," Travis admitted.

She studied him intently for a moment with her lips parted slightly. "I like you," she said suddenly. "If Sam and I make a baby, will you be my doctor?"

Travis heard Mrs. Weatherbee's quick intake of breath. Across the table, Milam's gaze was discreetly averted.

"I've never turned away a patient yet," Travis said. As Bunny giggled, he heard Sam's voice at the other end of the table, giving him the opportunity to shift his attention. Sam was answering Weatherbee, but talking louder, his words audible to the whole table.

The nation was growing soft, Sam said. Instead of sitting around lamenting business conditions, people ought to be out creating their own business conditions. That's what he had done when he was starting out.

Travis had long noticed a failing in self-made men. They believe they have cracked the hard kernel of life and stand ready to preach their philosophy to anyone who'll listen. Sam was no exception. Sam had never forgotten his days as a young roughneck, a go-getter with nothing but his own brass and guts. As Sam started telling the story of his first oil well, Travis reflected that Mrs. Weatherbee shouldn't have been so shocked at the revelation Sam and Bunny were trying for a baby. It was in keeping with Sam's philosophy: Take life for all it's worth.

The story of Sam's first oil well was a common one around town. But hearing Sam tell it gave the tale a new meaning.

Sam had acquired the lease on borrowed money and the promise of more. He ordered a drilling outfit C.O.D., then went out and tried to raise the money. When the equipment came in by rail, he still didn't have the cash. Everyone who had money had his own row to hoe in those boom-town days, and no one was interested in a partnership with an ignorant-talking ex-ranch hand.

Desperate, Sam spent his last few dollars for a jug of moonshine. Late that night he struck up a conversation with the railroad yard guard, a homesick Alabaman. Friendship blossomed under Sam's charm and the influence of the jug. In the early hours of morning, with the railroad guard passed out behind a pile of pipe, Sam loaded the equipment on borrowed wagons and disappeared.

Hearing Sam laugh as he recalled that night, Travis realized that to this day Sam still didn't consider the act stealing. It was just shrewd business. Having the sheriff after him added spice to the excitement of a big financial deal.

Fortunately, the whole county was in confusion with the oil boom, and the sheriff had other, more serious criminals to track down. Sam fenced off his lease, plowed up the telltale wagon tracks, and drilled day and night, hiring men on promise, hiring more when they gave up and quit. When the well blew in Sam hadn't eaten in three days. It flowed over the top of the derrick twenty-two hours before they could get it capped. This was in the days of unlimited production. When the sheriff found him, Sam was on the way to becoming a rich man. The moonshine incident in the railroad yard was laughed off as a big joke.

Sam continued his stories in the living room after dinner. He stood at the bar, an oversized Havana in one hand and a glass of brandy in the other, his guests seated in a semicircle around him, unsegregated. Travis had heard most of the stories before, but some were new. And they were all in the same theme . . . the overzealous investor who wound up with one hundred and eighty percent of a dry hole . . . the shady maneuvering to buy up leases . . . doctored drill samples . . . stolen pipe . . . legislative schemes. . . .

Shortly after eleven, Sam suddenly switched the topic to hunting. He described his last hunt in Alaska and the completion of his North American game collection with the killing of a Dall ram at three hundred yards on uneven terrain. He told of the climb, the exhilaration of watching the sheep through the spotting scope, the long tedious stalk, and the climax of the successful shot. Then he turned to Travis.

"You haven't seen the trophy, have you, Doctor?"

Travis recognized the gambit: You've drunk my liquor and eaten my food; now, damn it, we'll go to the basement and talk business.

"No, sure haven't," Travis said.

"We'll go down, then, if you like. I don't suppose the ladies would be interested. . . ."

Sam led the way to the elevator, Travis following. Milam, Weatherbee, and the mayor, still seated, looked uncertainly at each other, not knowing if they were included in the safari.

"This way, gentlemen," Sam said in clarification.

The elevator was small for five, but they crowded in. Sam punched the button and they dropped rapidly.

The entire house was built over the combination rifle range and trophy room. On the paneled walls hung the head of every game animal on the North American continent, excepting two bears, an elk, and a moose mounted whole. Dominating the room from the far end reared a giant Kodiak bear, almost twice as tall as a man, his forepaws brushing the ceiling. It had been rumored that when Sam McIntosh found his Kodiak bear wouldn't fit into his trophy room he summoned a contractor and had the basement floor lowered three feet.

Sam flipped on a series of small spotlights so they could see the ram's head better in its place of honor over the fireplace at the end of the room. It was, or had been, a magnificent animal, Travis thought, its huge horns curled back in regal rakishness.

"An excellent trophy," Travis said. Weatherbee, Milam and the mayor murmured their agreement. Sam stood, legs spread, and gazed up at the specimen, smiling as if he and the animal shared a secret.

"I think I'm prouder of this one than any of the others," he said. "Except the Kodiak, of course."

Travis had heard the story of the Kodiak many times. Sam had shot him first at a hundred yards, and the bear had turned and charged, covering eighty yards and absorbing five well-placed soft-nosed bullets before the last one downed him twenty yards away.

They strolled down the range to the Kodiak. Just looking at the beast gave Travis cold chills. He wondered if he would have the courage to stand and face a brute like that, charging. In the wondering he came as close as he ever had to understanding Sam and his pride in killing.

Sam sank onto the big leopard-skin couch across from the bear. "That was one day I'll never forget," he said. He looked up at Travis. "You do any hunting, Doctor?" he asked for the fourth or fifth time since Travis had known him.

"No, I'm afraid not," Travis answered again.

"You should. Nothing else like it. Even with your schedule you ought to be able to get up to Colorado for deer, or even some weekend wing shooting around here. That new lake ought to bring in lots of water fowl."

Travis almost grinned in admiration of Sam's knack of maneuvering the conversation right to the topic he wanted. Sam followed through smoothly by turning to the mayor.

"By the way, Hiram, how's the lake project coming along?"

The mayor glanced nervously at Travis before he answered. "Fairly well, Sam. The consulting engineers have recommended the lower site, and although I haven't had a chance to study it thoroughly, I believe it to be the most feasible."

"How is support shaping up?" Sam asked.

Again the mayor glanced at Travis. "I think it will carry at the polls," he said.

"We've been building support through the newspaper," Milam said. "We've had a long series of front-page stories, showing the need. . . ."

"That's fine," Sam interrupted. "But what I'm concerned about is the council. Mark my words, gentlemen. If the city administration is not one hundred percent behind this thing, the election will fail. Weatherbee, you're for it, aren't you?"

"Of course," Weatherbee said.

"What about you, Doctor?"

"I'm not against it," Travis explained patiently. "I just want to get the hospital program on the same ballot, or at least placed before the voters in the same election."

"I figured Cal Masters would be against it," Sam said. "That old bastard is against anything that smells of progress. But I thought you was more growth-minded."

Travis realized that Sam probably didn't know of Cal's illness, and the knowledge kept him from following an impulse and making a heated reply. Still, he felt called upon to defend the old rancher. "Cal is as honest in his beliefs as any of us," he said.

Sam looked at him for a moment. "Maybe we can compromise. I don't think the hospital plan should be on the same ballot, or even in the same election, because it's a tax item. Our best selling point on the lake is that it's a nontax project."

"We've been stressing that in our stories," BeeBee said.

"What do you want in the way of compromise?" Sam asked Travis.

"The hospital program."

Sam sighed deeply. "You've been muddying the water with these speeches, getting people confused. Why, even some of the hospital board and the medical association are beginning to turn on you. Did you know that?"

"I know."

"We've got to present a united front, convince the public we know what in hell we're doing. Now, Travis, suppose we have a gentleman's agreement that the next civic project will be the hospital improvements, creation of a hospital district, or whatever is found to be the best way to go about it. How would that set with you?"

"I've been hearing that ever since I've been on the council," Travis told him. "I've already committed myself to a plan of action. I don't think it will be detrimental to the water program, and I've already seen plenty of evidence of public support."

"From women," Sam said. "Travis, you're a good doctor and an intelligent man. But when it comes to politics, you've got a lot to learn. It's the men that pay the taxes. The women get out and have their meetings and all, but when the chips are down, the men still wear the pants. If you can't sell something to the men, it won't go over at the polls."

Travis tried to keep his tone polite. "I disagree," he said. "I think that if something threatens their home, their children, women are quicker to recognize it and more militant in combating it than the men."

Sam tried a new tack. "Why do you think this is more important than water. Isn't your attitude a little selfish?"

Here it was again—the implication he was trying to promote a free place to practice. Travis selected his words carefully before he answered, and he made an effort to keep his irritation from showing. "It's the sick and injured who need a hospital, not the doctor," he said evenly. "We're discussing what's best for our citizens, not the medical profession."

"Let's talk about what's best for the medical profession," Sam said. "I'm sure that if we have another drought like we had in the

Fifties there's a good number of your patients that will have to leave town to find work some place else. But if we get this new lake, new industries, there will be more patients for you. That's better for them, better for the medical profession." He spread his hands and laughed.

Travis heard his own voice rising in anger. "Sam, you've got enough water out here to go for a swim in your living room. But do you realize it's likely that if you suddenly needed medical treatment you wouldn't get the best possible?"

Sam's humor vanished, and Travis knew he'd hit a raw nerve.

"Don't worry, son. If I needed medical attention, I could afford the best," Sam said in a low voice.

"I'm not talking about six weeks of diagnostic studies at the Mayo Clinic," Travis told him. "If you and your wife should have a car wreck some night and be brought into the emergency room of our hospital, there's a likelihood you would not get proper treatment immediately. There might be unnecessary suffering and risk. That's what I'm talking about."

Sam's face turned beet-red. "Never underestimate the power of money, son. I would be treated."

"Not if I were on duty and another human being needed what facilities we have more than you," Travis said evenly.

Sam glared at him for a long, uncomfortable moment. Travis was aware of the mayor, Weatherbee, and Milam transfixed by the unexpected flare of emotion. The mayor opened his mouth as if to say something, but closed it before making a sound.

Then Sam laughed. "You should have been a businessman, Travis. There's just one thing better than a good bluff, and that's a man who's not bluffing."

With the tension broken, Travis suddenly realized how bad his behavior had been, considering he was a guest in Sam's home. "I'm sorry," he said. "I've been rude. I was just trying to make a point."

Sam laughed again. "You made it. I thought you was turnin' rabble rouser on me with all those speeches. But I can see now you got a point. That doesn't make me like your attitude on the lake any better, though." He stared up at the towering Kodiak for a moment. "I need some time to think about it."

He bounced to his feet. "Y'all come here. I got something I want to show you."

They followed him back down the long rows of animal heads to the fireplace. He unlocked one of the gun cases flanking the mantel and took out one of the rifles. The stock was beautifully grained and finished. Travis knew without being told that it was an expensive weapon.

"A three-seven-five magnum," Sam said. He handed it to Travis. "Try it for size. It isn't loaded."

Travis aimed the rifle at an antelope head on the wall. Although he wasn't a hunter, the gun felt good, like being behind the wheel of a powerful sports car.

"Nice," Travis said.

The gun was passed around for critical examination and praise. The mayor held it up to read the letters on the receiver.

"Want to try it out?" Sam asked.

For a moment Travis thought the mayor was going to drop it. "No," he said quickly. He handed the gun back to Sam. "It's too much for me," he said.

Sam took some cartridges from a drawer of the gun case and loaded the rifle. He handed it to Travis. "I'll put up the targets," he said.

Travis held the gun uncomfortably as Sam trotted the full length of the house to the target racks. Travis had never fired a gun bigger than a twenty-two, and that had been years ago, on farms and ranches, when he was traveling with his father. This gun, he knew, was a bear-stopper.

"Be careful with that thing," the mayor said too low for their host to hear.

Travis had been pointing the gun at the ceiling, but with the mayor's warning he remembered that Marilyn and the other women were up there somewhere. He decided it was safest pointed at the wall.

Sam put up the bull's-eyes and stood to one side.

"Have at it, Travis," he said, raising his voice to cover the distance. From the full length of the room, Sam blended in with all the animal heads.

"You trust me more than I do," Travis yelled. "Hadn't you better come back up here?"

"No, I'll call your shots."

The targets looked small. Travis brought the gun around, unlatched the safety, took aim at the target on the left, and fired. The sound startled everyone except Sam. It was surprisingly loud. But the recoil was less than Travis had expected.

"Good," Sam called. "But slightly high and to the right. Try again."

Travis took aim and fired.

"Bull's-eye," Sam yelled, almost with the report of the gun. "Try the other target."

Travis took careful aim and fired.

"Dead center," Sam said.

Travis put the rifle on safety and let Weatherbee try it. The realtor's shots were high and to the right as he flinched. Sam trotted back to reload the gun for Milam.

"Damned good shooting, Travis," he said with enthusiasm. "You have a good eye. I haven't been able to do a thing with this gun. Here, let me see something."

He put the gun up to Travis' shoulder and measured the results like a tailor.

"The stock's too long for me," he said. "And I've been reluctant to let anyone mess with it because of that finish. But it's just a fit for you."

Milam's shots were low, and Weatherbee fired two more high and to the right. When Sam offered to reload for him, Travis declined. He didn't want to push his luck.

"What's stopping the bullets?" the mayor asked. "Isn't there danger they'll ricochet?"

"That whole end of the room is lined with cotton bales," Sam explained. "Even if you miss, there's cotton behind that beaverboard."

Travis remembered that cotton is marketed by weight. "You're going to have some valuable cotton bales some day," he said.

Sam laughed and dug an elbow into his ribs. "That's right. I figure I'm goin' to get back every penny I spend on ammunition when I sell those bales."

"You might even put in for a government subsidy for storing farm surplus and make a profit," Travis said.

Sam roared with laughter and slapped Travis on the back. "Hot damn, I never thought of that. See, what'd I tell you, Doctor? You should've been a businessman."

Sam seemed to forget the angry clash as quickly as it happened. But for Travis the embarrassment lingered. He had told the baby-sitter they would be back, probably, by eleven-thirty or twelve. Now he had the feeling he shouldn't be the first to leave Sam's dinner party under the circumstances. There also was the possibility that with his going he would become the subject of discussion.

Midnight passed with him at the bar listening to Sam, the mayor, Weatherbee, and Milam solving the town's economic troubles. He knew meaningful glances were coming from Marilyn, sitting over with the women, but he kept his gaze averted.

He was standing there, wondering what he was going to do, when Cabrito entered and announced a telephone call for Milam.

BeeBee came back from the telephone visibly upset. "I'm sorry, but we'll have to say good night," he said. "I've just learned that my sister, Sharon, is leaving for Europe. We'll have to drive straight to the airport if we see her before she leaves."

"Hell, I thought maybe she'd finally settled down," Sam said. "Can't she make up her mind which side of the Atlantic she wants to be on? Where's she goin' this time?"

BeeBee seemed uncomfortable. "I don't know. She just said she was leaving. I didn't think to ask. Paris, probably."

Travis remembered that moment of recognition in the dark of the parking lot behind City Hall and the expression on Sharon's face as David Hartwell entered the car. He wondered if there was any connection between that rendezvous and her sudden trip to Europe.

As BeeBee and his wife prepared to leave, Travis saw his opportunity.

"It's getting late," he said to Marilyn. "We better not abuse Sam's hospitality."

The mayor and Weatherbee expressed mutual amazement and concern that it was so late, adding that they, too, must be going. So they all moved toward the front door together. As the others thanked the hosts and said good night, Sam kept a tight grip on Travis' arm.

"I want to talk to your knotheaded husband for a minute," he explained to Marilyn.

With the flurry of departures in the parking area, Sam led Travis into the moonlight a few steps away from the door. The night air was cool, and the lawn soft underfoot. Down the hill below them the Japanese garden and lake were outlined by gentle floodlights. Behind them, at the door, Travis could hear Marilyn and Bunny talking.

Sam turned and faced him. "Travis, I admire you," he said. "You're a man of principle. I know that. But for God's sake, don't get in the way of this lake."

"I'm not in the way of it," Travis said. "I'm just trying to put it in the right perspective."

"Now, don't misunderstand me," Sam said. "I'm thinking of you when I say this. The lake project is going to go through. I know, I let on I think it's nip and tuck. You got to keep those people downtown scared or you won't get nothin' done. But it'll pass, Travis, 'cause it's progress, and if you're not one hundred percent behind it, you're going to get hurt, and I'd hate to see that. Old Cal Masters has his life behind him. Nothin' can touch him. But you're different. You're young. You have your medical practice to think of."

"I'm trying to keep my professional life apart from this," Travis explained.

Sam snorted. "Don't kid yourself. You've gotten out and made some noble speeches for a noble project. Fine. It's probably helped your practice and raised your standing in the eyes of a lot of people that count. I'm all for it. God knows, I realize the worth of self-promotion. But everybody that is anybody in this town is for this lake, Travis, and if you're not fully with them, then you're against them. That's the way they think. No matter what they think of you as a doctor, they'll remember this."

Travis tried to keep the returning irritation from his voice. "I didn't make those speeches for self-promotion. I think people know that."

"I'm a businessman, Travis. I look at the results. And whether you like it or not, you are a businessman. You've got to look ahead at what the results will be if you get fouled up in this. If you vote against this lake, BeeBee Milam will ban your name from his newspaper. I know, it's childish and it's stupid. But just having your name left out of the paper would hurt. That doctor in front of your name is advertising, whether you'll admit it or not."

"I think I could survive not having my name in Milam's newspaper," Travis said.

"Sure. But that's just a sample of what I'm talking about. Multiply that by fifty, a hundred, a thousand, and you get the idea. You can't afford to have all the leading people in town down on you. No businessman can. Think it over."

As they walked back to the doorway Marilyn looked at Sam and smiled. But her voice had no humor. "Well, do you still think my husband is knotheaded?"

Sam laughed. "You're married to him," he said. "You tell me."

In the car, on the way back to town, Marilyn held her curiosity as long as she could. "You're mighty quiet," she said finally. "Sam must have really turned you across his knee."

"He just warned me to fall into line or I'll lose all my patients-with-bank-accounts," Travis said, keeping his eyes on the road.

"That's something to consider."

"Yes," he admitted. "That's something to consider. He also suggested my speeches have been good advertising and self-promotion."

She glanced at him quickly. "Well that's a cynical, thankless attitude. I don't think I like that at all."

"Maybe it's what others are saying," he told her. "Maybe Sam was trying to let me know."

"Why should we care what others think? We know the truth."

"Do we?" he asked her. "I don't. Right now, I'm all confused. I should consider you and the children."

"I don't care about money. Doing the right thing is far more important. Frankly, some of those stories Sam told tonight about stealing equipment rather shocked me. I would rather have our peace of mind than his millions."

"Sam called me a man of principle, so I guess I'll have to agree. But if my practice goes to pot and I can't send our children to college and give them the start in life they want, I'll have no peace of mind."

For several blocks Marilyn didn't answer. "I would hate to think Sam is right," she said finally. And she said no more about it. Outwardly, they went on as if the night had never happened. But Travis thought of it often, and no doubt Marilyn did, too.

When he arrived at his office Monday morning there was a long, narrow box on his desk.

"A messenger service brought it first thing this morning," his receptionist said.

Travis unwrapped the box. It was the rifle he'd fired in Sam's basement. There was no card. He called the messenger service and had the rifle returned. The delivery boy seemed confused.

"Any message?" he asked.

"No," Travis told him. "The package will be message enough."

# *Part Five*

## CHAPTER THIRTEEN

In the first days after Sharon Milam left for Europe, David Hartwell felt himself dropping back into the old, familiar rut. The firm resolutions he had made that night in the motel faded under two frustrating attempts to talk to Helen about Ronnie. Both efforts ended in tearful brawls.

On Monday he received a twenty-page report from Chief Dan McDowell on the highway investigation. Despite its length, the report had little new information. The ex-convict, Ratliff, thus far had made no contact with Berger. McDowell still believed they should wait patiently for developments.

In David's frustration, it was with something akin to relief that he plunged back into the man-killing task of shaping up the proposed city budget for the coming fiscal year.

Each year the battle to hold the line became worse. In some years he could count on a nominal tax increase. But now, with the lake proposal nearing the polls, he knew there was no chance for more revenue. There was only one answer: expenses had to be slashed. This had to be done in the face of rising operative costs, the need for more equipment, and the annual demands for across-the-board wage increases.

In most facets of administration, David had been able to devise his own, improved methods. But in hammering out a new budget he still used the time-honored system. He had each department head draft a preliminary proposal. With the human elements involved, each usually ran ten to fifteen percent above the budget of the preceding year. David knew this was inevitable, for each supervisor had promised his staff—at some time during the year—that in the next budget he would request additional equipment, repairs, raises, and more men.

With this fattened proposal in hand, David then went over the figures face to face with each department head, finding out what he absolutely had to have, and what he could do without for another year. This brought each section of the budget down to a battle of wills. David just depended on his being the strongest. It was a lousy system, often causing ill-feeling that took months to cure. He only used the method because he could find no other.

The present series of skirmishes had been the worst in his career. Last year there had been the highway program to work in, and all departments had been curtailed sharply. This made their current demands more rational. He'd had to agree to Police Chief McDowell's plea for new squad cars. Most had more than a hundred thousand miles on them, although they were only two years old. The Street Department needed new graders and trucks, and he had to include them as a matter of simple economy. If the department didn't do the work, the city would have to hire a contractor. The Sanitation Department had asked for new trucks, and he'd had to give in there, too. Many of the older garbage-disposal trucks were the open type, and in a Texas wind they make a mockery of the city's anti-litter campaigns. There'd been too many complaints; they'd have to be replaced. The Fire Department had asked for two new pumpers, and there was no arguing against that, either. The city was below minimum specifications, and if the insurance rates were raised, there'd be hell to pay.

Other requests had to be denied: a new fire station and the remodeling of two others; a street-paving plan; new employees; a new parking lot for the Police Department, a new blacktopping machine for the Street Department. . . .

Worst of all, word had gotten out during the last few days that there would be no pay increases this year. Already there was grumbling. If David could just trim the over-all budget slightly, laying aside enough for even a token raise, it would do wonders for morale.

But with the way things were shaping up, there seemed to be little hope. He had to do more trimming, somewhere. He went over the preliminary budgets repeatedly, hunting anything significant he could slash. And when he found the answer it was so simple he couldn't understand why he hadn't thought of it right off.

The Water Department figures contained a sizable outlay for a series of water main loops to serve certain fringe areas of town. It was a long-range program. A sharp jump in the number of residences in these areas had overloaded existing mains, lowering pressure. But the situation wasn't critical, now. Old John Traynor, the water director, had worked out a five-year plan, and in the last two years the sections with the most complaints had been fixed. There was no sane reason why the other loops couldn't wait until after the lake project went through.

On Wednesday afternoon David broke the news to John. As he expected, the old water chief was infuriated. It took all of David's skill to keep John from handing in his resignation.

David tried to make John understand the reasons. He praised the main replacement plan as one of the best programs ever originated within the city staff—which was true—and promised it would be carried to completion at the opportune time. He reminded John that in the new lake the Water Department was getting more of an outlay this year than all other departments combined. Then, to soothe John's injured feelings, David included a couple of minor procedural changes John had long advocated.

The two-hour conference had sapped David of energy. Yet the satisfaction of the tremendous cut in the budget left him elated. As he walked to the door with John he was eager to get back to his desk and learn how the figures now balanced. So when he saw Cal Masters waiting in the outer office, talking to Stella, he couldn't help his first reaction of irritation.

Normally he would have been glad to see Cal. But this was a bad day. Since he'd called Cal only the day before to set up a meeting with the newspaper reporter, Tom Kencaide, David assumed that was what Cal wanted to see him about. Now he was sorry he'd gotten mixed up in Kencaide's project.

Cal must have sensed David's thoughts, for his manner was apologetic. He stood by Stella's desk, nodded a greeting to John as he left, and made no move toward David and the inner office. "I just thought I might catch you in a slack moment, David," he said. "I can come back later, if you're busy."

"Oh, hell, we're not that busy," David said. "We've just been knocking the kinks out of the preliminary budget. You know how that goes. Come on in."

"I'll not take up much of your time," Cal said as they walked in to David's desk. "I should have called first."

Sometimes Cal could ramble for an hour about his morning ride into the river bottom, the birds and animal tracks he'd seen, the freshness and the greenness of the land. Maybe it was partly envy, but David often found these discourses irritating, and he was too keyed up to listen to one today. He turned his swivel chair to face Cal and spoke quickly to keep the initiative.

"I do have a wrestling match coming up in about thirty minutes with Dan McDowell over the police budget. And I don't know if I've got enough strength left to take Dan on today or not. In the last two hours I almost broke John Traynor's heart and he almost put me in shape for a mental institution."

Cal smiled. John Traynor was one of the few city employees whose career spanned back to Cal's days as mayor. David knew Cal would remember how obstinate John could be.

"You are busy, then," Cal said. "I'll come back some other time." His hands gripped the arms of the chair as he started to rise.

Now Cal's apologetic manner was even more irritating to David than the unexpected visit. "Hell, Cal, keep your seat. What's on your mind?"

Cal hesitated. He looked uncertainly around the office, as if assembling his thoughts. "It's just that something has come up in the last few days I think you—as city manager—should know about."

David nodded, using silence as a weapon.

Cal leaned forward, put his elbows on his knees, and spread the palms of his hands and looked at them.

"I shouldn't have come here today," he said again. "I wanted to tell you under more favorable circumstances, but now that I'm here I guess there's nothing else to do but go on with it." He raised his head and looked at David. "I thought you should know that I've just been given an examination by Travis and his cohorts. I have cancer, and it is likely I won't live out my full term on the council."

The last few words carried too much meaning for David's mind to absorb instantly. He sat, stunned, looking at Cal's pale blue eyes, while the full impact came to him.

"Oh, Lord, Cal," he heard himself say. He tried to add something more appropriate, but nothing came. Cal stopped his trend of thought.

"Now, David, this is a city matter. If I didn't think we could discuss it on that basis, I wouldn't have told you."

David found himself unable to speak. He nodded again to show that he understood. More to regain his composure than anything else, he got up from his desk and closed the door to the outer office.

"I'm awfully sorry to hear this," he said, fumbling for words. Then his helplessness made him seek a way out. "They're doing so much in medicine these days, surely. . . ."

Cal cut him off again. "David, no one should have any regrets when an old man dies. Especially if that old man has none of his own. As for the miracles of modern medicine, life itself has been enough of a miracle for me."

"Is there pain?"

"Not much. But I didn't come here to talk about that. I said a minute ago I have no regrets. I was wrong. There is one—maybe two. The first is havin' to leave my ranch—you know how I feel about that. My children and grandchildren are interested in other things. But that's a personal regret. The other isn't. David, what I hate worst is havin' to give up my council seat. I'm worried about who they'll replace me with."

"Nonsense, Cal. I'm sure they'll appoint some responsible person."

"I know. Things will keep movin', changin'. But I see a trend in our civic affairs that frightens me."

"What's that, Cal?"

"I'm not sure. We've talked about my views on things enough that there's no need to rehash them now. I've been a cantankerous old bastard at times, I know. They've accused me of bein' against progress, and maybe I have been. But until now I really hadn't taken the trouble to study the reason."

He paused and stared at his hands. David waited, the awareness of Cal's death sentence growing heavy within him. Cal looked up and met his gaze.

"David, I know now what I've been fightin' all these years—the injustices we've been doin' the individual. Our city government is the one closest to the people, and even we have forgotten the individual. Every major action the council has taken for years has been for the benefit of the economy, not the benefit of the individual."

"What's good for the economy is good for the individual, isn't it?"

"Not necessarily. We've wooed new industry and more people rather than raise the standards of service for the people we have. We haven't given the people of this town one thing more than what we've absolutely had to—and sometimes not that much. We haven't built a museum, and our history is as colorful or more so than Europe's. We don't have a single art gallery, water fountain, or monument. Not a single statue. Our library is a disgrace, not fit for a city one-fourth our size, and I don't guess we'd have that if Andrew Carnegie hadn't shamed us into makin' a start. Our symphony orchestra is a social club, a prestige clique, privately financed. Do you realize we haven't built one single thing of beauty in this town?"

"Do you think that's what people want? Art and culture?" David asked gently.

"They've been fed so much hogwash for so many years by that Chamber of Commerce and by that newspaper I don't think they have any idea what they do want," Cal said vigorously. "But I do know they've lost control. I think they realize they have. That's the reason they have no confidence in us. How many men on the council do you think are honestly concerned with the welfare of the individual?"

"I'm not a politician," David said pointedly. He was in no position to discuss personalities of councilmen, even with Cal, and even under the circumstances.

"My mistake. Well, you can't answer that, so I'll do it for you. Only one, Travis McNiel. Look at the rest of them. Weatherbee is all business. He thinks in volume. Wentworth is awed by the chamber, and he'd no more go against them on an issue than Weatherbee. The mayor doesn't go to the bathroom unless he gets it cleared by a chamber committee. Byron is the one that'll fool you. He's a man of many causes, a believer in conservatism in all things. But he's self-righteous and vicious. He has no respect for the individual. And Berger. He's a church man, they tell me, but I fear he's the most dangerous of all. He seeks power. He wants to run the whole town."

"What makes you say that?" David interrupted. He wondered if Cal had heard of the highway transactions—or knew any facts in the many things McDowell suspected.

"I've talked to him, and I can see into him. He's full of hate. He's consumed by ambition. But I honestly can't say which I fear the worst—him or the chamber. My point is, I want to build the Travis McNiel minority of one into a majority."

"I don't know how I could help," David said. "I can't get out and campaign."

"I'm not asking you to hand out bumper stickers or handbills, or even to take part in politics. All I want you to do, David, is to stay independent. The chamber has to be reminded every once in a while that their paperwork and charts and committees don't run the city government. City Hall does, or at least it should. I just want you to remember that the primary foundation of city government is the individual, and I hope you will always be more concerned with making sure that the garbage of that housewife on the North Side is hauled away on time, or that the holes in the pavement in front of a man's house are fixed."

"I've always felt those things are important," David told him.

"I know. That's why you've had my wholehearted support. That's why I came by to warn you of the possibility you may lose the support of my council seat. And I wanted to make sure you keep your perspective after I'm gone."

"I'll try," David promised.

"Good. I'll be gettin' along. I've got a lot of things to do. I'm goin' to talk to quite a few people about this—doctors, ministers, schoolteachers—people who should take an interest in City Hall and don't. I'll let you know who your friends are."

David walked to the door with him and stopped, his hand on the knob. "Cal, please come by any time. Whenever you feel like it. And if there's anything I can do, just let me know."

They shook hands. Cal's grip was warm and firm.

"That's nice to know. Thank you."

As David opened the door and Cal went out through the outer office, Stella seemed to realize from their faces that something unusual had happened. Then, as Cal left, she apparently became aware that she was staring, for she turned quickly back to a notepad. "Chief McDowell just called," she said. "He will be a few minutes late. A prisoner has hanged himself at the jail."

David had no desire at all to continue with the budget study. Not today. "See if you can reach him," he said. "Tell him . . . that something's come up here, too. Tell him in the morning will be fine, or tomorrow afternoon. Whenever it's most convenient with him." Then he decided to go all the way with it. "And I'll be out of the office for the rest of the day," he added.

He got his Stetson from behind the door and left, ignoring Stella's surprise. He didn't tell her where he was going, for he didn't know.

The sky to the southwest of town boiled with violence. Huge thunderheads towered white in the sun at their tops, but below their crowns they churned dark with wind and moisture. The storm moved in swiftly. When David left City Hall the thunder was still rumbling off in the distance. By the time he drove the twelve blocks to the Key Club the first gusts of the front were driving sand, dirt, and old newspapers along the street.

David stood by his Olds for a moment, holding his hatbrim against the wind, and studied the rolling clouds. He hadn't heard of a tornado alert, and he thought for a moment of getting back into the car to see if he could get a weather report on the radio. But then he decided this was only a rambunctious spring thunderstorm. He stood watching it approach until the first raindrops came. Then he dashed across the street to the doorway of the Key Club. From the shelter of the entry he waited until the rain built into a wind-lashed torrent. When he was satisfied it was no more than a heavy squall, he turned and went inside.

As he had expected, the club was practically deserted. He took a small table in the corner, as far as he could get from a group of Jaycees, the only other early-drinkers.

He ordered Scotch and water and sat thinking about Cal. In the years since Helen had taken to excessive drinking,

David had felt the need of alcohol as a crutch less and less. But this was an exception. Why, he wondered, did he never know how much people meant to him until he lost them? His feeling of regret toward Cal was nothing new. It seemed he had to learn the same bitter lesson over and over.

The first had been his mother, when he was fourteen. She'd always had a heart murmur—some childhood disease. No one ever explained to him that she had such a feeble grasp on life. Her death one cold, rainy night had left him stunned, but he hadn't learned. He let his father live out his last years in neglect.

First, there was the war, He had written occasionally, a quick V-mail letter, but they must have seemed few to a lonely old farmer. Then, after the war, there had been the GI Bill, college, and the start of his own family. There just hadn't been much time.

When word came of his father's death, David realized what he had done, but only then. Again, too late.

His mother, his father, and now Cal.

He should have given Cal more time, just as he should have given others more time. Today, if absolute courtesy hadn't demanded, he would have turned Cal away.

After Cal who? Helen? Ronnie? Christine?

He sat and drank and thought about things for a long time. The irony of it mocked him: David Hartwell, the leader of men, couldn't cope with a fifteen-year-old boy, a sixteen-year-old girl, and a woman too weak to face life. Maybe his approach was all wrong. Maybe his personal feelings interfered.

He lost count on drinks, but their effect helped him think objectively. The immediate need, obviously, was to do something with Ronnie before it was too late. He tried to analyze the situation just as he would any other problem.

What was Ronnie's trouble?

Lack of discipline.

What could he do about it?

Nothing. He hadn't time to watch the boy, and Helen wouldn't. There it was, a simply stated problem.

All right, what would he do if the city had a situation or job it couldn't handle? That was easy. He'd hire it done—call in an expert.

And what facilities exist for a boy with discipline problems? That, too, was easy. Military academies.

A good, logical conclusion, he decided, rather proud of his ability to stand off and take the long-range, impartial view. The idea grew. A stiff school might help Ronnie's academic standing, too. His present level was poor preparation for college. The more David thought about it, the more enthused he became. There was a good academy in South Texas, and the Southeastern states were full of them.

He began to think of what he would say to Ronnie. He couldn't keep from believing the boy might like going away for a while. Maybe they could sit down and discuss it, and maybe he could make Ronnie see it would be for his own good. An entirely new relationship might be established between them if he could just get the boy to accept this as mature judgment. . . .

Realizing that Ronnie should be home from school by now, David signed the bar chit and left the club.

The storm was over, and now the warm afternoon sun was raising steam from the still-wet pavement. For a moment after the heat hit him, David considered leaving the car and taking a taxi home, thinking of the possibility of the city manager being picked up for drunken driving. That'd be a lick. But his car in plain sight across from the Key Club would be a night-long advertisement of what had happened, so he decided to risk driving.

When he arrived home a rock 'n' roll record was going full blast in Ronnie's room. Helen was in Dallas and Christine, Calla Lilly said, was "out with that boy again."

David went up to Ronnie's room and knocked. At the boy's answering voice, he pushed the door open. Ronnie was on his bed, listening to the record, deafening inside the room. David went over to the record player and set the pickup arm in its cradle.

The sudden silence was momentarily disturbing. Ronnie didn't move. He just lay on the bed, eyes wide, staring. David looked around, found a chair, and turned it to face Ronnie.

"I want to talk to you," he said.

David was aware of his awkwardness. He remembered how his father had always seemed so awkward in these man-to-man talks, and he'd wondered about it even back then. Now, he still didn't understand the reason for the father-son awkwardness, and fought it, trying to make himself talk objectively.

"I have an idea," he went on. "I want to see what you think about it." He paused, trying to think of some way to ease into the subject, but he could find none. "How would you like to go to a military school for a while?"

Ronnie's thin body twitched nervously on the bed. "If you want me to," he said.

David was prepared for most any reaction other than this hangdog attitude. "Damn it, it isn't a question of what I want," he said, exasperated. "It boils down to what is best for you. You're getting damned close to being a grown man. You've got to start thinking like a man. And one thing a man needs is self-discipline. The military is a good place to learn these things."

When it came, David found himself welcoming Ronnie's first hint of protest. Anything was better than this lack of spirit.

"Why now?" Ronnie asked, his voice barely audible. "I'll have to go into service eventually anyway. Everybody does."

David tried to explain. "As I told you, the doctor believes your home life isn't proper, and no doubt he's right. Any child—teen-ager—needs discipline, training. I can't be here to give it to you, and your mother won't. It's as simple as that. A military school would give you what you need, prepare you for life, where we've failed. Then, when you go into the military, on to college, or whatever you do, you'll be much better prepared."

"What about Christine?" Ronnie asked, his voice trembling. "You going to send her to military school? She's growing up in this house too, you know."

David studied him a moment before answering. Sibling rivalry. As an only child, he'd never experienced it. He'd always known Ronnie felt resentment for everything he did for Christine, but this was the first time Ronnie had brought it into the open. David decided to be firm.

"If Christine needs something we can't give her, then I guess we can find a strict girls' school for her. Thus far, I haven't seen any indication she needs special attention."

"You better look around, then," Ronnie said, mumbling so low that David wasn't sure of the words.

"What?" he asked sharply. "What did you say?"

"Nothin'," Ronnie mumbled, lowering his head, staring at the bedspread.

David tried to keep from reading meaning into the remark. The temptation was strong to accept Ronnie's word. But David knew he had said something; he wanted to be sure of the exact words. "Ronnie, if you know something, tell me."

Ronnie didn't answer.

"I heard what you said," David told him. "You said I ought to look around. Well, I have. I've tried to look after both of you, and as far as I can tell, there's nothing wrong with Christine. Her grades are good. She leads an active social life, and she has a lot of friends. I wish I could say the same for you. But that's all I have to go on. If there's something else I should know, tell me."

"I didn't mean anything," Ronnie said without looking at him. "I just said it."

David thought that over, wanting to believe him, yet doubting. He decided to drop the subject, sensing he would accomplish nothing by pursuing it.

"We were talking about you. What do you think about the idea of a military school?"

"I don't know," Ronnie said without looking up. "I guess it'd be all right."

Suddenly David was tired of the whole thing. "Well, we don't have to decide right now. There's plenty of time. I'll have Stella send for some literature, then we can talk it over. But I want you to be thinking about it."

Not until he was back in his room, lying on the bed with the walls spinning, did David realize what he had done. He had just introduced Ronnie to another drunk in the family.

It wasn't until the next morning that he remembered he hadn't thought to ask Cal if he wanted to call off the appointment with Tom Kencaide. He should have asked, for Cal probably wouldn't want to be bothered, now.

## CHAPTER FOURTEEN

They rode along the river, Tom on a sturdy black Quarter Horse, Cal ahead on a skittish roan.

Below them, the river rippled shallow across graveled shoals, the water slightly muddied now by the runoff from yesterday's rain. Ahead, at the bend of the river marking one corner of Cal's ranch, the red clay bluffs rose steep, carved by centuries of flood, sharp in contrast with the smooth flood plain. Cal's roan picked his way through the salt cedars, following the narrow path the Herefords had traveled on their way to water through the years, as the Longhorns had before them and maybe even the buffalo before that.

Cal's back was stiff and erect in the saddle, his body leaving all movement to the roan. Tom made no attempt at conversation, for he knew the way of the old-timers . . . a time for speech, and a time for silence. Now was the time for quiet, for Cal was at work, his practiced eyes scanning the soft earth, reading stories in a language few Americans know any more—the language of the ground. Churned dirt where two bull calves played in youthful exuberance . . . the tracks of a coyote, the mission apparent from the way he traveled . . . the path of a mother skunk and her brood . . . droppings showing the jackrabbit population . . . the tracks of quail and chaparral. . . .

Tom didn't know the language, and he couldn't see these things. But he knew the messages were there. He remembered how often ground-sign was mentioned in the stories of the old-timers. So he understood Cal's preoccupation.

There was a strange sense of peace and tranquillity around them, with only the sounds of the horses breathing, the hoofs, and the wind in the salt cedars. Tom had overcome his earlier doubts about riding the Quarter Horse. At first, when Cal suggested it, he had thought the old rancher must be joking. Tom had ridden before a few times—park and rental stable animals—but never a high-strung, spirited purebred. He'd given in only when he saw that Cal really wanted—for some reason—to show him the ranch. Cal apparently considered the tour a normal prelude to talking business and had promised to have Tom back at the ranchhouse early enough for him to get into town and to work on time.

But work and this afternoon's scheduled interview with Berger seemed far away. The black, nervous, and uncertain of his rider at first, had settled down now to an almost lazy walk.

They passed under a lone cottonwood. Cal turned the roan up the bank, out of the riverbed, and Tom followed, feeling the muscles of the black bunch for the quick lunges up the steep slope. When they reached the top Cal reined in, stood in the stirrups, and swept off his hat, his thick white hair ruffled by the wind. Tom pulled the black up abreast, and for a moment his mind was stunned by the broad sweep of land before them.

The grassland stretched a full two miles into the distance unbroken. The far end of the pasture was edged by a grove of trees. Across this ground, an ancient flood plain for the river, more than a hundred fat Herefords grazed. A few of the closer cows raised their heads briefly, regarded them with indifference, and went back to grazing.

Tom knew now why Cal had brought him down the riverbed. The sudden confrontation with the big pasture held the same emotional surprise of a first trip to the rim of the Grand Canyon, or of stepping topside on a ship coming up the Hudson River and being introduced to the New York skyline at close quarters.

"I didn't know there was country like this around here," Tom said, thinking of the miles upon miles of mesquite and scrub oak.

"I've taken care of the land, and it's taken care of me," Cal said. "Do you know cattle?"

"Very little," Tom admitted.

"Then I will have to brag. That is one of the best foundation herds in Texas. Not as well-known as Tom Medders, Bridwell, or Hull-Dobbs, perhaps, because I haven't exhibited in years. But I used to give them a run for their money, and I've improved the stock greatly since then. I hope you'll excuse the braggin'."

"Looks to me like something to brag about," Tom said.

"I only tell you this because you strike me as bein' able to appreciate the man-hours that've gone into this ranch in the last hundred years. They say the only way to get a good rancher's foundation herd is to wait until he dies. That's what worries me now. I wish I knew what is goin' to happen to it when I'm gone."

Tom didn't answer. There is nothing to say when an old man talks of death. The black stirred beneath him, raising the faint, rich smell of leather and horse sweat.

"Let's go see about the salt cakes in yonder trees," Cal said, putting his bootheels to the roan's sides.

They started across the pasture, riding abreast. The heat of midday was building around them, but here in the open there was more wind. From somewhere far off came the call of a bird, a mournful sound, a cry of a lost soul.

"What is that bird?" Tom asked.

"Killdeer."

"He's a cheerful cuss."

Cal smiled. "I've always rather liked him. I guess it's a streak of my nature that I sometimes enjoy being sad."

Tom remembered past sensations of homesickness, the wash of foreign seas alongside a ship, and the cry of a seagull.

"I know what you mean," he said.

"I wish you had come out a while back," Cal said. "I was down here one mornin' and the wild geese came over. Filled the whole riverbottom with their sound. For eighty years and more I've watched them fly over, north in the spring, south in the fall. I suppose hardly anyone has time to listen to them any more, but it's always been one of the great pleasures of my life. I wouldn't miss it for anything."

"I've never heard them," Tom admitted.

"Too bad. I suppose city life has compensations, but it would take many to match that for me."

They crossed through the herd at a walk. Cal stood in the stirrups, and from the way his eyes moved, Tom knew he was counting, so he kept quiet. Finally, they reached the shade of the trees. Cal swung down slowly from the saddle and dropped the reins, leaving the roan to graze. Tom did the same with the black, then followed Cal over to the rough wooden troughs.

Cal studied the salt cakes. "Enough here for two, three days yet, I guess." He sat on the edge of a trough, laid his hat on the bare planks beside him, and looked out over the herd. "David Hartwell tells me you have a big idea," he said.

It was a statement, but a question, and Tom knew that this was the time and place Cal had chosen to talk business.

"An idea," Tom said. "I don't know whether it's a very big one or not."

Cal looked off into the distance for a moment. The cottonwood trees around them were shedding, and the fluffy seeds drifted down as gently as snow. "What kind of a newspaper do you have in mind?"

Tom explained, as briefly and simply as he could. Cal listened in silence until he had finished.

"A newspaper standin' on its own. Not a small dog yappin' at the heels of the big newspaper." Again, it was a statement, but a question.

"I have my own idea of what a newspaper should be," Tom said.

"What about income? How would you compete with the big newspaper with the stores?"

Tom explained what he knew of the attitudes of the city's advertisers toward the newspaper, about Arlene, and how he was confident of her abilities.

Cal considered this for a moment. "Suppose the Chamber of Commerce was backin' somethin', and you saw fit to oppose it. Wouldn't that cut down on advertisin'?"

"It might," Tom admitted. "But I don't think the loss would amount to much if I gave both sides of the issue full treatment and kept my own views confined to the editorial page. I think most advertisers would see the fairness in that."

"You have a higher regard for their sense of fairness than I do. But be that as it may. What about your subscribers? You know, and I know, that for the most part people don't give a damn what happens at City Hall. I don't blame them. Most happenings up there are the driest, dullest events imaginable. What makes you think they'd pay to read about them?"

Tom felt new admiration for the old rancher. He had hit the core of the matter, the weakest point of the idea.

"I'll try to make people see how those happenings affect them," Tom said. "I think people would be more interested if they got real news, and not just a promotion piece on every civic issue. Then, too, there'd be other local news, trials, that sort of thing, that I could cover in depth, make readable." He thought over what he had said. He had missed the point of what he'd had in mind. "I guess my main purpose would be to *get* people interested," he explained.

Cal nodded. "How much you think this journalistic experiment would cost?"

Tom took a deep breath, remembering all warnings he'd ever heard not to be conservative. "To do it right, ten thousand," he said. He explained briefly the cost estimates he'd made on printing, circulation, promotion, office expenses, and expected revenue.

"What kind of terms are you prepared to make?"

Tom decided honesty was his best course. "I don't know. I had thought something like a fifty-fifty split on profits, after guaranteeing minimum salaries. Our labor against the capital. But I don't know much about these things."

"You don't drive a very hard bargain."

"I'm not in much of a bargaining position."

"Don't sell yourself short. You've got youth, ideals, talent, ambition. Those are things more valuable than money."

"Do you think the idea has possibilities?"

"Of course it has," Cal said. "There was a time when I would have been very interested. A few years ago, or maybe even a few months ago. But now, I don't know. I need time to think about it. Let's ride on back to the house so we can be more comfortable while we talk."

The Masters ranchhouse, a rambling two-story white frame, stood on the crest of a hill, dominating the countryside for miles. Clippings in the newspaper files said it was built in the early 1880s by Cal's father. These stories, written by reporters of years past, said Cal's father had settled on the ranch in 1866, pioneered the cattle drives north to the railheads in Kansas, prospered, served in the Texas Legislature, reared a large family to meet assorted tragedies, and died in his sleep one winter night in 1897, leaving the ranch to Cal, his only surviving heir.

Tom followed Cal toward the corral below the ranchhouse, both their horses in a dead run. After entering the bull trap a half mile from the corral, Cal had put the roan into a trot, then a lope, and finally to a gallop and all-out run. The black, his racing instinct stirred, tried to keep up, but Tom held him back, dubious of his own ability to stay in the saddle. The black fought the bit so frantically that Tom was more fearful of the head-tossing than running, so he let the reins out and leaned low over the saddle horn. Wind whistled in his ears as the black swiftly closed the gap to the roan, his hoofs thundering against the earth flying beneath them. They passed Cal and the roan, but before they reached the corral the black faltered, began to lag, and Cal and the roan swept past through the gate ahead of them.

They tied the horses to a railing in the post-oak corral. The horses were still wild-eyed, excited, breathing hard. Cal was laughing, and three of the Mexican ranchhands were watching, grinning, from the door of the barn.

"Work's good for a horse, same as for a man," Cal said. "I always run them a little to work the fat off. They get lazy if you don't."

Tom was still puzzled as to how the roan managed to come on again so strong right at the finish. "I thought the black was outrunning him."

"Blackie's a Quarter Horse, best for short distances," Cal explained. "But he'll burn himself out if you run him much more'n four or five hundred yards. This one's got Thoroughbred in him. Gives him more stamina."

Cal loosened the belly girth to give the roan more breathing room. Tom did the same for the black.

"We can leave the saddles on," Cal said. "I'll have someone come out and take care of them."

Tom walked with Cal up the slope to the house. They went up the steps to the front porch, and Cal held the screen door open for him. As Tom entered the front room, he had the sensation of moving back sixty years.

Across from the hall door, facing them, was a huge native stone fireplace, decorated by a set of Longhorns a full eight feet across. Below the horns hung an old rifle. The furniture—a rocking chair, an arm chair, and an old couch—were of time scarred oak, with leather strips crisscrossed to hold feather-stuffed cushions. The bare hardwood floor had no pretense of polish, and in the far corner the large oak roll-top desk was piled with papers, testifying that this was not only a living room, but a headquarters for the ranch and extensive oil holdings.

Cal hung his hat on a set of elk horns to the right of the door. "Have a seat and make yourself at home. Would you care for a drink of whiskey?"

There was a tone to the question that let Tom know Cal wanted a drink and a drinking companion. It was almost noon, and Tom didn't want to go in to work with liquor on his breath, especially when he had the afternoon interview with Berger. But under the circumstances, he didn't feel like refusing. He rationalized that lunch would mask a single drink. "That sounds good," he said. "Just a little water."

Cal went into the kitchen. Tom crossed to the fireplace and examined the rifle. An old Sharps. He had seen them in museums. He heard Cal's voice in the other room, then Cal's returning bootsteps. Cal saw him looking at the gun.

"Belonged to my father," he said. "That was his favorite until repeatin' rifles became common."

Tom looked around the room, taking in the over-all effect. "I like this," he said.

"It lacks a woman's touch, that's plain," Cal said. "My wife was never happy here. The house in town was my first anniversary present to her. That's the way I got involved in city politics. If she'd been happy with ranch life, I suppose I'd have lived the rest of my days here and never thought of town as more than a place to get groceries. But once I became involved, it got to be a habit. So I stayed on in town after she died."

Cal's wife, Tom remembered from the clippings, died in a flu epidemic.

"I left the house here pretty much the way it was," Cal added. "Sentimental reasons, I suppose. Sometimes, if I'm tired, I stay here overnight instead of drivin' back to town, so it's handy. And I have Henry here to look after things."

The Negro, tall and lean and almost as old as Cal, came from the kitchen carrying a small tray with the whiskey. Tom took the offered drink and thanked him. Cal took the other and motioned toward the door.

"Let's take them out to the porch where it's cooler."

They walked out to the two cane-bottomed rocking chairs facing the single elm, Old Smokey, and Cal's pickup truck in the front yard.

"Whenever I see something of the past, like this ranchhouse, I'm always amazed at how things have changed in the last half century," Tom said.

Cal chuckled. "You're amazed. Say, I wish I could tell you just half the changes I've seen. When I was a boy, here, the only way to travel was by horse, wagon, or on foot. Now they're gettin' ready to send a man to the moon."

Cal took a pillbox from his shirt pocket. He held it in his open palm for a moment as if undecided whether to take one or not. Then he put it back into his shirt pocket unopened. A mocking-bird fluttered in from somewhere to the south and began a song in the elm.

"I grew up hearin' talk of Indian raids," Cal said. "In those days, a wood and flint arrow with a bit of feather on it was still a thing to be feared. Now we got arrows that'll span the oceans, kill hundreds of thousands of people in the twinkle of an eye. Yes, I've seen changes, boy, but it chills me to think of the things that may yet come in your lifetime."

"Maybe it's best not to think of them," Tom said. "They may never happen."

"I know that's the popular view, but I'm not convinced it's right. If the people on the frontier hadn't faced up to the dangers and met them, I'm sure our nation's history would have been vastly different."

"We've lived with it for nearly twenty years now," Tom said. "Maybe we can develop a philosophy, learn to live with it."

"Perhaps. I hope so. But it seems to me there is something lacking—a moral standard, a certain personal attitude of courage—that was prevalent in my younger days." He was silent for a moment. "I wish I could explain it better than that. You see, it was different, then. All over the range were men who had fought on both sides in one of the bloodiest wars in all history, fought with the Mexicans along the border, fought with the Indians, and lived constantly with the dangers of the trail and life in the open. Their example was all around us. It was a wonderful heritage to grow up with. It is a heritage that has all but faded away, I fear."

"I saw some admirable cases of heroism in Europe and in Korea," Tom said. "I think the mettle is still there."

"Battlefield heroics are one thing. I'm talkin' about something deeper, the courage to keep to principles when all else is threatened. I see a tendency to compromise that disturbs me. We are givin' up our rights, little by little, the same rights our fathers fought for—that you've fought for. Do you read the *Fort Worth Star-Telegram?*"

"Yes," Tom said. He usually looked through the exchange files in the office during the evening.

"Then you know of the ruckus they had there once. The Recreation Board wanted to sell a golf course to the university so it could build dormitories, and the people who owned homes around the golf course were protestin'. The board made a statement of policy at the time, and I want to read part of it to you."

He fished in his billfold for the wrinkled newspaper clipping, put on his glasses, and hunted down the column until he found the right place.

"The board said, 'Anytime a city grows, each person has to give up a little of what he thinks is his own.'" Cal lowered the clipping and whipped off his glasses. "Now, isn't that a hell of a thing? I don't know who wrote this, but it sums up exactly what I've been fightin' all the years I've been in city politics. Our country was founded to give the individual freedom, and now all levels of our government seem to be askin' him to give up this freedom, bit by bit, day by day, in the name of growth and to keep the economy healthy. Good Lord, we're givin' away our birthright."

"Maybe it's the fear of nuclear war," Tom suggested. "Maybe people are unconsciously putting themselves more and more under the care of the government for protection."

Cal considered the theory. "Could be you're right. As you know, I'm not a learned man. I have no idea as to the cause. But I do know there's danger in this dependency on the government. Thank God the cattle industry has stayed relatively clear of it. I don't know what I would have done if we'd gotten into it as deep as the farmers."

He seemed to be thinking aloud now. Tom sat still and listened.

"All that's just a part of it, though," Cal went on. "People have forgotten how to live. I guess that's the biggest change

I've seen in my lifetime. There's never the time any more to enjoy friendship. I think as much of David Hartwell as I did my own son that was killed in the first war. But David was always so busy. We never had much time together, except for a little huntin'. I enjoyed Travis McNiel. A fine man, and a good doctor. I knew his father, too, a preacher who delivered sermons like he had God standin' right behind him. Travis is a man who thinks deep thoughts and feels things deeply, but I never got to know him well."

The use of the past tense gave Cal's rambling such a finality Tom could think of no comment, and Cal seemed lost in thought. They sat for a time in silence.

Finally Cal became aware of his lapse. "I'm sorry. I guess the exertion of that ride this mornin' has made me tireder than I realized. I've been prattlin' like a senile old man."

Tom noticed the short shadows in the yard. "I've got to be going," he said. "I've been so relaxed I almost forgot that I have to work this afternoon."

"Be glad to have you stay for lunch," Cal said, repeating an earlier invitation.

"I really can't," Tom said. "I have an appointment in town."

Cal followed him out to Old Smokey.

"I've enjoyed our talk," Cal said, his hand on the car door. "And I'm quite interested in your idea. But like I said, it comes at a bad time. Give me a few days to think it over. You'll be hearin' from me."

The morning had left Tom in such a good mood he hated to ruin the day in an interview with Berger. He was certain Berger would be no more than civil, if that. He was wrong. Berger met him at the door, shook his hand with surprising warmth, and promptly offered to take him on a tour of the distributing plant.

So Tom followed the squat, bald little man across the wide concrete floors listening to figures on the number of beer cases that could be expedited daily, how fast a truck could be loaded with the modern conveyer system Berger designed and installed, and how the industry was finally ridding itself of the unnecessary expense of handling empties.

This was a side of Berger Tom had never seen. He was thrown off stride. He thought he had prepared himself for any eventuality, but this sudden affability confused him. This wasn't the mood Tom had in mind for sharp, needling questions about Joe Garzek.

It was Berger himself who opened the way to the subject. After the tour he led Tom through a heavily paneled door lettered PRIVATE into a small, secluded room equipped with a bar, stools, and a long beer cooler.

"We can't sell it without a place for customers to sample it," Berger explained. He went behind the bar and opened two cold bottles of Alamo.

Tom slid onto a bar stool, relieving his feet of weight. Berger's alert, nervous eyes were watching him.

"I know why you're here," Berger said. "I've heard about you nosing around, asking questions. I even know about you going to see the DA." He smiled, apparently to show he held no ill will.

"If you knew what I've been doing, why did you agree to see me?" Tom asked. Berger put his elbows on the bar and spread his hands.

"Because I want to lay my cards on the table with you. I want to show you you're wrong. You've been talking to the wrong people. A man can't get anywhere in this world without making enemies, and that's all you've been doing, talking to those sons a bitches uptown. I've got plenty of friends. I couldn't have been elected to council if I didn't. Why don't you get out and talk to some of them? Then you'll hear the other side."

"I'm willing to hear the other side," Tom said.

But Berger seemed to be swept up in his own chain of thought. His face reddened with anger. "I know what those bastards uptown say. I know the talk they put out. They claim I got some kind of a secret empire built up down here on lower Main. Sure, I got some things going for me, but I don't have a secret club like they got uptown. They don't think anybody can come in here from out of town and make a success of himself. Well, I showed them different, even if they do make me put up twice the collateral I need for a loan at the bank and look down their noses at me at chamber meetings. I've beat them at their own game and they don't like it."

Tom didn't understand exactly what he meant. "Then this is just a rumor they're spreading. You don't have any other business interests?"

Berger studied him a moment before answering. "I said I'd lay my cards on the table with you. All right, I will. Sure, I've got a little money tied up in some other ventures. I don't advertise what they are because I've got to get along with the Liquor Control Board, the beer company, my customers, and lots of other people. If something else goes sour, I don't want it to queer this operation here. Hell, look around. Every bank president uptown has got money in other things, but they want to be known as bank presidents. I want to be known as a beer distributor, because that happens to be my principal occupation. What's wrong with that?"

Tom didn't answer. There was a moment's silence.

"Do you know Joe Garzek?" Tom asked quietly. He thought he was ready for any reaction, from another angry tirade to more evasion. But again Berger fooled him.

"I imagine I know more about him than you do," Berger said caustically.

"What about this story he's telling about police harassment after trouble with your company? What's your side of that?"

"His trouble with the police is no concern of mine," Berger said heatedly. "I saw it coming on, and I could have told him. Frankly, I was glad to lose his business, because it's the rowdy bars that give taverns and lounges a bad name, hurt the whole industry."

"He operated that tavern two years without a single arrest. I've checked with the police records."

"Let's just say he let things deteriorate for two years until conditions finally came to police attention. It takes a good man to handle a bar out there. Most of the customers are airmen. Younger, less experienced drinkers than you get in an ordinary bar. You got to watch them, cut off the flow of beer before they're too far gone to make it back to the base, and do it without making them mad. Some people can do it, but not Garzek. I could see he'd let things get out of control a long time before the police stepped in."

"What about Garzek's trouble with your company? What's your side of that?"

"Garzek signed an order for forty cases of beer, and that's what the truck delivered. If it'd been anybody else, we'd have taken back what he didn't want and that'd been the end of it. But that's what I get for doing business with a mental patient in the first place."

Tom must have shown his surprise.

"You didn't know that, did you?" Berger said triumphantly. "I told you I know more about Garzek than you do. His wife committed him about four years ago. I don't know why. You're the newspaperman. You find out. They kept him out at the state hospital over six months, and I've heard he's still under a doctor's care. From my dealings with him, it seems to me he ought to be back in the nut house."

Tom was taken aback by this, but what was even more unsettling was that he had no trouble believing it. He remembered Garzek's affinity to tears and his quick, rabbitlike mannerisms. He felt quick anger at himself for not suspecting.

"I've still got that sales order Garzek raised so much hell about," Berger said. "It's in the office files. Do you want to see it?"

There was no point in looking at it. If Garzek was right, the order had been altered. If Garzek was wrong, the order and signature were genuine. Either way, Tom probably wouldn't be able to distinguish the difference.

"No," he said. "I've caused you enough trouble for one day."

Berger smiled. "No trouble at all." He extended his right hand across the bar. "No hard feelings, are there?"

"Of course not," Tom said, and they shook hands.

"Come back any time," Berger said. "The beer cooler here is always open to the working press."

Tom realized that in some unexpected, freakish way word of his talk with Berger might get back to Houston Collier. So that night he told Collier about it.

"That's what I like about my staff," Collier said. "They follow orders so well. I thought we'd agreed to forget about Joe Garzek."

"I didn't think it would do any harm to talk to Berger," Tom said lamely.

"Well, let's hope not," Collier said. "I don't know what'd happen if BeeBee should hear about it. He doesn't pay his reporters to go out and get the newspaper into messes with advertisers whenever they feel so inclined. But I want to know. Are you through with it now? Are you convinced?"

"I guess," Tom admitted.

And he was, almost. He checked with a contact at the state hospital and yes, they'd had a Joe Garzek as a patient four years ago. The diagnosis was, of course, confidential, but speaking off the record, yes, he had an extremely disordered personality when admitted. He had responded well to treatment, however, and was soon discharged for further, private treatment. Yes, delusions of persecution would be compatible with his type of disorder in its more advanced stages.

Tom realized that any logic should convince him that Garzek was nothing more than a harmless little man with a series of imagined wrongs. Every newspaper has to deal with one almost daily. With experience, most newspapermen learn to recognize them, pacify them by listening sympathetically, and send them on their way with no more thought than a brief reflection on the varied types a city room attracts. Apparently in Garzek Tom had failed to recognize the symptoms, attributing the tears to an emotional, Mediterranean background.

Still, there were so many other things that didn't add up, small, nagging doubts—the looks he'd seen on the faces of bar owners as he'd questioned them, the similarity of Garzek's story and that of the South Side bar owner, Al Fowler. There were too many places where Garzek's and Fowler's descriptions of Berger's beer distributing operation paralleled. He also remembered the way the police had acted, the warnings.

No fact alone was significant, but taking them together they still seemed to mean something.

He was sitting at his desk, thinking about this, when he saw Collier striding rapidly across the city room toward him. "You have any idea where Hartwell is?"

Tom considered. Hartwell had been out of pocket a great

deal lately. He seemed to have no set habits. "I might be able to locate him."

"Well, get on it, then. J. Marvin just called from the emergency room at the hospital. Hartwell's daughter has just been brought in after a suicide attempt. They can't find Hartwell anywhere, and they've asked us to help."

Tom picked up the phone, considering the possibilities. He canceled home and office, first places anyone would try. Stella, Hartwell's secretary, might have an idea. After that the Key Club, the Chamber, Cal's town place. . . . He thought ahead to what he'd say if he should contact Hartwell. "How bad is she?" he asked Collier.

"J. Marvin said she made a damned good try. She may not make it. I think that's why they're trying so desperately to get ahold of Hartwell."

## CHAPTER FIFTEEN

Dr. Wayne Callihan was the duty intern when they brought Christine Hartwell into the hospital emergency room. This was fortunate for all concerned, Travis thought later, not because Callihan was a better doctor than his fellow interns, but because he aspired to become a society doctor.

Without being obtrusive about it, Callihan was continually aware of the social standing and probable income of the patients each practicing physician attended in the hospital, and dwelled at length upon why that doctor attracted his particular clientele. Travis knew Callihan had long envied him in his daily contacts with the mayor, members of the council, Chamber of Commerce executives and business leaders, and he was highly critical of the lost opportunities in that Travis didn't follow up these contacts on the social level.

With his awareness, Callihan knew immediately that Travis was Christine Hartwell's family doctor. He also realized within the first thirty seconds that the girl's chances were borderline. And, conscious of the workings of promotion and esteem, Callihan also knew this was more than just another suicide attempt. There was apt to be some Monday morning quarterbacking on how this case was handled, both medically and administratively.

Callihan didn't want the responsibility. He had seen Travis enter the building by the rear entrance a few minutes earlier. He immediately had Travis paged.

Travis was in the maternity ward nurses' cubicle, writing directions for the night nurse, when the call came. He took the elevator to the lower level, still not convinced the patient was the Christine Hartwell he knew. He could not reconcile a suicide attempt with the shy, sweet-natured girl he'd treated for tonsillitis last winter.

But it was Christine. She still lay on the ambulance stretcher, the curves of her lithe young body outlined by the sheet, when he hurried into Emergency. The two ambulance attendants stood awkwardly inside the doorway, gaping at Christine, as Callihan checked the girl's pulse rate.

If it had been a man on the stretcher, or even an elderly woman, the two ambulance attendants would have been waiting outside in the hall for the return of their stretcher with their usual studied boredom. Now what chivalry they possessed had been jostled. He could almost see them thinking: what a waste. If she was going to throw her life away, why didn't she give me a part of what was left. I would have helped her. Anything would have been better than this.

Callihan looked up at Travis without expression.

"What did she take?" Travis asked.

"Don't know," Callihan said. "Some kind of barbiturate would be my guess."

Travis knelt by the stretcher. The pulse was weak, but rapid. The skin was cold and clammy. The respiration was slow and labored. He turned Christine's head and pushed back an eyelid. The pupil was constricted, but reacted to light. He pinched her arm hard, then slapped her face twice without response.

"Put her over there," Travis said, pointing to the table by the new respirator. He went over to the ambulance attendants while Christine was being moved. J. Marvin Olds, the police reporter, was standing behind them.

"Didn't you find a bottle, anything?" Travis asked.

"She was in a little foreign car out in the park," the ambulance driver said apologetically. "I started to look around, but a cop told me to get movin' with her."

J. Marvin Olds stepped through the doorway. "I found a pill on the floorboard of the car," he said. "Might be she dropped it."

"Let's see it," Travis said impatiently.

"The police have it," Olds said, also apologetic. "But it was blue. What the junkies call 'blue devils.'"

Amytal. Aprobarbital, a barbiturate of intermediate duration. That figured.

Travis hurried back to Christine and went to work: gastric lavage with potassium permanganate solution; sodium sulfate solution deposited in the stomach as a saline cathartic. The work was delicate because there was no gag reflex. Then they put her under the respirator.

After that he started a close watch on the vital signs—respiration, pulse, blood pressure, temperature, skin color, cardiac rhythm, pupillary size and reflex; corneal, tendon and gag reflex, and response to pain—hunting for evidence of improvement. But he knew it was too early to start building hopes.

When he looked up a few minutes later the ambulance attendants were gone, but two policemen had taken their place by the doorway. Travis left Christine in the care of the nurse and went over to them. "Have you been able to contact the family?" he asked.

The small one did the talking. "Mr. Hartwell isn't at home. But Mrs. Hartwell's on the way down here."

"Did you find a bottle with the girl?"

"No bottle. She musta thrown it away. But we found this on the floor of the car." He held out a small blue capsule. Amytal. "Can we talk to her?"

"Good Lord, no," Travis said. "She's in a coma."

"Maybe we better stay till she wakes up, then," the cop said dubiously.

"You may have a long wait," Travis told him. "Besides, she's going to be in a highly confused state of mind when and if she does come around. I doubt if she'll be able to remember right off what did happen."

"We have to make out a report," the cop insisted.

"Well, put down that I insisted you not talk to her for a day or two, at least. I'll take the responsibility. Right now, I imagine the best thing you could do would be to find David Hartwell."

They hesitated, reluctant to leave. If it had been a prostitute from lower Main they would have shrugged and walked away. But they knew this case had to be handled right. Their superiors would be asking all kinds of questions, and they wanted to have the answers.

"We'll be back later, then, just to see how she's doin'," the cop said. They turned and went out. Behind them, Travis saw J. Marvin Olds still waiting.

"How is she?" Olds asked quietly.

"You're not going to use anything on this, are you?" Travis countered.

"I don't know," Olds said. He leaned against the doorjamb. "Used to, a few years ago, I could tell you exactly what the policy of the paper would be. Now, I don't know. I'm just here for information. Somebody else will decide whether to run it or not."

"She's just fifteen or sixteen," Travis said. "If she lives, that'd be a hell of a thing to come back to."

"She's the city manager's daughter. That makes it news."

If it was an advertiser's daughter Milam damned sure wouldn't run a story on it. But Hartwell's daughter, he probably would. Milam had always seemed to dislike Hartwell. Travis didn't know why. Remembering what he saw behind City Hall that night, Travis reflected that maybe there *was* something between Hartwell and Milam's sister, and maybe Milam knew. If so, Hartwell's daughter shouldn't be made to suffer.

Perhaps if they thought Christine was going to pull through they'd start thinking ahead to the consequences of a printed story.

"You can tell them she's in very critical condition, but she's got a good chance to pull through."

Olds nodded. "I heard the cops say they can't find Hartwell. Maybe the newspaper staff could help. They're used to tracking people down."

"I'm sure he would appreciate it," Travis told him.

J. Marvin went across the hall to the phone in the registration room. Travis called Marilyn and told her he wouldn't make it home for dinner. Then he hurried back to Christine. There was no appreciable change.

Another ambulance came, bringing a man who'd lost two fingers in a power mower. In shock, he kept telling repeatedly how it got dark before he'd finished mowing, so he'd turned on the yard lights. He just stooped down to move the garden hose, and he didn't realize he was so close to the mower. . . .

Callihan clucked sympathetically as he worked. The man's wife and a tall teen-ager, apparently a son, entered the hall and stood outside the door, peeking in.

Travis was leaning over Christine, looking for a slight improvement in respiratory volume, when he heard a gasp behind him. Helen Hartwell was standing in the doorway, her face drained of color, her hands to her mouth. She was on the verge of hysteria. Travis moved quickly across the room and took her by the shoulders, gripping hard so his words would sink in.

"Helen, we're going to need your help. You've got to get hold of yourself."

The deep sob that came from her throat might have meant anything. She nodded to show she understood. Travis caught the faint smell of gin on her breath, but if she had been intoxicated earlier, she was cold sober now. Travis led her out into the hall.

"Listen to me. Christine is going to need you more in the next few hours than at any time since she was born. You've got to help her. Can you do it?"

Helen looked around wildly. "Where's David?"

"She doesn't need David," he told her roughly. "She's going to need you, her mother. You help her. We'll find David."

He could see her fighting for self-control. The wife and son of the mower-mangled man had turned from their own drama to watch Helen.

"How is she?" Helen asked in a calmer voice.

"She's a very sick girl," Travis admitted. "But she has a great deal working in her favor, so she has a good chance. I still don't know exactly how much poisoning she has. She took Amytal, a barbiturate. Now think. Do you have any idea where she got the pills? Were there any around the house?"

Helen put a hand to her mouth. "I have some. A doctor in Dallas gave me the prescription. I couldn't sleep."

"Where are they?"

Helen started to open her purse, then hesitated. "They're on my dresser at home."

"That's probably where she got them," Travis said. "How many were left?"

"I took two in Dallas, and, I believe two or three since . . . I just can't remember. A bottle about that high, and it was about three-fourths full, I think."

"Is there anyone at home now?"

"Calla Lilly, and Ronnie."

"Get Calla Lilly to go upstairs and look for that pill bottle. If it's gone, we at least will know where she got them. You can use that phone in there."

He showed her the phone in the registration unit. She picked up the receiver, then hesitated. "Doctor, is she going to live?"

He considered the question for a moment, then decided to tell her the truth. "I don't know. The poisoning affects the respiratory system, and the main danger is hypoxia—not enough oxygen in the blood. But, as I said, she's got much in her favor. She's young and healthy, and there's less danger of complications—pneumonia, infection, things that I'd worry about if she were older. If she can hang on twenty-four or thirty-six hours, she'll make it, I think."

Helen called and ascertained that the bottle of pills was gone. She turned to Travis, her disbelief plain. "She had no reason to do it. She must have taken them accidentally some way, experimenting."

Travis evaded a direct answer. "There'll be plenty of time to worry about that later."

Shortly after ten two Negroes, both drunk and bleeding profusely, were brought into Emergency from an East Side cutting match. Before long, their relatives were crowded in the hallway outside, the wives and mothers making considerable racket. Adding to the noise, four policemen moved through the crowd in a vain effort to find witnesses to the stabbing.

With the uproar, Travis decided to move Christine out of

Emergency. He thought there was definite improvement in respiration, and he figured that when she came out of the coma it would be much better for her to be in a quiet, private room rather than in the aftermath of a Negro knifing.

As usual, the hospital was full. A dozen patients were scheduled to be released early in the morning, but he had no authority to move any of them. Finally, he decided on the small room off the charity ward, just down the hall from Emergency. It wasn't much, but it would do overnight. Ordinarily it was used for terminal cases from the ward, a place where they could die with least intrusion on hospital routine. The room was empty at the moment. The old man who had occupied it the last two days had died during the afternoon.

Travis made arrangements for a special nurse to stay with Christine the remainder of the night. Helen insisted she would stay, too, and Travis agreed.

"I'd like for you to be here when she begins to come around. I want you to stay with her, talk to her like she's three years old. Don't let her talk about it now. I just want you to let her know she's loved, wanted."

He offered to arrange for a rollaway bed, but Helen insisted she wouldn't sleep anyway—at least not until David was found. Travis said he'd go check once more with the police on the search.

The police dispatcher said two men were working full-time on it. They had alerted every possible point, he said. Sooner or later Hartwell was bound to show up somewhere.

A growl from his stomach reminded Travis he'd skipped dinner, so he went up to the main floor and into the deserted hospital kitchen. He raided the leftovers in the big multidoored refrigerator and took his tray back to the stainless-steel table in the rear of the kitchen.

He ate slowly, thinking of Christine. There were several theories in the back of his mind as to the cause of her suicide attempt and he didn't like to think about any of them. He already was dreading the next phase of the case. Emotional wounds are usually more messy than physical injuries, he'd found.

Of all human failings, Travis considered suicide the most disturbing. Suicide seemed to be what set man apart—a demonstration of his free will, the choice to reject his mission on earth.

Every other creature on earth followed his mission—the microbes in their wars, the birds in their migrations, the jungle hunters, the spawning fish. Only man seemed confused, in doubt as to his life role.

In pursuit of this general curiosity, Travis had intended, years ago, to go on into psychiatry. But by the time he'd finished internship Marilyn had been working seven years to help support him. He didn't feel it would be fair to allow her to go on working. Besides, they'd put off having children all those years, and that had been her deepest desire. So he had given up all thought of further formal study, thinking he could read, do his own research on the side. But it hadn't worked out that way. It was all he could do to tend to his practice, keep up with advances in general practice, and—in past months—fulfill his hospital board or council duties.

He believed that in the individual human mind someone would, some day, find important answers to life's mysteries. There was a missing element in death. He had seen death, felt its presence many times, and never understood it. Suddenly a patient was gone, leaving a cadaver. Something had happened inside that patient that surpassed his medical knowledge. And Travis could never bridge the gap between what he saw and knew and his father's sermons on hellfire and salvation.

Always, there was the puzzle, the difference between the living, breathing patient and the cold, still cadaver. Somewhere, there was a middle ground between his experience and his father's faith. But he couldn't find it. This was what he couldn't explain to that church minister, Dr. Anderson. With no more understanding than he possessed, he would be a hypocrite in church.

He put his plate on the drainboard and went back down to Emergency. All was quiet, now. He went on down the hall and checked on Christine again. There was definite improvement, and he began to feel growing confidence she was going to live.

When he went back up to Emergency, intending to stretch out on a cot in the registration office for a few minutes, J. Marvin Olds was waiting for him. "They've located Hartwell," he said.

"Good. Where was he?"

"Up in his plane."

"I thought of that. But I didn't think he'd be up flying around at night unless he was going somewhere."

"That's what fooled us," Olds said. "Tom Kencaide called out there right off to see if a flight plan had been filed. But he didn't think to check with the tower to see if he was up on a local flight until a few minutes ago. He ought to be here in a little while. How is the girl doing?"

"Better," Travis said, relieved now that he wasn't forcing his optimism. "I think she's going to be all right. Is the newspaper going to run a story?"

"I'm afraid so."

"Damn it, why use that poor kid as a political pawn?" Travis asked angrily. He thought wildly for a moment of calling BeeBee Milam at home. He knew it wasn't his place, but someone should be looking after the girl's best interests.

"What'll the story say?" he asked. "I mean, will it use the words 'attempted suicide'?"

"No, the law protects her there. It'll just say she was found unconscious in her car in the park, and was taken to the hospital for treatment of an overdose of barbiturates, and that a note was found beside her."

"A note?"

"The police have it," Olds said. "But I read it. There's no doubt it was a suicide note."

Travis considered it briefly, then decided his next question was justified professionally. "Did she give any reason?"

Olds seemed to go through the same type of introspection. "It was addressed to her parents, saying she is pregnant, couldn't face the shame and humiliation, and that she thought this would be the best way out."

"Oh Lord," Travis said. That was one of the possibilities that had lingered in his mind all along. Now, the police had the note. The whole Police Department would know by morning, and it'd be general conversation at City Hall by noon tomorrow.

There was no longer any logic in calling Milam, he decided. The news story might even serve to minimize uglier rumors. But Travis had to voice the thought uppermost in his mind.

"This will just about kill David Hartwell."

# *Part Six*

## CHAPTER SIXTEEN

David eased back on the wheel, opened the throttle even wider, and felt the power of the engine take him higher into the night. When he reached eight thousand he leveled off, eased the throttle, and breathed deeply in the exhilaration of the thinner air.

There was no moon. All light came from the stars, his instrument panel and wingtips. He turned back north, keeping his altitude, until he could see the city again, a huge star on the horizon. Then he turned east, keeping the big star in sight.

The letter was in his shirt pocket beneath his light flight jacket. He could feel the weight of its folds against his chest. But he didn't need to read it again. He knew its every word.

He realized the courage required to write such a letter, and its cost in pride. Sharon Milam must have inherited more spunk from Shotgun and Thirty-Thirty Milam than he'd given her credit for. This was a facet of her he'd never seen. The letter left him mystified, feeling Sharon must have a far more admirable, complex personality than he'd realized. He had to admit this new Sharon was even more of a temptation than the old.

Phrases of her letter kept running through his mind: "I know you are unhappy with your present life. I am offering you another . . . I have all the money we would ever need . . . we would spend our time in the study of our love, both physical and spiritual . . . I would deny you nothing . . . we would live wherever you want, go wherever you want, as man and wife or as man and mistress. As long as we were together, I wouldn't care . . ."

There it was: the kind of life men dream about. Paris, the Riviera. Barcelona. Hunting in Africa. Maybe a secluded island in the Mediterranean or the Caribbean. Wherever their inclinations took them.

When he had made his decision before, it was against the prospect of a messy divorce. Sharon's proposition had changed that. Now he could go to Helen and say, "We have no marriage. I'm leaving you, but I'm leaving you and the children everything we have." That way, there should be no room for castigation from anyone. After the children's college trust funds, there would still be enough to support Helen comfortably the rest of her life. Not the way they had been living, maybe. But she would be left with more material things than most women get out of life. He would walk away without a dime in his pockets.

And by giving up all that was his, he wouldn't have such qualms about taking Sharon's money and going to her kind of life. Her proposition made it into a trade. Besides, if they later got married, maybe he could unshackle some of her inheritance and earn their living by increasing the income.

There would be trouble. BeeBee Milam apparently knew nothing of his affair with Sharon. The scandal would bring a violent reaction, for Milam had always disliked him. David didn't know why. Maybe the things that attracted Sharon to him repelled BeeBee. Milam would fight him all the way, but that didn't worry David. Legally, Milam's hands were tied. Sharon was an adult and the money was hers.

He would have to drop his old life completely. He would be an exile, severed from all present relationships—his friends, even his children.

Sharon had realized this. "I cannot offer, in good faith, to make up for the loss of your children's love. I can only promise to replace their love, in time, with the love of other children. . . ."

Other children. That was a pleasant thought, even if it was incongruous with an idyllic life in some tropical paradise.

Another life . . . another chance. . . .

The lights of the city had faded away on the horizon. He banked the plane to the northwest, knowing intuitively where the city lay. He eased the wheel forward, losing altitude and picking up airspeed. He had just sighted the bright star of the city on the far horizon when he heard his call on the radio. . . .

When David got to the hospital, Travis McNiel was waiting for him just inside the rear entrance. David was scared and confused. All he could think of was to find Christine. As Travis came forward to meet him, David didn't give him a chance to speak. "Where is she?" he demanded.

"David, she's going to be all right," Travis said quickly. "Everything is under control."

"What happened?" David asked. Damn it, no one would tell him anything.

Travis took his elbow, held him. "She took an overdose of barbiturates—some of Helen's. She's had a close call, but apparently the poisoning isn't as bad as we first feared. If there are no complications, she should be all right."

The meaning of the words began to come through to him. "An overdose? She tried to . . ."

Travis nodded, and David understood then why no one up to now would tell him the truth. But he couldn't make himself believe it. "Why?" he heard himself ask.

"I don't know all the details," Travis said. "There'll be plenty of time for that."

David stepped past Travis and looked into the emergency room. A young intern was sitting at a desk reading what appeared to be a medical book. A nurse and an aide were working at a sterilizer. There were no patients in sight.

"Where is she?" David asked again.

"This way," Travis said.

He followed Travis down the corridor and around the corner toward what he remembered as being the charity ward. But just outside the ward Travis pushed open the door to a room. David blinked, trying to adjust his eyes to the semidarkness.

Helen was sitting in a chair in the middle of the room, alert, intently watching the small figure on the bed. When she heard them behind her she arose and looked at David without expression. A nurse came toward them and whispered to Travis, then moved silently back against the wall to give them room. Travis took his arm and pulled him close. "She's still in a confused state. I wouldn't waken her," he whispered. "Be better if she sleeps it off."

David nodded to show he understood. Then he moved across the tiled floor as silently as he could.

The corner where Christine lay was the darkest of all, and she had her head turned toward the wall, so he had to move between the bed and the wall to see her. She seemed pathetically small in the long bed, and despite the darkness he could see the pallor of her face. Either the lights played tricks or her face was thinner, too.

He was still trying to understand what had happened. Easing back from the bed, he looked at Helen. She met his gaze confidently, and moved ahead of him toward the door, motioning for him to follow. He could tell from her co-ordination that she was sober. He followed her out into the hall. She stopped outside the door and lit a cigarette. Her hands were steady, but he knew from the redness of her eyes that she had been crying.

"We've been trying to reach you for hours," she said. But it wasn't an accusation. It seemed more of an apology.

"I took the plane up," he said. He had told her once, long ago, when they were much closer, why he liked to go up alone, and she had seemed to understand.

"I thought of that first thing," she said. "They told me they checked."

"I didn't file a flight plan," he explained. "It didn't occur to anyone to check with the tower until just a while ago."

They stood awkwardly for a moment in the deserted corridor, both hesitating to put their fears into words. From the charity ward David heard the dry, hacking cough of an old man, followed by a gagging sound. A nurse hurried by and disappeared into the ward.

"She almost died," Helen said. "When I first saw her in the emergency room, so white and still, I thought she was dead."

At least he had been spared that. But there was so much he hadn't been told. . . .

"What happened, anyway?" he asked.

"I don't know. She took some of my pills—I've forgotten the name—and Dr. McNiel said it's just lucky they found her in time, that she didn't take any more than she did, or that she wasn't more susceptible to the drug."

"I know that," he said, trying to keep his irritation down. "Damn it, what I want to know is why—why she did it."

Helen's voice sounded strangely faraway. "I don't think it really matters, David. What matters is that we've failed her, some way."

He was saved from answering by Travis, who came out of the room.

"I think everything's under control until morning," Travis said. He smiled at Helen. "You've been a big help. If you want to go on home, I'll have the nurse call you if you're needed."

"No, I'll stay," Helen said firmly.

"I'll run get Calla Lilly," David said.

"No," Helen said loudly.

Her forcefulness caught David off guard. "If you're sure," he said. "It wouldn't take but a few minutes."

"I'm sure," she said, still looking at him in a half-defiant way.

Travis seemed embarrassed by the exchange. "There are some formalities down at the office, David," he said.

David stood looking at Helen, puzzled by her sudden show of temper. He hesitated, uncertain. "I'll be back in a few minutes, then," he said.

Helen nodded, dropped her cigarette into a sand receptacle, and went back into Christine's room. David went with Travis down to the registration room across from Emergency. Travis turned to face him, leaning against a desk.

For the first time David noticed the haggard, tired lines around the doctor's eyes. "I know you're doing a lot more than anyone could expect on this," David told him. "I want you to know I appreciate it."

"I'm just thankful it wasn't worse," Travis said. He stared at the floor, as if searching for words.

David felt his stomach constrict with the foreboding the situation wasn't as good as he'd been led to believe. He voiced the first fear that came to mind.

"Is this going to affect her some way, permanently?"

Travis didn't seem to be listening. He answered almost absently, as if thinking of something else.

"No, I don't think so. Residual damage isn't common, even in severe cases. Sometimes there is neurological damage from severe hypoxia—lack of oxygen in the bloodstream—but I'm fairly confident now that we got her in time. I wouldn't worry about it."

Travis paused to push the telephone on the desk to one side so he could put his full weight on the desktop. David waited impatiently for him to go on.

"I wanted to be here when you came, because there are a couple of things I felt I should tell you, and I didn't want to trouble Helen with them. To begin with, J. Marvin Olds was here. He got the information from the police, and I understand there's going to be a brief story in the morning paper."

David knew he should be angered, and that he probably would be later, but now it seemed such a trifling thing. "I guess that can't be helped," he said.

"No, I guess not," Travis said. "Paper's probably already out. But I thought you'd want to know." He hesitated. "The other is a little more serious. I understand Christine left a note, and that the police have it. I thought you might like to get it cleared up with them tonight. I'll go down there with you, if you'd like."

It took David a moment to comprehend what kind of a note Travis was talking about. He still couldn't make himself accept the fact that Christine had tried to kill herself. He understood Travis' offer; if a medical doctor would take the responsibility, the police probably would be more inclined to drop the case in his hands, and there would be less unpleasantness all around.

"I know you're tired, Travis," David said. "But I sure would appreciate it."

Travis reached for the phone. "Chief McDowell called earlier. I promised I'd let him know when you were ready."

Dan McDowell was waiting for them in his office. With him was a Lieutenant Tomlinson.

The lieutenant was neat and trim in his uniform, but McDowell had a faint stubble of beard, his slacks were rumpled, and he wore a faded short-sleeved sports shirt loose at the collar. He shook hands with David and Travis, his face serious. David realized it was now nearly midnight. Ruefully, he remembered that he had been thinking of summoning Dan up to his office for a hard-nosed talk in an effort to get the highway right-of-way investigation moving again. After Ronnie's escapade, he had hesitated. And now this. . . .

"Dan, you shouldn't have stayed up," he said lamely.

"I'm just down here to help out any way I can," McDowell said. "You know Lieutenant Tomlinson, don't you? He has charge of the case."

Tomlinson was carrying a small metal clipboard. As David and Travis shook hands with Tomlinson, McDowell arranged chairs for them.

"How is the girl, Mr. Hartwell?" Tomlinson asked.

"She seems to be doing fine, thank you," David answered, taking the offered chair. He was growing impatient to get on with it. "I understand there was a note. . . ."

"Yes, there was," Tomlinson said slowly. He carefully slipped a piece of notepaper from beneath some forms in the clipboard.

David took the note. He recognized Christine's handwriting. She'd never gotten completely away from a childish scrawl, yet there was a feminine flair to it.

*"Dear Momma and Daddy: I'm sorry for all the trouble I've caused. I can't bring this shame upon you. I have been foolish and I am pregnant and I can't go on with it. I love you both."* There was the scrawl of her signature, then a P.S. *"Don't tell Ronnie why I did it."*

David sat stunned, trying to absorb the full impact of the words. He looked up helplessly and found all eyes averted. He looked at Travis, who was staring at the floor. He realized then that Travis had known.

When Travis looked up, it was at Chief McDowell, not David. "Since this is not a psychiatric case, and the girl is under medical care, there won't be any further action, will there?"

"Lieutenant Tomlinson is of the opinion—and I agree—that this is a family matter. I'm just glad she was found in time."

David heard them talking, but he was hardly aware of what was said. He was wondering who it had been. Christine was going steady with that young high school kid, but surely. . . .

He fought to regain his composure. He knew he should say something. "I want to do everything legally. . . ."

Tomlinson was quick to interrupt, his voice gentle but firm.

"The only time we ever take action is when it's necessary for the subject's own safety, or the safety of the family. When they need action to obtain professional care for the subject."

"And the report?" David asked.

Again he didn't have to explain. "I make my report direct to Chief McDowell," Tomlinson said. "It is confidential. But there were ambulance drivers, other officers, quite a crowd around. It's surprising how small this town is, sometimes."

"I understand," David said. "Thank you."

He waited until later, when they were in the car again and on the way back to the hospital, to speak to Travis about it. "You knew all the time, didn't you?"

"Not for sure," Travis said.

"Who else knows?"

"I have no idea," Travis said. "As the lieutenant told you, this can be a small town, in some ways, when it comes to rumors. There are some people that have little else to do, I guess. I wouldn't pay any attention to them."

With his sense of frustration and helplessness growing, David turned his anger on the cause of it all—that boy Christine had been dating, Buddy. Smart-aleck Buddy Nowell. He wondered if Buddy knew.

"I've a good mind to go right out there tonight and beat that little son of a bitch to within an inch of his life," David said, louder than he'd intended.

Travis looked at him, startled. "Who?"

"The boy."

"No," Travis said firmly. "I know how you must feel, but that would be the worst thing you could do. After all, they're still children. Besides, anything like that would only give truth to the rumors."

"Well, the truth will be obvious anyway, if I don't do something." He tried to clear his mind, make it plan ahead. "How in hell am I going to get her out of this mess?"

Travis didn't divert his attention from driving. "Let's don't try to make any decision tonight. With your permission, I'll examine her as soon as it seems advisable—perhaps in the morning. Let's don't cross any bridges until we come to them."

At the hospital, David didn't know whether to tell Helen

about the note or not. Christine was still asleep, and after checking her once more Travis left, instructing the nurse to call him at home if any marked change developed.

Helen would have to know about the note eventually, David reasoned. It might be easier on her now, and it would give her time to absorb the idea. He motioned to her to follow him out into the corridor.

"Travis and I went down to the police station and cleared things up there," he told her. "And I'm afraid I have some more bad news."

Helen stood looking up at him. With the dim night lights behind them, Helen was thinner, younger in the soft shadows, almost the Helen of twenty years ago.

"The police? Can't you fix that?"

"Yes, that's all over, dropped. But Christine left this note."

It was a cruel thing to do, but he knew of no easy way. He simply handed her the note. She turned it to catch the light. As she read, David followed her in his memory. When she reached the last line she slumped against the wall and broke into sobs. He reached to take her shoulders, but his hands stopped before he touched her. He couldn't recapture the lost rapport in a single night.

"I knew it," she said between sobs. "Somehow, I knew it was that from the first." She turned and looked up at him again. "What are we going to do?"

"Let's don't think about it now," he said. "She's alive, she's going to live. That's the important thing."

"What are we going to tell Ronnie?"

He hadn't thought of that. Ronnie would be getting up in a few hours and going to school. With the story in the newspaper there was no way of keeping it from him.

"I'll go out and talk to him about it. He's old enough to know. I'll tell him everything—except about the note."

"Perhaps it would be better if he didn't go to school today."

"Might be," he said with the gnawing return of frustration.

Already he was beginning to feel the effects of the rumors, even before he'd had any time at all to devise ways of contending with them.

Helen insisted that she would spend the rest of the night in the chair by Christine's bed. So, with nothing else he could do at the hospital, David drove home.

He went up to his room and undressed, thinking that a warm shower might be relaxing. As he peeled off his shirt he automatically emptied the pockets and checked the contents. Christine's note and Sharon's letter were side by side.

He stretched out on his bed in his shorts and reread Christine's note several times, searching for any hidden meaning that might have escaped him before, but he found nothing.

Then he reread Sharon's letter, this time with more thought. Had he seriously considered accepting Sharon's proposal? Or had he daydreamed about a life with a sex goddess in the same way he'd daydreamed about making a killing in oil, or getting a ranch some day like Cal's? Right now, he didn't know. He had been thinking of Sharon in terms of himself. Somehow, morality seemed to take on new aspects when thought of in terms of one's own children.

Finally, he got up from the bed, picked up his cigarette lighter from the chest of drawers, and went into the bathroom. He touched Christine's note to the flame and turned it carefully so most was consumed by the time he had to drop it into the water. Then he burned Sharon's letter and flushed the commode.

He took a warm shower and lay down again, but he couldn't sleep. He kept thinking of the new day and of how he was going to face it. He thought on ahead, of the future. . . .

He dozed for a while. A noise awoke him. He lay for a moment before figuring out that it was the morning paper striking the front-door screen. Pulling on a robe, he went down, got the paper, and took it back to his room.

The story wasn't as bad as he'd feared it might be. It was placed far inside, only three paragraphs saying simply that Christine Hartwell had been treated for an overdose of barbiturates. It would not have seemed too malicious if it hadn't mentioned that a note was found in the car. He threw the newspaper into the wastebasket.

By the time he dressed, it was good daylight, and he heard Ronnie stirring. David went to his door and knocked. "Ronnie, I want to talk to you a minute," he called.

Ronnie opened the door, then went to the bed, his baggy, rumpled pajamas somehow pathetic. He got back into bed, sitting back against the headboard, and pulled the covers up around him like a shield.

David sat down beside him, uncertain as to how to start. He didn't know for sure how much Ronnie knew. Helen had told Calla Lilly just to tell him Christine was ill and they were taking her to a doctor.

He tried to think of an opening gambit and none came. He'd always been self-satisfied with his easy banter in business, and the way he could progress right to the point at hand and dominate the situation. But now, he felt foolish and awkward in this fourteen-year-old's sleep-swollen eyes.

"I thought you would like to know that your sister is much better this morning," he said.

Ronnie blinked.

David paused, groping for the right words. He knew he not only must cross the barrier between the normal adult and adolescent world, but he somehow must cut through the boy's insulation from this family incident. Ronnie clearly felt no identification with the family situation.

"Something happened last night that's going to affect all of us," David told him.

The boy sat and stared at him.

"Christine has been very ill. But she is better, now. She almost died from an overdose of barbiturates. She found a bottle of pills in your mother's room and, well, took too many of them."

"On purpose?" Ronnie asked.

David could only nod.

"Why?" Ronnie asked guardedly. "Why did she do it?"

Again, David hesitated. "Apparently she was confused, mixed up," he said. "Maybe you've noticed how girls that age tend to overdramatize things, to take things too seriously. She made a mistake. I'm partly to blame, I suppose, and your mother. Somehow, we've failed to make you children understand that we love you, that we're here to help you, that you should come to us. I know I haven't been a very good father."

"You have, too," Ronnie said forcefully. Then he seemed embarrassed and lowered his head.

Warmed by Ronnie's reaction, David put a hand on his shoulder. "Well, anyway, I've made mistakes. What I'm trying to say, Christine is going to need our help. There is a story in the morning paper about it, and there may be all sorts of rumors. That can't be helped. But since we live together, constitute a family, we are responsible for each other. We are going to have to show her—show others—that we won't stop loving her just because she made a mistake. Does that make sense to you?"

Ronnie nodded, his eyes wide now.

"And you can help your mother a great deal, too. This has been quite a shock to her, and you know she isn't well, anyway. It would do her much good to know her son is someone she can depend upon."

Ronnie was fully awake, frowning. "Would it help if I went on off to military school now?" he asked.

"Good Lord, no," David said, stunned.

"I mean, it'd sort of get me out of the way," Ronnie added.

He had to make Ronnie understand exactly how he felt. "Look," he said earnestly. "I don't want you to go away. You're going to be grown and out on your own all too soon. That was a mistake on my part, thinking of sending you to military school. I sometimes have to consider two or three plans at City Hall before I come up with the right one. That was an early idea, and if I'd have thought it over properly—considered everything—I'd have realized it wasn't a good one." He paused, studying Ronnie's puzzled face. "You don't *want* to go, do you?"

"No," Ronnie said quickly.

"Good. As I said, we need you here. From now on, when you or Christine have a problem, I want you to come to me with it. If I don't have time, I'll take time, because you are the most important to me. Will you do that?"

Ronnie nodded. "Can I see Chris?" he asked.

"Of course. But it would be best to wait until this afternoon, at least. She's still a very sick girl."

He started for the door, then remembered. "Since Christine was still in junior high last year, I imagine most of the kids remember her. This will probably be the main topic of gossip for a while at school. If you'd rather not go today, I would understand."

Ronnie thought about it for a moment. "I'll go," he said.

"Good. I'm proud you're taking that attitude. And if you'll hurry and get dressed, I could sure use some company at breakfast."

While Ronnie showered, David went to Christine's room and found the pajamas, bedjacket, and slippers Helen wanted. Then they went down to breakfast.

On a hunch Stella might be in a few minutes early, he called the office before he left the house. He told her he wouldn't be in until after noon, and maybe not then. From her lack of surprise, he knew she either had heard about Christine or had read the news story. So he was ready when she solicitously asked if there was anything she could do. He appreciated the offer, he told her, but he could think of nothing. Yes, Christine seemed to be recovering nicely. Yes, he would tell Helen to be sure and call her if there was anything she could do. He hung up the phone feeling as if he'd cleared a big hurdle—his first contact with the world since it had happened.

Twenty or thirty people waited at the out-patient clinic outside the charity ward when David got to the hospital. When he walked into Christine's room, it was empty.

"She has been moved upstairs," a nurse said behind him. "Room four-oh-one."

He thanked her, and was on four hunting for the room when Helen intercepted him.

"Dr. McNiel is with her now," she said. "We'll have to wait in the lounge."

He couldn't keep from feeling resentment that he hadn't been there when Christine awoke. But Helen said she still seemed dazed, and had said nothing, shown no emotion. With the hospital attendants there to help move her upstairs, they hadn't been able to talk at all, Helen said.

David walked with Helen down the hall to the lounge, a small inset off the corridor with plastic-covered, tubular-steel chairs and couch, and Coke, cigarette, and candy machines. Since it wasn't regular visiting hours, the alcove was now deserted. Helen lit a cigarette and smoked, nervously, glancing up each time someone passed by in the hall. David sank into a chair. They sat for a long time in silence, both near exhaustion. The long vigil was beginning to tell on Helen. The lines around her eyes had deepened, and he could see the hand holding the cigarette tremble.

He turned his head to the wall, closed his eyes, and was almost on the point of dozing when Helen spoke. "When this is over, I'm going to leave you, David."

Her voice was matter-of-fact and unemotional. He studied her face a long moment and decided this was just a sudden outburst of feeling, a reaction from all that had happened, and his best comment would be none.

"I mean it," she added, glaring at him defiantly. "I'm unhappy, you're unhappy, and look what it's doing to Ronnie and Christine. We haven't had a marriage for ten years, and I'm getting out of it while I can still salvage some of my self-respect."

"I don't think I could be blamed for what loss your self-respect has suffered."

"I didn't say I was blaming you. I did a lot of thinking last night, and I came to some conclusions. One of them is that it's my fault for giving in to you as much as I have. I should have had more backbone."

He didn't understand. "Giving in?"

"Yes, I've let you have your way in everything."

"How? I sure as hell never wanted things the way they are."

"That house, for one thing. I should have refused to live in it. Then I let you bring in that black wench to run it the way you wanted it run. That was my biggest mistake."

"I didn't tell her to run it any way," he protested. "I hired a maid because I thought you could use the help and because we could afford it."

"If there was to be a maid hired, I should have hired her," Helen said. "She had me buffaloed from the minute she walked in. It's my fault for letting her, letting you, get away with it. I should have had it out with her right off, but it was easier to just retreat a little every day and keep the peace. First thing I knew, I was a guest in my own home, and I didn't even know how it happened."

He listened to her with growing concern. But he was too exhausted to feel anger. "Why didn't you say something about it?" he asked. "I didn't know how you felt."

"I just told you. If I had realized how I was letting people walk all over me, I'd have done something about it."

An orderly came in to use the Coke machine. They waited until he gathered up the bottles and left.

"I've been doing some thinking, too," David said when the orderly was gone. "There's no doubt in my mind that we've got to make a drastic change in our pattern of living, but I don't think divorce would solve what's wrong."

"I'm not seeking any solution," Helen said. "I just want out."

He didn't want to argue about it now, so he didn't answer. They sat waiting, the little rapport they'd found in the night now gone.

Helen was facing the hall, so when she suddenly tensed, David knew she'd seen Travis. They both got up to meet him. Travis was smiling slightly. He led them back into the lounge. "A false alarm," he said.

In his fatigue, David was slow to comprehend. Then when he did understand, he couldn't believe it. He hadn't even considered the possibility.

"These modern teen-agers are so sophisticated we forget sometimes they're not as knowledgeable as we think they are," Travis explained. "She was late, and assumed the rest."

Helen made a stifled sound in her throat, then hurried down the hall to Christine's room. David stood, uncertain.

"You're sure?" he asked.

"Positive," Travis assured him.

David's mind fought to absorb this sudden turn of events. "When can we take her home?"

Travis frowned. "She's had quite an emotional experience. I think it'd be a good idea to keep her here another night or two. Then, if there are no complications, she should be able to go home. But David, I would like for you to talk to a good family counselor about her."

"You mean about the whole family, don't you?" David asked.

Travis' face reddened. "We're talking about Christine," he said.

David realized his question hadn't sounded at all the way he'd intended. "I'm serious," he said. "It's certainly no secret, I guess, that my home life has been in a mess lately."

Travis shook his head. "I'm not qualified to discuss that, David. But I'll recommend someone."

After Travis left, David went into Christine's new room. She was lying face down on the bed, sobbing. Helen was sitting on the edge of the bed, an arm around her shoulder. David walked around to the other side of the bed. He sat for a moment, listening to her cry.

"Everything is all right, now," he said finally. "There's no need to cry."

"You read my note, didn't you?" Christine asked, her words muffled by the pillow.

"Yes, but don't worry about it."

She buried her face deeper in the pillow, wracked by deep sobs. Helen kept patting her shoulder.

"You should have come to us," David said.

He intended the remark as assurance, but Helen took it as an admonition. She looked up at him sharply. "We've never given her any indication she should. You can't blame her for that."

Christine had stopped crying and lay quiet. David leaned forward and put a hand on her other shoulder. His voice sounded husky and strange.

"Christine, we don't have to tell you what you have done is wrong. You know that. But I want you to know that we—your mother and I—realize the mistakes you've made are mostly our mistakes—most of them mine. What happened doesn't change our love for you in the least."

She turned her head and looked at him, her eyes red and moist. Then she threw her arms around him and buried her head in his shoulder, her body shaking again in deep, agonizing sobs. He picked her up bodily and sat in the chair, holding her. He closed his arms around her, wondering at his awkwardness.

This was the first time since Christine was eleven years old that he had held her on his lap.

## CHAPTER SEVENTEEN

Afterward, when it was all over, Tom could see the grim humor in the fact that—out of all those who tried—Joe Garzek was the one who blew the whistle on Councilman Berger.

On that Monday night, events stood poised like a string of dominoes. Drama was the only thing needed to set the whole string in motion. And Joe Garzek provided that. If Tom had seen the possibilities, perhaps the price would not have been so great. But he had no way of knowing, that Monday night.

He was working late. It was the eve of the crucial council meeting and vote on the water bond program. Dr. Travis McNiel was out making speeches again, whipping up his support for the showdown. BeeBee Milam was determined no angle was to be missed in putting the journalistic prod to the councilmen and public. BeeBee himself had written—with the help of his promotions man—a front-page editorial declaring that opponents of the water program were tampering with the city's destiny. The effects of the decision now by the council, he said, would be felt for generations to come—either for good or for evil.

Tom was writing the banner story. He had skipped his customary dinner with Arlene, sent out for a sandwich, and worked doggedly on finding a fresh approach. He tried to work in all the promotion element he knew BeeBee would demand, and yet disguise the drum-beating enough so the story would be halfway palatable to the reader. He had written the same material so many times, freshness seemed impossible.

Around him, the city room was busy, too. A Canadian cold front had swept down across the Panhandle on the heels of a ninety-eight-degree day, dropping temperatures, rain, and hail up to the size of tennis balls, uprooting trees, and—in a few rural communities—leveling outbuildings and houses. The city itself had escaped serious damage. But twelve miles northwest of town two tornado funnels had touched down in open country.

There had been an Indian legend of uncertain origin but wide circulation that the river valley was "naturally protected" from tornadoes, and that the city was safe. But three springs ago a similar cold front had spawned a tornado which traveled ponderously across the south edge of town, killed six persons, injured twenty-two, jammed all emergency facilities, caused more than one million dollars of property damage, and in general played hell with one old Indian legend. The memory of that day lingered with the public. The proximity of the two new tornadoes would have been the day's top story if BeeBee Milam had not already decreed that the water program story should be the banner. No one in the office would dare countermand an edict from BeeBee.

Now, the danger to the immediate area from the storm was over. The city desk was tracking the disturbance south and eastward, following it by telephone with the aid of rural correspondents. Outside, Tom could see that the storm had turned into a steady, soaking rain.

The writing of the long promotion piece had been the logical end of a long, disappointing day for Tom. He had heard nothing from Cal Masters after their talk a week ago. The waiting was tedious, but he felt it would be psychologically wrong to contact Cal . . . at least this early. So he could only wait. Also, Tom had a new worry in Hartwell. Since his daughter's close call last week, Hartwell had been unavailable. Tom could understand his desire for privacy after what had happened, but Hartwell wasn't delegating his duties. Tom was beginning to feel he was losing touch with the activities on his beat, and this disturbed him.

Shortly after nine, he had finished the story and was reading it over, making minor changes, thinking about these new worries, when his phone rang.

"Tom, this is Olds," J. Marvin said. "What was the name of that tavern owner forced out of business out there by the air base?"

"Garzek. Joe Garzek."

"Thought so. They had a routine disturbance call out at his home a few minutes ago, and the patrolmen have just radioed in a Code Twenty-Six. I'm fixin' to run out there, and I thought you might like to be in on it."

Code Twenty-Six, Tom remembered, was a call for assistance. "Sure," he said.

"I'll swing by. See you out front. And you might grab a photographer on your way out, just in case."

Tom took the lake story to Houston Collier and hurriedly told him of Olds' call. While Collier turned to the intercom to summon a photographer from the darkroom Tom wrestled into his raincoat, wondering if in some weird fashion his talk with Berger could have set something in motion.

"Let me know soon as you can if it's worth anything," Collier said as Tom waited impatiently for the photographer.

Loaded with cameras and gadgets, he came down the hall, still buckling straps. He was a tall, thin youth of twenty-three named Kevin Parker, and had been with the paper only two or three months. He was known for good pictures, eccentric mannerisms, and for carrying four times the necessary equipment.

Tom held some of Parker's gear in the elevator so he could pull on his raincoat. Then they stood on the sidewalk in the rain a couple of minutes before the staff car came wheeling around the corner.

As J. Marvin pushed the car door open for him, Tom heard the crackle of static from the police radio. "This may be good," J. Marvin said as they climbed in, Tom up front and the photographer in the back seat. "They've just put in a call for some traffic units and the tear gas squad."

J. Marvin gunned the car down to the next intersection, came to a lurching full stop, then ran the red light. It had been awhile since Tom had ridden with J. Marvin on a fast-breaking story, and he'd almost forgotten what a maniac he could be behind the wheel. Now, as they weaved through downtown traffic at up to forty miles an hour, he began to wish he'd told J. Marvin to go on and driven out himself in Old Smokey.

He sat, tense, watching the traffic stream past, trying to imagine elfish, meek-mannered Joe Garzek causing all this commotion. There must be a mistake. It couldn't be the same Joe Garzek.

"Have you been able to learn what's happening out there?" he asked as soon as they'd cleared most of the downtown traffic and he felt he could risk dividing J. Marvin's attention.

"Somebody holed up in the house," J. Marvin said. "The neighbors reported hearing gunshots inside, and he won't let the police get close."

It surely must be some other Garzek, Tom thought. He wished he had taken time to check the address in the city directory or crisscross. He couldn't remember Joe Garzek's street. Still, he did happen to remember the telephone number, and this would be the right exchange area for the prefix. . . .

J. Marvin went to the inside lane as they entered the expressway. The windshield wipers slowed momentarily as he accelerated, and rain blurred their vision. J. Marvin leaned forward over the wheel, trying to see.

"Sons a bitches," he said, and it took Tom a moment to realize J. Marvin's remark was directed at the windshield wipers. When the engine got them up to a smooth eighty miles an hour the wipers started working again. They were in a fifty-five-mile-an-hour zone.

Tom suddenly realized how tense he was, watching J. Marvin shoot between the slower-moving traffic and the raised curb of the median strip. He was tempted to ask J. Marvin to slow down, but he knew he'd never hear the last of it if he did, so he kept silent. He turned to see how the other passenger was taking it and found Parker's gaze locked on the speedometer.

"Twenty-fifth," J. Marvin said. "We turn off at Twenty-fifth. Where in hell is it?"

Tom peered out through the rain, orienting himself. He saw a sign flash by. "Next exit," he said.

J. Marvin began braking and pulling toward the exit lane. Again Tom tensed, half-expecting the car to go into a skid on the slick pavement. J. Marvin always seemed to know just how far to push his luck. They barreled down the narrow exit lane. As they left the freeway and sped down darkened residential streets, Tom began to remember the neighborhood—lower middle class homes, built not long after the war. Now the area appeared shabbier than he recalled.

Ten or twelve blocks off the expressway J. Marvin raised a hand and pointed. "There it is."

Ahead, the intersection was blocked by a squad car. Farther down, there were more police with spotlights trained on a small frame house. A traffic officer waved them to a stop. J. Marvin pulled up beside him and rolled down the window. The rain had tapered away to a slow drizzle.

"Better leave your car here," the officer said, recognizing J. Marvin. "If you take it on up there you're apt to get it shot full of holes."

J. Marvin put the car in reverse and backed quickly to the curb. They scrambled out and hurried toward the cars a half block away.

"Keep down," the policeman yelled at them. "There's been some shootin' up there."

They ran at a half crouch. Suddenly a gunshot, surprisingly loud, startled them, and Tom instinctively dropped to the wet pavement. Glass tinkled on the concrete somewhere up ahead. Tom looked up. J. Marvin was squatting in the street and Parker was running on ahead all stooped over. Tom moved on up even with J. Marvin.

"Sounded like a shotgun," Tom said, surprised at the steadiness of his voice.

"Yeah," J. Marvin said. "That young picture-taker's goin' to get his tail full of buckshot if he doesn't get down."

Parker was running in a crouch, but with his long legs and frame the precaution was more comic than safe. He stopped behind a car and aimed his camera at two policemen who were peeping over the hood, pistols drawn. Tom saw them jump when the flashbulb went off.

J. Marvin laughed. "He's determined to get shot by one side or the other." He shaded his eyes with one hand against the glare of lights. "I see Lieutenant Mills up there at that first car. Let's go see what he knows."

They moved up past the first three cars, parked bumper to bumper. The fourth, sitting right in front of the spotlighted house, was about fifteen feet beyond, leaving an unprotected gap. J. Marvin didn't hesitate. He ran across the open space with long strides, and Tom followed him. Parker stayed back beside the first car.

The lieutenant turned around, pistol in hand, as they came up beside him fast, seeking the protection of the car. They squatted in the rain beside him.

"What in hell are you two doing?" he demanded. "Who let you up here?"

Parker flashed another picture and a policeman yelled at him.

J. Marvin was breathing hard. "I came up here to ask you questions," he said between breaths, "and you ask me two before I can even get my mouth open."

"Get back there before you both get shot," the lieutenant ordered.

"I'm too old to worry about it," J. Marvin said. "And Tom here has been shot at more than your whole police force put together, I imagine. I doubt if a little more lead under his hide will make any difference. Besides, he may know the man inside there."

The lieutenant looked at Tom with new interest. "Garzek?"

"Is that him shooting?" Tom asked. He still couldn't believe it.

"I think so. What does he look like?"

"Small, dark. About forty-five or fifty. High forehead and a rather big nose."

"That's him," the lieutenant said. He wiped the rain from his face and leaned his back against the car fender for support. "I got a good look at him through the window when he yelled something at us a while ago. What kind of a guy is he?"

Tom thought of how Garzek had been, the last time he'd seen him, worried sick, given to tears. "He's done some time in the state hospital," he said. "But I understand they considered him nonviolent. He always seemed very meek and gentle."

"Well, he's violent now," the lieutenant said. He turned to look down the street. "What in hell's holding up that tear gas?"

"Maybe he would talk to me, if I called to him," Tom said.

The lieutenant considered the suggestion briefly. "No, I don't want anyone hurt. There's a car on the way with a speaker, too. Maybe you can talk to him through that, if . . ."

The shotgun boomed again, cutting his sentence off. Behind them, there was the sharper report of an answering pistol. Cursing under his breath, the lieutenant whirled.

"I told you to hold your fire," he yelled.

"What kind of load is he usin'?" J. Marvin asked.

"One time it'll sound like birdshot. The next time buckshot. I think he's just shooting up old ammo."

"What about his family?" Tom asked. "Does anybody know if they're in there?"

"Nobody knows anything except that they heard some gunfire and called us. When the two patrolmen got here he began shooting up their car. How many kids he got?"

Tom tried to remember. "Two, maybe three. A girl and two boys, I think, all school-age."

"I was afraid of that." The lieutenant turned to yell at the officers crouched behind the car where the pistol had been fired. "You clowns hear that? There may be some kids in there." He got up on his haunches and looked at the house again in desperation. "I got to get back where I can do something. I've got to get a couple of units in behind the house before we put the gas in there, and evacuate this block." He started to make the dash to the car behind, then hesitated. "Let's roll the car back, so we won't be exposed."

They tried to push the car back, but it was in gear. Tom opened the car door, reached across the seat and pulled the straight-shift lever into neutral. Then they rolled the car back slowly, Tom turning the steering wheel to guide it into the bumper of the car behind. The four cars then gave them a fairly solid shield until they got out of the field of fire.

At the corner, the crowd had grown, and now the police had rope strung across the intersection. Two or three hundred people were standing in the rain, watching. Others stood on nearby porches. Parker was busy now photographing the crowd.

"I'm goin' to see if I can find a phone," J. Marvin said. "I'll let Collier know what's goin' on."

Tom studied the small frame house, trying to think of it as a tactical military problem. It sat farther back from the street than its neighbors, and there wasn't any way to sneak up on it from the front. Maybe if someone went behind the flanking houses, then crawled along right next to the house, below the level of the windows, they could get gas grenades in without getting hurt.

He walked over to where the lieutenant was sitting in a squad car using the radio. He stood in the gentle drizzle, listening, while the lieutenant directed two units into each end of the alley behind the house.

As they waited, they heard the shotgun again.

"I think he's shooting at the lights," the lieutenant said. "If he is, he's a lousy shot. He's only hit one so far."

The radio came to life again. "We got the back of the house lighted," a voice said. "And there's a woman layin' dead in the back yard."

The lieutenant picked up the microphone. "Car two-four-oh. Are you sure she's dead?"

"Ten-four," the voice said. "Looks like she was hit in the head by that shotgun at close range."

The lieutenant put the microphone back on the dash. "This puts a new slant on things," he said to Tom. "Your friend in there is a killer. If he's killed once, he'll kill again, and I'm taking no chances. When the tear gas gets here, we're going to hit him from all sides, and he'd better come out without that gun."

Tom thought of mild-mannered Joe Garzek, the way he'd talked of his family. This just didn't seem possible. "Let me try to talk to him," he said. "Maybe I can get him to come out."

"We'll see," the lieutenant said.

Two more units came up the street toward them, red lights flashing. The traffic officers parted the crowd at the edge of the intersection to let them through. When the first car door opened, Tom saw the hulking All-American build of Police Chief Dan McDowell climb out and hurry toward them. "What's the setup?" he asked the lieutenant.

The lieutenant gave McDowell a quick rundown. "Kencaide knows him," he added. "He might be able to talk him into coming out."

"Think he might listen to you?"

"Might. He blames police harassment for the failure of his tavern. I've noticed he seems to be aiming at the signs on the police cars. Maybe he's shooting at authority."

"Good theory. Let's hope he doesn't switch to uniforms. Did he talk like a nut?"

"No. Matter of fact, I felt he had a legitimate complaint."

McDowell stared at him for a moment. It seemed as if he started to say something, then changed his mind. He turned and yelled at the cars behind him.

"Bring that bullhorn on up here," he ordered. He turned back to the lieutenant. "Get some men with the tear gas around behind the houses on each side. They can come up on his blind side and get up under the windows. If we don't do any good talking to him, I'll give the signal, and they can fill the house full."

"And if he comes out with the gun?"

"We got no choice," McDowell said. He touched Tom's elbow. "Come on, let's see if we can talk any sense into him."

Crouching low, they moved up the line of cars to the front of the house again.

All was silent in the house now. The soft drum-roll of rain on the pavement was the only sound. Then McDowell raised the speaker to his mouth. He squeezed the trigger and the amplifier boomed loud in the night.

"Garzek, this is Police Chief McDowell. We have the house surrounded. Come out with your hands up and nobody will get hurt."

The shotgun answered. The pellets slammed into the other side of the car and Tom thought he heard some whistle over their heads. Again there was the tinkle of glass on the pavement.

"You still want to try?" McDowell asked.

"Yes," Tom said. He could see a detective creeping up to the far side of the house next door. They were getting ready with the tear gas.

McDowell handed him the amplifier. "Just pull the trigger when you want to talk," he said.

Tom aimed the horn up over the fender of the car and pressed the trigger. "This is Tom Kencaide, Mr. Garzek," he said. "I want to talk to you. I'm going to stand up. Don't shoot."

"No," McDowell said. "Don't show yourself."

The voice of J. Marvin Olds came from the shadows of the car behind them. "He knows what he's doin', Chief."

Tom wished he felt the calm confidence J. Marvin's voice carried. "I don't think he'd shoot me as long as I don't force him to by scaring or cornering him," he explained to McDowell.

He heard McDowell unholster his pistol. "Well, go ahead if you want to. I guess a faceful of birdshot wouldn't be fatal at this range."

Tom once had lived with fear a long time before he'd learned to overcome it. The way, he'd found, was to put it aside for the moment of danger, to concentrate on what had to be done.

Slowly, he raised his head above the hood of the car, concentrating on steady movements that wouldn't alarm Garzek's troubled mind. He forced himself to stand for a moment before raising the speaker again, giving Garzek plenty of time to see him, study him. There was no movement in the house that he could see.

Then, carefully, he raised the speaker and pressed the trigger. "This is Tom Kencaide again, Mr. Garzek. I can't talk to you from here. I will walk up to the edge of the porch, Mr. Garzek. I won't come any farther than the edge of the porch. No one will hurt you."

"You got more guts than brains," McDowell said behind him.

Tom lowered the speaker and handed it to McDowell. "If he was going to shoot, he would have done it by now," he said.

"Let's hope so," McDowell said.

Tom walked slowly around the front of the patrol car, taking careful, measured steps, knowing how nerves strained to the breaking point react. He'd once seen a man killed from the sudden rattle of a canteen cup.

As he stepped upon the curb, the lights behind him, he could see better. At the corners of the house, the detectives were ready with the tear gas, waiting for the signal.

The panes were gone from the window where earlier Kencaide had seen the flash of the shotgun. Now he could see the outline of a figure in the darkness of the room. He slowed even more as he got near the edge of the porch.

"Don't come closer," the figure said. "I don't want to shoot you."

The voice was strange, and Tom tried to evaluate its quaver.

"I don't want to see anyone get hurt, Mr. Garzek," he said. "That's why I'm here."

From somewhere behind him a new, more powerful light came on, and with it Tom could see Garzek plainly, squatting behind the window sill, holding a twelve-gauge shotgun. In seeing for sure that it was Garzek, Tom realized that all along he had doubted.

But as recognition came, he also could see that this was a Garzek he'd never seen before, a Garzek that months of worry, strain, and fear had pushed over the thin red line of insanity.

The light, shining into his eyes, sent Garzek into a frenzy. "Make them turn it off," he yelled, waving the shotgun erratically.

"I'll try," Tom said.

He didn't want to startle Garzek by yelling, so he turned, pointed to the light, and made a cutting motion across his throat with a forefinger. McDowell called to someone and the light went out.

"Tell them go away," Garzek said. "I don't want them here."

"I can't do that, Mr. Garzek. But I can keep them from hurting you. If you'll put down the gun, and walk out with me now, they won't hurt you. I promise you that."

"No. Make them go away."

Tom stood for a moment, thinking, searching for a new line of argument. Maybe if he reminded Garzek of his responsibilities. . . .

"Where are your children, Mr. Garzek?"

"I don't have children," he said.

"But you told me you have," Tom insisted. "Remember? You told me about them, and the little girl who was to have her teeth fixed. Remember?"

"I got no children," Garzek said in a flat monotone. "I got no wife."

Now Tom understood. He knew the meaning of it all . . . the bursts of gunfire that had disturbed the neighborhood, the dead woman in the back yard. He was familiar with the phenomenon of the mind sometimes rejecting memories and facts too terrible to accept. Mrs. Garzek and the children were dead. Tom was certain of that, now. And the knowledge sent a burst of new fear through him. There probably was only a thread of recognition in Garzek's shattered mind, and that thread might go at any moment.

A light flashed. Thinking it lightning, Tom stood transfixed, waiting for the sound of thunder. Then he remembered Parker and the flashgun. He wanted to turn and yell at him, but he didn't dare.

He tried to think of something to say, anything.

"Mr. Garzek, we were going to try to do something about the man who ruined your tavern business. Remember? I still want to help you."

"It not work," Garzek said from the shadows. "But I write letters. Everybody know."

Tom could make no sense out of that. But he knew this incoherence might be symptomatic of further mental deterioration. He began laying groundwork for a retreat.

"Mr. Garzek, they gave me only a few minutes to talk to you.

I'm running out of time. I've got to go back. Please come with me. I promise I won't hurt you."

"No," Garzek shouted. "Make them go away."

Tom stood in the rain for a moment, thinking of a way to retreat. He was afraid Garzek might suddenly anger at his leaving and pull the trigger. Maybe if he thought Tom was going on a mission for him, he wouldn't fire.

"I'll go ask them if they'll leave, Mr. Garzek. I don't think they will, but I'll ask them."

Carefully, he turned his back to the darkened window and crossed the wet lawn, moving faster than he had on the way up to the house a few minutes before, yet controlling the urge to break into a run for the safety of the patrol car. He forced himself to take careful, steady steps, feeling the muscles of his back and shoulders tense as he waited for the roar of the shotgun. As he walked the last few feet and the sound still hadn't come, he couldn't resist. In two quick strides he dived behind the far side of the police car, scraping his palms and kneecaps as he hit the wet concrete.

Chief McDowell and J. Marvin were squatting behind the car, waiting, watching him.

Tom felt weak and giddy. He kept to his hands and knees, breathing deeply. "Didn't do any good," he said when he could talk again. "I think he barely recognized me. He's pretty confused."

"What about the children?" McDowell asked.

"I didn't see them. I think they're dead, though. When I asked about them he said he didn't have children or wife."

He didn't have to explain his reasoning to McDowell or J. Marvin. McDowell said an ugly word under his breath.

"I guess there's nothing to do but get on with it," he said. He turned and estimated the size of the crowd behind them at the intersection. "Whole town'll be out here pretty quick if we don't get this over with." He cupped one hand and yelled to the car behind them. "Sergeant!"

A policeman, crouching low, came up quickly and knelt on the pavement. He was carrying a sawed-off shotgun with a black glove over the muzzle to protect it from the rain.

"Sergeant, I want you to get there, between the cars, when

we put the gas in. He'll probably come out the front door. If he's carrying the gun, don't let him get far enough out to hurt anyone. If he looks like he's going to use it, hit him high. If he's just carrying it, hit him low."

The sergeant nodded to show he understood and moved back to the rear of the car.

McDowell picked up the amplifier. "Turn on that big light again, Roy," he said, and the huge light across the street bathed the whole scene again.

"Tear gas," McDowell said, and before the sound of the bullhorn had died away two tear gas shells went through the front windows. Tom heard window panes shatter from more at the rear of the house. The detectives fired another volley, then retreated to wait.

Tom found himself holding his breath. He peeked around the front of the police car. There was no movement in the house, no sound. Beside him, J. Marvin let out a long sigh, showing he, too, had been holding his breath. Garzek endured the gas an unbelievably long time.

"I don't see how he's standing it," J. Marvin said finally.

The front door of the house burst open and Garzek staggered out, half-falling off the front porch, but keeping to his feet. He was carrying the shotgun at port arms.

"Drop that gun, Garzek," McDowell barked over the amplifier.

As if in answer, Garzek raised the shotgun. But instead of aiming at the car, he pointed the gun at the side of the house next door and fired.

For a moment Tom didn't understand. Then he realized Garzek was blinded by the gas and was firing at the echo. Since the almost windowless wall of the house next door was a perfect sounding board, the echo was probably as loud or louder than the original sound.

"He's blinded," Tom yelled, hoping there was some way to save him. But he was too late.

The sawed-off riot gun roared and with it there was the sickening slap of double-ought buckshot tearing into Garzek. He went down so hard his feet were silhouetted for an instant higher than the rest of the body, giving it a curious rag-doll quality in the death moment.

The body quivered once and was still.

There was a distinct interval when time hung suspended . . . a motionless instant in which they all shared the experience of realization that they had witnessed the end of a life . . . that before their eyes a man had preceded them in death . . . a man who also had heard his own heart beat, whose brain had also thought thoughts . . . a man who had been one of them, and now was no more. . . .

Two policemen approached the body with drawn pistols and broke the spell.

Even before the officers ascertained Garzek's death, the crowd broke through the police line at the intersection and swarmed across the street for a closer look at the body.

McDowell swung the amplifier in their direction. "Everybody stand back," he yelled. "I mean it!"

The police formed a new cordon at the curb in a quick compromise, giving the curious a closer look at the gore, yet keeping them clear of official function.

Tom and J. Marvin moved inside the cordon and up onto the lawn. The body lay face down. McDowell knelt, felt of a wrist, then picked up the shotgun, pointed the muzzle upward, and levered two shells out onto the lawn. J. Marvin picked them up.

"Number six birdshot," he said as he handed them to McDowell.

McDowell put them in the right pocket of his raincoat. "Let's get in there and see about those kids," he called to the lieutenant.

The lieutenant and a detective were putting on gas masks. They fiddled with straps and adjustments an agonizingly long time before they finally entered with flashlights.

In a few minutes one of them found the switch to an evaporative cooler. With so many windows gone, the squirrel-cage fan started moving the gas outside.

As the crowd at the curb began to get the fumes a few ran, coughing, but most held their ground, seeming to relish the discomfort as if they, too, should suffer a little for the privilege of being there.

McDowell entered the house without a mask. Tom and J. Marvin waited at the door while the lieutenant and two homicide detectives went in. They followed as the inside lights began to come on.

Tom immediately wished he had waited outside. Through the glaze of water forced to his eyes by the gas, he saw the small figure of a girl lying in a pool of blood in the kitchen door. Someone called from the rear of the house and they went down the hall to a back bedroom. Both of the boys' bodies lay huddled together on the floor.

"I'll say one thing, he did a good job of it," J. Marvin said. He looked at his wristwatch. "It's getting late. I better find a phone and call in something for the mails. Looks like Garzek pulled this one out by the roots."

The severed phone cord lay at their feet.

"I don't suppose there's any chance of using all we know about Garzek," Tom said, trying to think of a way.

"No. But we can say he was despondent over business failure, and that he was a former mental patient. We know that. I'll put something in about his blaming the police for the failure of his tavern, but Collier will cut it out. Shall I tell Collier you'll have a separate story on your talk with him?"

"I'll do it if Collier wants me to," Tom said. He felt a strong reluctance to write anything at all about this, since he couldn't tell the whole story.

A flashbulb went off behind them and they turned to see Parker taking pictures of the children's bodies. As they watched, he switched cameras and took another.

"Why the two cameras?" J. Marvin asked him.

"I got color film in this one," Parker said, focusing again.

J. Marvin lifted his eyebrows, looked at Tom, and shook his head sadly. "I guess he's hopeless," he said. He scowled at Parker. "You got to be more careful, boy. You damned near got Tom shot out there a while ago when you popped a flashbulb while he was up here talkin' to that nut, not to mention almost gettin' shot yourself, runnin' around all over the place like a wild man. I guess we wouldn't have any trouble findin' another picture-taker, but good reporters are hard come by."

Parker grinned doubtfully, not sure whether J. Marvin was serious or joking. "Aw, if he was goin' to shoot Tom, he'd have done it before he got that far up the walk."

"I'm not too sure of that," J. Marvin said. "And what if he'd shot Tom right after you took that picture, before you could reload? You might have missed a good picture."

"No, I had my Rollei ready."

J. Marvin shook his head sadly and sighed. "Well, come on, you picture-taker. There's a corpse in the back yard that might make a good color shot." He turned to Tom. "I'll go on next door and use the phone. Maybe I can find out the names and ages of the children and get some 'I heard the gunshots and thought it was a car backfiring' quotes."

Sickened by the gas and carnage, Tom went back into the living room. He heard Chief McDowell in the hall, attempting to use the dead phone to call a peace justice for coroner duty. Someone told him the phone cord had been severed, and he sent one of the patrolmen out to a radio unit. Then McDowell came on into the living room.

There was no evidence of violence around them, except for the shattered window. McDowell looked at the draperies, the Italian Provincial furniture, the carpeting. "She had nice taste," he said.

Tom nodded.

"That was a brave thing you did tonight," McDowell said.

"But useless."

"No. I wanted to know about the children. I didn't have the over-all picture until you talked to him. With all you went through, I hate like hell to have to ask you to give a statement on it tonight, but I'm afraid I must."

"I don't mind, but I don't think you're going to like it," Tom said.

McDowell looked at him closely, started to ask a question, then checked himself as if realizing they could be overheard. "You mean it's tied in with what you mentioned earlier tonight?"

"Yes."

McDowell frowned. "We'll go down to the station and take it in my office, then," he said.

"Do you mind if I phone in a story first? Won't take but a few minutes."

"Not at all," McDowell said. "Tell you what, I'll be through here in just a minute. We'll go down in my car and you can use the phone in my office."

Tom nodded.

As McDowell went back into the rear bedroom, Tom began thinking through his conversation with Garzek, of the statement he was to make. He decided he would tell all, not that there was much chance of its doing any good. The statement, no doubt, was destined for private files. There might be an investigation within the Police Department, but that, too, would be kept secret.

Only the surface facts would be publicized. He glanced at his watch, evaluating the time-worth of the story. Too late for the East Coast morning newspapers, but the wire service story would hit the West Coast about right for the final editions. He even imagined the headline, maybe at the foot of page one, maybe somewhere far inside, something like:

POLICE KILL BERSERK GUNMAN
AFTER WIFE, 3 CHILDREN SLAIN

Tomorrow, the story would be fresh for the hungry East Coast early afternoon editions, then dropped out for later, fresher news. A little splash in a very big puddle. And the story behind the story might never be told.

There was still one puzzling thing—Garzek's incoherent talk just before Tom left him. At the time, it hadn't made sense.

Now, remembering the shortcomings of Garzek's English, Tom began to see a different meaning.

"It not work," Garzek had said. In front of that darkened window, Tom had thought he meant the effort to help him hadn't worked. Now, with time to consider the possibilities, Tom wondered if he meant their trap with the tape recorder hadn't worked.

And "I write letters. Everybody know." At the window, Tom had understood it as "everybody knows I wrote the letters." Now, Tom thought Garzek might have been saying "I've written some letters. Now everybody will know."

Garzek could have written and posted some letters. The more Tom considered that meaning, the more sense it made.

No way to sue a dead man for libel.

## CHAPTER EIGHTEEN

"As I'm sure you all know," Mayor Milner said, leaning forward into his microphone, "our principal item of business tonight is to take action on the recommendations of our consulting engineers on the proposed new city reservoir, to consider the proper site, and to discuss a probable date to present the proposal to the city voters for approval or rejection."

From his vantage point, Travis McNiel listened to the mayor's opening formalities without bothering to concentrate on the words or meaning. These opening speeches were the mayor's specialty, his weakness, a thing to be tolerated.

The council chamber was full, Travis noted with deep satisfaction. Down front, more than thirty Chamber of Commerce officials spread an aura of importance over the meeting by their presence. In vain Travis hunted for Sam McIntosh, thinking that perhaps, just once, Sam would condescend to attend a council session. But these were second echelon chamber officials—staff officers, the colonels and brigadiers. The four- and five-star generals had again delegated their authority. Travis saw the manager of Sam's department store, the executive vice-president of First National, and two officers from Sam's oil company. Sam was well-represented.

On the far side, a block of ranchers, landowners, and oilmen sat ill at ease, ready to protest if the proposed high-water mark began to move in their direction.

And the remaining three-quarters of the auditorium was filled with women—Travis' women. He had the support. If he only could find some way to use it.

Travis never had high hopes for scuttling the lake program. And now, facing the other members of the council, he thought he sensed a new undercurrent, a new attitude toward him. His opponents had devised a plan, he was sure of that. He sat listening to the mayor introduce civic leaders to polite bursts of applause, wondering what the plan could be.

Councilman Byron, he figured, had no doubt received considerable emphatic and unsolicited advice since his last deviation from chamber policy. Being a politically ambitious man, Byron probably would switch his allegiance back with the majority tonight. The belief was bolstered by the fact that Byron had avoided Travis before the meeting, and even now would not meet his gaze.

This left only Cal. Travis had been able to talk with Cal only a minute in the hall, earlier, since there had been no pre-council warmup session, and he was disheartened at how fast the old rancher's health was deteriorating. Cal had lost much weight, and he obviously was in pain. It showed in the deeper lines of his face, the set of his mouth. Travis could see the signs clearly the length of the council table as Cal also applauded the introductions.

Beside Cal, Berger seemed even more high-strung than usual. He kept fidgeting, glancing at the audience, Hartwell, the mayor, Kencaide, his eyes never still. Watching him, Travis noticed that Berger's glance kept going back to Tom Kencaide. Maybe Berger was re-evaluating the reporter in the light of the story in this morning's paper. Certainly, Kencaide had done a brave thing. That much was plain from the picture on the front page of Kencaide standing on the lawn in front of the darkened window, talking with the crazed gunman inside. But what impressed Travis more was Kencaide's restraint and modesty in leaving the feat for others to report. A first-person account of the heroics would have cheapened an otherwise courageous, unselfish act. But Kencaide's story had been a brief, poignant piece about the man who was killed. The incident had raised Kencaide in Travis' eyes. Maybe it had in Berger's, too.

The mayor started introducing the consulting engineers, signaling the start of the quiz session. Travis heard the audience stir. He saw that his clubwomen were now sitting more alert, intent, awaiting the anticipated forensic fireworks. Travis forced himself to be more attentive, hoping he wouldn't disappoint them.

"Since the time the consulting engineers made their recommendations," the mayor was saying, "the members of the council have had an opportunity to study the many complexities of the issue. Tonight, we are here in an attempt to answer any and all questions, both from the council and from members of the chamber, other civic leaders, and from the general public. The council has been burning the midnight oil over this for some time, so we will begin with them. Gentlemen?"

Travis thought it best not to take the initiative immediately. He let Weatherbee open the questioning.

"I think the end result we are seeking is cheaper, better water, and more of it," Weatherbee said. "Could you give us a brief comparison of the difference in cost and quality at the three sites?"

The question had the earmarks of too much rehearsal, Travis thought. The engineer—the same smart-aleck Travis tangled with at the last session—had the answer ready. And from the long, involved answer, Travis knew the Lone Grove Site—the one farthest from town and the most expensive—had been decided upon. Wentworth confirmed this by asking for comparative evaporation figures, which again showed the superiority of the Lone Grove Site.

Travis was certain now that the rest of the council had met and decided upon a course of action. They were entirely within their rights, he supposed, to meet and exchange viewpoints on the matter. Still, it rankled that he and Cal had been excluded.

He raised a hand to gain the floor for the next question. "I believe I asked last time for an estimate on the critical point in the city's growth curve where the lake would fail to pay for itself."

The engineer was ready for that one. He turned his charm on Travis. "Yes, Doctor, I have those figures. We compute that what you call the critical point, without an increase in water rates, would be a consumption of slightly more than twelve million gallons of water daily throughout the term of the bonds."

"As I understand it," Travis said, "our average daily water use is now something below ten million gallons, year-around. Am I right, then, that if the city doesn't grow, doesn't use more water, then we will have insufficient revenue to meet payments?"

The mayor interrupted. "Travis, I think you're getting into a problematical field. All our figures are estimates, highly flexible.

As you know, our sole commitment here is to purchase a certain amount of water from the water district at a specified rate. The water district can float the bonds on that basis. We can meet our obligation, I'm sure, by holding our present facilities—which are virtually paid for—in reserve. Or, if we should run into trouble, we could arrange to adjust the principal retirement. . . ."

"Or raise the water rates," Travis heard himself say.

There was a burst of appreciative laughter from the women in anticipation of the heated exchange they'd come to hear. The mayor scowled at Travis, frowned at the audience, lifted his gavel, then reconsidered and laid it down again. He waited until the disturbance had faded.

Travis regretted the gibe. But in the mayor's interruption he had sensed something that angered him. The mayor had a new attitude toward him. There probably had been some discussion about the problem of Dr. Travis McNiel, and the mayor had been warned not to let the radical physician get the floor and confuse issues.

"I'm just trying to point out the complexities in the doctor's line of questioning," the mayor said, nettled. "We could argue all night about it and not get anywhere."

"There's no argument intended on my part, Mayor," Travis said. "I'm only attempting to set some boundaries. I wouldn't sign a personal mortgage or any financial commitment of my own without first examining all the possibilities I might not be able to make good on the contract. I think the people of this city would expect us to do the same."

"I believe the doctor has a good point," Weatherbee said.

The mayor's anger was slow to fade. But Weatherbee's support of Travis caught him off guard. "I only want to prevent wrangling," he said. "You may proceed, Doctor, if your point is constructive."

Travis turned back to the engineer. "The question was, will the city's present water usage, at present rates, pay off our proposed obligation at the Lone Grove Site?"

The engineer spread his hands. "As the mayor said, Doctor, that is a complicated question. If you are asking, just for conjecture, if the city's present water usage, over and above present facilities, will pay off the mortgage, the answer is no. But if the city has a growth of twenty percent over a twenty-year term—again supposing the bonds are twenty-year retirement—the answer is yes. Since the city has had an increase of several hundred percent in the last twenty years, I fail to see any significant element of risk."

"But there is a slight element?"

"A slight one, yes. But I would say the odds are so remote as to be impossible to compute. And as the mayor said, even in that eventuality there are other steps to take—placing present facilities in reserve, a stretchout of payments, a sales program of supplying water to other, less-fortunate communities, or"—he shrugged—"an increase in the water rates."

This time he got the laugh, and Travis smiled to show he, too, could take a joke.

When the chamber quietened, Weatherbee asked for the floor. "Like I said, I think the doctor's got a good point. But we're not going to grow without taking risk. In every house I build I take a risk. There may be nobody to buy it. But I got faith there is, or I wouldn't build it in the first place. I think we got to have faith here. Faith in our city. If we think negatively, risk nothing, we gain nothing. If we think positively, have faith, we grow."

There was a burst of applause, led by the Chamber of Commerce section down front. Weatherbee must have had that speech ready, too. In fact, it was now evident the whole hearing was well-prepared. Travis could see he was accomplishing nothing by fighting the water program on its merits. It had been drafted by the best engineers in the Southwest, and he was only making a fool of himself in trying to punch holes in it.

He waited for the applause to fade. "Like they say on television, the questions of the panel do not necessarily reflect the views of the questioner. It is merely a method of seeking the truth."

The audience applauded, and even the mayor smiled, evidently to show that he no longer harbored ill feelings over their earlier clash. But he tapped the gavel lightly three times for order.

"Are there any further questions from the council?"

There were others, all picayunish and answered with ease by the engineers. Travis decided to keep quiet. His questions brought nothing but animosity, and he felt a deep reluctance at the moment to add to his apparent, growing reputation as the council's reactionary.

He became aware that Cal was not taking part in the discussion. The old rancher was bent forward, his head lowered. Alarmed, Travis thought of getting up to go see about him, but at that instant Cal raised his head and looked at Wentworth, who happened to be speaking. Still, Cal's color, actions, and general appearance worried Travis.

Finally, the council quiz was concluded, and the mayor invited questions from the audience. This took up another hour, for there were several oilmen and ranchers concerned over the exact high-water mark of each proposed lake.

As time wore on, Travis began to sense a restlessness in his clubwomen. This was not the militant battle they had expected. But Travis could do nothing to relieve their boredom. He had to await his cue.

"Are there any other questions from the audience?" the mayor asked. "The council?" He waited a respectable length of silence. "Do I hear any motions from the council?"

Travis spoke quickly, for he knew that whatever motion the mayor was seeking was well-rehearsed. "Before we take action on the consulting engineers' recommendations," he said, speaking to the mayor, "I would like to give the council the benefit of some community sentiment on this project in relation to another need of the city."

Travis had expected immediate opposition and had boned up on sections of the city charter pertaining to councilmen's rights, and rules of parliamentary procedure. But he was totally unprepared for the mayor's reaction.

The Gray Ghost smiled, looking up at the women. "Well, Travis, I suppose that since you have invited all these lovely ladies out this evening, we certainly should take advantage of the opportunity to hear them. If you will be so kind as to introduce them. . . ."

Travis knew, then, that it was all cut and dried. Feeling he was falling right into their trap, he picked up the list of names.

"I would be happy to, Mayor. First, Mrs. Bobbie Jo White of the Ben Milam Pre-School Association. . . ."

If he had written their speeches himself, Travis could not have gotten more from his troops. Their presentation, appearance, and effectiveness were perfect. All were attractive, well-groomed women, intelligent and articulate, experienced in speaking before audiences.

Yes, they realized the city's need for water, for industrial expansion. The water rationing of a few years ago disturbed them. But recently they had heard Dr. McNiel speak, and they had visited the hospital. What they saw and heard worried them far more than the water shortage. They believed the city council would do well to consider the hospital needs. From what they had seen, they believed the hospital program should come first. Their presentations varied, but the gist was the same. As he listened, Travis watched their effectiveness.

The council members were impressed. Their undivided attention told him that. Perhaps he had preached to the council so long on the hospital they had become immune to his pleas. Now, the same arguments from a parade of attractive young matrons—each representing a sizable block of voters—jarred them. He could see it in their faces. And he didn't know if it would affect their plan, because he still didn't know what their plan was. . . .

Twenty representatives of twenty groups, speaking only two, three minutes each, changed the whole atmosphere of the council chamber. He could feel it. He even felt new respect in the glances of the other councilmen.

"That is all, Mister Mayor," he said as the last woman finished. "I certainly don't think I could add anything to that. I only wish to thank the ladies I have called upon, and all those who have attended this session tonight in the interest of the hospital program."

The Chamber of Commerce section led the applause. The mayor sat frowning, his head lowered as if in deep thought. Then he raised his head and looked at Travis. Here it comes, Travis thought.

"Doctor, as you know, the lake program is too far advanced to get the hospital program on the same ballot. Also, the issues, being of different nature, would be incompatible on the same ballot. Or at least, that is the belief of the majority of the council. Do you concede that is the majority opinion?"

Travis was thinking ahead, trying to see the trap before he fell all the way into it. "It has been in the past," he said cautiously.

"This is a time when we should be seeking unity," the mayor said. "Both of these are needed projects. We all agree on that. And these lovely ladies have made the need for the hospital program even more plain tonight. We all agree on the need for both programs, we just can't agree on the relative importance. Isn't that right? Isn't it true you are not against the lake project itself?"

"That's true," Travis said warily.

"Our city has a wonderful future before it," the Gray Ghost said. "We must prepare for tomorrow in every way we can. If tomorrow comes, we must be ready for it." He paused, letting the audience reflect on his words. "Now, I've been talking with several other members of the council, Doctor. If we . . . tonight . . . adopted a resolution to solve our hospital problems as quickly as possible, appointing you as a committee of one from the council to work up new cost estimates from the existing plans with the architects, would you be able to give your support to both projects?"

Travis wanted to be sure he heard right. "You mean an election, as soon as possible?"

"As soon as you, the hospital board, and the architects can work up the estimates, with, of course, the legal limitations of public hearing and election notice. Also, it might be wise to follow the lead of some other state municipalities and create a hospital district, and I believe the rest of the council will agree with me we should utilize your talents in looking into that possibility. But that can wait. The point is, from tonight on, the full council would be working together, unanimously supporting both of these excellent projects, striving to accomplish both as quickly as humanly possible, preparing for tomorrow. How does that sound to you, Doctor?"

Travis knew that every person in the council chamber was looking at him, waiting. He sought to find the holes in the proposition, but could find none. Still, he had the feeling this was not victory, but defeat. There was an unknown facet, somewhere.

Maybe he had worked so long against the water program the idea of voting for it would require time to accept. That was the only reason for his reluctance, he decided—the strangeness of the idea. For despite the mayor's careful terminology, the proposition was one of log-rolling, pure and simple. He and the support he'd drummed up were a threat to the water program. By the agreement, they would gain the support of his troops. That was why they'd chosen tonight, with his audience present, to make the benevolent gesture.

All logic failed him. He could only think of the new hospital wing, a new recovery room, a new emergency room with proper facilities. "That sounds fine," he said.

The enthusiastic burst of applause that followed his words was unexpected. Travis' troops regarded the offer as a clear-cut victory, capitulation by the opposition.

But something in the mayor's unsmiling, hesitant manner told Travis the show wasn't over yet.

The Gray Ghost waited patiently for quiet. "There is only one other councilman who has opposed the lake program," he said. "And he, too, has been a strong advocate of the hospital program. Cal, could you see fit to follow the doctor's lead, and make support for both projects unanimous?"

Travis saw he'd put Cal in a terrible position. That had been the hidden facet he'd sensed but hadn't had time to find: the pressure this would put on Cal as the lone holdout.

There was a long moment of silence. Then Cal leaned forward slowly to the microphone. "Mister Mayor, surely you know that I am too old and too obstinate to compromise. However, I will put your mind at ease. This is my last council meeting. My health is forcing me to resign."

A murmur of surprise swept through the audience. Travis studied the expressions at the council table, one by one. Hartwell knew, he believed, and the mayor. But Cal's announcement stunned the others. Even Tom Kencaide at the press table below them sat motionless, pencil poised, staring at Cal, his reportorial objectivity apparently shattered.

The mayor recovered first, probably because of prior knowledge. "I'm sorry to hear that, Cal," he said. "I really am. We have had our differences through the years, but I think you will be the first to acknowledge that we've agreed and worked side by side far more often than the few times we differed, which unfortunately received more notice."

Cal nodded affirmatively.

"I know I can speak for the whole council," the mayor said, "when I say we regret illness is forcing you to take this action."

Cal looked out over the audience. "I know it has been said often that I am against progress," he said slowly. "But all I ever asked is that we be sure where we are goin', certain of what it is we are tryin' to do, exactly what it is we want to accomplish. Somehow, I think we never knew. I don't think you know now. If I thought makin' this a huge, sprawlin' smokin' city would better the lives of those who elected us to council, I would vote for this proposal. But I don't think it would. Therefore, I oppose it. But since I'll not be here to take the consequences, I'll not jeopardize the measure at the polls. I will abstain from voting tonight, Mister Mayor. Since you have my verbal resignation, the council may, in effect, vote unanimously."

The voting, then, was a formality. The city attorney was instructed to draft a resolution saying the council endorsed the hospital program as proposed by the hospital board and planned to work for its completion with all possible speed, with Travis as committee chairman to carry out the details. The vote on the water program was anticlimactic. The recommendations of the consulting engineers for the Lone Grove Site were approved in full, a public hearing was called six weeks hence to iron out the details, and date of the election was set tentatively for June second, which they reasoned was as early as possible legally, and still not so late that summer vacations would interfere with voter turnout.

As the mayor was recognizing and thanking various groups that had attended, Cal Masters arose slowly, reached for his Stetson on the hatrack behind him, and went quietly out the back door of the council chamber. This wasn't unusual. Often, when councilmen were in a hurry, they left early. Travis had done so himself at times when he wanted to visit a patient at the hospital on the way home, for sometimes the mayor's closing speeches seemed to stretch indefinitely.

But the way Cal reached for his hat, the way he looked neither to right nor left on his way out, alarmed Travis. He sat for a moment in indecision, then hurried out after him.

The hall was deserted. Travis went into the men's restroom and looked. It was empty. He hurried down the stairs to the next level. Cal was standing at the foot of the stairway, leaning heavily on the railing.

Travis took the stairs down to him two at a time. "What is it, Cal?"

"My head. Feels like it's about to split open."

"Look at me. How is your vision?"

"That's why I stopped here. Everything's blurred."

Travis heard footsteps behind them. Hartwell was coming down the stairs. "What happened?" he asked.

"Cal is feeling ill," Travis explained. "Could we take him down to your office?"

"Sure. I'll give you a hand."

They half-carried Cal down the hall to the office and put him in the big chair behind Hartwell's desk. Then Travis tried to make a quick analysis. There was no apparent paralysis or impediment of speech, and Cal's mind seemed clear. Yet Travis knew something had happened. If it was what he suspected. . . .

"I think we had better check you into the hospital," he told Cal.

"No. I'll be all right, soon as I get my strength back," Cal protested. They heard the crowd from the council chamber spilling out into the stairwell, the footsteps and talk echoing in the halls. "I'd rather not see anybody, though, right now," Cal added. "Don't let them know."

Hartwell went out and closed the outer door, then came back and closed the inner office door behind him, giving them a double buffer that muffled the sounds.

"We'll just check you into the hospital overnight where we can keep an eye on you," Travis told Cal. "If you're feeling better in the morning, I promise we'll release you."

"I reckon you're right," Cal said reluctantly. "I'm feelin' right poorly. But let's wait until everybody else has left the buildin'."

While they waited, Travis called and made arrangements. Fortunately, there was a private room available.

With Hartwell's help, Travis took Cal to the hospital. They helped get him togged out in a white gown and into bed. Then, over Cal's protests, Travis called Cal's eldest daughter, and she alerted the family.

By one A.M. it was clear that Travis' fears were justified. Cal apparently had cancer of the brain. Travis had seen the terrible swiftness of brain cancer before, and he had heard of pancreatic cancer spreading to the brain, although he'd never seen a case himself.

Shortly after dawn, Cal's pain began to ease, but with the relief came the first signs of paralysis. Travis knew then the end was near. He got the family's permission to call in two specialists. They agreed that Cal was apt to go into a final coma at any time and that there was nothing anyone could do.

Late in the morning the head nurse called. "Mr. Masters is asking for you," she said. "He seems very insistent. I thought you would want to know."

Travis had gone back to his office for a couple of hours. He had almost finished his office workload. Tired after being up all night, he had intended to take a brief nap. The nurse described Cal's condition as unchanged, but Travis knew Cal would not have sent word unless he considered it important.

Despite what the nurse had said, Travis found Cal weaker. Paralysis was further advanced. Still, his mental processes seemed clear.

"I'd like to speak to you privately, if I may," Cal said.

Travis nodded to the nurse. She went out silently, leaving Travis and Cal alone in the room.

"How long?" Cal asked.

"Don't ask me that," Travis pleaded. "I have no way of knowing."

"You promised you would be honest with me," Cal reminded him.

Travis re-evaluated his promise in the light of the moment.

The truth probably wouldn't have any effect on the inevitable outcome. "I am being honest. There is no way of knowing. The paralysis probably means the pressure is affecting your motor reflexes. This condition may last for days, or it could worsen in hours."

"Will those awful headaches come back?"

"It's possible, but I don't believe they will. The nerves or blood supply to the portion of the brain causing those headaches may be pinched off or numbed, now."

"What will be next?"

"We can't be sure. But a coma, most likely."

"Then I'll just . . . go to sleep," Cal said.

Travis didn't answer, but his face must have let Cal know the truth.

"Thank you," Cal said. "Knowing what to expect makes it easier. I never liked a dentist who told you what he was going to do wouldn't hurt, when he knew damned well it would." He smiled. "You know, I thought that when the time came, I would be afraid, but I'm not."

"I'm glad."

"Your father, in a sermon one time, said death is life's greatest adventure. He said that all life is preparation for death."

Travis remembered that sermon. He had heard it many times.

"Your father saved me from a life of sin," Cal said. "Did you know that? He was the turning point in my life. He helped me to find myself."

"No, I didn't know that," Travis said, embarrassed, feeling this was something he had no right to hear. "You shouldn't be talking so much. I warned your family not to tire you. Then I come in here and talk your leg off. Some doctor I am."

He picked up his bag, but Cal was not to be turned from the subject.

"That's why I asked them to call you. You are the son of the man who gave my whole life meaning. It would make me feel much better, now, if you were to pray with me."

For a moment Travis thought Cal's mind had been affected. "Cal, I'm a doctor, not a minister. Dr. Anderson was here from your church. I'll get them to call him back. . . ."

"You're a Christian, aren't you? You believe, don't you?"

"Yes. But . . ."

"You were near to him. You played in the brush arbors as a boy. I saw you. You grew up with the Word of God preached to your ears almost daily by the greatest preacher I ever heard. And you were his son. I would rather have you pray for me now than any ordained minister alive."

Travis started to protest again, but Cal was rambling.

"You've probably heard I was a wastrel in my early days. I was. A regular ring-tailed tooter. Then one night I was all liquored up with a couple of other boys, and we heard about your father's camp meetin'. We thought it was a different kind of camp meetin'—you know, where they roll on the floor and speak in the unknown tongue. We used to go watch those for sport—there wasn't much entertainment in those days."

"You shouldn't be talking so much," Travis said again, wanting to hear, and yet knowing he shouldn't. Cal went on as if he hadn't been interrupted.

"But it wasn't that kind of a meetin'. We listened from the edge of the crowd, and the other boys laughed. I didn't. What your father was sayin' got through the liquor to me. I was sober when I left. And the next night I went back, alone. When he asked for sinners to come forward and be saved, I went. He changed my life, gave it purpose. He taught me to pray, and because of him, I am not afraid now."

"He taught you to pray?"

Cal nodded. "He said, 'Prayer is love, not words. All the eloquence in the world is useless if there is not love, and if there is love no words are needed. There can be prayer without words, but there can be no prayer without love.'"

"Yes, I remember that," Travis said, wondering why he hadn't recalled it before.

"Would you say something for me now?"

Travis wanted to help, but he knew his own inadequacies. Cal was expecting too much. "I'm afraid I'm not my father's son when it comes to religious matters," he said. He saw disappointment on Cal's face. "I could quote some Scripture, if you'd like," he added.

"Please."

Travis lifted his head, closed his eyes, and searched for words. "The Lord is my Shepherd, I shall not want. . . ."

The words came easy, for he had learned to recite the Twenty-third Psalm before his fifth birthday, and in the years since he had gone over it in his mind many times. But now, as he spoke the words, a strange thing began to happen. The old, familiar phrases took on meaning. He felt warmth in his body, a communion of mind, and he knew that for the first time in his life he truly was praying.

"He maketh me to lie down in green pastures; He leadeth me beside the still waters. He restoreth my soul; He leadeth me in the paths of righteousness for His name's sake. Yea, though I walk through the valley of the shadow of death, I will fear no evil; for Thou art with me; Thy rod and Thy staff they comfort me. Thou preparest a table before me in the presence of mine enemies; Thou anointest my head with oil; my cup runneth over. Surely goodness and mercy shall follow me all the days of my life; and I will dwell in the house of the Lord for ever."

Then, without pausing, Travis said the Lord's Prayer. When he finished he stood for a moment, regaining his perspective, knowing he had undergone an experience as moving and perhaps as important as Cal had at that camp meeting forty years ago.

"Thank you," Cal said without opening his eyes, and Travis knew Cal had measured the depth of his prayer.

Overwhelmed by his own emotions, Travis picked up his bag and fled from the room.

At six that evening Cal went into a coma. They called Travis at home, where he was taking a nap, and he hurried back to the hospital. There was nothing he could do. Cal never fully regained consciousness. Only once did he rouse, but there was no rationality. He raised his head, seemingly excited. "I hear the wild geese," he said. "It must be spring again." He looked around the room, confused, then sank back on the pillow. At 3:10 A.M. respiration stopped as the growing cancer halted impulses from the brain's respiration center. Two minutes later the heart stopped beating, and Cal was dead.

# *Part Seven*

## CHAPTER NINETEEN

In the southwest, the contrail of a jet bomber was etched white against a blue sky. David stood watching the progress of the unseen plane as it moved over the church steeple and disappeared behind the roof, leaving a long stream of wispy cotton.

David was lined up with the other honorary pallbearers, waiting for the casket to be placed in the Byron Funeral Home hearse, the many eloquent words just spoken about Cal Masters alive, discordant in his mind.

The eulogy had been apt. Cal Masters had been a fine friend, a Christian, a leader in the community, and he would be missed. But somehow the real importance of Cal Masters had been glossed over. Now, as David waited, he tried to decide what had been left out.

The pallbearers stood straining under the weight of the heavy casket. There was a delay of some kind within the hearse. He couldn't see the trouble because of the shining black door. The crowd stood silent, waiting patiently, collectively ignoring the mechanical aspects.

The afternoon sun felt warm. David shifted his stance slightly and looked for the plane again, thinking it might have come out from behind the church by now. But it was gone, the contrails stretched into slowly widening curves where the high altitude currents reshaped them.

Inside the hearse the difficulty was solved with a metallic click, and the pallbearers slid the casket in with an audible rolling sound. It was secured by another click, then the funeral home attendant stepped out and closed the hearse door. He was sweating profusely from his efforts and paused to wipe his face with a white handkerchief.

With the ritual of the hearse over, the crowd on the sidewalk turned and started for the cars. David walked with the council members to the long black Cadillac limousine awaiting them with open doors, a driver standing by its side.

"He certainly looked natural, didn't he?" the mayor asked in a low voice beside David.

David gave the expected answer. "Yes, he did."

But Cal hadn't seemed natural at all. There was too much of Cal that was sky-blue eyes, soft warm voice, and gentle presence. That cold body in the casket wasn't Cal.

The driver directed them into the limousine, evidently according to size. Travis and the mayor, both long and lean, sat up front with the driver. David and Weatherbee, both short of leg, sat on the dropseats amidship, facing inward. Wentworth, Byron, and Berger, all broader of beam, were given the rear seat.

In the crowd from the church David had seen Tom Kencaide. He couldn't help sneaking a glance at Berger now, wondering how much Berger knew of Kencaide's statement after the Garzek slayings. Berger gave no sign. His face was expressionless.

Ahead, Byron's No. 1 assistant climbed into the hearse, apparently the signal to start the motors. The police motorcycles roared to life, and they started the long drive out to Memorial Park.

"A fine sermon," the mayor said.

"Fine-looking family," Weatherbee said.

"Yes," the mayor agreed. "As you all probably know, I handled his legal affairs—we were quite good friends, really, despite our differences. Anyway, I've had the pleasure of meeting the whole family in the last couple of days. Wonderful people, and the grandchildren all alert, clean-cut youngsters. Cal may have made a late start in life, but he more than made up for it."

"I guess, when you come right down to it," Travis said, "Cal's devotion to his family and the family life of the community was one of his most admirable traits."

There was a brief murmur of agreement. Travis had been closer to Cal in some strange way than any of them, David reflected. In one death he had lost patient, friend, and council ally. Today, Travis was even thinner and paler than usual.

The procession turned onto Lamar, the oncoming traffic pulling to the curb as they passed. David turned in the bucket seat to look out the window, hoping to avoid further conversation. Apparently the others felt the same way, for there was none. When they reached the highway, the police escort moved on ahead and the procession picked up a little speed.

David studied what Travis had said about Cal, assessing the truth in the remark. Perhaps that was what he had found lacking in the eulogy—Cal's old-fashioned virtues.

The limousine slowed to follow the hearse off the highway and into the cemetery. Looking back, David could see the full length of the procession, stretching back more than half a mile, the headlamps bright despite the strong sun.

As the car eased to a stop, the mayor opened the door and started to get out, but Byron's No. 1 assistant had left the hearse and walked back to their car. "Please wait in the car until everyone is parked," he said in funereal tones.

The mayor closed the door again. Since the driver had turned off the engine, and with it the air-conditioner, David lowered his window. Now, with no buildings to hinder, there was a good breeze from the southwest to ease the heat.

The cemetery was green with spring, the grass trimmed, the headstones straight, the walks graveled and even. Reluctantly, David looked past the hearse to where Cal's grave waited. A green tarpaulin covered the mound of fresh dirt beyond, half-hidden with flowers and wreaths. A canopy trembled in the breeze over the grave. The hole itself was surrounded with a carpet of too-dark, make-believe grass which spilled over the edges, hiding the raw earth.

David always avoided funerals whenever possible. Few things affected him more. And in a way, the funeral of a friend or casual business acquaintance was worse, when he felt just far enough removed from grief to study death objectively.

Behind them, the passengers left the cars and gathered around the grave. Cal's family was escorted by Byron's staff. Then one of the assistants opened the limousine doors.

David lined up with the councilmen again behind the casket and followed it down through the silent crowd to where it was placed on an aluminum and web frame over the grave.

Another minister began speaking, but David couldn't concentrate on the words. His mind was cluttered up with the morbid thoughts that always came at these times—the claustrophobia of the closed casket, the way it looked inside, the corrosive action of the earth's acids, how things would look in a year, five years, ten. . . .

To divert his thoughts, he shifted his gaze to Cal's grandchildren. The mayor was right. They made a striking family—the boys tall, blond, and husky, the girls full-figured. As they bowed their heads in prayer he studied them. They ranged in age from fifteen through the early twenties, but they all had the same mature, unassuming confidence he wanted so much to see in his own children. Now Ronnie was even more hang-dog in appearance, and Christine, crying all the time, was sure she could never face the world again.

The minister concluded the prayer. There was a moment of uncertainty before everyone realized the services were over. The casket was to be left poised over the grave, in accordance with modern custom, sparing all the sight of its sinking into the ground, the scrape of shovels and the hollow thump of fresh dirt. . . .

David walked back to the limousine and waited. He had no inclination to linger, but the councilmen seemed reluctant to leave. They mingled with the crowd, talking. Finally Travis, who had been talking with Sam McIntosh, left him and came up the path toward David. "Marilyn brought our car out," he said. "Why don't you ride back in with us and come by the house for a drink?"

"I'd sure like to, but I'm afraid I'll have to take a rain check," David said. "The mayor has something on his mind he wants to talk over."

Travis looked back toward the grave. "I will always regret what I did to him in that last council meeting," he said. "I felt like I sold him down the river."

David considered briefly what he could say in the way of comfort without stepping beyond his official limitations. "No cause to feel that way," he said. "Cal knew that after all the work you've done, you had to accept their offer."

"Did I?" Travis asked. "I'm still wondering if I didn't get played for a sucker again."

"Why?" David asked. "It seems to me you got the promise of all you've wanted."

Travis nodded. "Another promise. I'm just hoping now that their written word is worth more than their verbal promises."

"You might come up to City Hall and monitor the city attorney in drafting the resolution," David said. "I'm sure you would be within your rights to insist that the wording measure up to the terms as you interpreted them."

Travis seemed grateful for the suggestion. "Thanks," he said. "I'll do that."

The doctor saw his wife and waved. He repeated the offer of a ride back to town and a drink, and again David declined.

At the moment, he didn't feel in the mood for company. He watched Travis walk up the line of automobiles toward his wife. David stood by the limousine, feeling the sun warm on his face, alive, breathing. . . .

He looked back at the casket suspended over the open grave and thought of Cal's life, compared to his own. He wondered what Cal would do in his shoes.

The mayor came up to the limousine, nervous, troubled, Cal apparently already dismissed from his mind. "David, I've got to talk to you. In private. Where can we go?"

The mayor's office downtown wasn't very private, David remembered. It was in an old building. The walls were thin. "City Hall is closed for the day," David reminded him. "My office will be deserted."

"Fine," the mayor said. He glanced around to make sure Berger was still out of earshot. "You hear about the letters?"

David nodded. "Chief McDowell called me as soon as he received his. I have a copy of it."

"Is it true?"

"It appears to be. There are some later developments I'll fill you in on."

"But this is terrible," the mayor said. "A city councilman. . . ." He glanced around to locate Berger again and chopped off what he was about to say. "Shh. He's coming."

"I'll meet you at City Hall, then," David said.

"About five?"

"Let's make it six," David said. "I have something I must do first."

The mayor appeared somewhat taken aback, but with Berger approaching, he didn't protest. "Six, then," the mayor said.

David got clearance from the tower and took off from Municipal Airport, leaving the throttle open wide, climbing fast.

He turned westward, following his compass heading until he saw the river. With the water a bright, shining ribbon curving far below, he turned upstream, watching the play of the sun on its surface.

He knew he should be thinking ahead to his talk with the mayor on the Berger affair. He still hadn't decided how much to tell, and he should be weighing carefully the consequences of each development of the last few hours. But he couldn't worry seriously about all that now. He'd always had an unfailing instinct for what was his own concern and what was in the purview of the council. When the time came, he could play this case by ear, too. He kept seeing Cal's body in the casket . . . the casket over the open grave. . . .

Gradually, the turns of the river became more familiar. He saw the bend below Cal's ranch where they'd hunted—the high bluffs on one side, the brush of the wide flood plain on the other.

As he passed over the ranch, he could see no changes in the green stretches of open grassland, the trees, the Herefords grazing, or in the sturdy house, corral, and outbuildings. Somehow, he had expected it all to look different.

He banked and went back over, losing altitude. The pasture down by the river was so smooth he was tempted to set down, but there might be an unseen hole. The risk would be foolish. He passed over the ranchhouse without seeing anyone.

He wondered what would happen to the ranch now. The daughters would have no trouble selling, despite the relatively small acreage. Still, the prospect of its going into a stranger's hands was a shame, for Cal had worked so hard, so many years. He had protected the land in drought and good times, without greed, keeping always to the long-range goal, with little thought to the profits of the moment.

David remembered what Cal had said in that last council

session. "All I ever asked is that we be sure where we are goin', certain of what it is we want to accomplish. I don't think you know now."

Cal had known. Somewhere in his life Cal must have decided what it was he wanted to achieve, for the evidence of planning was all around. He'd had extensive holdings in oil, considerable property in town, and other vague investments. He'd never talked about business, but David could see a pattern. Cal had held onto the ranch as a hole card—there was more than just sentiment involved. Cal had branched out. Yet, here was the roots. In any consideration, the ranch came first.

The signs of planning were plain in Cal's personal life, too. His young wife hadn't liked the ranch, so he'd made sacrifices there. Cal was no social mixer, but he'd seen to it that his daughters had the opportunity to meet the kind of husbands that would give them the things they wanted in life.

David remembered the way Cal had often wanted civic policy to go one way or another because of his children and grandchildren. Cal had called it selfishness, but it was really a part of the planning.

Again, David found himself comparing Cal's life with his own. It took no imagination to project his own life another few years. His wife, most likely, was headed for an institution unless the improvement she'd made the last few days was protected. His children would be leaving home unprepared to face the world and all it demanded of them. As for himself, there was the possibility—even probability—that eventually he would be booted out of office by a hostile council over some trifling issue. It had happened to older and wiser men. The rewards of all his worry and labor might be the loss of his job right when he needed it most. That was something to keep in mind.

The answer was plain. He should be planning his life—and for the life of his wife and children.

He stood up to the council on other issues. From now on, he would have to start telling the council what was his personal life and what was his official life. He would have to serve notice he was putting in a nine-to-five day, and no more—with the exceptions of council meetings and dire emergencies.

He turned back toward Municipal Airport.

The councilmen would never understand. They'd probably point out that he was on salary, not hourly wages. He'd just have to stand up to them. He would have to take the long-range view.

"I think it's hopeless, David," Chief McDowell said. "We can't get a thing out of him."

Through the open door at the end of the hall David could see the ex-convict, Donald Ratliff, seated in the interrogation room, two detectives standing over him.

"I don't care what we get out of him," David said. "Just as long as we get him tied to Berger. What was he burglarizing Garzek's tavern *for*, anyway? What was he after? You have any idea?"

"Just a theory," McDowell said. "I think he was after the tape out of the tape recorder Kencaide had put under the bar. When we went out to check on the recorder after the shootings, Kencaide noticed that about three-quarters of a spool had been run off, then rewound—the machine rewind makes a different pattern on a fresh spool. As I told you, the tape was blank. But I got to thinking. It seemed to me highly probable that Ratliff visited Garzek again to scare him, Garzek attempted to put their conversation on tape, and punched the wrong button."

David saw his line of reasoning. "That could have been the final straw," he agreed.

"Probably. Anyway, Kencaide mentioned that he had told the DA about the recorder. Now I happen to know the DA and Berger are just like that." He held up two fingers side by side. "So I figured Berger knew about the machine. But it's plain Ratliff didn't. I think he went out there on his own, just throwing his weight around. It seemed to me that if and when Berger learned of Ratliff's visit, he just might send Ratliff back out there to see if he could find the tape."

David understood then. Ratliff's arrest hadn't been an accident. "You mean you had a stake-out waiting for him?"

McDowell grinned. "Police work is just like defensive football. Figure out what the other guy is going to do, then be there. Anyway, we've got a warrant, and we're fixing to go out and shake down his room. Want to come along?"

David nodded.

They walked down the hall together. Ratliff saw them coming and looked up, squinting against the bright lights.

During his weeks of frustration, David had been unable to build a mental impression of Ratliff. Now, facing him, he found himself disappointed. Ratliff was an ordinary-looking man in his early thirties, rather heavy-set, with a stubby crewcut.

McDowell and one of the detectives exchanged glances, and the detective, with a barely perceptible shake of his head, signaled the lack of success. McDowell stared down at Ratliff. "All right, if that's the way you want it. But you're making a mistake. I can't promise you any deals, but it'd probably go easier on you if you'd co-operate."

Ratliff looked down at his jail denims. He didn't answer.

McDowell nodded to a uniformed jailer, who stepped forward and motioned Ratliff to his feet.

"If you change your mind, let us know," McDowell told Ratliff as the jailer started out with him. A muffled obscenity from the hall was the only reply.

At the fleabag hotel on lower Main, an old man with the scraggly remnants of a handlebar mustache escorted David, McDowell, and two detectives up to the room on the second floor, protesting with every step that Mr. Ratliff had been an ideal guest and had never given him any indication his business was dishonest. He was sure the room was just as Mr. Ratliff left it.

As David watched, McDowell and the two detectives searched the room. They methodically went through the unmade bed, the ancient bureau and chest of drawers, and the closet. There was nothing except a few changes of clothing, widely scattered and in disarray.

"You sure nobody's been up here rummaging around?" McDowell asked the old man, who was standing silently in the doorway.

"No, sir, not a soul," the old man said.

McDowell appeared dubious. "Looks to me like somebody's shaken this room down good." He nodded to one of the detectives. "Let's really give it the works. Maybe they missed something." He turned to the old man. "I think we'll stick around a while."

The old man shuffled away. One detective started pulling the drawers out and searching under and behind them. The other took a chair and climbed up into the closet, where there was a crawl-hole into the attic. McDowell looked behind the mirror, under chairs, behind the headboard of the bed.

It was twenty minutes later that McDowell and one of the detectives moved the bed and found a slight irregularity in the worn carpet beneath. Pulling the rug away from the wall, they found a manila envelope on the floor. Inside were a stack of legal papers and several sheets of notepaper filled with figures.

"Paydirt," McDowell said, shuffling through the contents. "Promissory notes between one Donald Ratliff and one Max Berger."

David studied the amounts as McDowell handed the papers to him. There was something vaguely familiar about the figures. Then he remembered. "Every one is in the amount of a land purchase along the right-of-way."

"Insurance," McDowell said. "Berger wanted protection against a double-cross, or a way to get the land if Ratliff got jailed again."

David was looking at the sheets of figures. "That's Berger's handwriting. I remember how he makes his fours, closing the top like that, almost like a nine. I've got some samples we can use for comparison."

"Good," McDowell said. "You've got what you want. This ties them together."

"Think it's enough to make a case?"

McDowell grinned. "David, I'm just a dumb cop that's caught a burglar. Now, there are a lot of things to take into consideration before filing charges against a city councilman. This looks like a policy decision to me."

"I don't know what to do about these letters," the mayor said from the chair by David's desk. "I certainly don't want any scandal in my administration."

"The situation is far more serious than just the letters," David told him softly, trying to prepare him for what was to come.

"You mean all this hysterical tirade is true?"

David nodded. "Making a few allowances for Garzek's obvious mental condition, it's all true."

The mayor seemed dazed. His left hand began to tremble. He spread it on his kneecap to steady it. "Then Berger *is* a crook," he said. "What are we going to do?"

"I'll tell you all I know," David said. "But I wouldn't attempt to advise you as to what action to take. It's a long, involved story. The only way I know to tell it is to go back to the beginning."

Starting with the land sale, David described the entire Berger case. The mayor sat bolt upright and listened in silence.

"This is terrible," he said when David had finished. "You should have told me about this before."

"Perhaps," David admitted. "But remember, we've had no proof before. Not until today."

The mayor breathed deeply, and as he spoke his voice trembled. "This might be enough for an indictment."

"McDowell thinks we might have a case. Ratliff matches Garzek's description, and he was identified in a lineup this afternoon by a friend of Kencaide's, another tavern owner, as the man who came into his place and set the quota on Alamo Beer. And, of course, there's still a chance Ratliff may talk. But McDowell and I feel that since so much is at stake, the disposition of the case is a council matter, rather than an administrative one."

The mayor was beginning to see the extent of the consequences. "Oh, my, no, we can't prosecute. It would cost us the water bond program, for sure. We would never win support at the polls, if this became public. And even if we got the program approved, a scandal like this might affect our municipal credit rating."

David wanted to be sure the mayor saw the danger in doing nothing. "Well, Berger has only sixteen or seventeen more months left to serve," he said. "You might wait and make sure he's defeated."

The mayor considered that for a moment. "No, we can't take the chance," he said. "There are too many risks for scandal—the beer thing, all those shoddy businesses, gambling, the right-of-way property. Any one of those things could come out into the open at any time. Besides, we would never know what use he was making of confidential council information."

"If the DA could be trusted, there might be a chance for an indictment on the beer shakedown alone—without mentioning the highway land. But Chief McDowell thinks the DA and Berger are rather close."

The mayor frowned. "Yes," he said, shifting his weight in the chair. "This is something else, a story that's going around in legal circles. Quite true, I'm afraid. I heard it from a dependable source. It seems that the district attorney went out to see some prostitute who was trying to get her boy friend out of jail. It was a trap. They had one of those mirrors, with one-way glass, rigged up in her room, with a movie camera behind it. The district attorney performed rather well, from what I hear. Anyway, Berger has the film. It's all been treated as a big joke, but everyone understands that there's nothing funny about it. The story is that's why the DA is soft on certain hoodlums."

"And I thought my revelations on Berger were a surprise to you!" David said.

The mayor frowned again. "Well, I knew he was associating with some . . . unsavory, I suppose you'd say . . . persons. But I had no inkling of anything like this." He tapped the arm of the chair impatiently. "I certainly wish I knew what to do."

David kept silent, even though he knew the mayor was soliciting his opinion.

"I think it might be a good idea," the mayor went on, "to get the council together with the chamber directors and see if we can't come up with a plan of action." He waited again for David's comment. When he saw it was not forthcoming, he asked for it. "What do you think?"

David hesitated. He didn't want any part of intracouncil politics, yet he felt he had to voice disapproval. The Chamber of Commerce would be the last place he'd take such a problem, if it were left up to him. Also, the whole matter was highly unethical, not to mention possibly illegal. He hedged.

"I don't know that such a group could take any official action. . . ."

"Oh, that wouldn't be the purpose. We wouldn't meet as a

body, just as a selected group of civic leaders called to discuss the problem and decide what to do."

David opened his mouth to put his views into plain words, then closed it again. He would say no more about it. Whatever happened, he was out of it. The wrongdoing was in the council, not in the city administration, and no one could blame him. Only if he became involved in the petty intrigues could he be open to censure. His subtle disapproval was lost on the mayor, who mistook his silence for acquiescence.

"I believe that's what we will do," the mayor said firmly. "I'll go down and discuss this with the chamber president first thing in the morning and see if we can set up a meeting in the next day or two. Let's see, it would be best, I believe, to have a luncheon meeting at one of the hotels, be less formal, and we'd all feel more free to air our views. Of course, I'll want to have you and Chief McDowell there, too."

Now David had no choice. He had to make the issue plain. "I don't believe that would be wise," he said.

The mayor was obviously taken aback; he really didn't understand. David spelled it out for him.

"Having the chief of police there would give the appearance of official charges—turn your discussion into a sort of kangaroo court. I don't believe Chief McDowell would be a party to it, and I don't think I should be, either. Also, as I said before, I believe this is a council matter. I don't feel the administration should be represented."

The mayor stared at him. "I suppose what you say is true, David. But let's not forget that some of those accusations in the letters do concern the city administration. I believe both of you should be there to answer those charges."

David couldn't keep the anger out of his voice. "The twelve policemen can be taken care of without discussion before the chamber."

"That would be true if it weren't a part of the Berger problem," the mayor argued. "There's more involved here, David, than mere discipline of twelve policemen and removing a disgraceful politician."

David could hold back his anger no longer. "That's so, Mayor. But the matter in the Police Department is Chief McDowell's responsibility, and as long as I am city manager, I will keep it so."

They sat for a moment in silence. David couldn't tell if the mayor's stern expression was from anger or injured feelings. When the mayor spoke, his voice was subdued. "Then you will not attend the meeting?"

"No. I don't believe it would be wise."

The mayor's shoulders slumped visibly. "I hope your absence is not misinterpreted," he said. "I will attempt to explain your views."

Only then did David understand the mayor's fears. "You mean you think there may be an effort to remove McDowell?" The possibility hadn't occurred to him.

"I sincerely hope not. But we must do something about Berger, and unfortunately the Police Department is involved. It is bound to come in for some heavy criticism."

"Well, let them solve the problem of Berger. But if they have any complaints on administration, they can come see me."

The mayor sighed. "Perhaps your way is best. But I can't help feeling that, in this, you are wrong."

After the mayor left, David sat alone in his office for a long time, considering what the mayor had said.

The Gray Ghost was right, he decided.

Like it or not, there was no way to avoid involvement. If there were any effort to remove McDowell, he would have to go to McDowell's defense.

And while he was butting heads with the council, he might as well get one thing straight: either he kept the city managership under his own terms, or the council could have *his* resignation. In fact, the way things were shaping up, maybe he'd better start planning in that direction.

## CHAPTER TWENTY

Two days after Cal's funeral, the Jaycees officially opened the water bond get-out-the-vote campaign with a "colorful downtown parade" and selection of a "water bond queen."

Tom Kencaide was not required to cover the noontime festivities. The afternoon paper had the events more than adequately staffed. Tom could have rewritten the P.M. stories. But he went downtown on his own initiative, for he had long been a student of West Texas parades. He never missed a chance to see one and marvel at the progress the pastime had made through the years.

During the early Depression Thirties of his boyhood there hadn't been much to parade. Now a parade was ready-made, awaiting the signal to spring into existence. The horse had a new role—a symbol of civic enterprise. Sheriff's posses and riding clubs had brought about the change.

In most every town, no matter how small, there was at least one posse or club. In the bigger towns, there were more, and maybe a mounted Shrine patrol. When word of a parade went out, these clubs got to work deciding how many members could represent their club and town, carrying their banners hundreds of miles in every direction.

Tom watched the parade from the corner of Fifth and Main, basking in the warm noon sun. The flag-bearers, winners of earlier queen contests, led, followed closely by the high school band playing "Stars and Stripes Forever." The mayor and Isaac Webster, Chamber of Commerce president, came by next in an open Cadillac convertible. For once, Tom noticed, the mayor's attention wasn't on his public. His Honor and the Chamber leader seemed engrossed in some deep, troubled conversation.

More than a hundred and fifty horses, three other high school bands, and the queen candidates riding in open convertibles made up the main body of the parade. The turnout of paraders wasn't bad, Tom thought, for such short notice. Twelve ancient autos from an antique club were decorated with posters promoting the water bond issue, some cleverly worded, urging "backward thinkers" to get into gear. To all this the Jaycees had added a burst of inspiration peculiar to their organization: three camels trucked in from a circus at Houston. These were bedecked with signs warning that the area was destined to become a desert if the water bond program failed on Election Day. The camels were led by Jaycees dressed in flowing white robes reminiscent of Rudolph Valentino and the Sahara. A Jaycee sound truck brought up the rear, urging sidewalk viewers to "vote as you please, but please vote."

The parade was better than average, Tom thought. The horses were still sleek with winter fat, and the bands good after almost two semesters of instruction. But most of the queen candidates were at least two years too young, and the floats were fewer and more conservative, apparently because of the hesitancy of business firms to wholeheartedly back a political issue, even under the guise of "getting out the vote."

After the parade was over, Tom stood on the corner a while and watched the passers-by, analyzing the smiles of faint embarrassment which to him confirmed a general self-consciousness of the secret, unspoken hope that some Easterner had been present, and would notice the casualness of the natives at the sight of real horse manure on the streets.

Tom considered going to a movie before work, but he realized that there wasn't time, now. So he strolled on into the newspaper office to pick up his mail. On top of the stack in his pigeonhole by the bulletin board was a note to contact the mayor.

Remembering the mayor's apparent intent preoccupation in the parade convertible, Tom wondered if His Honor had a news announcement of importance, or if he wanted a firsthand report on his statement after the Garzek slayings. Tom went to a phone immediately and returned the call.

"Got a few minutes?" the mayor asked. "I'd like for you to drop over. It's rather urgent."

The mayor's office was only a little more than a block away. "I'll be right over," Tom said.

He walked up Main to the old Burnet Building and climbed the creaking stairs, braced for a stern quiz on the Berger-Garzek affair. So he was thrown off guard momentarily when he was met with a friendly handshake and ushered into an inner sanctum of law books, roll-top desk and ancient wooden swivel chairs.

"Better brace yourself for a big surprise," the mayor said with just the trace of a smile. "I have a pleasant duty to perform with you."

"Me?"

The mayor leaned back in his chair and ran the fingers of one hand through his long, gray hair. "As you probably know, I am executor of Cal's estate. Officially, I'm retired, but I still do these things for long-standing clients. There's a letter among Cal's personal effects concerning you."

He picked up an envelope from the papers on the roll-top desk and handed it to Tom. It was addressed to "*Thomas Kencaide*" but not sealed. Inside was a single sheet, paper-clipped to a First National Bank deposit slip for ten thousand dollars in Tom's name.

Stunned, Tom read hurriedly through the brief letter, dated two days before Cal's death.

*"As you will notice by the enclosed, I have deposited ten thousand dollars in your name at the First National Bank. I could have gone through a bunch of red tape and stipulated how the money is to be spent, but I deem it unnecessary. We both know what the money is for. I trust you will spend it wisely. Lastly, I wish you every success in your endeavor. I believe that in helping you to realize your ambitions, I can best serve the things I believe in. So you see, this is a selfish gift after all."*

Below the text was the scrawled signature, *Cal Masters,* in black ink.

The mayor gave Tom time to reread the letter and absorb its meaning. "I saw no reason to delay this, since it is not a part of the will," the mayor said finally. "The money was taken from Cal's account two days before his death, under his signature, and I'm fairly certain it won't be contested. This is, if there's a logical explanation. . . ."

He left the question hanging. Tom's first inclination was to ignore it, leaving the mayor to guess what the money was for. Then he saw what the mayor was implying. Explanation now, before the will reading, should kill any budding ideas the heirs might have on filing suit to recover the money, or any possible claims Cal had been unduly influenced in his weakened, ill state just before his death.

"I had talked to Cal about backing me in a small, independent community newspaper," Tom explained. "That's what the money is for. I had no idea how ill he was."

"I'm sure there will be no difficulty with the money, then," the mayor said. "Everyone knew Cal's interest in civic affairs and his outspoken dissatisfaction with the present newspaper. I assume, from Cal's generous gesture, that you two shared essentially the same political philosophy."

"I suppose so," Tom said, still not completely recovered from the surprise. "We'd never talked much, though—he wouldn't have much to do with anyone from Milam's paper. I didn't get to know him very well until recently."

"Too bad. He was a wonderful man, and the community will miss him." The mayor frowned. "I think now, the way things are going, we should have listened to him more."

The mayor was silent for a moment. Tom thought the mayor was going to continue on that theme, perhaps taking his regrets on into talk of the Berger case. But he seemed to break off his meditation abruptly.

"Well, if you saw eye to eye with Cal, then I imagine you and I will be at odds occasionally," the mayor said, smiling slightly to indicate he really didn't believe what he was saying. "Before the fur starts flying," he added, turning more serious, "let me offer my congratulations to the new publisher. I have every confidence you will have a publication that will be a genuine benefit to the community."

"Thank you," Tom said. They shook hands.

"What are you going to call your newspaper?" the mayor asked.

Tom searched in his mind momentarily before he realized that there wasn't a name yet. "I haven't decided," he admitted. "And I'll have to recover from this before I'll be able to think of one."

"Well, I can see you're starting from scratch."

Tom still couldn't believe that there were no strings attached to the money, that it was really available and in his name. "Aren't there some papers for me to sign?"

"Just the checks as you need the money. I'm sure there'll be no difficulty. In fact, I imagine the family will be happy to know Cal kept his interest in such things right up to the last. You might, after a decent length of time, call them. I'm sure they'll appreciate it. But the money is such a small part of Cal's holdings, the withdrawal will hardly be missed."

Tom thanked the mayor again and was back out on the street

before he began to comprehend the vast change the last few minutes had made in his life. From contemplation of a time-killing movie out of sheer boredom an hour ago, he now had so much before him he didn't know what to do first.

The enormity of the project facing him was frightening. A name would only be a start. He'd have to find a printer, select type, decide whether to do his own photography and set up a darkroom or hire it done, make arrangements with an engraver, outline and put into action a promotion compaign, figure out a distribution system, and work out an arrangement with Arlene to handle the advertising. He didn't even know what to try to charge for advertising. That would have to be figured.

Tom walked the streets for a while in a daze, uncertain what to do first. After a time, it dawned on him that he wasn't a free agent yet. He'd still have to give Milam a two-week notice. And Arlene would have to give notice at Sam McIntosh's department store.

Telling Arlene, he decided, would be his first move. But when he told her he wanted to seem much calmer than he felt now. He went into a lounge and ordered a beer, hoping it would have a sedative effect on his system. It didn't, so he ordered another.

He unfolded Cal's letter. As he began to read it again, his vague feelings of uneasiness crystallized. He began to understand what it was that worried him. It wasn't the mechanical aspects of starting the newspaper. However formidable, he knew he could lick them. Cal's letter reminded him of the depth of the legacy. It was the moral responsibility that weighed heavily upon his mind. He was setting out to assume leadership of a certain element of thought in the city. This would have to be done in exactly the right way.

He thought about the problem. Factual, probing stories presenting all sides of each civic discussion would show his honesty. But to demonstrate leadership and purpose, the newspaper needed sharp, concise editorials taking a positive stand *for* something. He needed some good, thought-provoking ideas right from the start to put across the role the newspaper expected to take in civic affairs.

The lake project wasn't the answer. To come out for—or against—the lake now wouldn't make an impact one way or another. He needed a completely new platform, a series of front-page editorials that would set every thinking person in town to talking about the new newspaper. No promotion scheme ever devised could put across the paper's purpose and sincerity and get the circulation off to a good start better than that.

Finally, he felt calm enough to phone Arlene. "I've got some good news that won't keep until tonight," he explained. "Cal Masters left us the money for the newspaper. Ten thousand, no conditions or anything."

The phone was silent so long he thought they had been disconnected. When Arlene did speak, her voice betrayed little surprise. "Oh, that's wonderful, Tom. I had a feeling he was going to do that."

"What made you think so?"

"He came to see me two days before he died."

Tom couldn't keep the surprise out of his own voice. "Why didn't you tell me?"

"He made me promise not to."

"Sounds like you're way ahead of me. Maybe you'd better fill me in."

"I will," she said. "Tonight. Oh, Tom, I'm so happy for you—for us. I just wish it had happened some other way. I can't keep from being a little sad, too."

"I know."

"I won't be worth a tinker's damn the rest of the day, I'm so excited."

"Try not to think about it," he told her. "We have plenty of time."

That afternoon, he found out what his advice was worth. He went through the motions of making his City Hall run, unable to concentrate, knowing he must be acting like a sleepwalker. He didn't see Hartwell.

When he got back to the city room, he went over to Houston Collier's desk. "Could I talk to you for a minute?"

They went into the conference room. Tom sat on the edge of the big table, and Collier tilted a chair backward, bracing his right foot on the edge of the table, staring at Tom quizzically.

"I don't know how to say this," Tom began. "I hate like hell to do it, but I'm resigning. I've got a little capital, and I'm starting a weekly paper."

Collier just sat and grinned at him. "Cal Masters," he said.

"He came to see you, too?"

Collier nodded.

"Looks like I'm the last person in town to know about this," Tom said.

"No, he was very discreet. I knew him back in my reporting days, you know, when he was mayor. He just wanted to find out what I thought of you as a newspaperman, and what I thought of your character." Collier's grin broadened. "I didn't ask any questions, but I had my suspicions." He offered his hand. "Congratulations."

"I may be back here with my tail between my legs," Tom said. "But at least I'm going to try. If two weeks' notice isn't enough, I'll stay until you can find someone."

"You might make it," Collier said. "There's always a market for anything good, and I imagine you'll have BeeBee climbing the walls with the first issue. Of course, I can't give you any help, but there's no rule against our being friends, seeing each other every once in a while, and if discussions should come up . . ."

Somehow, Tom had known it would be like that with Collier. "I thank you for that," he said. "It's nice to know. How do you think BeeBee will react to some competition?"

Collier thought it over before answering. "He'll try to ignore you for a while. Then, if you really put it over, he might try to buy you out. Failing in that, he might start trying to compete with you on local coverage."

"Won't that be the end of me? I mean, with all his resources, BeeBee could bury me."

"No, I don't think so. By the time he gets around to the effort, you'll be on the ground floor, with people coming to you with their troubles. When the policy of this paper changes, if it ever does, people will know why. Also, remember that BeeBee has never conducted an aggressive operation. He'll be learning, too. Really, I'm glad to see this, Tom. If we can get to play newspaper with a couple of competing sheets, it may be the best thing that's happened to this town in a long, long time."

That night, Tom soon learned that Cal's legacy had brought about a new estrangement in his relationship with Arlene. Their new life was being thrust upon them without time for adjustment.

After dinner, they went to her apartment and put on some records. They talked, still filled with wonder over the sudden development. Even yet Tom found it difficult to believe that Cal had talked with her.

"What did he say?" he asked. "Tell me everything you remember."

She thought for a moment, nervously biting her lower lip. Then she closed her eyes, a trick she had for remembering.

"He called at the store and said, 'Miss White, this is Cal Masters, Tom's old reprobate friend on the City Council,' and I was so surprised, I don't remember exactly what I said, but I asked him how he was, or something. Because he said, 'Tolerable well,' I remember that. Then he said, 'Miss White, Tom has come to me with a business proposition, and since it involves you, too, I wonder if we might have lunch together and discuss it.' I hadn't gotten over my surprise, and with the luncheon invitation on top of everything, I'm afraid I was embarrassingly long in accepting, but he went on joking with a line about this being our little secret, that he didn't want you to know he was courting me behind your back. I know now he was just giving me time to recover."

"Sounds like a good line to me," Tom said. "I'll have to remember it."

She frowned at the interruption, then went on. "I finally accepted, and he said he'd be waiting at the elevator, if that was satisfactory. I had seen his picture in the paper, and on television, of course, and I knew he was as old as the hills, but I wasn't prepared. He looked ancient."

"He aged twenty years in the last six months," Tom told her. "I should have realized how sick he was from that."

"He was the nicest old man," she said. "He said something about how he should have known you'd have the prettiest girl in town, or some blarney like that, and he had the most gentle, courtly ways. When we got outside the store he asked me if I minded walking to the Petroleum Club. Can you imagine an eighty-year-old man asking me if I minded walking two blocks?"

"That kind of consideration was what women gave up when they got the vote and started competing with men for their jobs," Tom said, teasing.

She gave him a mock glare. "Do you want me to tell this, or discuss your views on suffrage?"

"I'll be quiet," Tom said quickly.

"After we ordered, he started asking me what I thought about prospects for the newspaper, from the standpoint of advertising. I told him I thought there would be no trouble, that it would be just a matter of getting out and selling it. Then he asked me about several specific firms, and we went on talking in that vein for a while. . . ."

"Which firms?" Tom asked. "You're not telling all."

"Oh, fifteen or twenty," she said impatiently. "I can't remember them all now. He seemed concerned over the bigger stores, especially groceries, and I explained a little of how chain stores handle their advertising. I told him who the advertising managers are, and which ones have some say-so in their advertising budgets and why I thought they'd welcome another outlet—things you and I have been over and over. He just sat there listening, nodding every once in a while to show he understood or agreed. Then, after we'd finished eating, or rather after I'd finished—he just picked at his food—he suddenly asked me, 'What are the things you admire about Tom?'"

Tom laughed. "I guess that stopped you."

"Of course not. I told him I admired you for your ambition, how you worked your way through school, your sense of professional ethics, your old-fashioned, unabashed patriotism, your loyalty—even to that damned newspaper—and . . ."

"Come on, now," Tom said, embarrassed. "What did Cal say to all that?"

"He seemed to agree. He said, 'I have a feeling he will succeed in this. Tom is a determined young man, and with your help, I don't see how he could fail.' Then, on the way back to the office, he asked me to keep our talk a secret a few days while he made some arrangements."

She was silent for a moment.

"That all?" he asked impatiently.

She closed her eyes again, trying to remember. "All except one thing," she said finally. "Just before we got to the office he said, 'This will be a fine thing for the city. But you know, it's the personal element of it that appeals to me the most. I think I would like very much to be associated with you and Tom.'"

"He knew then that he didn't have long to live," Tom said. "He must have known the day I was out at his ranch, too."

"When we got back to the store, he said he had enjoyed having lunch with me, and hoped to see me again. I . . . I said something about maybe we three could get together . . ."

She trailed off in midsentence.

Tom thought of something. "What time was that?"

"A little after one-thirty. I had left early and was late getting back, I remember. We were gone more than an hour."

"And the banks close at two," Tom said. "He must have gone straight to the bank and deposited the money after he left you."

"I wanted to tell you about it, but I'd promised him I wouldn't. When he died—I heard about his death on the radio that morning before I left for work—I decided not to tell you—at least for a while—because I knew how disappointed you'd be."

"There's a good chance I may be disappointed yet," he told her. "Ten thousand dollars isn't much money in this day and time."

"You've always said it could be done for that."

"If it can be done at all," he corrected her.

He sat studying her mood, trying to fathom what was in her mind as to a working relationship. He decided to take the warm plunge.

"What I mean, I've always thought of this project as sort of an impoverished partnership. The paper probably can't pay you anywhere near what you're making—at least for a while."

He knew instantly that he'd said the wrong thing. She glared at him in genuine anger.

"I don't recall ever saying anything that would give you the impression I was interested in this for the money."

Tactless or not, he had no alternative but the truth. "I don't know what you expect of me," he confessed. "I don't know if you want to go ahead and get married first, or what."

"You're sure not putting it very romantically."

He sighed. "I've proposed to you innumerable times, under every romantic circumstance my limited budget and imagination could devise. Then you say you'll marry me, but you won't discuss a date. I sure don't think I ought to assume now this changes things—that you will marry me out of simple economic expediency. I don't know what to do."

Her anger faded. Suddenly she began to laugh. "You should see the expression on your face."

"The picture of a man at the end of his rope, I presume."

She took his hand. "I suppose you're right, I've gotten about as many proposals out of you as a girl can expect out of one man. Therefore, I'll propose to you this time. Thomas Kencaide, will you marry me?"

"Yes," he said emphatically. "Tonight."

"The time is the bride's prerogative," she reminded him. "Even for brides that do the proposing. But since you bring it up, how about a week from Sunday afternoon, the day after you get your divorce from BeeBee Milam, in a simple but elegant ceremony, with no one but immediate family and a few friends sworn to secrecy? Agreed?"

"Agreed," he said.

Afterward, they planned it all out. They would go to Santa Fe and Taos on their honeymoon, using the few hundred dollars Tom had in the Credit Union, for—as Tom told her—it wouldn't seem right to use Cal's money.

Then they would return and start laying the groundwork for the newspaper, aiming at a September 1 debut. They talked most of the night, planning.

"I still don't understand it," Tom said finally. "Here I am giving up the security of a weekly paycheck, no prospects but a long shot like this, and it's now that you decide to marry me."

Arlene gave him an enigmatic glance. "Kencaide, you sure don't know much about women," she said.

He reached across the couch, took her wrist, and pulled her toward him. "Well, let's never let it be said that I'm not willing to learn."

## CHAPTER TWENTY-ONE

When Travis received his summons to the secret meeting, his first reaction was to ignore it. He could see no reason why he couldn't be told the topic for discussion. He assumed, from the mayor's plea for secrecy, that the meeting was to reveal some grandiose, pie-in-the-sky program for the year 2000 dreamed up by a Chamber of Commerce subcommittee. If he had known the subject, and that he himself was to become the center of controversy, he wouldn't have gone.

Curiosity and a reluctant sense of duty led him to accept. He told the mayor to go ahead and put his name down, and later forgot about it. He would have missed the luncheon entirely if his receptionist hadn't reminded him at midmorning. As it was, he arrived late, after the others were well into the meal. If there was any talk of the matter beforehand, he missed it. The whole Berger affair caught him unprepared.

He realized from the moment he arrived that the meeting was not what he had supposed. Instead of the usual Chamber of Commerce rank-and-file drumbeaters, the entire hierarchy of twelve Chamber directors was present—the four- and five-star generals. The council—excepting Berger—and the city secretary brought the total in the hotel's long private dining room to eighteen, a much cozier atmosphere than Travis had expected. He was greeted with an almost frightening grimness. Sam McIntosh nodded curtly. There was nothing in his stern stare that hinted he'd once been Travis' genial host. During the remaining few minutes of the meal, there was little talk—all contrived and superficial.

The mayor arose and conferred with the caterer while the dishes were cleared. When the mayor closed and locked the doors behind the departing waitresses, Travis knew something far out of the ordinary was occurring. The mayor stood at the end of the long table facing the silent, attentive group. He frowned, more haggard and worn than ever before, Travis thought. He studied his audience for a moment, then cleared his throat nervously.

"I have called you together because something has arisen that could well jeopardize our city's future. This is a serious thing, involving personalities, and I must ask all of you on your sacred honor to keep confidential everything discussed here today until such time as it is decided to make this meeting public, if that should ever happen."

There was a brief murmur of assent, followed by the silence of anticipation.

"I have asked the city secretary to be here. I thought it might be a good idea to have notes on what is said here today, in case it ever is needed in the future. Does everyone concur with this?"

There was another general murmur of agreement, and Travis realized he was perhaps the only person in the room who did not know the topic to be discussed.

The mayor waited patiently until the city secretary unfolded his pad and prepared to make shorthand notes.

"First," the mayor said, pausing to glance sideways at the city secretary and make sure he was following, "I want to read to you a letter I received. I'm sure you all remember that unfortunate affair on the East Side last week when a man shot his wife and three children to death and then lost his own life in a gun battle with our Police Department. This letter came to me the second morning after that happened. The police chief received a similar letter and, although I haven't discussed it with him, I have heard from a reliable source that the district attorney got one, too. I will now read you my copy."

As the mayor unfolded the letter, Travis thought back, trying to recall all he could about the shooting. If it hadn't been for Kencaide's picture on the front page in connection with the story, Travis probably wouldn't have read the details, for he never relished that kind of news. A tavern owner, Travis remembered, despondent over business failure. He had never heard of the man.

The mayor adjusted his reading glasses and began:

"'Dear Mr. Hiram Milner, Honorable Mayor. You do not know me. But I want to tell you what kind of a man you have on your council. That Mr. Max Berger. Before I lose tavern because of big mortgage, I buy beer from him. He send men in to tell me if I not buy more beer, I have trouble. When I tell him this free country, I no need more Alamo Beer, he send policemen to arrest boys in my bar. Mr. Mayor, for two years I not have one arrest. Then in four months arrests every night. Soon no customers, I go broke. I go to sheriff's office, he say it inside city. I go to see Mr. Kencaide on the newspaper, and he can do nothing. I afraid to go to liquor control board again. Maybe they take away my license because of arrests, say I have trouble spot. I run clean place, Mr. Mayor. No drunks, no minor children. For two years I have no arrests. I go broke because of big mortgage. I know nothing more I can do. But I want you to know what kind of man you have on your council, Mr. Mayor. Joe Garzek.'"

Travis couldn't believe that the mayor had summoned them together to hear such a tirade of hysteria. The letter undoubtedly was the work of a disorganized, disoriented mind. Travis recalled, then, that the news stories had said the man was a former mental patient. Travis raised his hand to get the floor, but Chamber director Sam McIntosh spoke Travis' thoughts without the preliminaries.

"That guy sounds like a nut to me, Mayor. Good Lord, I've had worse poison pen letters than that myself. I can't see anything to get worked up over. Hell, he's not the first guy to go broke because of a big mortgage."

Sam got an appreciative laugh from the directors, but the mayor didn't smile. "I'm afraid it's more serious than that, Sam," he said. "Police Chief McDowell has conducted an extensive investigation, and all preliminary reports seem to bear out Mr. Garzek's accusations. We have the man in jail who apparently was threatening Mr. Garzek. He has been positively identified by another tavern owner. Gentlemen, there is no doubt Councilman Berger has been using twelve members of the police department for his own gain."

"Still seems like a police matter to me," Sam said. "It's their job to catch crooks, even when some of the crooks are cops."

"But not when the crook is a city councilman," Walt Weatherbee said from across the table. "We can't afford a scandal, Sam. We just can't afford it."

"Gentlemen," the mayor pleaded. "Please hear me out, then

we can hold a discussion. There are, I'm afraid, more serious things to consider. Mr. Secretary, will you please help me with this map?"

The city secretary cleared an area of the table and turned a chair upside down, the seat on the table. Then he helped the mayor thumbtack a city map to the chair legs. There was a brief commotion as the mayor's audience moved into positions so all could see.

"This shows the route of the latest intercity highway project. The shaded areas here, adjacent to the future bypass right-of-way, are choice sites for motels, restaurants, that sort of thing. Gentlemen, all those lots were purchased in two days by a Mr. Donald Ratliff. The dates of the purchases are immediately after the proposed route was made available to the City Council, and prior to its release to the public. I regret to say this did not come to light until our city attorney began checking the plats for acquisition a short time ago."

The city secretary grunted, a long-standing signal that he was getting behind in his shorthand. The mayor paused and waited for him to catch up.

"This same Mr. Ratliff who purchased the property," the mayor continued, "is the man I referred to earlier as being identified as a strong-arm man for Councilman Berger's beer distributing firm. Through diligent work by Chief McDowell and his men, this Ratliff was caught burglarizing Garzek's tavern shortly after the shootings. We believe he was seeking a tape recording Garzek attempted to make of a conversation between them. In a search of Ratliff's room, Chief McDowell found a promissory note between Councilman Berger and Ratliff in the exact amount of the land purchases. We are certain Councilman Berger was using Ratliff as a front, and the promissory note was his protection so he could claim the land in the event something happened to Ratliff, and to preclude a double-cross."

There were a number of questions then on the man's identity, where he came from, and how he was caught, but Travis only half-listened, for he was just beginning to get the full import of the situation. Such misuse of political position would be far-reaching if brought to light. Every man on the council would be suspect. The city's financial rating might suffer, and public indignation would be long-lasting. Everything they had accomplished might be ruined at the polls when the bond issues came up for a vote.

Travis' uneasiness began to grow. This meeting didn't seem to be the proper way to handle this. If such accusations were to be made, it seemed Berger should have the opportunity to reply.

"I must confess," the mayor was saying, "that I had heard rumors in the past, and put little stock in them. Since this has come up, I've found our Police Department also has had numerous suspicions." The mayor searched through his notes, then began a long list of vague connections between Berger and various shyster businesses and underworld operations.

As the mayor ended his presentation, discussions erupted around the table. Travis understood by now that he was probably the most surprised of them all. There must have been much general talk going around town which he—being fairly well removed from the business world—hadn't heard. Travis raised his hand to get the floor. The mayor nodded toward him and tapped his water glass with a spoon for quiet.

"I arrived on this late, Mr. Mayor," Travis said. "And I've had no opportunity to talk to anyone before the meeting. Would you please fill me in on exactly what kind of body we constitute here. City Council? Chamber?"

The mayor frowned. "Neither, I suppose, Doctor. Let's just say we're meeting as a group of civic leaders, faced with a serious problem."

"Do we have the right?" Travis asked. "How can we sit here, and try, and condemn this man without his being here to give his side of it?"

A chorus of protests challenged him, but the mayor cut them off.

"Gentlemen, gentlemen, please. The doctor, of course, is right. We cannot try the man here. But Doctor, that is not what we are doing. We are faced with a delicate, explosive situation, and we need some top-level thinking as to how we are going to meet this thing. That is our purpose."

Travis did not carry the argument further. He felt he was too uninformed to debate.

"In fact," the mayor resumed, "that is what we need at the

moment. Some top-level thinking. I have given you every piece of information that I possess. Do I hear any suggestions?"

"Mr. Mayor," one of the Chamber directors said, "I make the motion we go on record as unanimously deploring the situation."

The vote was solemnly taken. Although Travis didn't vote for or against, the motion was presumed to have carried unanimously. Travis didn't protest. He asked for the floor again.

"Couldn't we instigate a recall election?"

The mayor frowned. "I think the proposal is worthy of consideration. Walt, do you happen to know what the city charter requires for a recall election?"

"It takes a petition signed by one percent of the total vote cast in the last election," Weatherbee said.

"How would we get out the vote?" asked Cecil Steward, City National Bank president, and a Chamber director ever since Travis could remember. "We would have to make some explanation," he added. "We'd have to make some issues known."

"Yes, I'm afraid that's true," the mayor said.

Sam McIntosh banged a fist on the table. "Why don't we just send a delegation to this guy and tell him we know what he's been up to, and if he doesn't resign and get out of town we'll ride him out on a rail?"

"That sounds more like it," someone said behind Travis.

"I think it could be worded a little more subtly, but I agree," Steward said.

McIntosh laughed. "Well, I didn't mean it quite that literally, Cecil. But that's the general idea. We can just let him know we're wise to him, and that if he doesn't resign he's in for some damned tough sledding. Might not hurt to hint he might face a jail term if he doesn't co-operate."

The mayor's frown deepened. "I've been advised, Sam, by all concerned in the investigation that our evidence is adequate for formal charges. But there is the questionable position of the district attorney in the matter. I understand he and Berger are rather good friends, or at least they seem to have some sort of an alliance."

"I guess we'll just have to extend our ultimatum to include the district attorney," Sam said.

"Well, anyway, we can't prosecute," the mayor said. "We can't let this become a public affair. But I do think your suggestion has some merit, Sam."

"What if Berger wouldn't resign?" Travis asked. "What if he called our bluff?"

McIntosh brought his fist down on the table again, making the coffee cups rattle in their saucers. "Then by God we'll let him know we're just as tough as he is, and that won't be any bluff. If we have to, we can beat him at his own game. A word from us in the right place would lift his beer franchise, and he knows it."

The outburst hit a responsive chord in several directors. They started a general discussion on meeting threats with threats, violence with violence.

"In other words," Travis said, "if Berger really is a hoodlum, we just show him we're no better than he is?"

They shouted him down. McIntosh was angry now. He turned in his chair to face Travis. "I bet you'd feel different about it, Doctor, if he was sending some thug into your office to tell you how many patients you could treat each day, how many operations you could perform each week. No, Doctor, if our Police Department can't protect our people from that kind of thing one way, then by God we'll do it another."

"The end justifies the means, then?" Travis asked.

Sam started to reply, but the mayor interrupted by banging loudly on his water glass with a spoon.

"Gentlemen, we're not getting anywhere by bickering. Travis, do you have an alternate plan?"

"If all this is true, the voter made the mistake," Travis said. "I think we should return the problem to him and let him suffer the consequences."

The mayor paused, then spoke directly to Travis. "I believe I speak for everyone here, Doctor, when I say, no doubt, that would be the ideal solution. However, we've already discussed and agreed that we must keep this disgusting affair out of the press and out of the hands of the public for the good of the community. Therefore, your suggestion, although ideal, is unfortunately impractical. Do I hear any other proposals?"

There was none. When it came to a vote, only Travis and Byron went against Sam's plan.

Discussion turned then to the best method of presenting the ultimatum. Approaching Berger at his office or home was unsatisfactory, they agreed. Sam suggested an executive council session, and several of the Chamber directors voiced quick agreement. Travis realized that this would hand the dirty work back to the City Council, but he didn't feel like arguing the point.

The mayor didn't seem to like the idea, either. "Well, that's a thought," he said noncommittally. "But I'd hoped we could bring some Chamber influence to bear."

"You can tell him the whole Chamber board concurred in asking his resignation," Sam said. "That'll give him something to think about."

The mayor searched the table for help, and found none. "Well, I guess an executive session would have advantages. We could be certain of privacy, and it'd be off the record. If no one else has a better suggestion . . ."

No one did. There was a preliminary stir as adjournment was anticipated, but Sam quickly regained everyone's attention.

"Mayor, as I see it, getting Berger off the council is only half the solution."

"How's that, Sam?"

"We still have a Police Department rotten to the core. If they were shaking down this Garzek guy, odds are good they're shaking down others."

The mayor went into his stern pose. Sometimes, when he was forced to do so, the mayor could assume amazing dignity. Watching him now, Travis couldn't help but admire his performance.

"I assure you that everything possible is being done to clean up the unfortunate mess in the Police Department," the mayor said. "It will be done quietly, with no publicity. The men involved will simply be transferred to other duties."

"That's not good enough, Hiram," Sam said. "We've got to get rid of them."

The mayor explained. "Those men are protected by civil service laws, Sam. The only way they could be removed from the force would be to bring charges against them. And I'm sure we don't want that. Every man who had a hand in this is known, and they'll all be watched closely in the future."

"Not good enough," Sam repeated. "When you clean house, you start at the top. I suggest we consider bringing in a new police chief. I just can't believe all this has gone on in the past without McDowell being aware of it."

"Now wait just a minute, Sam," Travis said. "That's a pretty serious accusation."

"This whole thing's pretty serious," Sam said. "If McDowell's not in on it, then he's been stupid as hell in letting them hoodwink him, and that's just as bad, in my opinion. Maybe we need a good, strict disciplinarian down there."

"We don't have the authority to fire McDowell," Travis said.

"What do you mean you don't have the authority?" Sam demanded. "He's a city employee, isn't he?"

The mayor intervened. "I'm afraid the doctor's right, Sam. The police chief is hired by the city manager. Of course, the council can make recommendations. . . ."

"You control Hartwell, and Hartwell controls McDowell," Sam said. "It looks simple to me."

"Hartwell would never fire McDowell," Travis said. "You'd have to remove Hartwell to get to McDowell."

"Well, I'm not too sold on Hartwell, either," Sam said. "He can go too, as far as I'm concerned."

"That would be a big mistake," Travis told him.

"Yes, I'm afraid I agree with Travis, Sam," the mayor said firmly. "Hartwell is a fine administrator."

Travis was surprised that the other councilmen didn't speak up in Hartwell's defense. Wentworth and Weatherbee sat expressionless, looking at the mayor. Byron's gaze was upon the tablecloth. Travis didn't know if they shared his opinion or not. He assumed they were reluctant to voice their views in front of Sam and the other directors.

"Well, you people have been working with him, and I haven't," Sam said. "You know him better than I do. But I still think we ought to give McDowell his walking papers, however you have to go about it."

"I have every confidence in Chief McDowell," Travis said.

Sam turned to face him again. "You have confidence in Hartwell and you have confidence in McDowell. But somebody was sure as hell asleep at the switch in this mess. Who was it?"

"All of us, I guess," Travis said.

"All of who?"

"Everybody—the public, the Police Department, the council, even the Chamber, maybe."

"I wasn't going to mention the council, but since you have, I agree," Sam said. "It seems some councilmen were asleep up there, too, sitting around and doing nothing while some peckerwood almost takes over the town. Maybe we need some new councilmen the next time around."

"Why don't you run, Sam?" Travis asked. "I think a term on the council would give you a new outlook on things."

"Gentlemen," the mayor said again, raising his hands in a helpless gesture that brought a laugh from the directors.

The mayor waited for quiet again. He seemed to be struggling with what he had to do. Finally, he seemed to come to a decision.

"Sam has suggested that the council recommend the dismissal of Police Chief McDowell. All those in favor raise their right hand."

Travis looked around with a sinking sensation. Everyone in the room had a hand up except himself and Byron. And when the mayor asked for opposing votes, Byron didn't even bother to raise his hand.

When the meeting was adjourned, Travis left without speaking to anyone and headed straight for the parking lot and his car, for he didn't trust himself at the moment.

Sunday was dry, dusty, and oppressive. The wind whipped around the house in gusts, made the doors creak, and sometimes set up a low moan under the eaves. The sky was yellow-brown with dirt, the sun only a halo in the haze.

Travis arose early, upset and jittery. He had lain awake most of the night, worrying about the council situation.

After breakfast, while Marilyn helped the children dress for Sunday school, he took a cup of coffee into the living room and picked up the morning paper.

There was a layout on page one of the Jaycee Water Vote

Campaign Kickoff Parade, with pictures of the camels marching down Main Street and the Water Election Queen riding in a convertible. But Travis didn't have to look through the paper to know there was no hint of a secret session of self-selected civic leaders, plans for an ultimatum to a wayward councilman, or a pending demand for the resignation of the city police chief.

The moral aspects of what they were about to do disturbed Travis. He wanted no part of it. Yet, as a council member, he was obligated to go along with the majority. He was worried, too, over the Chamber directors' attitude toward Hartwell. Travis did not consider him so expendable.

During his council term, Travis had learned the basic insecurities of politics. He had discovered that the foundations of city government lay on a restless sea of shifting sand. In the council's constant search for equilibrium, he had seen expediency overrule logic, pressures surmount good sense, and pledges dwindle to compromise. He had always considered these shortcomings in the same category with side-effects of life-giving drugs. He had assumed the democratic process would improve, just as medicine gradually solved its problems. But now, in his present mood, he wondered if there was any hope. The residual effect of human nature was a costly burden.

In Cal's death the council had lost one of its most stabilizing influences. Now, before Travis had time to recover from the loss—and his disturbing personal experience—the councilmen were being pressured toward firing Hartwell.

With the children off to Sunday school, Marilyn came into the living room. Usually on Sunday mornings Travis slept until the children left, then Marilyn came back to bed. Now, with their routine broken, Travis felt strangely awkward. Marilyn picked up the society section and took it to the platform rocker, facing him. "Want more coffee?" she asked.

"No," he said. He put the paper down restlessly, feeling again the gnawing guilt of these Sunday mornings, the memory of that experience with Cal still heavy on his mind.

"Would you like to go to church this morning?" he asked on impulse.

Marilyn's mouth opened in surprise. "Why, I'd never get ready in time, now," she said, flustered. "If you'd said something about it, earlier . . . Why don't you go, if you want. . . ."

"No, I just thought you might like to," he said. He tried to make his next question more conversational in tone. "Would you like to go occasionally?"

"Yes, I would like to very much."

"I wish I had known you felt that way. Why didn't you tell me?"

She seemed to be studying him, taking the measure of his meaning, his mood. "I thought, somehow, that you didn't want to talk about it."

Sometimes her understanding of his inner workings was frightening. "What made you think that?" he asked, trying to learn a little of how she came to know these things.

"Just the way you talked of your father . . . your reaction that time Dr. Anderson called and invited us to his church . . . the children going to Sunday school . . . our living pattern."

He sighed. He would never know how she constantly understood his every action. "You could have gone," he said. "My feelings shouldn't have kept you away."

"I didn't want to make you more uncomfortable," she said.

"I suppose we should think of the children, too," he said meditatively. "They're getting old enough to sit in church. They might not understand, yet, but the environment would be good for them."

She agreed. But, being Marilyn, she didn't push it. A few minutes later she was humming to herself as she put the breakfast dishes into the dishwasher. Judging from outward appearances, she soon forgot all about the conversation. But Travis remembered. It was in the back of his mind all day.

In the evening, after dinner, he went into the study and finished reading a research report on pancreatic enzymes, but his talk with Marilyn kept nagging him. He had no right to deprive her and the children of something that would enrich their lives, he told himself.

But he was much too introspective to believe that was the real reason the subject bothered him. Those few minutes at Cal's bedside had shaken him deeply. The truth was, he decided, that after all these years maybe he was ready to explore this vacuum in his life.

Why not now? he asked himself. What was he waiting for? He knew what he should do: obey the impulse he'd had all week. Many times, in the past, he'd called the Reverend William Anderson for others. Why not now for himself?

He found the number in the telephone book and wrote it on a corner of the enzyme article. He sat looking at it for a long time. Then he picked up the receiver and dialed. The minister answered before the third ring. "This is Travis McNiel. Could I talk to you for a few minutes tonight?"

"Sure, Doctor. About someone at the hospital?"

"No, nothing like that. It's, well, personal."

The minister hesitated. "Tell you what. I left some notes I need over in the church study. I forgot to pick them up after the evening services. Could you meet me there in about fifteen minutes?"

"Fine," Travis said.

It was as simple as that. Now, he was committed.

When Travis arrived the church was dark except for a light at the rear entry. He went in and was searching down the carpeted hall for the study when he heard the minister's voice through an open door.

"That you, Doctor? Come on in."

Anderson arose from his desk and greeted Travis warmly, his curiosity not completely concealed. He was wearing a dark suit and tie, reminiscent of the somber, heavy "pulpit suit" Travis' father had worn for preaching. This, the books and the wood-paneled closeness of the office gave their meeting a formality Travis hadn't anticipated. He began to get cold feet.

"I shouldn't have bothered you this time of evening, especially on your busy day," he said.

"No trouble at all," Anderson said, motioning Travis to a chair. "I had to come down and get these notes, anyway." He waited until Travis was seated. "What can I do for you, Doctor?"

Travis hedged. "I've always intended to become a member of your congregation. I would like to do so, if possible, now."

"Wonderful. That is very gratifying. Just you, or . . . ?"

"No, my whole family," Travis said quickly. "I'd like to do

whatever is necessary. I've been out of the church for a long time."

"The requirements aren't very rigid, you know," Anderson said, smiling. "All the members of your family are baptized, aren't they?"

"Yes."

"Well, there should be no hindrance. Have you and your wife been affiliated with any other church?"

"No . . . that is, not since our marriage."

"We can classify it a profession of faith, then," he said, his voice still edged with mild humor. "That will look good on the records for me. I'm not as evangelistic as I should be." He hesitated, studying Travis. "I knew your father, you know. He was rather famous in these parts. When you came here to practice, I was disappointed when you didn't join our church."

"I've been rather busy," Travis said.

"Yes, I know. When your children started attending our Sunday school, I told myself that. Still, on the time or two I called to invite you to church, I felt there was another reason."

He was looking at Travis seriously now.

"I fear I'm not the Christian my father was," Travis admitted.

"Few of us are," Anderson said. He studied Travis for a time in silence. "You believe in God, don't you?"

"Oh, yes," Travis said quickly.

"And from what I hear, you're living a fine Christian life. I can't imagine your harboring any great, agonizing guilt."

Travis had to grin. "No, my sins are rather insignificant, too."

"Then what is troubling you, Travis?"

Once Travis started, the words came easily. "It's like I said. I'm just not cast in my father's mold. I don't suppose I became aware of it until I was grown, but I'm simply incapable of . . . well . . . the things he was. I see people die, and I read the Bible, I study and hunt answers, and still I can't comprehend, as he did. I can't even pray. What I mean by that, I have no feeling of communication, except in one recent, isolated instance. The more I think about it, the harder I try, the more inadequate I become."

Anderson nodded. "I think I understand," he said. He got up from his desk and walked to the bookcase at the end of the room, standing for a moment. When he turned to face Travis again he seemed to be possessed by some secret knowledge. "In fact, perhaps God in His wisdom has sent you to the only person in the world who *can* understand."

He leaned against a table by the bookcase and smiled at Travis.

"I was just a young preacher when I first met your father. I had a little church out in the Shiloh community, and he came for a revival. I had thirty-two families in the church when he came, and fifty-eight when he left—almost two hundred souls. But instead of being overjoyed at having my congregation almost doubled, I was panic-stricken."

His smile widened, but he shook his head sadly, remembering.

"I was twenty-two, and that was my first church. I guess you can imagine how my sermons sounded, after those of your father. I've never experienced such a feeling of inadequacy before or since. Some your father won to the church began to backslide, and I felt responsible. Finally, I decided to give up. I went to see one of the elders, to tell him to ask for a replacement. And I'll never forget what he said when I told him all my doubts. That old farmer looked at me and said, 'Brother Anderson, we all serve the Lord in our own way. When my youngest daughter was near death last summer, you, not Brother McNiel, was the one who came to our house, comforted us and prayed for her recovery. It was you, not Brother McNiel, who saddled a horse and swam a swollen river to be with Sister Miller when she passed on last spring during the flood. There isn't a home in the community that doesn't remember some kindness, some service you have done. You are serving the Lord in your own way, Brother Anderson, just as Brother McNiel.'"

He paused, savoring the recollection.

"So I stayed," he added. "And I've never been the preacher your father was, but I've served the Lord the best I could in my own way. And, as I see it, Doctor, so have you. You ease suffering, you've spent long hours on the hospital board, the City Council, seeking community betterment. You've been serving, Travis, just as your father did."

"I've never looked at it that way," Travis admitted. "But still, accepting this doesn't solve my lack of comprehension."

"I don't think we can ever really comprehend, Travis, except in terms of faith. Your father was a dynamic man, and as I remember he spent every waking minute working at religion—reading the Bible, praying, preaching—he had no time for anything else. His faith was the product of a lifetime. Now, there are those who can accept faith blindly, and I envy them. For some of us, who have to temper religion with logic, faith is hard work, a long struggle. But I'm sure of one thing, Travis. You'll come nearer to finding serenity of mind inside the church than you will outside."

"I hope so," Travis said. "I will try."

After Anderson turned out the lights they walked out together. They shook hands again in the glow of the street light.

"I will be looking forward to having you and your family with us," Anderson said. "In the meantime, if you should want to discuss anything, don't hesitate to call."

"That's nice to know. Thank you," Travis said.

He drove home. Basically, he felt no different. But he sensed that, somehow, he had taken a decisive step. One worry was eased, giving way to another. That night, long after Marilyn was asleep, her head on his shoulder, Travis lay awake, thinking ahead to tomorrow's council meeting.

The special session had an illicit aura from the start. It was the first daytime meeting Travis could recall, and the council chamber wasn't the same in sunlight. The complete absence of witnesses added to the furtive atmosphere. There'd never before been a session without others present—the city secretary and Hartwell, if no one else.

Travis arrived at the council chamber shortly before noon. The mayor and Weatherbee were already in their places at the council table, waiting. They spoke as Travis went to his seat, but both seemed disinclined to talk. The mayor watched the door, nervously. Weatherbee cleaned his nails with an open penknife. They waited five more minutes, ticked off on the big Seth Thomas at the rear of the chamber, before Berger entered.

The wayward councilman nodded a curt greeting to them and went straight to his chair at the far end of the horseshoe. If he knew the reason for the meeting, he hid it well. Watching him, Travis could see no sign he thought this other than a routine session. He, too, sat and waited without comment.

If the topic was secret, Wentworth probably gave it away. As he entered the chamber he glanced at Berger, then quickly looked away to avoid speaking. His usual bouncy manner was subdued. He quietly took his place, gaze lowered as if he'd come to witness an execution. They waited in uncomfortable silence.

Byron was seven minutes late. He hurried down the center aisle, slowing only to glance over his shoulder at the clock.

"Sorry I'm late," he said. "I didn't realize my watch was slow. One of those damned self-winding. I guess I let it run down."

"No harm done," the mayor said.

Byron circled behind Travis' end of the table toward his chair, hesitated, then took Hartwell's place next to the mayor.

This seating arrangement was unfortunate, Travis thought, for it left the five of them facing Berger, who sat alone on the far end of the table.

The mayor tapped his microphone experimentally without result. The amplifier was off. "I don't suppose we will need this thing, anyway," he said.

He paused, going through that chameleon change Travis had seen many times, assuming a mantle of dignity as his shield against the distasteful job he had to do.

"Gentlemen, I have called this special session on a very serious matter. Our signal honor to sit on this council is a very sacred trust. I'm afraid I have reports that one of our councilmen has been violating that trust. Mr. Berger, these reports concern you."

Berger lifted his eyebrows slightly. "In what way?" he asked.

The mayor tapped an open sheet of paper. "I have a letter here, Mr. Berger, from a Mr. Joe Garzek." He began reading the letter.

Watching, Travis was certain that the contents were no surprise to Berger. His face was expressionless, but his gaze went from one councilman to the next, down the line, as if measuring up his opposition. Travis forced himself to meet Berger's eyes. Berger stared at him for a moment, then turned back to the mayor.

When the mayor completed his reading of the letter, Berger

leaned forward, forgetting that his microphone was dead. He raised his voice to compensate.

"Mr. Mayor, the man who wrote that letter was a mental patient. He wasn't responsible for his actions. But I assume you *are* legally responsible for *your* conduct. I advise you to be careful."

The mayor retreated further into his shell. "I will not be threatened, Mr. Berger."

"And I won't listen to this kind of crap. It wouldn't stand up one minute in a court of law."

"There's more, I'm afraid," the mayor said.

Berger thumped the council table. "If you're going to repeat a bunch of rumors and lies, I demand the right to have my lawyer here."

The mayor looked at him sternly. "I believe you should hear me out. Then, if you still want to be advised by counsel, I will repeat what I am about to say if you so desire."

The mayor shuffled through his papers. He stood, unfolded the highway map, and handed one corner to Byron. They turned it to face Berger. The mayor pointed to the shaded area.

"These choice sites along the proposed interstate bypass were purchased by a Mr. Donald Ratliff within days after the route was made available to the council. We have every reason to believe that he was acting in your behalf, Mr. Berger."

Berger's eyebrows lifted again. "That's a pretty serious charge, Mr. Mayor. I presume you think you have proof."

"We have," the mayor said, refolding the map. "Ratliff was arrested burglarizing Mr. Garzek's tavern the night after the shootings. In a search of his room, officers found a promissory note between Ratliff and you in the exact amount of the land purchases."

Berger was listening intently now. "So I knew Ratliff," he said. "So he owed me some money. What does that prove? I don't know anything about his goddamn land."

"It might interest you to know that Ratliff has been identified by another tavern owner as putting a quota on his sale of Alamo Beer," the mayor added. "Also, several scratchpads full of figures in your handwriting were found in his room. I am sure your relationship with this convict can be proved in court, if necessary."

Berger sat tense, alert, studying the mayor. Travis could almost see his mind working, wondering "how much do they know?" and "what can they prove?"

"What are you guys after?" Berger asked softly.

"I think it's obvious by now," the mayor said. "We want your resignation from the council. We want you to sell your business and get out of town. The Chamber directors are behind us unanimously in this request, and I also might add that there has been talk of stronger measures, but we have agreed that if you co-operate, there will be no further action."

"If I co-operate?" Berger leaped to his feet. "What right do you have to ask me to give up all I've worked seventeen years for? What makes you sons-a-bitches think you're so much better'n me?"

Beside Travis, Weatherbee jabbed a finger at Berger. "Because you've violated a public trust. That's what right we have," he said heatedly.

Berger snorted. "You're one to talk about morality, Walt Weatherbee. They tell me you used to be a good carpenter. What happened to *your* honesty? I could kick a hole in the side of any of the houses you build today, and you know it. You don't build houses for people, you build them for the FHA, quick turnover, quick obsolescence. I know some of your tricks, like jacking up the price for a hundred percent loan. I know about dummy buyers and loan kickbacks. Every decision you ever made on this council was made for the benefit of the homebuilders. Now I ask you, Walt, who's dishonest? You, or me?"

Weatherbee's face reddened. "I build as good houses as anybody in town, and I don't hire convicts to do it, either."

Byron leaned forward. "Name-calling isn't going to get you anywhere, Berger," he said. "You're the one facing criminal charges."

Berger turned on Byron angrily. "What's the matter, afraid I might start on you? Ask you why your ambulance drivers have fist-fights with others over corpses? Afraid I'll ask how much the markup is on those gilded caskets you sell to widows? Or the profit you make on that burial association of yours? You act like you hate to spend federal funds, Byron, but I bet you damned sure take all that oil depletion allowance you can juggle."

"Please, Mr. Berger," the mayor said firmly. "We'd rather not have any unpleasantness."

Berger glanced at the mayor, his eyes widening with a new thought. He hesitated for a long moment. "Of course you don't," he said slowly. He grinned. "Hell no, you don't want to go to court with this any more than I do. This is all a bluff, isn't it?"

"No, Mr. Berger, this is not a bluff," the mayor said.

But his voice lacked conviction, Travis thought. Berger seemed to sense this, too. He sat down again with a short, explosive laugh.

"I believe it is, Mr. Mayor," he said. "You wouldn't do anything to endanger your precious lake—which you hope will be named for you. Weatherbee has a vested interest—and you, too, Wentworth. The doctor doesn't want his hospital plan wrecked. And the chamber sure as hell wouldn't want the boat rocked. No, I don't think you'd risk it. You can go back and tell your Chamber directors, Mayor, that I'm not going to co-operate."

The mayor's face was ashen. "You're making a big mistake, Mr. Berger," he said.

"The more I think about it, the more I'm sure I'm not," Berger said. "I've got friends. I don't believe you'd even get it to trial, if you tried."

"Maybe we wouldn't have to," Weatherbee said. "All we got to do is put out the word in the right places, and you're out of business, Buster."

"My beer franchise, you mean?"

"Right."

"The only way the company can lift it is by legal process. And that puts us right back where we started, doesn't it?"

There was a long silence, with Berger grinning. The mayor's eyes were lowered in thought. Travis had known, somehow, that the mayor's bluff would be called. But not until now, facing Berger, did he realize why.

"You're quite a realist," Travis told Berger.

"I've had to be," Berger snapped at him. "I wasn't born with a silver spoon."

"I don't believe you're thinking far enough ahead, though," Travis said. "You're not examining the alternatives."

Berger stared at him in silence. He wasn't grinning, now.

"The mayor implied this ultimatum was unanimous with the council," Travis went on. "That's not quite true. You know what I wanted to do, Mr. Berger? I wanted to seek a recall election, making all the reasons known. I proposed we put this right back into the hands of the voters."

"That would wreck your hospital project."

"Might. And again, it might not. If it did, I suppose we could get by at the hospital as we have been, and I could just consider it the lesser of two evils. Anyway, that is what I intend to do if you do not accept the mayor's proposal."

"They wouldn't let you," Berger said.

"Who?" Travis demanded. "Who wouldn't let me? Mr. Berger, I am a citizen. I don't have to answer to the mayor, the other councilmen, or the Chamber. Any citizen can circulate a petition. I've packed this room before, and I can do it again."

"Are you threatening me, Doctor?"

"No, I'm not threatening you, Mr. Berger. I'm telling you."

Berger studied him for a moment, then glanced at the mayor. "And you wouldn't be able to stop him, would you? At least you couldn't last time."

Berger stared at the council table, frowning. He rubbed the top of his bald head several times in frustration. Then he looked up at Travis.

"You called me a realist, Doctor. All right, I'll be realistic. My business is worth money. If you start a hate campaign against me, it's going to cost me. There's nothing I'd like better than to fight it out with you, but that's a luxury I can't afford. Besides, this council work has taken too much of my time for the returns. You win, Doctor. Mayor, you shall have my council resignation."

"In writing," the mayor said. "And we shall expect you to be out of town within a grace period of, say, sixty days."

Berger shook his head. "You don't understand, Mayor. With my resignation, the doctor no longer has a cause. He has no weapon to run me out of town. And I'm not afraid of your bluff. This way, I lose nothing but my council seat."

The mayor opened his mouth, then closed it without a sound.

"Take his resignation, Mayor," Weatherbee said. "He's nothing but a cheap, two-bit hoodlum that'll be booted out of town eventually anyway."

Berger leaped to his feet again. "Two-bit hoodlum? I run a more respectable business any day of the week than you do, Walt Weatherbee, and you better keep your goddamn nose out of it."

"You'll keep overreaching yourself," Weatherbee said. "Sooner or later, we'll get you."

Berger left the horseshoe, stepped off the platform, and bumped into the front row of folding metal chairs, overturning two. The clatter as they hit the hardwood floor, echoing through the council chamber, seemed to unleash Berger's complete anger. He took a step back toward the council table.

"All right, you got me off the council. But if you start messing up my business, I'll get even with every one of you if it takes me a lifetime. And I'll be doing it from right here in town, too."

"I shall expect your resignation in writing, Mr. Berger," the mayor said. "You may use whatever phraseology you wish."

Berger wheeled, lashed out with his right foot, and sent another chair clattering to the floor. Then he walked swiftly up the aisle to the door at the rear of the council chamber and slammed it behind him, never looking back.

The violence of his departure left them stunned. The mayor was the first to speak.

"That was good thinking, Travis," he said. "I'm not sure how the Chamber directors will view the compromise, but as far as I'm concerned, you handled that magnificently." There was a murmur of agreement from Weatherbee, Wentworth, and Byron. "Unfortunately, that doesn't conclude our distasteful duties today," the mayor added.

He paused, apparently finding the prospect of facing David Hartwell with the request for Chief McDowell's dismissal even more difficult than delivering Berger's ultimatum. His reluctance was obvious as he picked up the house phone at his elbow and dialed.

"David," he said firmly. "Will you please step into the council chamber? We have something we must discuss with you."

## CHAPTER TWENTY-TWO

David Hartwell had tried to condition himself to the probability of the demand for Chief McDowell's dismissal, but as he heard it coming from the mayor, he still found it difficult to believe.

He had assumed that the Chamber directors, removed from the practical aspects of operating a city and given to theoretical assumptions, might demand that McDowell be replaced. But David had hoped the council members would rise to McDowell's defense and nip the request at the source. Now, as he listened to the mayor's carefully worded explanation, he knew he had been too optimistic.

Could he be wrong about McDowell? David remembered the gentle, efficient way Dan had handled things when Ronnie and Christine were in trouble. Could his defense of Dan be based mostly on friendship and gratitude? He thought not. With Ronnie and Christine, Dan's concern had also been with proper procedure. In the Berger investigation, Dan had always protected the suspects' civil rights. Dan was a good man.

Quickly, David sized up the situation. Travis would listen to reason. Byron was an independent thinker. But Weatherbee and Wentworth were influenced strongly by downtown pressure. With the mayor David wasn't sure. Sometimes the Gray Ghost could be swayed easily. At other times he could show surprising originality of thought.

Ironically, the margin of support David needed had just left the council chamber.

David regretted now that he had taken a seat at the deserted press table, facing the remaining members of the council like an errant schoolboy. But Byron had taken David's regular seat next to the mayor, and it was too late to move up to the council table without the reason being obvious. He sat listening to the mayor's lecture, seeking a clue to the tenor of the council's thoughts.

"The crux of the matter is, Mr. Manager, that our civic leaders believe that if the police chief had been sufficiently alert, this unfortunate affair never would have occurred. They feel he should be replaced."

"How does the council feel?" David asked.

The mayor glanced briefly at Travis before he answered. "We voted with the majority."

David could imagine the kangaroo court vote that was taken. He was sure now Travis was on his side.

"Chief McDowell was more aware of what was going on than we were," David reminded them. "Most of the information we have came from him."

"That's true, I suppose," the mayor admitted. "But we certainly believe he should have made that information available earlier."

"Chief McDowell is a man of high principle," David said. "I don't imagine he would have made the information available at all, if he'd known exactly how it was to be used."

The mayor looked at him sternly. "Do I understand that you are criticizing the way the council has handled this situation?"

"That's not in my purview," David said evenly. "City administration is, though, and I don't think we could have a better man in charge of the Police Department than Dan McDowell."

"I'm afraid that is not the consensus of our civic leaders," the mayor said.

David was beginning to find these references to the chamber irritating. "What do they know about running a Police Department?" he asked heatedly. "There's more to police work than just enforcing the law. If all the statutes on the books were strictly enforced, there'd be chaos. There has to be a certain amount of permissiveness. It takes a good man to walk that tightrope. Berger isn't the only ambitious, power-hungry man in town. We'll always have our Bergers. We need a police chief who can't be bought. As far as I know, Chief McDowell's integrity has never been questioned."

"No one is questioning his integrity now," the mayor said. "We agree that his record has been good in the past. Perhaps what we need is more discipline down there. At least, something went wrong."

"I believe in allowing a man to correct his own mistakes," David said. "Chief McDowell erred in assuming his men were as dedicated as himself. He has promised a complete investigation and steps to rectify the situation without undue publicity. Since he knows the personalities involved, I'm sure he can do that job better than anyone."

The mayor sighed deeply. "I see no purpose in arguing the matter further, Mr. Manager. You have the council's request before you. If you desire time to think it over, I suppose there is no great rush. But it is our firm recommendation that he be replaced as chief of police."

David gave the mayor a long hard look before he answered. "No," he said. He saw that his stand momentarily jolted them.

The mayor stared back at him. "Do I understand that you are refusing to fire him?" he said, spreading his hands in a helpless gesture. "Why? Surely, David, you understand that we cannot have a city manager who retains personnel detrimental to the best interests of the city."

"Mayor, it would be the simplest thing in the world for me to follow the council's recommendation. But I don't believe it is right. I've always been careful to define what is rightfully the council's domain and what is mine. If I started listening to everyone telling me how to do my job, I'd soon be in a hell of a shape. I have to do what I think best. If I started to compromise on what I believe is right, where would I draw the line?"

The mayor frowned. He stared at the council table for a moment before answering.

"Please reconsider, David. We all have to do things occasionally we don't like to do. This whole thing is distasteful to all of us, but it has to be done. We all have a certain obligation to the city."

David knew, now, what he had to do. After all the hours of struggling with the decision the last few days, the words came easily.

"If that's the way the council feels, then you have my resignation, Mr. Mayor," he said firmly.

They stared at him for a moment in stunned silence.

The mayor's face was ashen. When he spoke, his voice trembled. "If you feel that strongly about it, David, perhaps we could work out a compromise—keep McDowell on as chief of detectives, perhaps. We can certainly understand your loyalty toward him."

"There's more to it than that, Mayor," David said. He tried to explain. "This is a carefully considered action on my part. There have been events in my personal life during the last few weeks that have made me aware of my obligations—all of them. As you said, Mayor, I do have an obligation to the city. But I also have an obligation to my family which I have been ignoring to fulfill the demands of my job. The job isn't worth the price. I believe, reluctantly, that it would be to the best interest of all concerned if the council would accept my resignation."

There was another moment of silence. The mayor glanced nervously at the other councilmen, seeking help.

"What are these demands of the job you consider excessive?" Weatherbee asked. "The hours?"

"That's the principal thing. The city manager is expected to be too many places, both day and night, to do justice to his main task of administration. And any semblance of home life is beyond reach."

"Isn't that an occupational hazard?" Travis asked. "Wouldn't you still have the same problem if you went somewhere else as city manager?"

"I suppose so," David admitted. He decided he could trust them. "But I plan to stay here. This is confidential. I have been talking with Cal's family. It looks like with the help of the First National Bank and the kindness of Cal's daughters, I may be able to buy Cal's ranch and a good portion of his foundation herd."

Weatherbee laughed. "I'd think you'd get a little bored out there, administrating cows."

"I'm afraid I agree," the mayor said. "I can't see you as anything but a city manager."

Travis raised a hand for the floor. "Mayor, I believe the city manager's stand has shown how far from the proper sense of proportion we've been led. Let's see if we can't regain our perspective. Are *we* doing what we know is right? Remember the question Cal Masters always asked: are we doing this for the good of the people to whom we have responsibilities, or are we taking the advice of those who do not have those responsibilities?"

The mayor started to reply, but Travis went on. "I believe the city manager's view of our recommendation is just. Couldn't we take an informal vote now, without outside interference, on our recommendation for the dismissal of McDowell?"

The mayor frowned. "Doctor, we have already taken our stand."

"Not as a duly-elected body, we haven't."

"Well, I suppose it wouldn't hurt anything," the mayor said hesitantly. "Of course, we're not meeting in any official capacity today, either, but if anyone should wish to reconsider . . . will all those in favor of the recommendation raise their right hand?"

Wentworth and Weatherbee raised their hands.

"Opposed."

Travis and Byron responded.

The mayor's frown deepened. "Gentlemen, as I said, this is an unofficial vote, and I don't suppose I'm obligated to break a tie." He paused and rubbed his chin nervously. "I've been thinking, though, of what the doctor said a moment ago, reminding us of a question often asked by my late friend, Cal Masters, as to the source and worth of advice. I have the uncomfortable feeling we've been pressured into this by those who do not have the responsibility. The emphatic conviction of our city manager —in whom I have great trust—that we are doing a wrong has further convinced me. Also, since we are not a full council, perhaps we should take no important steps until we have two new members. I propose we just drop the matter."

Weatherbee and Wentworth didn't seem too unhappy over the mayor's decision, David thought. They probably had held out only because they assumed a report of their stand would get back to the chamber directors.

"I thank you on behalf of Chief McDowell," David told the council. "But as I said, my resignation is based upon personal reasons. This action doesn't alter that."

The mayor nodded. "David," he said slowly, "I'm sure if I explained to the Chamber directors—sort of put out the word that we're riding a good horse to death—we could ease this schedule of night meetings for you. There is no reason the city and the Chamber can't work in close harmony without so much personal contact."

"That's a good idea, Mayor," Travis said. "But I don't believe it goes far enough. I think the city has grown to the point where we should gradually expand our City Hall staff. Why don't we include the creation of an assistant city managership in the next city budget? I'm sure we could get some bright young trainee for eight to ten thousand a year who could take a tremendous load off the city manager—free him for higher level work."

The mayor considered the idea briefly. "That suggestion certainly seems to have merit, Travis. I think we should make every effort to retain our city manager. Walt, what do you think of that proposal?"

"I would have no objection if it can be worked into the budget without a tax increase," Weatherbee said.

Byron and Wentworth nodded agreement.

"Would that change your mind, Mr. Manager?" the mayor asked.

David laughed. He had never delegated much authority, but he supposed he could learn. "What can I say but yes?" he asked.

David lingered behind with Travis on the stairs. "I want to thank you, Doctor," he said. "Your support turned the tide back there."

"They would have reconsidered, I think, in time," Travis said. "Does this change your plans to buy Cal's ranch?"

"No," David explained. "It's partly an investment. But my two teen-agers are pretty thrilled over the prospect of becoming ranchers, and I imagine I'll spend most of my newly acquired spare time out there."

Tom Kencaide was waiting for them at the foot of the stairs on the first floor.

"The new publisher," David said. "Congratulations."

Tom took David's hand, feeling strangely embarrassed.

"Out after your first exposé?" Travis asked.

"No, I still have a two-weeks' notice to work out for BeeBee," Tom explained. "The exposés will have to wait. But I have enough on hand to last a while."

"I had a feeling the exposé business was going to pick up," Travis said.

They walked on down the corridor toward the front door.

Tom was wondering what had gone on in the secret session upstairs, but he knew he wouldn't learn from these two. Not now, anyway. He had thought that if he caught Berger on leaving the council chamber today, he might be angry enough to talk. But it hadn't worked out that way. Berger had been livid with rage, but when Tom stopped him, Berger gave a cool, collected statement that he was resigning from the council because of the press of business.

Now, watching Hartwell, Tom was certain something else had happened. The city manager seemed more relaxed, happier.

Tom remembered, as they went out the front door, why he wanted to see Hartwell.

"Would it be possible for me to see the transcripts of every council meeting for years past?"

Hartwell stopped on the City Hall steps and turned to face him. "Why, I guess so. They're kept in the basement somewhere."

Tom knew finding them would be difficult. He felt he should explain.

"I want to compile quotes from Cal . . . the exact quotes. I started outlining what I want my newspaper to stand for, and I went back in my notes trying to find that lecture Cal used to give on democracy. You know the one I mean?"

Travis remembered verbatim: "'City government should be the most perfect, because it's closer to the people. If it isn't, it's because the people aren't working at democracy. How can we expect to be world leaders, if we don't even work at governing ourselves?'"

"I only have rough notes," Tom said. "But I got to thinking what a good series Cal's ideas would make."

"Be a lot of work, but I think it would be worth the effort," David agreed. "When you get ready, I'll tell the city secretary to turn you loose in the files."

As they started down the steps, Travis offered to give David and Tom a lift, since his car was near, but both declined.

David walked with Tom to the parking lot, then drove home, wondering what kind of men would be chosen to fill the two council vacancies.

## AFTERWORD

In *The Wooden Horseshoe*, first published by Doubleday in 1964, Leonard Sanders, author of several novels and historical works, provides a detailed and revealing account of exactly how city government functions in a large Texas town in the early 60s. At least on one level that is what the novel appears to be about, and given Sanders' background as a newspaperman in two large Texas cities, Wichita Falls and Fort Worth, as well as three cities in Oklahoma, including Oklahoma City, one is not surprised by the attention to details only a trained journalist would observe and note.

The mechanics of city government and the inclinations of council members make for interesting, even fascinating, reading. As one suspects, power and self-promotion are as likely to be the driving forces behind a citizen's desire to serve on a city council as is a humble desire to serve the community. Sanders gives readers an insider's knowledge of the personal and official feelings and thoughts of council members as they deal with proposed issues for a highway bypass, a new hospital wing, and a new lake and recreation area, while simultaneously attempting to serve all the citizens' interests, including their own, without offending—and in some cases with intention to serve—the desires of the powers-that-be, the local newspaper owner and an oil tycoon. But even an intriguing novel dealing with innumerable political and personal conflicts should deliver a more substantial message, and this one does. On a deeper level, the novel is really about the daily external and internal struggles that the main characters face, and therein lies the beauty and value of this easily read, fast-paced novel: the themes of life, death, love, truth, and self-fulfillment are timeless.

Sanders achieves the expression of his themes by artfully weaving the lives of three characters in and around the city council's day-to-day business. David Hartwell, the confident, aggressive city manager, is an expert at juggling the issues and personalities within the council chambers, while failing miserably in balancing his professional life with his roles as a husband and a father of two teenage children. David is the kind of man we all know, the one with the perfect job, perfect home, and perfect family, on the surface anyway. So why are we surprised to learn that his wife is an alcoholic, his daughter attempts suicide, and his son is caught window peeping? The answer, as Sanders shows us, is because in real life, with real people, there often is a vast difference between appearance and reality, although we prefer to believe there isn't. Hartwell learns the hard way, as do most of us, that the consequences of real life decisions may force a man to rearrange his priorities.

Sanders' portrait of Dr. Travis McNeil, a young physician, is just as carefully constructed. Unlike Hartwell, Travis does have a successful marriage and family life and manages to balance the demands of his home life and his medical practice, deriving a sense of peace from each. The introverted son of a widowed minister, Travis is haunted by an inability to accept the religious convictions his father expounded, although his profession demands that he deal with life and death on a daily basis. The truth that he eventually faces is that he has avoided, for most of his life, formulating any convictions, religious or otherwise, of his own. His role as a councilman forces him to take a stand for what he believes is good for the entire community, an action that endears him to an old rancher who is dying of cancer. In being a comfort to the old man during his last minutes by agreeing to pray with him, Travis learns the value and the power of prayer and love, lessons the rancher learned years before from Travis' father.

Tom Kencaide is a Korean veteran and an experienced reporter for the local newspaper, and part of his news beat is covering city council meetings. It would have been easy for Sanders to take readers inside the council chamber using only Kencaide's perspective, but that would have been a mistake. We are allowed to view city administration from each council member's position, and besides, Kencaide, like Hartwell and McNeil, has his own story to tell. Like any good reporter, he seeks the truth behind any piece of news, for to him that is the measure of a reporter, as well as of a man. Unfortunately, such a stance places him in constant conflict with the paper owner's agenda, which the owner doesn't hesitate to promote on the editorial page. The result is that Tom's in-depth reports on some council members' manipulative actions are consistently ignored, leaving him continually frustrated with a job he truly loves.

As if that were not enough conflict in Tom's life, his girlfriend of two years sees in him a man capable of doing much more with his life, which Tom tries in vain to deny. He truly enjoys newspaper work, in spite of its frustrations, and will not consider other possibilities. Eventually a series of events, including the near loss of the woman he loves, forces Tom to take a close look at the two most important things in his life: the woman he loves and his work. He manages to salvage the relationship and achieve a high degree of self-fulfillment by starting his own small paper in which the truth behind any story will take precedence over all other considerations.

Sanders, perhaps deliberately, does not "flesh out" his characters physically. A reader does not get a mental image of the appearance of the characters. Instead, Sanders creates a clear inner image of each one. We understand exactly how they think and feel. We come to know their values and ideals, their frustrations, their fears, and their triumphs. In part because the characters are not tied to physical appearance, they become universal characters, and we identify with them, for they could easily be our friends, our neighbors, or other people we think we know, such as ourselves. So, we are not just entertained by a novel about the inner workings of a city council; we are enthralled by the internal motivations of average human beings, and there are few things more interesting than the study of human nature. I do not expect any more from a novel than *The Wooden Horseshoe* so aptly delivers.

Charlie McMurtry
San Angelo State University
San Angelo, Texas

The Author

Leonard Sanders is a former newspaper journalist and book-review editor for the *Fort Worth Star-Telegram. The Wooden Horseshoe,* originally published in 1964, was his first novel. Other titles include *Fort Worth, Sonoma* and his most recent, *In the Valley of the Shadow*. Sanders lives in Fort Worth, Texas.